# FROM OPPOSITE SIDES

BRYONY SIER

# FROM Opposite Sides

*ISBN number: 978-1-7394109-0-2*



Book design concept by *Helen Sier*
Book design illustrated by *Richie Evans.*

www.bryonysierbooks.co.uk
All images used within this book were designed in the Canva app.

BRYONY SIER

*For my beautiful Mam, Helen. You are my best friend. Thanks for reading every draft I wrote of this book and for the constant love and encouragement. You technically wrote this story with me! Love you.*

—B.S.

# Chapter One

SQUELCH. SQUELCH.

I never realised how much noise a pair of wet trainers could make. I'm annoyed—mostly at myself for thinking that riding my bike in a torrential downpour was a good idea. People are staring at me like I've lost my mind for choosing to venture out in this weather without a hood or an umbrella for protection. They don't realise that my only mode of transport is my rusty old bike, and I wasn't going to let a bit of rain stop me from getting to college in one piece.

I quickly pop to the toilets and place my head under a hand dryer, receiving odd looks from girls entering and leaving the bathroom. It gives them some clarity once I explain that I pedalled here in the rain.

Freckles cover most of my face, and fiery red hair tumbles down my shoulders, untamed and desperately needing a brush. I would probably look very ordinary if it weren't for my voluminous hair and the fact that I am the real-life version of Merida from the Brave movie, minus the Scottish accent. Most would also say that I am the spitting image of my mother, but I don't have her eyes. Mine are blue. Hers are more of a chocolate brown. That's what separates us in the looks department.

I leave the bathroom in a hurry to make it to class. I'm late again, but it's not my fault! I have a lot of trouble getting to class on time, considering my most reliable mode of transportation is my bike.

Jumping up the stairs, I push through some double doors and shriek when two boys come hurtling towards me down the corridor, almost rugby-tackling me to the ground.

"Hey! Watch where you're going!" I shout once I've managed to regain my balance.

One of the boys stops, whipping his head around to look at me. A gasp leaves my throat, my stomach and jaw dropping in perfect unison.

Rory Keaton is wearing his usual playful expression. He runs a hand through his hair and smirks at me. If his ringtone isn't *Danger High Voltage*, there's seriously something wrong with the world. Our paths continued to cross throughout high school, and he always seemed to be engaged in a fight or conflict, but the faint scars etched across his knuckles and along his jawline reveal a silent story of encounters that were not so easily won.

Rory is taller than most people, and I hate that I have to rise on my tip-toes to be considered a worthy opponent. His eyes are too green, reminding me of a cat: mysterious and unpredictable. They're framed by a tousle of dark, unruly hair. Blending into the shadows, nobody would notice him since he's always dressed in black clothing.

I cross my arms tightly across my chest. "Rory, I would be lying if I said it's nice to see you, so I won't bother playing nice."

A wicked grin breaks out on his face.

"Clemons, I was just about to apologise for nearly knocking you over, but with that attitude of yours, you can forget it."

My cheeks turn an even deeper shade of red.

He smiles an inch wider. "Bad hair day?"

*Be calm. He's just doing this to rile you up. Please don't give him satisfaction.*

"Pft!"

I spat in his face.

*Smooth.*

"At least I haven't shown up to college looking like Darth Vader. Seriously, it's embarrassing, dude."

*That sounded way better in my head.*

He's still grinning like I've amused him more than insulted him. "Darth Vader is one of the coolest supervillains ever, so you just complimented me."

*Damn. That backfired.*

"Nice trousers, by the way. Looks like something my Great Aunt Dolly would wear."

I glance down at my high-waisted, slouchy Mum jeans. They're a bit old-fashioned, but boy, are they comfy. I love them, so who cares what Rory Keaton thinks? I certainly don't.

"Wow, Rory. Is that the best you've got?"

He leans against the wall and shrugs. "As much as I'd

love to stay here and catch up for old times' sake, I've got to bounce. There's something important I need to take care of, and thanks to you, he's managed to get away."

Rory can't avoid a fight, so nothing has changed there. I stick my nose in the air and stare back at him, irritated.

"Who's ticked you off this time, then? Did someone disagree with you? Did they look at you the wrong way? Or did they just say no, and you couldn't take it?"

Rory steps towards me, cornering me against a row of lockers. I'm forced to share his breathing space as he lowers his mouth to my ear. His warm, minty breath tickles my neck, making me shiver involuntarily.

"Maybe you should focus on your issues, Skye. Like, why doesn't anyone seem to like you? I'm sure you'd get more than one valid answer if you asked yourself that question."

I appreciate that my teacher Ricky doesn't bat an eyelid when I claim my seat at the back of the classroom, and he carries on teaching like he hasn't just been interrupted, but I can't avoid the curious stares of my classmates. They must be wondering why I've turned up to college looking like a drowned rat for the millionth time.

The only thing that I remotely look forward to these days is my language and literature classes. I've always had a passion for writing. Whether I'm good at it is another question, but I love to write because it allows me to express myself. Writing brings so much freedom, and there are no restrictions—my mind can venture out and travel anywhere. Of course, living in a poor community means I am limited to a certain extent, but that isn't preventing me from following my dreams of becoming a journalist someday.

Rory's words continue to play in my head as I begin fishing around in my bag for a notebook and pen.

*Ugh. Get out of my head, Rory Keaton!*

The truth is, I have a bad reputation, and I don't miss the regrettable hookups in high school. Once you have slept with a boy, it can never be undone. You're forever branded as easy, desperate, a slut. When boys sleep around, they're not given a hard time about it. They're praised. They're put on a pedestal for the world to view and admire. My name was slandered around the halls. I lost respect, and boys forever had the wrong impression of me based on a few mistakes I made ages ago.

Digging around in my bag for the longest time, I realised I hadn't brought my pencil case today.

*This day keeps getting better and better.*

"Good morning, Skye!" Josie shouts, startling me out of my thoughts.

*I don't know which is worse, returning to my reality or revisiting my messy past.*

Josie Bryant always tries to initiate a conversation with me, and I don't know why. I'm the type of person who prefers to be left alone, and I thought I made that pretty clear. I wouldn't say that isolating myself is something to shout about, but I'm antisocial without meaning to be sometimes. I wear the same expression every day—one that gives off the impression that I'm constantly annoyed or angry at the world, which is partially true, but I often find myself wishing I was more approachable.

Josie settles into the seat in front of me and smiles. Her long brown hair is in plaits this morning, and she is wearing these big, floral glasses that look too big for her face. Large, puppy dog eyes continuously blink at me from behind them, wide and innocent. She is nerdy, enthusiastic about everything, and can make people feel welcome and at ease without even trying. She also tends to wear the most outrageous outfits to college that I wouldn't want to imitate simply because I couldn't pull them off.

Today, for example, she has opted for a bright yellow dress with big black stripes covering the front of it, some thick yellow tights and a pair of cowgirl boots. She looks like a walking, talking bumble bee but doesn't seem too fazed by it.

"Morning," I mutter back, lowering my eyes to the floor.

*If I don't say much, maybe she'll take the hint.*

"Do you always ride a bike to college?" she asks curiously.

"Yes," I say, opening my notebook to a new page and wishing she'd leave me alone.

"That must be exhausting! No wonder you're always running late to class."

"I'm late because of low-functioning technology, Josie. My alarm doesn't wake me up when it's supposed to."

She goes quiet for a second, like she's trying to figure out whether or not I'm joking.

"Oh right, fair enough. Have you thought about having driving lessons?"

*Here we go. I saw this coming.*

I'm one of those few college girls who can't afford to pay for a bike upgrade, let alone have driving lessons. I have no choice but to pedal my sorry butt to college every day, regardless of the weather.

*The struggle is real.*

I let her question go unanswered and return my eyes to the front of the class, where Ricky rambles about an important announcement.

"Lakeside College has had to shut down for the time being. The building is undergoing renovations," he says, gaining everyone's undivided attention.

I wonder why Lakeside's current dilemma is so important to us. Based on the richer side of town, it's an entirely different world that I'm comfortable keeping at a safe distance.

"As we are the closest educational facility in the area, students from Lakeside will be relocating here. They will be arriving today, so we must warmly welcome them."

Gasps of shock reverberate throughout the room, mingling with my own, and I feel the anxiety start sweeping over me, but before my thoughts can catch up, Ricky's voice interrupts the chaos.

"This is only temporary. There's no need to panic, but we must make slight changes around here," he reassures us.

It doesn't take long for the class to erupt, and almost everybody expresses their concerns simultaneously. I sit there and try to process this news, but I only feel uneasy about what changes will be made to my comfortable routine.

A flurry of voices drifts in from outside the classroom, and there's a knock on the door. It swings open, revealing one girl and three boys huddled together on the other side, exchanging glances and grinning at each other. It's irritating, but I won't be made to feel inferior. They are the ones who are trespassing.

"Welcome to Barnett College!" Ricky greets, showing indecent enthusiasm, which isn't returned.

I watch the rich girl's repulsed reaction as her eyes scan the room. Standing next to her is a tall, blond boy and judging by the look of pure disgust on his face, it's as if he's just walked into a crime scene.

Ricky chuckles when the intruders continue to remain in the doorway. "Are you going to sit down then, folks? We don't bite, I swear."

Slowly, the three of them sit down as close to each other as possible, but there is an empty chair beside mine, and the blond boy parks himself there. Ricky starts handing out some name tags so we can all get better 'acquainted,' and while I'm writing my first and last name on it, I tense up when I hear the blond boy say to his friend, "Ugh, this place stinks."

"I thought I was the only one thinking that. At least I'm not losing my mind," his Lakeside companion replies.

Blondie leans back in his chair as if he owns the place already. "It could be worse, Ed."

"What could be worse than *this*?"

"I've got nothing, never mind. I can barely move my arm without hitting the girl sitting next to me."

My grip tightens around the pen in my hand.

*He's got some nerve.*

The whole class takes turns introducing who they are and what interests them. I zone out for most of it, but when it's Blondie's turn, he doesn't seem to take this seriously.

"What was the question again?" he asks, acting dumb.

A few laughs travel around the room, and I roll my eyes as I finally turn to acknowledge him, noticing how good-looking he is. Most girls would say he is the total package, blessed with golden blond hair, striking blue eyes, perfectly sculpted cheekbones, clear skin, and angelic features, but I think it depends on a person's perception. Mine is unshaken. He's arrogant and royally stuck up. That makes him unattractive.

Blondie straightens in his chair, grinning to himself. "I don't need to introduce myself anyway, sir. Sooner or later, everyone will know who I am. I'm pretty hard to miss."

*Could he be any more arrogant?*

"Egotistical pig," I whisper under my breath.

"What was that, Skye?" Ricky inquires, prompting everyone to look at me.

*Oh, shoot.*

I may as well speak my mind now since the new boy isn't afraid to speak his mind.

"I was referring to a certain egotistical pig who thinks he's better than everybody else here. I won't mention his name because it's obvious who I'm talking about," I admit, receiving a chorus of gasps and amused laughter from around the room.

I glance in Blondie's direction again, only to find that he's already looking at me, the corners of his mouth tugging up.

"Woah, I think somebody's taking this a bit too personally," he says, studying me.

"Well, you have an issue with how we run things here. Stop complaining. You're stuck with us, so learn to deal with it."

He lets out a long sigh. "Thanks for that unfortunate reminder."

"Excuse me?"

"There I was, thinking you didn't have manners! Hallelujah! We're saved. There is still hope for us!" he exclaims dramatically, placing a hand over his heart. "Don't worry, *Skye*. We won't step on your toes too much," he adds, sneakily glancing at my name tag.

An incredulous laugh escapes me. "Are you seriously implying that you're better than us?"

"Those words didn't come out of my mouth. They came out of yours, but to answer your question, yes."

I narrow my eyes, hot anger burning through my veins. "Why? Is it because you're from a richer part of town? Does that automatically make you more capable than the rest of us?"

I realise I'm pointing at him aggressively, yet he isn't deterred. I'm usually good at intimidating people. It has a lot to do with my fiery red hair and fierce personality, but the boy I'm exchanging death glares with now is a new kettle of fish because he doesn't seem intimidated.

"Newsflash, it doesn't matter where you come from. This is the twenty-first century. Have you been living under a rock this entire time?" I continue, unable to control the anger in my voice now that it's officially been unleashed.

"Does this girl have a filter?" he asks nobody in particular. "It seems we've met the class viper. I can see this is going to be an issue."

"Yes, a big issue because you and your Lakeside crew don't belong here!"

"I don't even think *you* know where you belong," he snarls, eyes blazing.

Words seem to fail me for the first time in a long while. I search for them, but when nothing comes to mind, I realise I've lost this round. He's hit a nerve.

I slump down in my chair and fold my arms, glancing at Blondie's name tag for future reference.

Grayson Swain

*More like Grayson Swine.*

Grayson leans forward and whispers, "No need to introduce yourself. I know quite enough, Skye Clemons."

All the blood drains from my face.

This is going to be a long week.

# Chapter Two

It's fair to say that after spending two weeks with the Lakeside students, I'm exhausted and grouchier than usual. Writing an essay is not easy to master on a typical day, especially not when I'm expected to analyse a news article and then write ten thousand words about it, but I'm struggling to focus.

College life used to be so predictable and comfortable, but now it represents everything I hate, with many challenges to overcome and conflicting changes out of my control. The class isn't getting along anymore. There is such a divide that enjoying the lessons is becoming difficult. For once, I can relate to Shakespeare because we're in a Montague and Capulet situation where nobody's backing down or giving up the fight.

My head falls against my bedroom desk, and I close my eyes, the day's events returning to haunt me in one giant swoop. Grayson's annoying face appears in my mind, and I let out a tiny internal scream.

I sit up, take calm breaths through my nose, click my fingers, stretch my legs and tell myself to snap out of it.

*It's fine. This is just temporary, remember? The Lakeside students will be around for a while, but not forever.*

Miraculously, I feel less stressed and more motivated to finish this essay before it's due tomorrow. I manage to type the first three letters of a new paragraph into Microsoft Word but raised voices from downstairs cause my concentration levels to become non-existent, my sudden burst of inspiration flushing itself down the toilet to the point where it's untraceable.

Leaving my room to investigate, I reach the top of the stairs and notice our landlord standing in the passageway, his face bright red like he's been spending too much time in the sun. He scratches his beer belly hanging out of his paint-splattered work trousers, and I wonder if they are the only pair he owns.

Robert Knowles has never been the friendliest of people. He's foul-mouthed, grumpy, and seems to wear the same clothes whenever I see him. He doesn't have one of those understanding faces. Instead, he's stern and cold. I'm envious that he can turn his emotions on and off at will.

“I'm sick and tired of hearing the same old excuses from you, Julia! The rent is six weeks overdue!” he's shouting at my mother, every word that escapes his mouth laced with impatience.

“I—I'm so sorry, Rob! I've been struggling to make ends meet, but I promise you I will find a way to pay back what is owed,” my mother says, sounding choked up.

"I've been patient enough, but patience doesn't pay the bills!"

I hold my breath and close my eyes, imagining I'm on a beach. It's sunny, and Rob isn't there. I can hear the waves crashing against the shoreline, the wind lashing my face, and the salty air rising to welcome me. The best part is that I'm alone and at peace with the world. Nothing can spoil this moment of utter tranquillity except the harsh reminder of my reality, which is about to come crashing down again.

"I don't want to hear it! Get your life together and sort yourself out. You're an embarrassment!" Rob's voice slices through the air.

I almost trip as I descend the staircase, and my mother's eyes flash to me, her face stained with tears.

"Don't you dare talk to my mother like that!" I yell at him.

Rob's bushy eyebrows twitch as he looks up at me.

"You'd better stay out of this," he warns, waving a chubby finger in my face.

"Skye, please go back to your room," my mother begs.

Rob edges forward, and I take a giant step away from him. I'm never usually intimidated, but Rob is much bigger than me. I could never defend myself against him if things got out of hand.

"One day, that mouth of yours will get you into trouble," he snarls, scratching at his receding hairline.

"Go, Skye. Please go," mum pleads.

Reluctantly, I drag my feet upstairs and wait for the argument to end, but it only seems to continue, and at one point, I don't think it will ever stop. I must have dozed off during the fight, resting against a spindle on the staircase, because when the front door slams shut, I jolt awake in a cold sweat.

Rushing downstairs, I return to my mother's side. She still stands near the door, a vacant expression on her face. I wonder if there was a time my mother smiled and meant it. When was the last time she truly smiled? One minute, she seems larger than life; the next, she hits a wall again, unable to crawl back to the surface for air.

Stray tears roll down her face.

It breaks my heart.

"Rob was right. I am a mess. I don't know what we're going to do," she reveals, wiping her tear-stained eyes.

"Rob is a scumbag. We'll figure something out. Even if it means I have to get a part-time job."

"I tried to convince him to extend the rent deadline, but he wants the money by the end of next month."

Rob is not the understanding or gentle type. She should know that by now. There's no way he would extend the deadline, so trying to reason with him is pointless.

"How much does he want?"

"Over a thousand."

My eyes go wide. "Woah! How is it that much?"

My mother's shoulders rise and fall, entirely out of sync. Her reaction is making me panic more. I have no money to my name, and she only works at a local bakery in town.

"I forgot to pay the rent last month, so it's a back-dated amount," she explains, avoiding my gaze.

“Can't we sell some stuff? We could do a boot sale on Saturday at the market.”

“And how do you suppose we get there, Skye? You can't exactly transport our belongings on that beaten-up bike you always ride. It's not like we've got anything valuable to sell anyway,” she snaps, voice rising.

I'm starting to feel the first beads of sweat.

Rob will not let this go, and we'll have to think fast. Otherwise, we'll be thrown out onto the streets and might be dragged into something neither of us signed up for.

* * *

Sleep wasn't possible last night, and it has influenced my mood. Forget that I barely managed to finish my assignment on time; I am one hundred percent certain that it's not my best work. If anyone chooses to mess with me this morning, they will face my wrath. I didn't bother putting on makeup. I probably look like a walking zombie. I may as well have 'do not disturb' written across my forehead.

I spot Grayson sitting at my table, invading my workspace, and I realise I have a bigger problem on my hands. A girl is sitting in his lap, and I'm guessing she must be his girlfriend. She's stunning, of course, in every form of the word—a model. With a face like that, I'm sure she's bound to have had plenty of opportunities to show it off.

“Is that *her*?” the girl whispers, spinning to Grayson to discuss me openly.

It's a pity I don't care what either of them thinks.

Otherwise, their comments might mean something. Her words are just wasted on me.

She plants a territorial kiss on Grayson's lips and smirks triumphantly. If she's anticipating a response, she may want to give up on the idea because I don't find Grayson even remotely attractive, and I know he doesn't think much of me, either. His girlfriend seems like the type who thrives on attention—practically lives and breathes it. That must be exhausting.

"I'll see you later, babe... if you survive," she says, throwing me another sly glance as she leaves the room.

My face tightens, and I let my gaze land intentionally on Grayson's. He's holding a pen between his teeth, his mouth curling up into an almost smile, but there's no warmth behind it.

"Class viper, we meet again," he says smugly.

I flinch at the nickname, rolling my eyes as I claim my seat. "You'd better watch the ink doesn't spill in that pen. You wouldn't want to ruin your pearly whites."

"Aw, thanks for caring."

"Don't misunderstand me. I'm more concerned about how much ink would go to waste."

This seems to shut him up until Ricky starts collecting our essays. Grayson is calm when he hands his paper over, whereas I'm in the middle of a mid-life crisis.

"That was so easy!" he cries, leaning back in his chair once Ricky is out of earshot.

Eddie chuckles, and I hear him chewing a sweet loudly from behind me. He must be eating with his mouth open because the sounds he's making should not be audible to the human ear.

"Dude, we aced it! Top marks, I reckon, hands down!"

Above my head, they give each other high-fives.

*They're acting like a pair of toddlers competing for a gold star.*

Grayson gives me a sideways glance, and I narrow my eyes in preparation for what he will say next.

"Did you finish your assignment on time, Skye?" he asks, sounding suspiciously nicer than usual.

*I'm not an idiot.*

He's not asking me this to be friendly or out of the goodness of his heart. He has a hidden agenda.

"Yes, not that it's any of your beeswax, Swain."

"Ah, it's natural to panic a bit. Don't worry if you don't get the results you want the first time around. You could always resubmit when the opportunity presents itself."

I hated Grayson Swain the moment he arrived at this place, but now he is my sworn enemy. He is underestimating my ability to write.

"You may have had the top score back at Lakeside, but Barnett College is not known to take it easy with the marking scheme. Be prepared for disappointment."

"All the more reason for you to be worried. I'm one of the top students at Lakeside. That will not change, especially considering who I'm up against."

"Not everything has to be made into a competition, Grayson."

He blinks a few times like he's developed a slight twitch in his eye. "Whatever. I'm done with this conversation. It's boring."

"Good, because my eyes were starting to hurt just looking at you."

He opens his mouth, then closes it. I grin triumphantly, satisfied with his inability to invent a quick comeback. I've managed to get the last word this time. I deserve a pat on the back or some form of recognition. A gold star would be equally as satisfying.

I face forward, determined to get him out of my system. I need to stay focused. This class is my only source of normalcy in an otherwise chaotic world, and I can't let Grayson Swain ruin the experience for me. I guess I'll just have to act like he doesn't exist.

"If we were to conduct a news interview, for example, how would we approach it?" Ricky is asking the class.

"You would—"

"First, you would schedule the interview," Grayson says, cutting across me.

*So rude.*

"State the blinking obvious Albert Einstein." I direct my full attention towards Ricky again and say, "One of the main procedures would be to conduct research. You can't interview without research."

Grayson places a hand over his heart dramatically.

"Thank you, Skye. I'm so happy you're comparing me to one of the brainiest men ever."

"There's this thing called sarcasm."

"Never heard of it."

Ricky sighs heavily and shakes his head. "Would both of you cut it out already? You're acting like a pair of bickering schoolchildren!"

"Sir, when will we be doing some work?" Shelly pipes

up, making me want to hit her over the head a few times with her stationary kit. She's a popular member of the Lakeside crew and might be more stuck up than Grayson himself if that's even remotely possible.

Ricky maintains his composure, and I have no idea how he does it.

“You need to be able to work together, and group discussions are a good way to generate ideas.”

Shelly pops her gum and snorts. “We used to work individually at Lakeside, which suited us just fine. We didn't need much guidance, unlike these Barnett college wannabes.”

The class erupts, and Ricky tries to be the voice of reason but can't be heard above the noise. Grayson throws a rubber band at me, signalling that the war has just begun.

~~Capulets vs Montagues.~~

Lakeside vs Barnett.

*Let’s do this.*

If we were in Romeo and Juliet, the battle scene would involve swords and knives, but as alternative weapons, we have stationary, a couple of rubbers, and a few pencils, which will have to do.

Another elastic band is fired in my direction and bounces off the tip of my nose.

*Something in me snaps.*

Reaching for my pencil case, I throw it at Grayson full-force, but instead of striking him, it makes a loud smash against the glass window pane. He laughs at my failed missile attempt, so I smack him over the head with my notebook while his eyes are still closed.

He casts the iciest glance my way. “Woah! What the hell? This college is bloody bonkers. You’re crazy!”

I'm about to invent another comeback, but Ricky's voice invades the room, silencing the class in seconds, “That's enough! This is not acceptable! Quite frankly, I'm disappointed!”

“Me too! I thought this college would at least have computers that function. I can't even comment on the Wi-Fi. It only works in certain areas of the building. I have to lean out of the window to get internet access,” Grayson exclaims, throwing his hands in the air.

Ricky approaches our table, eyes narrowed. He can be pretty terrifying when he wants to be. From being the gentle giant we’ve all come to know and love, he’s suddenly transformed into a predatory lion within seconds. I was never introduced to this side of him until the Lakeside students arrived.

A smile takes over my entire face when I notice Grayson visibly tremble as Ricky continues to stare him down, and then everyone retreats quietly to their seats.

Ricky walks over to the whiteboard, eyeing us all carefully. “No one is happy about the situation, of course, but you have to accept that this is how things will be for a while. You can criticise my work ethic all you want, but I won’t alter my teaching or methods of instruction for anyone.”

I do a little victory dance in my head, and I'm dying to chant, ‘Go, Ricky! Go!’ but something tells me it wouldn't be appropriate.

“Barnett College students, this rule applies to you also. Your behaviour has been just as unacceptable. You can continue to hate each other, but I expect you to put your differences aside in my classroom."

A few hushed whispers travel around the room.

"If you can't tolerate it here any longer, feel free to go, but remember that finishing this course is the only way to get to university. We are the best you will get at this point."

Nobody moves or says anything, and I realise how much I've missed learning in silence.

Arriving at the library, I'm happy to find it mostly empty. I can hear a few people tapping away on their keyboards and the sound of pens greeting paper, making a constant scratching noise. I sit behind a computer screen and print off some sheets for upcoming assignments. It's not urgent, but I must take my mind off the madness that is going on inside my brain. The distraction serves me well until the printer decides it doesn't want to cooperate.

My mother told me not to worry about the rent situation, but it has been pretty much all I've thought about, especially considering she earns a pittance and will struggle to pay Rob his money back by the end of next month.

Seeing as I'm already on the internet, I quickly search the Indeed website, carefully scrolling down the list of job vacancies. To my horror, there seem to be few. I've always known that Barnett lacks opportunity, but I only realised its severity now.

I change the miles for my next search and the page refreshes. My eyes zoom in on a new post that wasn't there before. It was put on the system virtually ten seconds ago.

I click on the link and read over the brief job description.

# WE ARE HiRiNG

We currently need a cheerful, motivated, hardworking individual to join our team at Trinity stables. Experience is not essential, but a genuine love for horses and a willing attitude are.

Urgently needed!

**Stable hand**

Part-time positions

**Benefits:**

- Competitive salary
- Paid vacation and holidays
- Medical, dental, and vision insurance

If you are interested in this job opportunity, please send your resume to

**Trinitystables@gmail.com.**

We look forward to hearing from you!

I can't apply for this, can I?

I don't have any experience with horses, and it would help if I liked them. Why would someone from Lakeside hire me when there are probably more experienced people? There would be little use in applying because they presumably already have someone in mind for the role.

I close my eyes and let my head hit the table, telling myself to give them a brief rest, but before I know it, I'm transported into a distant memory.

*Mummy is going out again.*

*A man fills the doorway, and I hide behind mummy's leg as he smiles at me, showcasing a row of crooked teeth.*

*I wish mummy was staying with me and not going somewhere with this scary man. Sometimes, she's gone for days, and I worry she will forget about me.*

*Mummy walks out of the house, and a cold shiver travels down my spine when the strange man winks at me before shutting the door behind them. I rise onto my tiptoes to peer through the letterbox, my eyes searching for any sign of her changing her mind.*

*She doesn't.*

*Sadness consumes me.*

*The babysitter offers no comfort, so I curl into a small ball on the floor, close my eyes and let my imagination whisk me away to a castle where mummy is my fierce protector against the evil warlocks.*

*The hours pass, and my attempts to imagine I'm elsewhere aren't working because a glimmer of hope is lost. Not even my imagination can save me now.*

*Nearing Midnight, I'm relieved to see my mother return home, but she breaks down under the weight of her emotions, sobbing uncontrollably.*

*"What's wrong, mummy?" I ask her, concerned.*

*Her tears are seemingly unstoppable, and her pain is so palpable that it tugs at my heart, making me want to weep alongside her.*

*"It's fine, Skye. Go to your room. I'll come and see you in a second," she manages to utter between sobs.*

*Reluctantly leaving her side, I retreat to my room and slip under the covers, anxiously waiting for her to tuck me into bed. Seconds turn into minutes, minutes into hours, and still, mummy does not come.*

*The realisation settles in.*

*She's not coming, and it's because of the monster.*

*It won't leave mummy alone.*

*I'm sad now because the monster has won.*

*It always wins.*

I shoot up from the table, and my eyes flash open, the memory still fresh.

When I was seven, I was aware of my mother's depression. She kept it a secret from everybody else but couldn't hide it from me. She pretended everything was alright on certain days but found it difficult to get out of bed on other days. Her strategy was moving on to the next object or person, but it was never successful.

Although the days were moving ahead, she was still comfortably trapped in the past, most of the damage done before I came into the picture. Now, she lives her life behind a false smile and identity. She only reveals her most genuine self when she's behind closed doors.

That's when she breaks.

I notice that the printer has finally responded to my demands, and I start collecting the papers, hoping that nobody saw me taking a nap on the desk. As much as I don't want to apply for the Trinity job, nobody else will come to my mother's rescue. I have nothing to lose, only something to gain if they miraculously want to hire me.

Mustering up the courage, I attach my CV to the email and fire it off into the universe, where my fate awaits me.

# Chapter Three

"I've got something to tell you all," Ricky says, encouraging the class to look up at him with equal amounts of horror because we all know how his little announcement ended the last time he had something to tell us.

Another college invaded ours, and a war broke out between the original and new students, resulting in the biggest divide in college history—a Shakespearean Montague vs Capulet battle within a classroom environment, minus the swoon-worthy Romeo and Juliet.

"We have to start focusing on the class project that will take place over the next eight weeks. You will be expected to get to know your partner intimately."

"Ooh, I like the sound of that. Sign me up, sir," Eddie says, causing some boys to snigger amongst themselves.

*Ugh. Disgusting.*

"Sir, can't we choose our partners to save you the trouble? Maybe it would be easier for the Lakeside students to stick together and vice versa," Grayson suggests, making a valid point for once.

"I agree. I'd rather work with someone I like," Shelly comments, even though nobody asked her opinion. The girl is entirely unavailable. You don't exist in Shelly's world unless you were born and bred in Lakeside.

"The pairs have been decided, and I've chosen them for a reason. The main purpose of this project is to get an insight into another person's background. It's a reflection piece. It would be too easy to pair you up with a friend you've known for years. Some of you will not be happy with my decisions, but nobody is swapping partners," Ricky continues as if he was never interrupted.

We're all sitting at the edge of our seats while Ricky reads the list out loud. I don't know what he is trying to accomplish by doing this, but if he's expecting us to start building friendships with the Lakeside students, he can forget it.

"This is exciting, isn't it?" Josie whispers, spinning around in her chair to face me.

I stare at her like she's living in an alternate universe.

"I couldn't think of anything worse. I hope I'm not paired up with—"

"Grayson and Skye, you are the last pair," Ricky interrupts me mid-sentence, sending my poor heart into overdrive.

I turn instinctively towards Grayson.

*There is no way I am working with him.*

*It's not happening.*

*I refuse.*

Averting my eyes, I grit my teeth.

Disappointed is an understatement. I'm concerned for my health. I don't know how I'll cope with having Grayson around for longer than five minutes when I can barely cope with him in class.

How the heck will I survive a few weeks with the guy?

"Sir, you can't expect me to work with Skye on this. I can't afford to fail," Grayson speaks up, mid-panic.

*My days of holding back are over.*

I grip my chair and twist around to face him.

"I'm the one that can't afford to fail! I am not happy about this either. We're not compatible."

"It's true! She drives me insane!" Grayson agrees.

"And he's impossible!" I conclude.

"I've paired you two because you're always fighting over your different opinions, yet you're more alike than you think," Ricky says.

"Are you kidding me? We're complete opposites!" Grayson scoffs as if the idea of us being close to similar is impossible.

"I couldn't agree more! We are from completely different worlds!"

"What if that's the point?" Ricky counters, silencing us. "This project is called From Opposite Sides. The goal is to discover your partner's childhood, interests, and hobbies. We all live extremely distinct lives as individuals. Therefore, there may come a time when you'll be requested to tell someone else's story. Think of this project as a trial run. It accounts for seventy percent of your final grade this year."

*I feel like I am going to throw up at that reminder.*

"This might seem like a disaster, but you will thank me when you write exceptional pieces. You might even find you get along better once it's completed."

There is nothing to learn about Grayson Swain other than he comes from a wealthy family, owns a red Bugatti and enjoys making my life miserable. Therefore, I have no interest in finding out anymore aside from the obvious.

I can attempt to persuade Ricky to change his mind.

*It's worth a shot.*

After class, I'll make it my mission to ensure Grayson is no longer working with me on this assignment.

"Sir, I need to talk to you about something."

*Good start. It's better to get straight to the point. I want a partner switch and will not leave until I get one.*

I am more of a writer than a public speaker, so now that I'm standing in front of Ricky, the nerves kick in almost immediately.

Ricky stops sorting through some papers on his desk to look at me and says, "Go on."

"I'm all for supporting diversity and equality and whatnot, but please, can you pair me with somebody else for the project?"

Ricky shakes his head, and my stomach does that disappointed flip.

"Grayson was just asking me the same question."

*That little weasel. He beat me to the punch. I wanted to be the one to ask for a partner switch first.*

“My decision hasn't changed, Skye. Nobody is swapping.”

I clutch my folder tightly, willing myself not to cry.

“Why Grayson Swain, though? I would have been fine with anyone else, but you know how much we clash. It will be difficult getting to know him when we don't like each other.”

Ricky gives a slight nod, and for a split second, I think maybe I’ve persuaded him to see things my way.

“Skye, this might be the breakthrough you need. You're a great writer, but you’ve always held yourself back. It would help if you found your muse. You need to ask yourself, what makes you stand out?”

What if I never find my voice as a writer?

If I don’t, what else could I do with my life?

I dream of leaving Barnett eventually, but sometimes, that goal is shut down because it seems unrealistic.

“Maybe I'm just not good enough,” I say, feeling sorry for myself.

“One thing you are not is a quitter. Don't be afraid to let people get to know you—the real you. Grayson is your polar opposite, but you could learn from each other if you're willing to try.”

I'm not ready to share a private part of myself with the world or Grayson. I'm not prepared to take the mask off yet. I gather my bag and make my way out of the classroom, firing Ricky one last glance.

“Thanks, sir. I'll keep that in mind.”

I start walking down the busy corridor. The crowds of people become a blurry mass of colour, and I'm just tailing after them, another person who doesn't belong—another person pretending that she does.

It's a miracle I can get home because I am truly exhausted. The thought of taking a hot shower is all I can think about as I walk inside my house and steer my bike into the narrow passageway, teeth clattering while I struggle to shut the door behind me.

Our floral wallpaper is starting to tear in certain places and urgently needs replacing. The whole house could use a makeover if we could afford to pay for the damage. A draft comes in from somewhere, and the winter months are the worst. Even the central heating can't help to provide enough warmth.

After watching a few episodes of *Tipping Point* with my mother, I eventually shower and retreat to my room to finish studying for the remainder of the evening.

While I'm waiting for Microsoft Word to load up, Batman decides to make his presence known. At a distance, you might assume that he is a dog or some wild animal on the loose, but he is just my dysfunctional cat. I called him Batman because I have the biggest crush on Michael Keaton, and I'm a huge Batman fan.

Batman is supernaturally clever, with big googly eyes and thick black fur. In the daytime, he does nothing but sleep. At night, he's very much alive. He doesn't like anyone else's company aside from his own.

Our gazes lock across the room, an intense stare-off unfolding between us. He leaps onto the windowsill, and without hesitation, he propels himself into the night, disappearing into the shadows beyond. I don't know when I will see him again, but he always returns, usually with a vengeance.

I return to my computer screen and type the project's name into the header section on Microsoft Word.

**From Opposite Sides**

The title itself is making me feel nauseous already. However, I am beginning to understand the inner workings of Ricky's mind. This is a creative assignment if it can be executed well.

I'm staring at my computer screen for the longest time until my phone buzzes on my desk.

It's an email.

My heart leaps into my throat when I read who it is from.

FROM: TRINITYSTABLES@GMAIL.COM

SUBJECT: TRINITY STABLES APPLICATION

Dear Skye,

As you're probably aware, we have had a high volume of applications for this position. I'm sure you understand that narrowing them down has been difficult. However, we would like to schedule an interview with you.
Is tomorrow at five O'clock suitable? If you can make it, please let me know so I can send over the address.

Kind regards,
Michael

*Holy crap.*

# Chapter Four

IT TAKES FORTY-FIVE MINUTES TO GET TO LAKESIDE ON FRIDAY. The houses are neatly aligned, with private driveways, balconies and freshly cut front gardens. Open bay windows give visitors a glimpse into the kind of life the Lakeside students lead. I must keep reminding myself to close my mouth whenever I turn into another street because it's hanging open in amazement.

One thing I notice is how quiet the area is. There's hardly anybody around. Back in Barnett, the streets are loud and chaotic. The streets and roads at Lakeside are dead—lifeless even.

Do people even live in these houses, or are they there to look pretty?

My breath catches when I notice a luxurious, white mansion appearing up ahead. It looks like it's rolled straight out of a movie and has the power to make you fall in love with it at first sight. A sweeping staircase ascends gracefully towards the front door, and skeletal trees are everywhere. I can imagine how beautiful they must bloom in the summer. A marble fountain peeks behind the trees, creating a soft, melodic, gurgling sound.

*I can't believe somebody lives here.*

**12, Crescent Road, Lakeside.**

*This is it, the address from the email.*

I've only ever seen houses like this in photographs or on TV—never up close. The people that live here must be millionaires. I don't want to walk any closer because if I damage something, I'll never be able to pay for it. Everything about this place is over the top, expensive and intimidating.

I place my bike in the driveway and run up steep steps to ring the bell, rehearsing what I will say in my mind continuously.

*Be calm and collected. Try to avoid fidgeting. Hold eye contact. Most of all, give it your best shot.*

The door opens to reveal a man in a black tuxedo. It's so startling that I do a double-take.

*Are we in Bruce Wayne's mansion right now?*

*Is this Alfred?*

I'm finding it impossible to swallow.

My throat has dried up.

I lick my lips and force a smile onto my face.

"Uh, hi. I'm here for the Trinity interview."

"What is your name?" Alfred's doppelganger asks, looking me up and down, disinterested.

"Skye Clemons, but my email is Skyeclem@Yahoo.-co.uk, just in case you've got that written down somewhere and need me to clarify."

After an entire minute, the Alfred lookalike opens the

door wide so I can join him in the hallway. White shimmering tiles, cream carpets and open space living instantly blind me.

*I'm scared to breathe in here.*

"Follow me," he says, walking swiftly ahead, his back as stiff as an ironing board.

I let him lead the way, eyes flickering from one side of the house to the other. Every room seems to carry on, like a never-ending story. I'm paying so much attention to all the intricate details that I don't notice a giant dog bounding towards us, jumping up at me from every possible angle.

"Buckie. No," Alfred orders casually.

Miraculously, the dog ducks his head and leaves us, but anxiety sweeps over me until I find it hard to put one foot in front of the other.

The man stops outside a large wooden door, and I almost walk straight into him. He spins sharply towards me, his face wholly stripped of emotion. I'm curious if he's ever smiled in his lifetime. He looks me up and down again, making me feel self-conscious. I'm wearing my smartest clothes for the interview—a simple white blouse, flat shoes and casual black trousers. Pedalling proved trickier than I thought, so the bottom of my trousers got a little muddy along the way. That is why I'm under this guy's scrutiny.

*I think that coming here was a huge mistake.*

"Mr Swain will see you now."

I freeze, positive I heard him say, Mr Swain.

"Uh... sorry, what was that?" I ask him, dread rising in my chest.

"Mr Swain insists on meeting all the applicants who have applied for this post. He's very passionate about the work at Trinity and wants to hire the right person for the role. Best of luck."

His words of encouragement are not enough to reassure me because I am about to be interviewed by Grayson Swain's father.

"Come in," a male voice orders from behind the door.

Every single muscle in my body has become taut with fear. If Mr Swain is anything like his son, we're about to engage in a hostile and uncomfortable conversation. There's still time to turn around and forget that this ever happened. I don't have to go through with it. I'll slip quietly out of the door. Nobody will ever suspect that I was here.

"Come in," Mr Swain repeats, a tinge of frustration in his voice.

I don't know what compels me to open the door, but I'm already inside the room before I can think twice about my decision.

It's bright and surprisingly cosy. A man is busy sorting through some papers on his desk. The smell of freshly made coffee lingers in the air, along with an expensive cologne that belongs to the formally dressed man sitting in front of me. Above his desk, there is a family photograph hanging on the wall. I notice Grayson is in the picture straight away. His eyes are drilling into me from across the room.

The pressure is building in my chest.

*This was such a bad idea.*

I feel like I've stood there an eternity until Mr Swain

finally looks up from his workload to acknowledge me. Our eyes meet, and I stare into the ocean's deepest depths. It sounds corny, but there's no other way to describe his eyes. They're so startling. I can't stop staring into them.

Mr Swain's entire presence has the power to turn heads. He is much younger than I thought—a similar age bracket to my mother, possibly in his late thirties, and his hair is honey-blond. He's wearing a designer suit that must have cost him a fortune, and everything I had planned to say in this interview has been completely erased from my memory. I'm unprepared and speechless.

"Please take a seat and introduce yourself," he instructs.

Carefully, I sit in an oversized armchair that swallows me whole.

"Uh... hi, I'm Skye Clemons. I'm seventeen and a half." I scramble for something else to say and end up with, "I'm here for the interview."

His eyebrows rise for a split second, and I blush bright red. Mr Swain leans forward, his smile never wavering. It's not one of those fake, overly-done smiles, either. It seems genuine.

"Tell me a bit about yourself, Skye."

*I loathe talking about myself.*

"Um, well..."

*Come on, words, don't fail me now.*

"I'm committed and determined, and I—"

He holds a hand in the air, preventing me from saying more. "I've heard this speech from the last five applicants. What makes you so different from the last person I just interviewed?"

*That's a fair question. I wish I knew how to answer it.*

I feel my face flood with colour.

"Um, I've..." *got nothing.*

More heat creeps up my neck.

*This is a disaster.*

"Why should I hire you, Miss Clemons?" he asks, his voice firm but not unfriendly.

Even if it means I leave without a job after this, I will give him what he wants—a different approach. It's not the end of the world if I don't get the position.

"Look, I'll be honest with you, Mr Swain. I am a college student from Barnett. Opportunities are scarce there, but I've never let that stop me. I work hard, and I believe in hard work. I didn't come here expecting this to be a walk in the park. I came here knowing that I would probably be less experienced than Applicant A and maybe even less qualified than Applicant B. Still, I refuse to compare myself to your previous candidates because no two people will be alike. To answer your question, I think you should hire whoever you think suits the role best. I'm just here to try, like everybody else."

His warm smile returns, and I don't find him intimidating anymore.

"Have you had any prior experience with horses?"

"I used to feed some in the field when I was about five, but that was a long time ago."

He chuckles, and the sound catches me off guard.

"That's not quite the kind of experience I was referring to, but I admire your honesty."

"Honesty is the best policy," I pause and quickly add, "Sir," just in case he's used to people calling him that.

I let out a shaky breath.

I am under Mr Swain's watchful eye, and I don't know whether that should scare me.

"If you were to get this position, you'd work two days a week. The role is pretty hands-on. You will clean the horses, groom them, brush their coats, and oil their hooves. In addition, we'd expect you to clean the stables, saddles, bridles, and other riding gear, fitting them on the horses. Any new bedding needs to be put down, and you would also need to get the horses ready for riding lessons and dressage events."

My brain has already reached its capacity.

That's a lot of information to take in.

"You wouldn't be working alone, of course. So, you can learn these things."

I nod. "Right. Yeah."

"Are you in college every day of the week?" he asks, moving on to something I can answer.

"I'm in college on Mondays, Tuesdays and Wednesdays, but I'm free every other day of the week, including weekends. I don't usually do much, so my timetable is flexible."

In simple terms, I don't lead the most active or superior lifestyle. It's boring now that I think about it.

"What are you studying at the moment?"

"Language and Literature."

"Oh, that's interesting. My son has just transferred to Barnett College, and he's studying the same thing. You might have seen each other around. His name is Grayson."

I can hardly dig myself out of this one now, can I?

If Mr Swain finds out that I'm in the same class as Grayson, he will probably mention it at the dinner table tonight, and my chances of getting this job will be even lower than when I first stepped foot into this office.

"Funnily enough, we're in the same class, but he doesn't know I've applied for this job, so I'd rather keep that information low-key if possible."

"Hm. Well, it's a small world." *Too small.* "What are your plans for the future? Are you hoping to become a writer someday?"

"That's the dream. Although, my tutor recently told me that I need to start branching out and broadening my horizons. He said I need to find my voice as a writer, which is another reason I'm here. I want to try something new and do exactly that."

I can't tell if he's pleased with my answer or not. Despite his infectious smile, he does have a pretty good poker face–similar to Grayson.

"I wouldn't normally hire someone without experience, but I think you've got a lot to offer. So, with that in mind, would you like the job?"

I stare at him, dumbfounded.

"Uh, aren't you supposed to tell me if I've got the job by the end of the week? Isn't that usually how it works?"

"I've never been a fan of tradition."

"Are you one hundred percent sure, though?"

"I could've easily hired the person that came in

before you, Skye, but I respect your honesty. It's refreshing. The job is yours if you want it."

*If I want it? Is he kidding?*

*This seems too good to be true.*

"I–I accept."

"Great. Let me give you a tour of the stables."

It's only a short walk from Grayson's house to Trinity Stables, but I feel sick as soon as we arrive. Never in a million years did I think I'd be offered this position, and now that I have accepted it, I'm worried I've just made the biggest mistake of my life because I officially work for Grayson's dad now, which means there's a strong chance I might bump into Grayson at the stables occasionally.

The farm is enormous, which doesn't surprise me. These people have money up to their eyeballs. They could probably swim in it. The sun shines directly on a lake, giving off the illusion that it's alive. Luscious mountains tower above the lake's surface, radiating a calmness that ripples and dances within the steady water below. Trees and flower beds surround the area, flooding the place with life and warmth.

Mr Swain frequently glances at me over his shoulder, checking that I'm still following him and haven't gone off to explore alone. He asks me questions I'm struggling to answer, and because I seem to have lost my ability to speak, I just nod along with everything he says.

Silence is all I can manage.

When we finally reach the stables, the harsh smell of horse manure hits me straight in the face. I can practically taste it. I'm tempted to pinch the end of my nose, but I am aware that Mr Swain is observing me, and if I can't deal with the smell now, how can I be expected to work here?

There are separate stalls for each horse, and a couple of the animals are looking at us from behind them, dark eyes following our every move.

*I wonder if horses can sense fear because I've got plenty of it.*

"I will have to introduce you to our other stablehand. He will be on the same shift as you, so you will see a lot of each other. Getting acquainted as soon as possible will be good for you both. You will get to meet him next week. He isn't here today," Mr Swain says.

"Uh, okay, cool."

*Really? Of all the words I could have used, I went with uh, okay, cool. How original.*

"Anyway, I'm confident you will enjoy it here. If you run into any issues, please don't hesitate to contact me. I won't always be here, but I like to stop by when I can. I expect you to be at Trinity next Friday at seven in the morning. The working hours are long, with late finishes."

*That's what I'm worried about.*

"Any questions?"

*Ask him if Grayson visits this place a lot.*

*Ask him.*

*Go on.*

*Ask him!*

"No. None that I can think of."

That's going to cost me.

# Chapter Five

Baking is a regular human activity, but my mother only bakes this much when she's stressed. She's made various cupcakes, all crafted to utter perfection. Some have sprinkles on top, others are made entirely out of chocolate, and the rest are just plain sponges with the right amount of jam in the middle. As mouth-watering as these creations are, it's a little over the top.

I sit at the table and watch her rush around the kitchen like a mad woman. We've already got enough cake to last us an entire week.

"Try a cupcake, Skye. They're so good!" she cries, giving me an encouraging nod.

Reluctantly, I pick up a cupcake and take a small bite out of it. The flavour is delicious and melts in my mouth, but I can't enjoy the experience as much as I would like to because these cakes represent a build-up of emotions and show signs of decline rather than improvement. I'd like to believe that on good days, my mother is getting better, but, in the end, the outcome is never promising.

"They're lovely."

This brings a smile to her face, but I know that what I'm about to say next is going to jeopardise the happy mood that she's in.

"Are you okay?"

She doesn't spare me a glance as she continues to rummage through containers and jars.

"Mum..."

Her eyes snap to mine. Lines crease her forehead. Nobody outside of the house ever sees this side of her. Instead, they see what she wants them to see.

"What? I'm fine," she snaps, a bit forcefully.

"You can talk to me, you know? I'm here."

"Everything is okay, Skye. Stop fussing."

I desperately want to believe her, but lately, I've realised that trusting what she says is not worth it because, half the time, she's unwilling to admit that there's a problem.

"So, what time do you start work tomorrow?" she asks, changing the subject entirely.

When I first told my mother I got the job at Trinity, she was thrilled to hear about it, but once she found out that I had to travel over to Lakeside, her excitement died almost instantaneously. I knew she would worry about the long-distance thing, but her reaction confused me. Anyway, I've thought no more about it since then because I don't want to be negative. This job has come at just the right time, and it's preventing us from being evicted, so it'll be the perfect solution if I can stick it out until I've made back the money we owe Rob.

"I start at seven, so I'll probably have to leave at six to give myself plenty of time to get there," I say.

Mum stares vacantly into space for another second or two. "I'm proud of you, Skye, but this is all my fault. You shouldn't have needed to search for a job because I screwed up."

I give her hand a quick squeeze.

"Hey, don't be so hard on yourself. I'm happy to help if it keeps Rob off our case."

Mum nods her head painfully slowly. After a while, she tells me that she's going to bed, which is alarming since it's only three in the afternoon. She blames it on all the baking and that it's tired her out, but I'm not convinced. She's mentally falling apart right in front of my eyes.

It's only when I find myself alone in the kitchen that I feel her absence.

* * *

Walking into Trinity Stables for my first day of work, I keep telling myself it's just like any other day.

I'm supposed to meet the other stablehand this morning, but Mr Swain forgot to mention his name or what he looks like, so I don't know how to find him.

Making my way towards the red barn atop a small hill, the sliding doors are already open, so I take a few steps forward and peep my head inside.

"Hello! Is anybody in here?"

My voice bounces back at me and alerts a few of the

horses. I apologise for disturbing them and then tell myself off for being so ridiculous.

"Hello!" I shout again, receiving nothing but a low grunt from a chestnut mare who looks ready to attack me after I rudely interrupted her beauty sleep.

I jerk my head up and twist around when a storage cupboard door opens, and out walks my co-worker.

*Right. This is it. Just be cool.*

I adjust my hair, check my breath and prepare to greet him with as much enthusiasm as possible.

*Hi. I'm Skye Clemons. I'm the new stablehand. Nice to meet you.*

Pretty straightforward. No big deal.

The boy lifts his head, and I get a better glimpse of his face, which sends my heart plummeting. I don't even have to look at him twice because he's easily recognisable.

I notice Rory Keaton's dark brows and hooded stare. Black clothing must be his favourite colour because that's all he wears. He hasn't seen me yet, or maybe he is just choosing to ignore my existence. I'm standing there, engulfed by an old baggy jumper I bought from a jumble sale years ago and a pair of denim overalls that are incredibly unflattering on the eye.

Rory's head whips up, and he does a double take like I've scared the living daylights out of him. I don't know whether to run, laugh, cry, or smile. Smiling takes a lot of effort, and when his famous smirk appears, my plans to greet him with a positive attitude have been terminated. I am back to being my usual grumpy self, thanks to him.

"Well, this is a surprise, Clemons. I didn't pin you

down as the horse-riding type," Rory says, his grin spreading.

*It looks like Mr Swain has kept him in the dark about this little arrangement.*

"I'm not here to ride the horses. I'm the new stablehand."

Rory stares at me for a long second and then bursts out laughing. "Seriously? You're the new stablehand? I doubt you know the first thing about horses."

I match his curiosity with a frown, placing both hands on my hips. "I know quite a bit."

He runs a hand through his tousled brown hair and laughs under his breath. "Oh, is that right? You won't need my help then. You can figure everything out yourself since you're so knowledgeable."

I watch him walk away, and my stomach twists. I might not like Rory, but I'm counting on this job. I have no choice but to suck it up and accept that he is officially my co-worker. We will need to find some common ground for this to work.

"Wait!" I call out, bringing him to a stop. "Fine. I lied. I don't know anything about horses or this stablehand stuff. Now, can you help me?"

Rory spins on his heel, refocusing his expression. "What's the magic word?"

I stick my nose in the air and shake my head roughly.

"Forget it."

"Alright. See you later. Good luck!"

Off he trots like a tall black stallion, blending into the shadows.

Stubbornness is my speciality.

It takes all my willpower to cry, "Please!"

He swivels, holding a hand close to his ear. "What was that? I didn't hear you."

I stomp my foot on the ground, and it seems to get a negative response from the horses. The black one is grinding its hooves into the gravel aggressively and neighing at the top of its lungs. If this horse could speak English, it would say, 'I'd like to stomp on your head.'

"Please," I say reluctantly, meeting Rory's gaze.

"Alright, I'll help you out. It's not like I have much of a choice. Mr Swain expects me to train you since you have no experience."

I can tell he's still trying to figure out why Mr Swain hired me instead of a more experienced applicant. I've been wondering the same thing.

"Try to keep up. I don't like having to explain myself twice. Also, you've ticked off Luna with all that foot stomping. You'll need to cut that out. The horses don't like it," he adds, inhaling deeply.

Luna, who was otherwise known as Chestnut a few seconds ago, is breathing heavily through her nostrils when I dare to glance in her direction again.

"That's a girl?"

Rory taps her on the back, and she neighs in appreciation. "Yup. She's as tough as steel and in popular demand. Seems to prefer the male stablehands to the females, especially fiery ones with bright red hair."

I touch my hair subconsciously.

"By the way, you might want to pin some of that up. The horses might mistake it for food and won't hesitate to bite it when your back is turned."

Taking orders from Rory is not going to be easy. I'd have no trouble listening to anyone else's demands, but I *know* Rory. That makes this situation incredibly awkward, not to mention completely out of my comfort zone.

He dumps a bucket of hay at my feet, and I stare down at it, perplexed.

"What exactly are you expecting me to do with that?"

"The first thing we do when we enter the stables is feed the horses. Otherwise, they are a pain in the backside, especially Dante." He gestures towards the black horse with a white stripe across its nose, proudly trotting around in its stall.

*Yikes.*

If I were the other horses, I wouldn't want to get on the wrong side of Dante. Compared to the rest, he stands out without even having to try. Dangerously beautiful. That's how I would describe him.

"Okay, so how do we feed them? Do I fling the food over the fence?"

Rory's laughter bounces off the walls, and my face burns with embarrassment.

"Wow. Remind me again why Mr Swain thought hiring you would be a good idea?"

"Just be helpful for once in your life."

Rory sighs and pulls me towards another stall. A petite horse is waiting on the other side of it, bushy tail swinging behind him. This guy could use a haircut. His fringe is hanging in front of his eyes. I'm surprised he can see anything at all.

"Okay, are you ready?" Rory asks, snapping me out of

my staring competition with the horse version of Cousin It.

"Huh? Ready for what?"

He rolls his eyes. "Pay attention, Clemons. I told you that I'm not going to be repeating myself."

Slowly, Rory opens the stall door, and we get a glimpse into the horse's world. It's not at all glamorous. There is manure everywhere and tons of flies buzzing around. One lands on my sleeve, and I quickly swat it away with my hand before Rory can take note of how much I'm freaking out.

He raises the bucket and pours the food into a white wall container. The horse is there in a flash, devouring everything inside it.

"This little guy is called Albatross. He's been at the stables for a while—one of our oldest horses. Still in good shape," Rory says, tapping him lightly on the back.

"Why hasn't anybody given Albatross a haircut? The poor guy can barely see because his fringe is longer than his face."

Rory's eyebrows shoot up.

He's acting like this is the first time he's ever heard anyone say that, and I'm finding it hard to believe.

"He hasn't complained."

"He's a horse," I remind him.

"Really? I had no idea," he mumbles sarcastically. "Stick to the job description, alright? You're not here to give the horses makeovers."

That's disappointing.

A few of them could use one.

. . .

I have never cleaned up so much poo in my entire life.

All horses do is poo, sleep, eat, and repeat. My job is to clean up as much of it as possible, using a pitchfork and wheelbarrow to transport it from the stables.

When I think we've outdone ourselves for the day, Rory leads me to the field, where we start all over again. I'm sweating through my clothes, and the bottom of my back feels like it's been trampled on by a herd of horses. I probably smell like something rotten, not that anybody cares.

Rory is shovelling away like an absolute pro, and I'm seriously lagging behind. I've been trying to lay low in case Grayson shows up unexpectedly, making my day even more difficult. If he does happen to appear while I’m mucking out after the horses, I don't think I would ever live it down. He would go to extreme lengths to humiliate me in front of our college class.

I bet his version of events would go a little something like this.

*'Guess what, guys? The funniest thing happened the other day. I saw Skye Clemons picking up horse poo on my Dad's farm. It turns out she works at Trinity Stables now. I should've taken a picture. It was priceless.'*

The sun beats down on my back, making my burning thirst impossible to ignore. The lake looks tempting enough to dive in, but bathing on my first day of work doesn't sound like the wisest idea. Besides, I only have a couple more hours left, and then I can go home.

Rory doesn't say much while we work, and that suits me. Neither of us are social butterflies, and we’re not willing to start now. So, we continue to work in total silence. It's not uncomfortable or strained, just mutual.

By the time my lunch hour comes around, I can't wait to sit down. I collapse onto a bench outside and delve into my sandwiches. I didn't realise how hungry I was or how much work would be involved in this stablehand business. I already feel so exhausted, and it's not even the end of the day yet. I've got another three hours of hard labour left to complete, and then I've got to face another round on Sunday.

*What has my life become?*

A loud neighing sound almost causes me to choke on my overcooked chicken. I turn sharply to the left and spot Rory riding Luna across the field. They compliment each other. It's the perfect pairing with Rory's stern demeanour and Luna's solid frame.

It takes me another long second to realise that a girl is riding alongside Rory, her light blond hair shimmering in the sun. It looks romantic — like a scene from a movie.

The two of them are engaging in what looks to be a pleasant conversation. It makes me feel a little left out and even more alone. This is unfamiliar to me; the horses, the routine, the responsibility. I'm unsure I can do such demanding tasks, but I won't give up. It's not in my nature. No matter how hard this gets, I will not surrender to my anxiety.

It'll get better.

It has to get better.

. . .

Lunch lasts roughly half an hour, although it feels like two seconds. I'm thrust back into the unknown, and Rory is in the middle of introducing me to two horses that have just returned to the stables. They are almost identical, but their personalities couldn't be more different.

"Dijon is full of love but doesn't know his own strength. He's a powerhouse," Rory explains, stepping into Dijon's stall with a confidence I wish I could borrow.

I hang back in case I somehow end up spooking the horse. Maybe it doesn't want me invading its territory. I'm still practically a stranger.

"He also loves listening to music. Watch this."

Rory grabs his phone, and a song fills the stables. Dijon instantly begins to sway back and forth, bobbing his head to the beat. It's the funniest thing I've seen in a long time.

"And then, in the next stall, we have Henry. We tend to call him a grumpy old man. I'll tell you why in a second."

I watch as he heads into Henry's stall as if it's the most natural thing in the world. I would be terrified. Horses up close are far more intimidating than those in photographs or at The Grand National.

"Most horses love being fussed over and can't get enough of it," he says, "but Henry is quite timid. You can show him some love, and then he'll be like, no more now. Get out of my personal space. I'm not interested. He's a bit standoffish."

Rory speaks with so much passion. The way he talks about the horses already makes me smile, and I quickly have to pack it in every time he opens his mouth. The last thing he needs is an ego boost. I can't afford to get distracted by this new version of him.

"So, how did you end up working at a place like this?" I ask, eager to hear a bit of his story.

"I got into some trouble last year..." he starts.

*Ah. That's not unusual. Trouble is his middle name, after all.*

"A couple of boys and I vandalised the farm, so as a consequence, we were told we could either do community service or pay off our debt by working here for a couple of months. I was the only one who chose the second option, and once I paid my dues, Mr Swain offered me a job."

He lets out a long sigh.

"Honestly, I don't know where I'd be if it weren't for this place. It keeps me sane and centred."

I don't like Rory very much, but if he's found something that makes him happy and keeps him out of trouble, then good for him.

"Do you go to college as well?"

Aside from that one time when he was chasing someone down the corridor, it has just occurred to me that I've never actually seen him around campus.

"College isn't for everyone," he says with a shrug.

"So if you don't go to Barnett College, how come I bumped into you there the other day? What were you doing chasing that boy around? It looked pretty intense..."

A dark shadow looms over his face, and I stop there because I've clearly said something I shouldn't have. I'm thankful when Mr Swain walks through the stable doors at that moment, wearing top-of-the-range riding gear, I suspect.

*Has he come to check that I haven't burned the place down already?*

"Mr Swain, I wasn't expecting to see you today. Is everything alright?" Rory asks, stepping forward.

"Everything is fine. I wanted to see how things were going. How has your first day been, Skye?" I like the way he pronounces my name—with meaning and respect.

"It's been a little overwhelming, but at the same time, I'm enjoying getting to know some of the horses' names and their unique personalities."

"I can imagine that it has been a lot to process. But it will get easier once you start coming here more regularly."

Is he Grayson's biological father?

This man is incredibly kind, and Grayson doesn't appear to have a single kind bone in his body.

"You can take the rest of the afternoon off, Skye. I need to have a chat with Rory about something."

I'm being cast out, knowing that whatever they're about to discuss does not include me. I'm not wanted, and I'm not trusted enough yet, either. I guess it's none of my business, so I leave them to carry on and don't speak another word as I whisper a silent goodbye to Trinity Stables and hello to my old life.

# Chapter Six

THE CHAINS COME LOOSE ON MY BIKE WHILE I'M ON MY WAY TO college, and I almost crash into a lamppost. I bend down to observe the damage and shuffle myself and the bike closer to the edge of the pavement so I'm not blocking the public path. My shoulders automatically stiffen when I hear a loud laugh behind me, along with the expensive slam of a car door.

"The mystery has finally been solved," Grayson says, standing over me, the sun appearing from bchind a ray of clouds, bringing out the blond tones in his hair.

"Go away," I snarl under my breath.

He swings his car keys around, trying to act cooler than he is. "Ouch. You've hurt my feelings."

"I seriously doubt it."

"Is that any way to treat your partner for the project? I'll have to report your hostility to Ricky."

My gaze turns icy.

"Right now, you're nothing but a local pedestrian. And tell Ricky whatever you want. I don't care."

Grayson glances down at my bike with a judgemental look, his brows pulling together. "I've always wondered why you habitually show up late to class. This explains it. Do you seriously ride that rusty old thing to college every day?"

I sigh under my breath, tired of this conversation.

"Yes. The correct term is bicycle, by the way. I thought you were good at English, grammar boy."

"There'll be nothing left of that soon. It looks like you bought it from a scrapyard."

I rise to stand, meeting him at eye level.

"You're suddenly an expert in bikes now, are you?"

"I can spot a cry for help when I see one. This poor bike has endured enough sweat and tears. It's coming to its ultimate end." He glances down at my greasy hands, and I quickly stuff them into my trouser pockets. "You might want to visit the lady's room, by the way. You've got grease all over your face."

My hands automatically cup my cheeks.

"I do?"

"Hah! No! I can't believe you fell for that! Now, you definitely need to wash your face. It's looking a bit shiny, class viper," he says, chuckling as he struts towards the college building.

I imagine running Grayson over with my bike.

That would surely wipe the annoying smirk off his face.

I'm five minutes late to class, and the urge to strangle the culprit only strengthens.

I stink of rusted metal and something else.

*Wait a minute...*

I lift the back of my shoe and gasp.

I've stepped in dog's mess.

No wonder people looked at me funny while I was walking to class. I thought that a drainpipe had burst somewhere, but nope. It's me.

I stink.

Grayson covers his nose, and I don't have time to run away because his eyes travel south, and he gets more than he bargained for. A large grin takes over his face, and he can't control his giggles.

"Uh oh... it looks like the class viper has had a bit of an accident, folks," he says, laughing at me.

*I want to crawl into a hole somewhere and hide.*

Fleeing the room, I reach the nearest toilets and stick my shoe under the tap. I soak the back of it with some soap and hot water. The dog responsible for this creation must've eaten a big meal beforehand.

Why can't dog owners clean up after their dogs?

It's not fair that the general public has to suffer like this.

I wobble slightly whilst sliding my shoe back on, and when I re-enter the classroom, I refuse to look at Grayson because I can still hear him chuckling. It's incredibly irritating.

"Since you've all got a lot of work to do, I've decided to let you use this lesson time to focus on the project," Ricky says, making me want to head butt the table.

*I'm never going to catch a break. Ricky is starting to push my buttons with all these unexpected lesson changes.*

The class starts to move around, and I force myself to look at Grayson. He's staring out the window, aggressively tapping his pen against the desk.

“This is pure torture,” he mumbles, shaking his head.

“Well, I'm not exactly thrilled about it either, Einstein!”

“You have a bad temper, Skye,” he declares, pointing the pen at me and waving it in my face like he's casting a spell. I wouldn't put it past him. “Let's talk about that. Do you have anger issues?”

“Only as far as you're concerned. I have a serious problem with you.”

“Okay, so when did this unhealthy obsession start?”

I snort at him. “Get off your high horse.”

*No pun intended.*

“It's natural to think about me every so often. Lots of girls do. I can't help it that I'm irresistible.”

“More like infuriating with a capital I.”

“Ooh, that's a big word. Did you learn that yourself?”

I throw my hands up. “You're so full of crap.”

“I believe you were the one that was full of crap a couple of seconds ago... quite literally.”

I point my chin up to the ceiling, averting my eyes.

“Well, I haven't found a single good quality in you yet, and that's alarming.”

“Ditto.”

I arch an eyebrow. “At least I can admit that I've got flaws. You can't even acknowledge that you're no different from me.”

Grayson tilts his head and slumps down in his chair,

looking agitated. "We have absolutely nothing in common, Skye."

"Good. I'm glad!"

We don't say anything for a few moments. Both of us glare at each other across the table, nostrils flaring. Out of all the people in this class, why did Ricky have to pair me with Grayson? We're halfway into our first week of working together, and we've done nothing but argue.

To make matters worse, Ricky happens to be walking right up to our table at that exact moment, and the tension is palpable.

"How are you two getting along?" he asks cheerfully, seemingly oblivious.

I wave a hand in Grayson's direction, dismissing him.

"We're not... getting along, I mean. I can't even talk to him right now."

"Me neither. She's a right drama queen."

"Referring to yourself again, are you Grayson?" I counter with a fake smile.

Ricky places a hand on the table, interrupting us before the real fight begins.

"Can I see your notes, please?"

We present him with the notes we've taken so far, and he glances at the single page, perplexed.

"This is all you've got?"

"Uh, we've mostly been getting to know each other on a no-note-taking basis," Grayson says, feeding Ricky a load of BS so we don't get into trouble. "Also, Skye didn't want to take notes. I kept telling her we should, but she wouldn't listen."

I gape at him.

“You're talking trash! I never said that! Don't put words in my mouth!”

“Here she goes again, playing little Miss Innocent. Don't let her fool you, sir,” he says with a grin, winking at me.

*I am going to kill him.*

“This is not good enough. You don't have time to mess about or call each other names. You've both got to start shaping up. Otherwise, neither of you will be passing this project, and I would hate to see that happen. I really would,” Ricky says, shaking his head disappointedly.

I exchange worried glances with Grayson, knowing he's thinking the same thing I am.

We're screwed.

* * *

Waking up at six in the morning is not fun, especially when I have to pedal the whole forty-five-minute journey to Lakeside.

I come across a large, black motorbike in the car park. I can only assume that this piece of machinery belongs to Rory. It looks like something he would own. I can't imagine Mr Swain ever taking this for a spin, but who knows? Maybe underneath all that expensive clothing and fancy hair gel, there is a daring side to him just waiting to be unleashed.

Rory is busy preparing food for the horses when I walk into the stables. The cold chill bites through my clothes, and my teeth chatter, creating a noise that is startling enough to attract his attention.

He glances at me, then back at the ground.

"You're late," he huffs.

Usually, I'm the one that's in a bad mood. I'm about to experience what it's like to be on the receiving end of one.

"Sorry. I would've gotten here sooner, but I underestimated the traffic."

"Whatever. You don't have to explain yourself to me. You're here. That's the main thing."

*I'm starting to wish I was elsewhere but go figure.*

"I've already filled the food buckets, so you can start feeding Albatross and Luna."

"Right. I can do that."

*I think.*

I pick up one of the buckets and wobble towards Albatross's stall. He's watching me intensely while I try to juggle the bucket and open the gate.

"Hi, Albatross. I'm new, so please go easy on me, buddy."

*I'm talking to the horse as if expecting it to reply. I need to stop overthinking this.*

I tug and tug at the lock, but it doesn't budge. My foot slips, and I lose balance, legs almost doing the splits as I attempt to keep myself above ground level and out of Albatross's way.

"What the hell are you doing, Clemons?"

I jump at the sound of Rory's voice from behind me, and we almost bump heads when I swivel around to face him.

His eyebrows draw together.

He's not amused.

“I—I can't open the gate,” I tell him, sounding weak and pathetic.

Rolling his eyes, he pushes me out of the way and flips the lock up and down. It opens wide, like an actual miracle.

“How did you do that?”

“Don't tell me I have to teach you how to open a lock now as well? That was never part of the deal.”

“I'm perfectly capable of doing that myself, thanks.”

“Good, because I wasn't offering.”

He turns away from me, and I march into Albatross's stall, holding the bucket firmly in my grasp. I don't expect Albatross to start desperately trying to eat out of it while we're still attached. He sticks his head right in, and I'm forced to back up against the wall.

“Uh... a little help, please.”

A wicked grin slips over Rory's lips.

“How will you ever learn if I'm always helping you, Clemons? First-hand experience is always the best kind.”

I glare at him and try to get a better grip on the bucket, but Albatross is much stronger than he looks.

“I should have warned you... Albatross is an eating machine. Bring food in here, and all the power is in his hands.”

“Oh, well, thanks so much for the heads up,” I mumble sarcastically, lowering the bucket and granting Albatross full access before I leap through the gate and close it, my heart beating fast in my ears.

One down, one more to go, and Luna is giving me a

look that says, 'I don't trust you. Come any closer, and I won't be held responsible for the consequences.'

Without Rory's guidance, I click the lock open by myself this time. Luna allows me to enter her stall and set down the bucket, but then she moves so fast that I barely have time to step out of her way. I trip over my foot and land in a mountain of poo.

The stable is suddenly alive with laughter.

The main source?

Rory Keaton.

Luna is bobbing her head up and down, making a deep-throated sound. She's joined the let's-all-laugh-at-Skye movement by the looks of it.

My morning routine consists of helping feed all six horses, cleaning and replacing any soiled bedding, and trying not to collapse from pure exhaustion while undertaking a series of chores and demanding tasks.

We’re back in the field by midday, scooping up more poo. We've also gained an audience of three sheep named after Shirley Bassey, Etta James and Barbara Streisand. I think it adds a nice touch, but after meeting them face to face, I’ve realised that Etta is quite the character and has a sassy attitude, certainly living up to her household name.

I slump down on a bench at lunch and start unrolling the foil around my sandwiches, barely sitting there for two seconds when I overhear laughter and a speedy conversation from nearby.

Grayson's laugh is unmistakable.

Ducking behind the bench, I slowly pop my head around it to track his whereabouts. He's a few feet away, and his model-like girlfriend emerges behind him. I won't be able to move from this spot without being seen.

*Universe, why does it feel like you are constantly trying to trip me up? It's not fair.*

Grayson is holding Luna by the reins, and I hear him say, "We'd better head out now before it gets dark. Practice makes perfect."

Practice?

If he's practising for something, he must visit the stables often. If so, I will find avoiding him in such a closed-off environment impossible. We will inevitably cross paths, but I can delay that part if I stay one step ahead of the game. There must be a book or sign-in sheet around here, keeping a record of the regulars. It's a good thing I only work here twice a week.

*Maybe I should only write my first name on the sign-in sheet from now on.*

A hard tap on my shoulder frightens me, and I lose my balance, toppling over and receiving a close encounter with the earth. Rory towers above me, amusement mixed with annoyance dancing across his face. I can't tell which is worse.

"What the hell are you doing now?"

"Ssh! I'm trying to keep a low profile."

"From who? The horses?" he guesses, crossing his arms. "You're hard to miss with all that hair, Clemons."

He has a point. My hair is a bit wild, but I can't help that it blows up like a frizz ball and demands special attention.

"Ha ha, very funny. Now, please go and bother someone else. We still have approximately ten minutes left for lunch, and I'd rather continue eating mine alone."

He stares right at me then, his eyes searching mine. I don't know what he's expecting to find.

"Who are you hiding from exactly?"

"That's none of your business."

"Tell me, or I'll give away your location."

My jaw drops. "You wouldn't."

"I would."

Rory sucks in a large breath, and I quickly yank on his arm, pulling him down to my level. He stares at me, eyes wide and questioning.

"Grayson. I'm hiding from Grayson Swain," I say, a little breathless.

"Why?" he asks, batting my hand away.

"Because if he finds out that I work here, he'll only end up giving me a hard time about it."

His grin widens. "What's your grand plan? Are you hoping to avoid him like the plague? Play dress up for a day so he won't recognise you?"

When he puts it like that, this whole plan of mine sounds ridiculous and unachievable.

"Come on, be real. This is Michael Swain's son we're talking about. He treats this place like a second home. I don't think you thought any of this through," he says with a laugh.

My cheeks get warm.

Trust Rory Keaton to come along and crush my not-so-high hopes. I know he's making sense, but I would never let him think that. I wouldn't want to feed his ego when he's got plenty to go around.

"This isn't just some casual hating game or childish vendetta, alright? I could lose my job. Grayson already makes my life a misery. I don't want to give him something else to laugh about. I will do whatever it takes to stay under the radar if it means I won't get fired."

"Here's a little piece of advice."

He leans in, and I get a strong whiff of his aftershave. He smells like a simple mixture of mint and soap. It's not a bad combination.

"This place might be big enough to play hide and seek for a while, but eventually, a person can do only so much hiding before they're forced to come out of the shadows and face the music. Grayson isn't going anywhere, and neither are you. If I were in your shoes, I would get the initial awkwardness over and done with."

"I know what I'm doing," I say, trying to convince myself.

"You have nothing to worry about then. Just don't come running to me when this goes pear-shaped."

I don't doubt it won't get messy because my life hasn't been smooth sailing. Nothing ever goes right, and luck never seems to be on my side, but this is a risk I'm willing to take. If I regret my decision further down the line, I only have myself to blame.

"I need this job, Rory."

"You're not the only one," he mumbles, pulling out an e-cigarette from his back pocket and inhaling.

A puff of smoke surrounds us for a split second before it's swept away by the wind, and something foreign passes between us. Working here keeps Rory out of trouble and seems to fulfil him, whereas I'm only here to settle my mother's debt. I didn't realise he might have something to lose, but I can see how much Trinity means to him.

Standing up, Rory abruptly spins on his heel and heads back towards the stables, leaving me with a lot to think about and a half-eaten sandwich I no longer have time to finish.

I've lost my appetite anyway.

# Chapter Seven

THE LIBRARY DOOR OPENS, AND GRAYSON'S EYES NARROW AT the sight of me.

We agreed to work on the project after college today, but he's kept me waiting for almost half an hour. We exchange death glares between us for a long moment, and then he sits opposite me like he hasn't just wasted my time. He doesn't even give me an excuse for why he's late, either. He continues to type away on his iPhone, ignoring me. I may as well be invisible.

I tap my nails against the table, expressing my annoyance. "Grayson—"

"What?" he grunts from behind his illuminated screen.

"We've got a project to complete, remember? We need to focus."

Grayson sighs heavily and places his phone on the table, finally meeting my gaze. "Okay, Miss Trunchbull, if you insist."

I breathe heavily through my nostrils, flipping to a

new page in my notebook and trying to soften my approach. "Look, I know this isn't ideal for either of us, but I'm sure you want to pass as much as I do."

He tilts his head and holds a hand over his heart.

"You deserve an award for that speech. It was so emotional."

"Ha, you're hilarious!"

"Thanks."

"It wasn't a compliment."

"I'll live."

I fold my arms. "On a serious note, I suggest we start when you're done being a child."

"Go ahead. Ladies first."

I take a deep breath. "How old are you?"

"A five-year-old could've come up with a better question than that."

"That's interesting because your response sounds exactly like something a five-year-old would say."

He sighs in defeat. "I'm seventeen. How old is the class viper, dare I ask?"

"Seventeen, but I'm going to be eighteen soon. Your immaturity makes far more sense now that we've covered the age difference."

His eyebrows scrunch together, and I give myself a little tap on the back for that quick comeback.

*This is quite fun.*

"What are you most grateful for?" I move on.

He raises a hand in the air, waving at me furiously.

"Hey, don't get ahead of yourself. I never said you could ask me two questions in a row."

I stare at him, unamused.

“Just answer the bloody question, Swain.”

He lets out a yawn. “This is stupid.”

Grayson isn't even trying, but that's his problem, not mine. To pass this project, my presentation is all I have to worry about. As long as I've got Grayson figured out, I don't need to worry about whether he's got enough information about me. That task is his to achieve and his alone.

“Whether or not the questions are to your particular taste is beside the point. I care about answering them quickly so we can move on with our lives.”

Grayson chews on the tip of his pen and then shrugs.

“I'm most grateful for my money.”

*That is such a typical thing for him to say. I should have seen it coming.*

My eyes shoot up to the ceiling in agitation. “Really? That's it?”

“In this day and age, you need money for everything. I'm grateful my family has enough to keep us going, and I've got a nice home to live in.”

I grit my teeth. “That's such a shallow thing to say.”

“You don't wear jealousy well, Skye.”

I lean forward, trying to catch what he's jotting down in his little black notebook, but he's blocking my view.

“Hey! What did you write in there?”

His gaze falls back on me. “I'm making a note of your jealous behaviour. It's not an attractive trait. I've just learned something about you.”

“You think that I'm jealous of what you have? Trust me, that couldn't be further from the truth.”

"So, money is of no interest to you? Is that what you're saying?"

"That's not what I'm saying at all. I don't see how life must only revolve around money."

"Almost everything we do requires money. It's a priority. Without it, we couldn't do anything," he argues, holding my gaze.

Grayson is blinded by his affluent lifestyle and, therefore, couldn't possibly empathise with a poor community like ours. He has no idea what it's like to worry about paying the rent, electricity bills or buying food to last the week. He's probably never had to worry about anything because he's got his whole life handed to him on a silver platter.

Grayson relies on money to carry him through every experience, but does money bring happiness? Does having the best clothes, car, and house define a happy heart? It may bring glitz and glamour, but some of the wealthiest people are miserable. They have everything, and yet it's still not enough.

"Money is important. I'll agree with you there, but wealth doesn't last forever. Every materialistic thing in this life is temporary."

"What are you most grateful for, then?"

*I don't even have to think about it.*

"My mother. She's been through a lot and had to raise me as a single parent. I appreciate everything she's done for me and all the sacrifices she's had to make. She's the only family I've got," I tell him, watching his eyes widen momentarily.

Even though there have been times when she hasn't been there and I've had to watch her health deteriorate, I love her more than anything.

I blame my dad for many of my mother's issues. I don't know who he is or what happened to him because it's such a touchy subject. I've thought about him extensively, but he's not worth my time. There's no point wasting my breath on someone who missed a chunk of my life and could have another family living on the other side of the world.

"What's your biggest fear?" Grayson asks, a tiny frown tugging at his face.

I have trouble answering this because I have too many fears to name. I fear losing my mother every day. I have a fear of failing. I fear the unknown and not knowing what's around the corner. Mostly, I'm scared I'll never be able to live a happy, fulfilling life.

"I don't like dogs."

"Care to elaborate?"

"I had an incident with one when I was younger."

"Must've riled the dog up pretty bad."

*Of course, he would defend the animal.*

"He attacked me! I still have nightmares of him trying to bite my hand off!"

"Can you blame him? He probably felt threatened by you and was defending his animal rights."

I narrow my eyes and present him with a heavy glare.

"I was traumatised."

There isn't an ounce of sympathy in his expression.

"I bet the dog was too."

I wave him away. “Your turn. What are you scared of?”

“Nothing.”

“Everybody's afraid of something. You're not immortal, Grayson. You're a human being.”

He glances out the window, avoiding my eyes. “I fear losing what I have, and I'm afraid of dying.”

I clap my hands together.

“See! It's not so bad being honest, is it?”

“No.” He shakes his head. “It's worse.”

* * *

It's freezing at the stables.

I greet Rory with a broad smile, which he doesn't return, and then I begin working my way through my morning chores, delivering horse feed to each stall and ignoring Rory's presence at every opportunity.

You don't have to like your co-worker, do you? Lots of people don't. You just put up with them. If you get along, that's always a bonus, but The Rolling Stones once said, 'You can't always get what you want.’

Rory is about to show me where the horse-riding gear is kept. We step inside a large storage cupboard, and he flicks on the light. The back wall is covered with medals, sashes and rosettes from competitions and events that have taken place over the years, showcasing a lifetime of memories and a caseload of history.

“Wow. This is incredible.”

The bright lighting draws out the dark circles under

Rory's eyes. “It's pretty cool, right? This is only two percent of them.”

“Really?”

“Yeah. Mr Swain is a big name in the horse-riding world. He probably keeps the rest of his awards at home. Grayson has won a ton of competitions as well. He’s a bit more vocal about it, though. He doesn't shut up about his achievements,” he adds as an afterthought.

That sounds precisely like Grayson. He's following in his father's footsteps and wants everybody to know it. I'm not interested in hearing about his extracurricular activities, but being here might work in my favour. If I can secretly dig for more information about him, it might help me score some bonus points with Ricky while helping to find out who the real Grayson Swain is. Then, I can write a killer essay about him and be one step ahead of the game.

I'm on the lookout for Grayson all morning, constantly glancing over my shoulder in case he appears out of the blue. I need to be prepared. Always. Nobody knows what will happen an hour from now or what the day has in store.

“If you can help me put a bridle on Henry, it'll speed up the process,” Rory says, making my stomach drop as he whizzes past.

“But I don't think...”

“You'll be fine. Make sure the bridle is the right way around when you put it over his head, that’s all.”

I reach Henry and try not to reel back from the dramatic height difference. If this horse wanted to, it could easily rear up on its hind legs and kick me into the next day. I tell my nerves to calm down and try fitting the harness onto the horse. It doesn't go well on the first attempt or the second. Henry keeps backing away, and my patience is wearing thin.

Coming up from behind me, Rory takes control. Gently, he lowers the bridle over Henry's head, making it look so easy. He turns to me, and I try to ignore how close we are, but I can feel his body heat radiating against mine. It's a bit distracting.

"For this next part, it's essential that we fit the saddle properly because if it's not the same width as the horse's shoulders, it will pinch the spine and restrict movement. If the saddle moves too much while riding, it will rub the horse's back, and we don't want that to happen."

"No pressure," I mumble, chewing my lip anxiously.

"Why don't you give it a try?"

"I don't think that's such a good idea."

Rory moves towards me, and now he's inches from my face. My heart picks up speed as he passes me a saddle cloth and reaches for my hand, helping me to guide it over the saddle area. The action feels intimate, and I try not to think about his hand on mine.

I lower the saddle onto the cloth without a hitch, and Rory helps me place it vertically so the fabric doesn't move underneath. We stare at each other for a long moment, and then he dips his head, breaking eye contact.

"We're expecting an important visitor today. Mr Frost has invested a lot of money in Dante. He thinks that he's going to be the next big thing. So, we must keep him happy at all times. I will take Dante to the field for training and prepare him for when Mr Frost arrives. Will you be okay to work on your own for a while?"

I glance around the empty stables, never feeling better about working alone. No Rory equals my idea of a perfect afternoon.

"Sure. I'll be fine."

Two hours later, I'm sitting in my usual lunch spot, which feels pretty satisfying. My morning has gone excruciatingly slowly, yet my lunch hour still feels non-existent and always seems to be over before it's truly begun.

I close my eyes and soak up the sun splitting through the clouds. The seasons have no boundaries, and neither does the concept of time. I've been working here for almost three weeks now, yet it only feels like I was interviewed by Mr Swain yesterday.

I would never have imagined working here a few weeks ago or that I'd be spending so much time with Rory Keaton, of all people. I'm still trying to figure out where we stand. He treats me like a stranger off the street, and I'm okay with that if it means we only have to tolerate each other for a few hours.

Raised voices disrupt my alone time, and my eyes are forced open. I glance towards the field where Rory seems to be having a heated discussion with someone. Curious about what's happening, I leave my sandwiches on the bench and head straight towards them.

"He's a bit nervous. Just give him a minute," I catch Rory saying to a man with barely any hair. He's stocky and short, and if I were to take a guess, I'd assume that he was important purely based on the way he holds himself.

*This must be the famous Mr Frost, who is on the frosty side.*

"Well, I haven't invested all my time, energy and money into this horse for it not to do as I please. He won't even allow anyone to mount him!" Every word spoken out of this man's mouth is deliberate and threatening.

Rory glances worriedly at Dante, then back at Mr Frost. "I understand your frustration, but this does not truly reflect who Dante is. He's having a bad day, that's all."

"A bad day?" Mr Frost repeats, shaking his head. "No. No. No. That won't do. It's not good enough."

Dante remains a good foot away, refusing to come any closer. Rory steps towards him, but the horse mimics his movements, taking a more considerable step back.

*I'm witnessing a stand-off between a boy and his horse.*

During my shifts at the farm, I have noticed Dante, and he seems to have noticed me, but we keep our distance. He's the only horse I'm not allowed to fit saddles on or go near very much. Rory says that's because he tends to rebel and is unpredictable, but something about him intrigues me.

Rory captures my gaze, and I'm sure I see some relief

melt his expression, but it's gone within a second. There is no trace of it ever being there.

"If the horse doesn't respond within the next minute, you can kiss my investment goodbye."

I don't care if Frosty over here returns or not. I don't think he deserves Dante, but for professional reasons, Rory doesn't want him to leave. I can see how much he's wracking his brain for a solution.

"I promise you, if you come back tomorrow, he will be more than ready."

"You're a determined young man, and that's admirable, but there's a lot of money at stake here, and I'm not going to waste any more of my time. Good day."

Rory's entire face drops to the ground, and I don't know what compels me to do it, but I start chasing Mr Frost across the field, determined to match his pace with my own. He's quick on his feet, but once I've managed to catch up, I make it impossible for him to escape without hearing from me first.

"Mr Frost, I think there's been a total misunderstanding."

"There sure has been. Taking a gamble on a horse nobody wants to train or go near is already enough of a challenge, but Dante has some real issues—issues I don't have time to fix."

"If you can spare five more minutes, I'd like to show you why Dante is worth investing in."

I may not know much about horses, but it's clear to me that Dante has potential.

Mr Frost has slowed down, and he's eyeing me with

enough curiosity to kill a cat. “Really? How are you planning to do that?”

“I have seen Dante in action. He truly is an impeccable horse.”

By 'in action,' I mean that I've just seen him parade around the field now and again, mostly minding his business and enjoying his own company. I have also witnessed his tendency to disobey simple instructions. On Friday, for example, he wouldn't allow Rory to go anywhere near him, and he even tried kicking me when I entered his stall without his permission. Rory did warn me not to get too close to the horse. I should have listened.

“So, I've been told. But unless I can see that with my own eyes, I have no choice but to assume he is not a competition horse, and that is what I'm searching for,” Mr Frost says, returning my attention to our conversation.

My heart skips when he picks up the pace again, but I won’t let him get away that easily.

“What if I proved to you that he is more than capable of being a competition horse?”

*Why am I acting as if I am an experienced rider?*

*I'm no expert.*

“Dante won't let anybody near him,” he quickly reminds me.

“If I can somehow mount Dante today, would that be enough to change your mind?”

*What the heck am I doing?*

I've never ridden a horse before—let alone a super intimidating one like Dante. I'll never be able to pull this off. Rory will kill me when this master idea of mine takes a wrong turn.

"If you give him one last chance, you won't be disappointed. I swear."

*Shut up. Stop talking.*

Mr Frost scratches his jaw in deep thought. "And who are you supposed to be?"

"My name is Skye Clemons. I'm the new stablehand."

"Hm. I will stick around to see if you can prove your point, Skye. Please don't make me regret this."

I can't bear to look at Rory as I escort Mr Frost back to the middle of the field. Dante hasn't moved an inch, and now the spotlight is on me. I'm about to make myself look like an absolute fool.

*If Rory couldn't control the horse, how am I going to?*

I approach Dante carefully while Mr Frost converses with Rory from the sidelines. He's filling him in on our previous conversation because, judging by Rory's piercing glare, he's not happy about this unexpected arrangement. I'm unqualified, nervous around horses and can barely swing my leg over a picket fence, let alone a horse's body, but here I am, very much alone in this scenario. All I have to rely on is the horse and myself, which isn't enough to reassure me that we will both be okay after this.

Dante's watchful eyes study me, wary of my intentions. He seems curious but continues to walk backwards, leaving tons of space between us. I hold a hand up and speak softly so I don't frighten him off.

"Hey, it's alright, Dante. Everything is cool. I know

you're not yourself right now. We all have bad days, but I need you to work with me here."

Dante charges toward me, and instead of jumping out of his way, I reach out and snatch his bridle, gaining control. We are sidestepping each other for a couple of minutes until he suddenly rears up, his powerful hooves soaring through the air. He doesn't necessarily kick me as such, but it was still dangerously close and could've ended differently if he had managed to land a blow. It may have resulted in me being crushed underneath his hooves.

"Whoa, boy, take it easy."

Dante lowers his head and returns his eyes to mine, sussing me out. He sniffs my hair and tugs on my ponytail with his teeth. The motion causes the elastic band to snap, and my hair bounces back into its rightful place, spilling down my shoulders.

"If you wanted my hair down that badly, you should've just said so," I joke as Dante snorts with amusement.

Feeling more confident, I reach out to gently stroke his nose. He responds with gratitude, his demeanour softening. Drawing closer, I secure a firmer grip on his reins, bridging the gap between us. We remain like this until I muster the confidence to mount his saddle. Lifting my leg, I'm ready to elevate myself onto his back when Dante jerks away, and I lose my grip.

"It's okay. I'm not going to hurt you," I reassure him.

It takes a few attempts, but eventually, Dante stops fighting me, and I've miraculously found a way to mount him. I hold onto the reins tightly, nerves and adrenaline kicking in.

*Wow. This is a powerful moment for me.*

I glance at Rory and Mr Frost, who are both speechless. Rory's expression mirrors his disbelief.

How on earth did I get to this point?

It was like an out-of-body experience. I had no idea what I was doing, yet my body seemed to know exactly what to do.

*Weird.*

Dante starts moving around, and I grip onto him for dear life. I may have conquered the initial fear of sitting on a horse's saddle, but I still need to be more confident to do the riding part.

"Well..." Mr Frost clears his throat more than once, seeming to have lost his voice.

"Looks like the problem is solved. Dante is ready for you, Mr Frost," I say, thanking the heavens above for having my back.

I haven't been able to wipe the smile off my face since my encounter with Mr Frost this afternoon. I can't explain it, but something happened on the field. I felt a spark in me ignite when I communicated with Dante. I am curious to know whether I just got lucky or if I genuinely have a hidden talent that I never knew about. Either way, nothing will beat the thrill of what I did today and how much I enjoyed it.

"Hey Skye, wait up!"

I cast a glance over my shoulder just in time to see

Rory sprinting towards me in the car park. I wonder why he's stopping to chat. We never usually say goodbye.

He flashes me a curious smile, his dimples surfacing.

"What you did today... that was cool."

*Oh. I wasn't expecting that.*

I'm not used to Rory paying me compliments. Should I thank him? Say nothing at all? What is the socially appropriate response?

"I'm just glad it worked out. If the opposite had happened, we wouldn't be having this conversation now. Instead, I'd probably be unconscious or in a hospital bed," I murmur faintly, positioning myself on my bike seat, my hands firmly gripping the handlebars.

"It was reckless, completely and utterly stupid, but at the same time, totally badass. Mr Frost was impressed. I haven't seen Dante connect with someone on that level before. You earned his respect somehow, and he is not easily swayed. Trust me."

"I'm happy to be of service. I would bow, but I'm still attached to my bike, so I'd rather not risk the embarrassment."

Rory isn't looking at me with his usual distaste. If anything, his eyes are kind and warm—two things I didn't know he was capable of. He throws me one of his most dazzling smiles, and I figure this must be what he does to lure girls in. Poor souls. He doesn't even have to do much except smile like that, and suddenly, girls are flocking.

I hate how my eyes fall into the same old trap, but I can't help but check him out. It's not like he has a six-pack or anything, and it's obvious he doesn't spend much time at the gym, but he's got enough muscle to appear stronger than the average person, and I can understand the appeal.

I'd better get out of here before I lose my mind, but Rory has already beaten me to the punch. He's settled himself onto the leather seat of his motorbike, and with a low chuckle, he revs the engine, fires me one last glance and speeds off into the night.

# Chapter Eight

BEFORE ATTENDING MY CLASSES FOR THE DAY, I HAVE A MEETING with my college adviser. We cover enrolment, scholarships and financial aid. I'm excited and nervous to start the next chapter of my life because I'm one step closer to following my dream, but I know I've got a long way to go. First, I must pass my language and literature course and deal with the Lakeside students, which is a challenge in itself.

The topic of University has been dropped into the conversation more than once, and while I am excited to be considering universities, I'm unsure where I want to go. Fear and a strong surge of doubt set in as I question whether I am genuinely good enough.

"Weigh up your options. Do your research," Janet says. She's a lovely woman who is very softly spoken, ideally suited to her role, but sometimes it's as if she's living in la la land.

I don't have many options.

If I got accepted to study at a university, I would have

no choice but to relocate, which isn't ideal. Am I being selfish by putting my dreams first when my mother is suffering and needs me to be her shoulder to cry on?

If I left, she would have to fend for herself, and she needs me. I can't just abandon my responsibilities here. I can't leave her.

"You have plenty of time to decide, but you should consider applying soon. You can secure a place that way," Janet continues as I overthink and invent worse-case scenarios.

*Maybe what I want isn't an option anymore.*

When I can no longer ignore the painful pleasures of being a college student, I meet with Grayson in the library to work on From Opposite Sides. His blond hair makes him stick out like a sore thumb, especially since the sun is shining directly on him.

He's sitting on a chair by the window and taps his watch impatiently as I slide into the seat opposite him. This time, I'm the one that's running fashionably late.

"You're approximately ten minutes behind schedule," Grayson grumbles, waiting for me to sit down and take off my coat.

I'm not ready to face another round of quick-fire insults, but we're getting quite good at this game. We've got it mastered.

"You deserve a taste of your own medicine, Swain. Now you know how it feels to wait an eternity for someone to show up. Not nice, is it?" I grind out, balancing my notebook on my knees.

Grayson folds his arms over his chest and wrinkles his nose. “I've only ever left you hanging for virtually a second, and that's not even an exaggeration.”

“More like half an hour, actually, and at least I wasn't trying to be late on purpose.” I glance down at my notepad and instantly feel like crying. All I've written down about him are three sparse lines. “Okay, let's regroup for a second. How about we have a normal conversation for a change?”

He stares at me as if I've grown five heads. “I thought we were already having a normal conversation.”

“Grayson, we never have normal conversations. Our previous conversations have usually ended up with one of us either storming away or kicking off. So, let’s try speaking to each other without throwing any insults or causing unnecessary drama. Do you think you can handle that?”

He scratches his chin in thought, purposefully taking his time to answer my question. “Hm, I don't know. Insulting you is slowly becoming one of my favourite things to do. I can't promise I won't slip up.”

I turn on a heavy glare, and he sighs, running his fingers through his hair, tousling it up. “Fine, let's have a normal conversation then... whatever that's supposed to mean.”

I try to think of a good starting topic but fall short when nothing comes to me.

“Um, so... do you prefer McDonald’s or KFC?”

Grayson bursts out laughing, attracting the attention of a group of friends playing chess in the corner of the library. They flash us accusing stares as their game is rudely interrupted, but Grayson is utterly oblivious because he's laughing so hard.

"Out of all the things you could have asked me, that was at the top of your list?"

"You put me on the spot," I hiss, trying to keep my voice down.

"You're the one who suggested we should try to have a normal conversation," he quotes with his fingers. "How's that working out for you, by the way?"

The disgusted look on my face is making him erupt with more laughter.

"Forget I even asked," I mutter under my breath.

"I'm more of a KFC kind of guy. Although, if I'm honest, I'm not a fan of either. Junk food is not good for the digestive system," he says.

"Hah, who would have thought?"

He presses his lips together, narrowing his eyes at me. "What's your favourite time of the day?"

"Why is that even relevant?"

"It's more relevant than having a conversation about fast food chains."

*Good point. I should have gone with something more original.*

I quickly scramble for an answer, "Probably the evening."

"Why?"

"Because the only time I feel totally at peace is when I'm asleep."

"That's deep."

I wait for him to insult me further, but I'm pleasantly

surprised when time passes, and he doesn't. Maybe he is taking this 'normal' stuff seriously after all.

“Any dreams you'd like to share while we're at it?”

I mostly dream about my dad. I can see his outline, but his face is always blurred. He tells me he will never leave again, which is usually when I wake up. I'll keep that story to myself for now, though. It's a bit too personal.

“I once dreamt that CeeLo Green tripled in size and started eating everyone.”

Grayson’s blue eyes twinkle with amusement, and his mouth twitches up. “Isn't that the guy who sang *Forget You*?”

“Yup. That's the one.”

He laughs again, and it suits him better than his daily scowl.

“That's so random.”

“I know! I don't understand why he was eating people or appeared in my dream, but it was terrifying.”

“I bet. I can't say I've dreamed about CeeLo Green eating people, but I remember watching *Goosebumps* on TV as a kid. There was this episode where a guy bought a fridge, and a ghost kept appearing to him from inside it. My parents didn't know I'd watched something scary, so I went to bed emotionally scarred. It gave me nightmares for weeks.”

“Goosebumps was the best! I was a fan of the books mostly. I don't think I ever watched the TV series. They were descriptive for young readers, but that made them great.”

*Hang on a minute. There is a good chance that we are bonding right now. It's a miracle.*

"Would you rather have Batman's skills, money, equipment, and lifestyle or end crime worldwide for good but be poor and unnoticed?"

Grayson stares at me incredulously.

"Blimey. There's a question. Uh... I guess I would rather..." he pauses for a moment, scratching his head. "Well, the most obvious answer would be to end crime for good, wouldn't it?"

"Yes, but is that what you would rather do?"

"Why does it have to be Batman? Couldn't it be Spiderman or the Hulk? Batman doesn't even have superpowers."

"But you can't deny that he's super cool and wears a cape... which he happens to pull off very well. He also gets a lot of female attention."

Our eyes meet, and I know he can't disagree with me.

"True. Selfishly, I would rather be Batman."

"I knew it!"

"But, I wouldn't choose to live that kind of life if I had the power to end all suffering. Nothing is more important than that, not even becoming Batman himself."

I incline my head, pleased with his answer.

He's redeemed himself for now.

"I have a cat called Batman."

He slaps a hand to his mouth and says in a high-pitched voice, "Shut up! Does he wear a cape, too?"

"No, but I was thinking of buying him one for Christmas."

Grayson's cheeky grin returns. "Sounds like a good

idea. Why don't you throw in a catmobile while you're at it—go for the full shebang?"

We share a laugh, and for once, I don't want to strangle him, which is a nice change. Grayson's eyes leave me in a flash when his phone vibrates on the table. He quickly answers a call, and I can tell who's on the other end of the line without guessing.

His uptight girlfriend.

"Sophie! Hey..."

He glances at me, and his scowl returns, erasing all the progress I thought we had made today.

"No, I'm free. I'm not doing anything important."

On the ride home from college, I make a mental list stating why I dislike Grayson Swain.

There are too many to name, but I list them anyway.

*- Talks too much about himself.*

*- Snobby.*

*- Selfish.*

*- Rude to people, not just me.*

*- He thinks he's the best at everything.*

I quickly swerve to avoid a streetlight and hold a hand to my heart when I dodge it. Even when Grayson isn't around, he's causing me to nearly crash.

"Skye?"

At the sound of my name, I turn my head in all directions until I spot Michael Swain sitting behind the wheel of his car. The window is completely rolled down so he can talk to me through it.

*What a coincidence!*

“Oh, hi,” I say, a little shocked to see him in this part of the neighbourhood. It’s strange seeing my boss outside of work. It’s like seeing an old teacher from school or something, which is always awkward.

“I thought I recognised you. How are you doing?”

“I'm okay. I'm just making my way home from college.”

Mr Swain smiles and taps the side of the steering wheel. “I'm heading back to Lakeside. I had some business to take care of over here. Do you live very far from this area?”

“Not too far. It's about ten minutes away—near the industrial estate.”

“Would you like me to drop you home?’

I wave at the air. “Oh no, it's fine.”

“Are you sure? I don't mind. I'm not pressed for time or anything.”

I don’t usually take rides from strangers, but considering he doesn’t count as a stranger anymore, I suppose it wouldn’t hurt. My legs are getting tired.

“That would be great. Thank you.”

I jump off the bike and steer it towards the car. It's a fold-up bike, so slotting it into the boot is easy. Sitting in the passenger's seat, I don't move or say anything for the first few minutes. I can't tell if the minty smell is coming from the car or Mr Swain. It's not unpleasant.

“Bit of a random question, but are you and Grayson close?” I ask, breaking the silence.

He blinks, startled, eyes flickering from the road and back to me again. “Why do you ask?”

“We're working on a project together at college.”

His eyebrows raise as the car starts moving down the street.

"You are?"

"Yeah. He hasn't told you about it?"

I thought he would have mentioned the project to his parents. Does that mean he's not close to them? Does he have mummy and daddy issues?

*I should start writing this down.*

"We're both busy nowadays," he hesitates as if he might reveal too much by finishing that sentence. "Anyway, tell me about this project."

"We've got to find out as much as we can about each other's lives. That's the whole point. It might help if I asked you a couple of questions. As long as you don't mind."

"I'm happy to answer your questions."

*Bingo.*

"So, considering you raised Grayson and live with him, you must know everything there is to know. What's he like?"

"Grayson is a good kid. He worships his mother and always puts her first. He's quite sensitive, too."

*Grayson?*

*Sensitive?*

That doesn't sound like the person I've spent all my time with lately. Maybe what I'm seeing isn't an accurate projection of who he is because am I staying true to myself whenever he asks me a question?

Probably not.

"What do *you* think of him?" he asks, turning the question back on me.

I can't exactly slate him now. That would defeat the purpose. I want Grayson's father to like me to a certain extent, so I can earn his trust and use it for my own personal gain. Of course, there is the other matter of him being my boss. He could fire me if I admit I'm not a fan of his offspring.

"Let's just say he's not afraid to voice his opinions."

Mr Swain chuckles like he knows what I mean.

"He's always been like that since he was a child. Making friends used to be very difficult for him. He got bullied in his first year of high school. All the other kids had sprouted up over the summer, but he was slow to follow. They teased him about that for months."

"Wow. That's horrible."

*Am I feeling sorry for Grayson now?*

*What is wrong with me?*

"Eventually, he had to move schools because the bullying got worse. We placed him in a private school, and he was much happier there. His grades are always spectacular. I'm proud of how far he's come."

It's nice that he cares about his son that much. I'm slightly envious of their relationship, and I hate seeing Grayson in a different light.

I still need to write this down, but my pen is lingering over the paper, and no ink has touched the page.

"Are there any other questions you'd like to ask me?"

Honestly, I can't think of anything else.

*And the award for worst interview of the year goes to Skye Clemons.*

"I—I think you've covered the main points," I tell him, defeated.

We approach a familiar stretch of road, and I instantly recognise the old abandoned car wash and my tattered old street sign. Mr Swain is glancing around, eyebrows slowly crawling up his forehead as he takes in the amount of litter on the ground and potholes in the road.

*It'll be a miracle he doesn't pop a tire.*

This is not his kind of scene. I can't picture him ever gracing these streets with his presence. He'd probably get mugged on sight. I'm not embarrassed. These are the streets I grew up on, every memory stored away, the good, the bad, the ugly. Yet, my heart has always longed for a different life.

A dog runs across the street, causing Mr Swain to break hard on the clutch. The car halts, and the dog scampers into the bushes. A bead of sweat trickles down his nose, and he adjusts his tie, composing himself.

I whip off my seatbelt.

*Better put an end to his misery.*

"You can drop me off here. I can walk the rest of the way."

"Don't be silly. I'll drop you outside your door."

"You don't have to do that. Honest. If my neighbours see you, they'll ask me questions because they are super nosey and like to know everybody's business. Plus, you'll attract a lot of attention because nobody owns a Ferrari in my neighbourhood."

His shoulders fall, but he doesn't object this time.

"That's understandable. I'll pull up here then."

Mr Swain parks on the kerb and helps me to pull my bike out of the boot. He stares at me so earnestly that I suddenly want to run up and hug him. It's inappropriate, of course, and I would never do that. I'm shocked that the thought even crossed my mind.

"Well, thanks so much for driving me home. I appreciate it," I say, breaking the stretching silence.

"That's alright. It was my pleasure." I start walking away but stop at the sound of his voice. "Rory was telling me that you showed great initiative the other day. Mr Frost is not easy to please, but you changed his mind about Dante and turned the situation around."

My mood brightens at the reminder. "Ah, it was nothing."

"Well, that's not what I heard. Keep up the good work, Skye." His praise is rewarding, and every word holds so much meaning. I don't think I've ever wanted someone's approval so badly, but Mr Swain's acceptance of me is valued.

"Can I ask you something? Sort of like a favour."

He nods firmly. "Go ahead."

"Can you not mention that you dropped me home today to Grayson?"

"Can I ask why?"

*No. You can't. It's complicated.*

"I would rather he didn't know, that's all. I want my essay to be a total surprise when I present it to the class. So, I would appreciate it if you could not mention anything about that as well."

I hope my words convince him because I have no other explanation. I could tell him the truth—that I'm worried Grayson will make fun of me if he finds out I'm working at Trinity, but I can't exactly admit that to my boss, can I? It wouldn't be practical or sensible.

"Alright. You have my word. I won't mention anything to Grayson."

"Thanks, Mr Swain."

I guess not all rich people are jerks.

This guy is the exception.

# Chapter Nine

My mother hasn't left the house for two days, and I don't understand how she can go to work when she can hardly get out of bed. How can she still look presentable when she's mentally falling apart? I think that's the worst thing about having an invisible illness. To the rest of the world, nothing seems to be wrong with her. The monster is unseen. Yet, to her and me, it's the real deal.

I'm washing the dishes when she finally joins me in the kitchen, flipping through a magazine at the table, still very much hungover from last night's antics. I got home from college yesterday and found her passed out on the sofa with an empty bottle of wine in her hand and an alarming amount of tissues piled up by her side. I've been cleaning the house because she was vomiting throughout the night, and I barely slept. My eyes are struggling to stay open.

"Ugh, I've got such a headache. It's my fault for drinking so much last night," Mum says, grimacing as she holds her head.

I lose grip on my cup, which falls into the sink with a sharp clunk. I've chipped the side of it, which is disappointing.

*That used to be my favourite mug.*

*Not anymore.*

"Why don't you go and lie back down, and I'll make us some tea?"

She looks up at me, her gaze full of affection. "Thanks, honey. Do you fancy watching a film or something?"

"I'd love that."

"Great. Before I forget, can you please put my phone on charge for me upstairs?"

"Sure. No problem."

"You're the best. What would I do without you?"

I rush upstairs at lightning speed because I'm beyond excited to spend quality time with my mother. We don't get to bond like this because she's either too busy, dealing with a mid-life crisis or has a male friend over. The fact that she wants to watch a movie with me is the best news ever.

I shuffle inside my mother's bedroom and realise that getting from one end of the room to the other will be challenging. She isn't necessarily messy, but her room becomes a dumping ground whenever she has an episode. She no longer cares that she's surrounded by filth and clutter that she'll eventually have to clean up or I'll have to clean up.

Clothes are spread sporadically across the bed, and a couple of empty plates and wine bottles are on the floor. I wouldn't dare look under her bed because goodness knows what I'd find down there. I notice her phone charger on the dressing table and reaching out for it, I trip over a wine bottle and accidentally bump into her desk, spilling some documents onto the floor.

*Crap. I'm such a klutz.*

I bend over to pick the papers up, but I notice my name on one or two of the documents, and curiosity gets the best of me. Automatically reading the small print, my heart is beating so fast I'm worried I will pass out.

# ACCOUNT SUMMARY

STATEMENT

ISSUED TO: SKYE CLEMONS

| DESCRIPTION | DETAILS | TOTAL |
| --- | --- | --- |
| August 18 | Bluebell | £250.00 |
| July 18 | Bluebell | £250.00 |
| June18 | Bluebell | £250.00 |
| May18 | Bluebell | £250.00 |
| @BLUEBELL | TOTAL AMOUNT | 50,000 |

*What the hell?*

At first, I wonder if my eyes are playing tricks on me, but no, this is real.

This is very real.

I notice several statements dating back to the year I

was born, all written the same way, with the same amount deposited each month.

*Bluebell.*

Why hasn't my mother mentioned any of this to me before?

Fifty thousand pounds is a lot of money.

Was she going to tell me that she'd miraculously won the lottery one day and that we were swimming around in cash suddenly? Is that how she'd planned to break the news? Did she think she could keep this a secret and that I would never find out?

I'm curious about this Bluebell character and why they've been sending money into my account for so long.

Who does that?

Better yet, who can afford to do that?

I am trying to figure out what to do with this information, but I can't continue asking myself questions I can't answer. My mother is the only person who can answer them and owes me an explanation.

I hurry out of the room and return to the kitchen, taking determined strides towards her. With the papers in my hand, she only has to take one look at them before fear clouds her expression. It's everywhere.

"Who is Bluebell?" I demand, clutching the papers tightly and waving them at her. I need to know what I'm dealing with here to process and try to make sense of what I've just discovered.

All the colour drains from her face, proving that she is far from innocent and knows something I don't.

Her eyes turn accusingly as she looks at the papers in

my hand. "Why have you been snooping through my things? That's private, Skye."

"These statements are addressed to me, so technically, I have every right to read them. Now, can you please explain what all of this means?"

"You weren't supposed to find those... not yet."

"Well, it's a good thing I did because I don't think you were ever planning to tell me about all this money, were you? How could you do that to me? How could you not say anything?"

I don't even care that my mother is sobbing uncontrollably into her hands. I don't feel the least bit sorry for her because she could have saved herself from this conversation if she had been honest with me from the start.

"I'm so sorry," she says. "I-I just..."

"Who is Bluebell?" I snap, getting frustrated.

"Those payments are—" she pauses, hot breath staggering out. "They are from your father."

I stare at her in complete shock, unable to form words. There's an aching in my gut, and it's getting more painful and harder to digest. I wish I could magically click my fingers and make this sensation disappear. I want it to disappear so badly.

"I don't understand."

"He pays money into the account every month. It's there to support you. When you turn eighteen, you'll be able to access it."

My mouth has gone dangerously dry.

"I can't believe this. You can send the money back. I

don't want it," I say, dabbing my watery eyelids with the end of my sleeve.

"Skye..."

"No! Seriously, send it back!"

My legs are already carrying me to the door as I swing it open and run out.

To know that the father I have never met has been trying to buy me this whole time is another stab to the heart. His money means nothing. I feel sick thinking about it. Not only do I feel more anger towards my father now, but I feel betrayed by the person I care about most. My mother kept this from me, and if I hadn't read those statements, would she have ever told me?

The world is a whip of colour. I'm not thinking about where I am or going; I know I can't go home. That's the last place I want to be.

I collapse under a flickering streetlamp. Aside from a stray cat watching me cautiously across the road, I'm alone. All I can hear is the sound of my heavy breathing followed by heaving sobs leaving my body, making my chest tight and my throat sore.

A large sum doesn't compensate for the years my father lost. He can't buy me or my affections. I could have used a male role model to point me in the right direction growing up—a dad to protect me from the dangers of this world. My birth father is out there somewhere, and he could be anyone. I could be passing him in the street and not know it. I used to spend so much time wondering who he was, and I hate that he's left a gaping hole in my heart.

Sadly, some wounds will never heal.

* * *

It might be my day off at the stables, but that doesn't stop me from turning up there unannounced. Going home is not an option right now, so the stable presents me with the perfect opportunity to escape from reality.

Dante seems to be waiting for me in his stall, making me think he knew I was coming. My eyes are still brimming with tears, and I know I shouldn't be here. My emotions are all over the place, and I am in no fit state to take Dante for a walk around the field, but that's precisely what I'm about to do.

Dante doesn't argue with me. Instead, he plods along, allowing me to take him by the reins and lead the way.

*I swear this horse can read my mind.*

Another wave of emotion sweeps over me, and the horse glances in my direction, his eyes wide with intrigue.

“I'm sorry that you're being dragged into this,” I whisper to him softly.

Reaching the field, I was only planning to do a couple of laps with Dante—just enough to free my mind and provide him with some exercise, but I'm missing the thrill of the chase and the excitement I felt when I first mounted Dante. I want to experience more of that again.

I approach him tentatively, watching his ears flatten as I attempt to place my foot in the stirrup. He moves away with an angry toss of his mane, leaving me grasping at thin air. After another failed attempt, he finally allowed me to mount him without much of a struggle. He moves through the field, bowing down to eat some grass, and I sit in the saddle, feeling on top of the world—like nothing can touch me.

Amid my daydreaming, Dante decides to pick up speed, and now we're full-on galloping across the field.

*Wait.*

*I'm not ready.*

*How do I stop this?*

Dante rears on his hind legs, flinging me backwards, the force of the fall knocking the wind out of me. I land awkwardly on my back and lie entirely still in the freshly cut grass.

"Skye!"

Someone is calling me in the distance.

Panic fills my body as the pain becomes more known, and a pair of bright green eyes stare down at me. Breathing normally becomes impossible. Not enough air is being transported into my body.

"Don't close your eyes! Dammit! Skye!"

Rory's voice sounds distant—like he's moving away, or maybe I am.

The last thing I see is complete darkness.

# Chapter Ten

I'M NOT DEAD, BUT I DON'T FEEL ALIVE EITHER.

My eyes flash open, and I scramble up in a panic. I'm in the staff room, lying on the recliner, aware of the sharp shooting pain in my knee, but I choose to ignore it for now. Too many questions are swimming around in my head, and I don't know where to start.

Noticing I'm awake, Rory rushes to my side.

"What happened?" I ask him, trying not to wince at every little movement I make.

"Aside from almost killing yourself? You're lucky that you didn't break your neck. I mean, what the hell were you thinking?" He shakes his head furiously.

I lower my eyes to the floor, ashamed. "I'm sorry. I just..."

"This isn't a playground. Just because you had a breakthrough with Dante last week doesn't mean it will happen again. Horse riding is way more complicated than learning to ride a bike for the first time. I don't think you understand that," he interrupts, making me feel like an incompetent child.

I bite my lip to stop myself from crying. Aside from the physical pain, I'm more emotional than usual.

"I wasn't thinking. I made a reckless decision, and it's inexcusable. Is Dante okay?"

I don't know what happened or why Dante reacted the way he did. Maybe he got spooked. I shouldn't have put either of us in that kind of position.

"He's fine. Why are you here anyway? You're not supposed to be working today," Rory replies, firmly clasping his hands together.

I blink a few times and let my gaze lower to my lap. The first tear rolls down my cheek, and I can tell he doesn't know how to handle this—me crying.

*I'll make it easier for him.*

I force a smile onto my face, even though it feels like the most unnatural thing in the world and say, "You know what, considering I've already caused you so much inconvenience, I'll spare you the details and get out of your way."

I rise to my feet, but the room starts spinning, and I realise how much of a mistake that was. Rory immediately comes up behind me, steering me back to the recliner. I'm thankful, but at the same time, I don't need his help. I didn't ask for it.

"You can't go anywhere yet. The doctor is coming out to see you."

"But I'm fine," I protest, holding my head.

"You might have a concussion."

"I'll get over it."

He inhales deeply, his breath trembling. "Not on my watch."

I might have fallen off the horse, but it must've been scary to watch it happen. Rory still seems a bit shaken up.

"Look, I know we're not exactly friends, but if something is bothering you... you can talk to me. I'm a good listener, believe it or not."

The silence lingers again, heavier this time.

I feel the pressure building in my chest, the air dissolving.

"If you can't already tell, my life is a shambles, and you are the last person I'd ever want to talk to about it."

Rory rolls his head back and looks up at the ceiling, agitated. "I know you've got your opinions about me, but I'm trying to be nice here."

"Why start now? Please don't do me any favours."

He tilts his head, wearing a look of pure exasperation. "Do you always think the worst of people?"

"Yes, and don't avoid the question. All you have ever done is judge me."

"I can't lie and say I've never thought bad about you, Skye, but you're a hypocrite. I'm sure you've judged me just as much as I've judged you."

I almost laugh at that, even though I know he's speaking the truth. I am a hypocrite. I'm just too proud to admit it.

"I spend very little time thinking about you, Rory."

"Same goes." His eyes sweep over me briefly. "But,

considering you had a near-death experience just now, I thought I'd cut you some slack."

My eyes automatically fill with tears, and I don't know why I'm crying. I can't pin it down to one cause because there are too many to name.

Rory's eyes are full of sympathy, and I hate it. His arms wrap around me, and he's surprisingly warm. I'm tempted to hug him back, but then I realise who is holding me, and I'm quick to stop it.

I push him away, and he stumbles backwards.

"What do you want from me?"

He lowers his head and stares at a spot on the floor, his eyes eerily distant. "Nothing. Forget it. I'll go and see if the doctor is here."

Without saying another word, he marches out of the room, and I allow myself to unravel.

I've already cried a river by the time Rory finally returns, accompanied by the doctor. He assesses me for any broken bones. Luckily, I don't appear to have any severe injuries. Aside from a few bruises and scratches here or there, I'm as good as new.

"So, is she going to be okay?" Rory asks. He's been in and out of the staff room so many times that I've lost count. He can't keep still for longer than five seconds.

Doctor Chi nods and starts packing away his medical equipment.

"Your girlfriend is going to be fine."

Rory's eyes pop open, matching my look of mortification. "She's not my girlfriend."

"Yeah, we're not together," I quickly add so he doesn't get the wrong idea.

"Oh, sorry. My bad. You can never tell these days," Doctor Chi replies, clearing his throat. "You're lucky you didn't suffer from a back injury, Skye. Rest that knee and try to avoid riding a horse without supervision or in general for the next few days. You must give yourself time to heal."

"Right. That's good advice. Thanks, Doctor."

"You had a lucky escape this time. Remember that."

Rory escorts him out, and I'm alone again.

The staff room is small and only has enough space for one recliner, a coffee table and an old vending machine.

*A packet of Haribo gummy bears is calling my name.*

I walk towards the machine and fish for change in my back pocket. Unfortunately, I only find a bobble and a few two-pence pieces, which won't get me far.

My phone buzzes in my back pocket, and I reach for it, reading the numerous messages I've received from my mother. It hasn't stopped lighting up with notifications.

MUM

Where are you?

Please come home.

We need to talk.

I throw my phone onto the recliner and rest my head against the vending machine.

*This feels like a bad dream. I want to wake up.*

"What are your plans for the rest of the day?"

I jump a mile as Rory fills the doorway.

"Bloody hell! You can't creep up on people like that, especially not when they've just fallen off a horse!"

He stares at me, unfazed. "I can give you a ride home if you want."

*Rory Keaton has offered to take me home.*

*I never saw this coming.*

Is it because he feels sorry for me?

Most likely.

Or does he want to get into my pants?

That sounds more like the Rory I know. He's heard about my past. He probably wants to get laid, and considering I'm 'easy' as people put it, he's set his sights on me to prove I can't resist him.

"How low can you get? I might have a reputation for sleeping around, but I no longer do stuff like that. So, no. I'll kindly decline your offer. You can see yourself out."

I walk towards the staff room door, open it for him and wait. When he doesn't budge and continues to stare at me, I fling my hands up in exasperation.

"Did you not hear me? I asked you to leave."

"Oh, I heard you. Loud and clear," he says impassively, his stare unflinching. "You've misjudged this entire situation. I don't want to sleep with you, Skye. You're not even my type."

His words swim around in my head, and I find it all insulting. I didn't even know Rory had a type. I thought 'girl' was his type. I can't read this boy, and that's the most frustrating part. He's a mixture of confusion and complication—two things I want to avoid.

"I'm annoyed that you think I only offered to take you home purely for that reason. Never mind. I won't bother asking again if you're constantly going to jump to conclusions like that."

His eyes shift away from me, and then he stalks away.

I don't know what I expected him to say, but that wasn't it.

*Now, what am I supposed to think?*

He doesn't want to sleep with me.

I should feel better knowing this, but it only makes me feel insecure and embarrassed for even assuming he did. He's never been interested. Simply put, I'm just a joke to him, and that's all I'll ever be.

* * *

Since learning about my father's financial arrangement, I've not given myself time to process it properly. I've mainly been listening to the doctor's advice—taking it easy while trying to work on the class project. I'm not getting very far because Grayson is a mystery. Attempting to write about him is useless, and I generally feel uninspired.

It's fair to say that Grayson does not get his personality from his father. It's impossible to compare them both. I find it funny how I can get along with his dad, and I've barely known him for five seconds, yet I can't be in the same room as Grayson without biting his head off.

I pop my earphones in and listen to *Nothing Else Matters* by Metallica. I'm not a massive Metallica fan, but their songs resonate with me, especially when I've got all this built-up anger and aggression with nowhere else to go. Halfway into the song, my bedroom door flings open, and my mother walks in, her eyes red and puffy. I pull my headphones out and stare at her expectantly, waiting for her to say something.

"I know you're angry with me, and you have every right to be. I was planning to tell you about the account and the money eventually. I should have done it much sooner. It looks bad, I know," she starts, on the verge of tears.

"Why all the secrecy?"

She squeezes her eyes shut, and a couple of tears spill out. "I thought I was doing the right thing by you. I was just trying to protect you."

I bring my knees closer to my chest. "You keep saying you're only trying to protect me, but who exactly are you protecting me from? My father?"

I genuinely don't know anything about the man.

Is he dangerous?

Is that why she never mentions him?

I must possess some of his features and characteristics. Part of him exists in me. I can't change the fact that I have a dad and that he chose to abandon me. It'll hang over my head for as long as I live.

She swallows, retracing her steps, treading carefully with her words.

"I know you must have questions, but I didn't want you to learn about the account and get your hopes up. I was worried that you might want to reach out to your father, and as far as I'm concerned, the man wants nothing to do with either of us."

*So, it's true.*

*My dad never wanted me.*

*I was an unwanted child.*

*He doesn't even love me.*

"I forgive you for not saying anything," I say, watching her shoulders sag down with relief, "but I am hurt that I was kept in the dark. I can handle myself. I've been doing it for years."

She nods, blinking back more tears forcing their way to the surface.

"I know. I'm sorry."

"My father means nothing to me. You don't have to worry about me ever wanting to reach out to him because I don't need him in my life. I've got you, and that's enough."

My mother collapses onto the bed, her gentle sobs rattling against me as I nuzzle my head into her neck. I believe people can change, and I'll never stop hoping my mother will get better someday, but sometimes even your biggest wishes don't come true. For now, I'm okay with not knowing who my father is. The past is the past, and I can't change that, but I can determine my future, and that's all I have to look forward to.

Once my mother has fallen asleep on the bed, I sit by my desk and start researching different universities. The closest to Barnett is three hours away, meaning I would have to live there permanently. Living alone is a nauseating thought, especially since I'd have to leave my mother behind. I'm not sure she'd even survive without me.

*I can still apply, though. I don't see the harm in that.*

I like the look of Sloanville University, so I click on the explore option on their website to see what kind of courses they offer. I scroll down the list until I find the journalism section.

Burying the rising fear, I begin my application.

# Chapter Eleven

RAIN THUNDERS FROM ABOVE, PAINTING THE SKY A RATHER depressing grey colour. The journey to Lakeside is long and painful. I got caught in a major traffic jam, had at least five cars beep angrily at me, and I almost fell off my bike on two separate occasions.

Call it paranoia or superstition, but I also couldn't help but feel like I was being watched from a distance. That feeling lingers until I finally arrive at the stables, and images of my last conversation with Rory flood my mind, making me forget all about it. I'm beginning to think that maybe I owe him an apology after I accused him of wanting to jump my bones the other day.

I find him searching the barn like he's lost his shoe or an arm.

"Rory, I just wanted to say..."

He walks away, leaving my mouth open and an unfinished sentence hanging off my tongue.

*Okay, so he's still mad.*

I follow him out into the yard and try again. “The thing is, I shouldn't have–”

His constant pacing makes me feel dizzy. He's barely giving me a chance to explain.

“Alright! I was going to apologise, but if you're going to be a jerk, I won't even bother!” I shout, throwing my hands up in surrender.

A sharp gasp leaves my throat when he looks at me. The worry on his face closes off into a pinched look of annoyance.

“Honestly, I don't care if you apologise, Skye. I didn't lose sleep over it, and right now, we have a much bigger problem on our hands.”

“What's the problem?” I demand, sounding harsh. I was supposed to be in apology mode, but that ship has long sailed.

“The horses are gone,” he sputters out.

I do wonder whether he's joking for a second, but as I glance around the barn, the lack of horses is astonishing and terrifying all at the same time.

“What do you mean? Where are they?”

Rory's jaw twitches. “The simplest answer is that a total idiot forgot to lock up, and the stalls were left open all night. Weren't you the last person to leave yesterday?”

I hope he isn't trying to shift the blame onto me. I've never locked up before. I didn't realise I had to start doing that now and let's not forget that I had just fallen off a horse. My head wasn't in the right place.

“I automatically assumed that you'd done it. I'm not even supposed to be working here on Saturdays.”

He blinks at me, then reels himself back. “We'll have to find all the horses before today's event.”

I turn to him, confused. “What event?”

“Mr Swain hosts bumper races at the farm sometimes.”

“What’s a bumper race?”

“A bumper race is for horses needing more track experience before attempting hurdles, dressage competitions or eventing. The track is always flat in a bumper race, and it’s great for introducing the horses to racing.”

“Oh. Right.”

“All horse owners in the area compete for a chance to win. We usually get a good crowd.”

*I still don't get it.*

He lowers his head. “Let’s split up—”

“And look for clues?” I finish, instantly regretting my tendency to act humorously in a situation gone wrong. My *Scooby Doo* references will not be appreciated at a time like this. Rory is making that perfectly clear.

“The horses couldn't have gotten far,” he says, shouldering past me. “We have two hours to get them back into their stalls, washed and ready.”

“And what if they're not ready by the time the event starts?”

He scowls. “Then we may as well consider ourselves out of a job.”

The craziest part about going on a horse scavenger hunt is that you'd think they'd be easy to find, but these guys know how to hide in good places.

Albatross, however, was found within the first ten minutes. He was sitting comfortably in the parking lot, chewing on his mane. I still think that he could benefit from a haircut. One of these days, if we don't get fired, I'd like to bring it up to Mr Swain. I'm sure he'd agree that strong action must be taken.

It takes at least another half an hour to detect Dijon and Henry, mainly because they have ventured far away from the yard. While Rory deals with Dijon, I lure Henry back to the stables, but his cooperation is minimal, and as I reach out for his reins, he gallops further away from me.

I remember reading up about thoroughbred horses a couple of nights ago. Of course, any horse can compete, but thoroughbreds are bred for riding and hunting, depending on their training. Henry is a class A example of what being a thoroughbred is all about—a little on the wild side, fast, muscular, and strong, but I can see why people call him a grumpy old man.

First, he isn’t approachable.

Second, he can't be won over by food alone.

Lastly, he's a lone ranger, making my job much harder.

“Hi, Henry,” I whisper confidently.

If the horse senses I'm anxious, it'll only feed its desire to escape.

“There's a strong chance I might get fired today, and I can't afford to lose this job. Between you and me, I'm desperate for money.”

Henry waves his head in my direction, and I step closer.

"I know you like your personal space, and I understand because I'm the same. I think we're similar, actually, you and me."

I never thought my voice would be soothing enough to reassure anyone, but Henry responds well to it. The horse is suddenly beside me, and I escort him back towards the barn. Rory is pacing back and forth across Dante's stall, and I instantly pick up on his frustration. His cheeks are flushed red, and sweat is sticking to his forehead. I can't even imagine how unflattering I must look in comparison, but it's not important right now. My appearance should be the least of my worries.

"This is a total disaster!" Rory cries, running a hand through his hair repeatedly.

"It'll be fine. Don't worry about it."

"It's not fine. I'm going to get fired, Skye. This job is the only thing that's keeping me afloat," he says, letting out a long string of curses, his reasons for being here a lot stronger than mine. I'm the one that deserves to get fired. I'm still a novice. Rory is good at his job.

"You're not going to get fired, okay? If this ends badly, I'll say that it was my fault. I mean, technically, it was. If I hadn't distracted you by falling off that horse yesterday, maybe none of this would've happened."

Rory's outward expression hasn't changed much, but I'm sure I catch a glimpse of some astonishment on his face as if I've surprised him by saying that I'll take the bullet.

He shakes his head violently.

"I'm the one who made a mistake. I was supposed to be in charge. I should have known better."

“Whoever's to blame is irrelevant. Stop being so hard on yourself. We've got a job to do.”

“You're right. Focusing on the what-ifs is never a good idea. Let's get all the horses back to their stalls and hope the rest of the day goes well.”

An hour later, people start turning up at the farm, wearing extravagant hats and glamorous outfits. They're expecting an afternoon of entertainment, but little do they know, they're about to experience the worst kind their eyes have ever feasted on because the horses have been running wild since this morning and are extremely tired. The only thing working in our favour is the weather. Despite the early rain showers, the day has brightened considerably, and let’s face it; Nobody wants to watch a horse race in a thunderstorm.

I catch Mr Frost praising Dante in front of a large crowd of onlookers, but he's failed to notice Dante's total lack of energy and how much that will cost him in today's race. It won't be long before the cracks start to show during the performances, and that's when Rory and I will be in the firing line.

I could be a better communicator. I mostly stand around and watch everyone else engage in conversation while I continue to blend into the background and remain invisible. I'm becoming increasingly queasy because I've realised that I'm on Swain property, which means Grayson is bound to show up sooner or later, and I need to remain in the shadows.

*Stay out of sight, disappear, and evade detection.*

*It can't be that difficult.*

"Good afternoon, Skye."

Mr Swain's voice startles me.

*My cover has been blown.*

I turn around to greet him. He looks pleased enough to burst and must be excited about the show. That makes sense. He is the primary host, which is something to be proud of.

"Uh, hi, sir," I say, unable to hide the tremor in my voice.

"What are you doing over here all by yourself?"

*Well, I'm hiding from your son and all the other guests simply because I don't belong here.*

"I just needed some time alone," I say convincingly enough.

"Me too."

That's surprising. I thought he loved the attention. Why else would you host an event like this if you didn't?

"I wanted to discuss something with you."

Oh no. It's never a good sign when your boss wants to discuss something. He's going to fire me. That's where this conversation is headed. I'm going to get fired before the show even takes place.

"Rory told me about what happened with Dante—that you had an accident."

I cover my head in my hands, deeply humiliated at the recent memory. "I'm so sorry! It was stupid of me to risk jeopardising my safety and Dante's. I was upset about something and let it get to me. It's no excuse and—"

Mr Swain waves a hand in the air, and I'm forced to stop talking.

“Skye, it's okay. You don't need to explain yourself or apologise.”

“I don't?”

“No. Accidents happen.”

“You're not going to fire me?”

Mr Swain laughs. “Fire you? Why on earth would I do that? Yes, on the one hand, you should not have mounted Dante without supervision, but you were brave enough to try, and that shows just how strong-willed you are. It's quite promising.”

I consider this for a minute, wondering what he means by that, but I don't have time to question it because Rory is approaching us fast.

*I hope that nothing else has gone wrong.*

“Sir, Grayson is looking for you. He says it's urgent.”

I glance at Rory sharply, noticing his firmly fixed gaze on me. Silent words pass between us, and a wave of anxiety overwhelms me to the point where I struggle to swallow.

*Grayson. Is. Here.*

Mr Swain nods, concerned. “I’d better go and check on him. Enjoy the rest of your day, Skye,” he says, working through the crowds.

Rory is a ball of tension, and I'm slowly starting to catch up.

“We're in serious trouble,” he says once Mr Swain is out of earshot.

“I know! Grayson is here.”

“Who cares?”

"Me! I care! He doesn't know that I work for his dad. Is that story ringing any bells?"

Rory lifts his eyes to mine and shakes his head. "You know what, Skye, I'm starting to think that maybe you're ashamed of this place—what we do, who we are, what we represent. If you don't want to be here, why did you sign up for the opportunity?"

My heart trips inside my chest.

"I had my reasons for applying for this job, not that it's any of your business, and I'm not ashamed!"

"If that's true, why are you so concerned about Grayson finding out you work here? Are you embarrassed? Is that it? Or do you think you're better than us—that the work we do at Trinity is beneath you?"

I feel weirdly emotional hearing him say that. Rory always manages to hit a nerve whenever I'm presented with his brutal honesty. I hate how much he's right in several ways and wrong in many others.

"Here's the truth," I start, looking him straight in the eye, "I would never think I'm better than anyone else, not even my worst enemy. Maybe I am embarrassed, though—not by Trinity or you or the work that goes on. That deserves nothing but high praise and respect. But if Grayson finds out I'm working for his father, he will never let it go. That's just the type of person he is, and believe it or not, I don't need the extra hassle right now."

*Not with everything else that's going on,* I want to add but don't.

Rory takes a deep breath, his gaze lifting upwards as a large plane glides across the sky. He focuses his attention back towards me again, and I wish the plane would suddenly take a pit stop so this conversation wouldn't have to continue.

“Are you saying Grayson has been giving you a hard time?”

“It's nothing serious, and I'm not saying I'm a saint. We're just as bad as each other, but he already makes fun of me, and I don't want to give him any more reason to flaunt his wealth in my face or rub it in. Does that make any rational sense?”

“I guess it does.”

“Despite what you might think of me, I have nothing but positive things to say about this place. I mean that.”

“Alright, I get it,” he says, wrinkling his nose. “I can see why you feel the way that you do. Grayson isn't a very likeable guy.”

Rory doesn't know I’ll leave this place behind once I’ve made enough money to pay Rob back. If everything goes according to plan, I'll be free to walk away in a matter of weeks, and Grayson will forever be kept in the dark about my time at Trinity Farm. It will be as if I never truly arrived.

“I think you might need a disguise,” Rory says, startling me out of my thoughts.

“I agree. Maybe I could wear some sunglasses.”

He laughs, shaking his head at me. “You’ll need more than a pair of shades, Clemons. Nobody else here has hair like yours—it gives your identity away. Grayson will spot you the minute we step onto the field.”

He’s not wrong.

“Okay... what are you suggesting I do?”

Rory folds his arms across his chest and flashes me a mischievous grin.

"I have something in mind, but you won't like it."

"I am *not* wearing that," I say, my voice laced with disgust as Rory holds up a horse costume he unearthed from the depths of an ancient storage cupboard. A tail and a horse head mask are attached to the full-length bodysuit—enough to give anyone nightmares.

Is this truly Rory's master plan?

How does he expect me to blend in by wearing this?

People will think I'm insane, and I'll likely be escorted off the premises.

Rory shrugs, his nonchalance baffling me. "It's not *that* bad."

"The costume has a horse's head and half a tail, Rory. It's horrific—not to mention utterly terrifying!"

I'm not even exaggerating in the slightest.

"Hey, you're hurting Dudley's feelings."

"The costume has a name?"

"Of course! Dudley is the farm mascot. We sometimes bring him out for entertainment purposes. The children love him."

My gaze reluctantly shifts to the horse's freakishly long nose and comically goofy teeth.

"Children actually like that thing?"

"Oh, yeah. They'll be excited to see Dudley back on the scene if you dress up as him for the day. Do it for the kids," he says, teasing me.

"I don't even think Dudley is wearable," I remark,

sceptically examining the thick layers of fabric and contemplating how one can breathe whilst remaining trapped inside this monstrosity.

Rory rolls his eyes dismissively as if I'm being dramatic.

"Wear it or don't wear it, I couldn't care less. But, if you really want to keep your identity a secret, Dudley is your guy."

*Just don't think about it.*

*Seriously,* ***don't.***

# Chapter Twelve

"WHAT THE BLOODY HELL IS GOING ON?"

"Is this a joke?"

"Run, Dante! Run! Do something, for crying out loud! Stop eating the damn grass!"

There are too many voices shouting at once.

Rory had vital information to share before I brought the Grayson subject up again and distracted him. Most horses are too tired to listen to their owners' instructions, and many have decided to nap midway into the race. I can't bear to look at Mr Swain because he will be disappointed that his event isn't going as smoothly as anticipated.

I search for Dijon and Henry and find them lying on opposite sides of the track, basking in the sun emerging from behind the clouds.

*At least they're getting some vitamin D.*

Dante is lagging, and Mr Frost does not look pleased with him. A horse like that should be in the top five by now. Frosty will kick up a fuss when this is all over, that's for sure. The whole event is chaotic, and the crowd looks like they want to kill the culprit. They take this horse-riding business very seriously.

Grayson is competing in the race, so luckily, I haven't seen much of him. He's riding Luna, who seems to have plenty of energy to spare. He picked the horse with the most stamina, and she's currently in first place. Gliding effortlessly across the track, Luna is winning by a long mile. A few of the other horses could learn a thing or two if they chose to stop being so lazy.

"How's it going in that costume, Clemons?" Rory asks, his attempt to maintain a serious face quickly crumbling.

Wearing Dudley isn't comfortable or fun. The guests' peculiar glances add to my discomfort, and I hope I don't pass out in this suit because it's unbelievably hot.

*I guess this is the price I must pay.*

"Not great. I thought you said the kids loved Dudley," I say, scratching my arms to eliminate a persistent itch.

I approached a child in the crowd earlier, and they fled in tears. Although it wasn't the reaction I had expected, I understood why they cried. I would probably be taken aback if a person dressed as a horse suddenly started speaking to me, so there were no hard feelings.

"They do love Dudley... sometimes."

I spin towards him, my anger palpable.

"What do you mean *sometimes*?"

"It's a hit-and-miss situation," Rory says casually, his attention quickly shifting back to the ongoing race.

I'm starting to think the children have never truly warmed to Dudley because he is not a child-friendly mascot. I bet Rory only told me that information to get me in the suit.

"Incoming..." Rory whispers into my ear.

I take a hurried step back from him, flushing red. "Can you not do that?"

"Do what?" he asks, puzzled.

"Don't lean in so close."

He smirks. "Why? Do I make you nervous, Clemons?"

"You wish."

"I was just about to warn you that Grayson has won the race, and he's heading this way... but that was five seconds ago."

"*What?*"

I almost choke on my tongue as my head swivels, taking in my surroundings. Grayson is busy chatting with Mr Swain, but he suddenly glances in my direction, his expression becoming a mixture of wonder, fear, and confusion.

*Where is the crowd when you need them most?*

"Crap! Crap! Crap! Grayson has seen me. What am I going to do?"

Rory laughs and pats me roughly on the head. "Relax. You're Dudley now, remember?" he reminds me, referring to my disguise.

I forgot about Dudley for a split second.

Grayson may not recognise me, but I don't want to take any chances. He steadily approaches us, his every movement purposeful and determined. I stand frozen because it's too late to hide or flee—not now that he's standing a few feet away.

"Bloody hell! Nobody mentioned Dudley was going

to be making an appearance today. Who's the poor soul in the costume this year?" Grayson exclaims, taking off his riding helmet to properly assess me.

Rory shrugs, feigning ignorance. "Beats me."

"How much did my dad pay you to dress up as our mascot?"

Caught off guard by his direct question, I remain silent, aware that I can't respond without revealing my true identity. He'd recognise my voice in an instant.

A flicker of frustration crosses his face when I don't answer him.

"Hello? Is anybody in there? Earth to Dudley..."

I keep my mouth firmly closed, and a crease forms between his brows, his patience wearing thin. Determined to stay in character, I keep my mouth firmly shut, but Grayson grows more suspicious.

"It's common courtesy to respond when someone asks you a question, especially if the boss's *son* asks."

Sweat breaks out across my forehead.

*I'm doomed.*

Just as the tension peaks, a man in a navy blue suit joins us, diverting Grayson's attention and saving me from further interrogation. His face is not one to be forgotten. He's undeniably handsome, with his clean-cut appearance, brown hair, and deep blue eyes exuding power and control. A striking resemblance to Mr Swain suggests a possible connection between the two. Perhaps they're friends or brothers with a taste for designer suits. I bet they don't even own a single pair of flip-flops.

"Sebastian! I'm so glad you could make it," Grayson greets the man, momentarily forgetting about Dudley.

"Congratulations on winning the race today, Grayson. I'm impressed."

"Thanks. It was almost too easy to claim the top spot this year," Grayson boasts, prompting an eye-roll from me at his constant need to show off.

Would things have been different if the other horses hadn't failed to race against the clock?

"I don't know what happened to the other horses. They were all over the place. It doesn't look good on your father's behalf. I'll be having words with him later," Sebastian says.

"Well, I can't vouch for the horses that didn't compete today, but Luna proved that she was more than worthy."

Fishing in his pocket, Sebastian pulls out a card and hands it to Grayson. He's probably just offered him a ticket of a lifetime, not that he needs any more money to his name. Fame could be of interest if Grayson wanted that sort of thing. He doesn't have to search for opportunities because they get handed to him.

How lucky is he to have been born into such privilege?

Sebastian's gaze falls on me, and he flinches, his reaction delayed.

"What on earth..." he begins, unable to finish his sentence, disbelief clouding his face.

Grayson explains, "This is Dudley, the farm mascot. I think he's lost his ability to speak this afternoon. He's giving me the silent treatment."

Feeling a tug on my tail, I whip around to find a group of kids running away, giggling and screaming.

Dudley has become the laughingstock of the farm, reduced to a child's plaything they can poke, prod, and treat like a piñata.

"Take the mask off, Dudley," Grayson commands, his tone authoritative.

"I don't think that's a good idea, Grayson. It might frighten the children if Dudley suddenly revealed his true identity," Rory quickly intervenes, coming to my rescue.

"Hey! What are you trying to say?" I blurt out, unable to contain myself, slapping Rory's chest with one of my fake hooves.

My hand flies to my mouth, hoping Grayson hasn't recognised my voice. Desperate times call for desperate measures, so I transform into a make-believe character—an imaginary horse in one panic-induced moment.

"Neigh!!" I yell at the top of my lungs, pretending to gallop away from them.

During my grand escape, I'm confident I overhear Grayson mutter, "I swear, Dudley gets weirder every year."

It's close to four o'clock when we've finally finished hosing the horses down, and I return Dudley to the storage cupboard where he belongs.

*I smell like horse fart mixed with sweat and endorphins.*

Dante whips his head over the fence to look at me as he continues to munch on some hay, and I give him a good pat on the back. I pull my hair away from my face and tie it into a loose ponytail, placing my hands firmly on my hips, the horse watching me curiously.

"Luna might've shone on the field today, but I know you've got a lot more to give. So let's try and get you in the top five next time, yeah?"

Dante neighs, and I take that as a sign of commitment. He lowers his head and allows me to rub his ears.

"You're a big softy, aren't you? I know you didn't mean to throw me off the saddle, and even if you did, I don't blame you. I'd like us to be friends if you're cool with that?"

Dante gazes down at me, his expression tender and a little soppy. Human beings are never this transparent. Animals aren't afraid to be vulnerable. Just like a dog stays loyal to its owner, a horse is reliable even if its owner is harsh and hurtful sometimes. If only people could remain faithful to each other. The world would be a much better place.

"Excuse me."

My chin jerks up, and I find Sebastian standing there, briefly looking over at Dante and then back at me. I don't know why he's still here. The event ended hours ago.

"Uh, hi. Can I help you?" I ask, a little curious.

"I'm looking for Michael. Have you seen him?"

"Mr Swain?"

"Yes, who else?" he grinds out impatiently.

"I haven't, sorry."

Sebastian rakes his gaze over me with this frustrated intensity, making the situation uncomfortable. He seems like the type of man who always gets what he wants, no matter the outcome and regardless of whose toes must be stepped on to get there. Something about him makes me a little uneasy.

"Do I know you from somewhere?" he demands, something unsaid sparkling in his eyes.

I shake my head, confused. I would remember seeing this guy around because he has such an unmistakable face—one that stops people in their tracks. I know that we have never met before.

"Uh, no. I don't think so."

He clears his throat and shakes his head. "Right. Never mind. If you see Mr Swain, please tell him I need to speak to him as soon as possible."

"Sure. I will."

He stares at me for a moment longer, then marches out of the barn. I glance at Dante after he's gone, letting out a breath.

*That was weird.*

# Chapter Thirteen

"Did someone's cat die?"

I sit up sharply and wipe the grogginess from my eyes, Grayson invading my lunch table.

I've sat through lectures all morning, unable to retain any new information. Despite catching up on sleep, I still feel exhausted. There's so much I need to do, and I am still trying to figure out where to start. I need to get my emotions in check. I don't even know what day it is.

"Seriously, did your cat die? I was only joking," Grayson says, eyebrows scrunched together.

"Nobody has died. Batman is fine."

I haven't seen my cat since last week, but I'm not worried. He occasionally ventures into the wilderness and always finds his way home. I must keep my window open if he returns unexpectedly and I'm not there to let him in. You'd think he would have gotten used to me by now, considering I am allowing him to take refuge under my bed, but I don't think he likes me. We have a love-hate kind of relationship.

"Phew, that was a close call." Grayson pulls out a little lunch box, and I stare at him, wondering what he's still doing here. Last time I checked, we agreed to study during lesson times and in the library. Lunch hours are strictly off-limits.

I fix him with a glare, which he happily returns. "Are you lost?"

"Why would you think that? I know my way around the cafeteria by now. It's bloody tiny."

"That's not what I..." I'm about to correct him but think better of it. I am not prepared to argue with Grayson today.

He picks through his sandwiches and starts munching away, making the most atrocious noises I've ever heard.

*He's annoying me already.*

"While I'm here, I have a question to ask you," he says, popping a crisp into his mouth and chewing like a horse.

"Not now. Can't you see that I'm busy?"

He exhales a small laugh. "Busy doing what exactly? Feeling sorry for yourself?"

*He's got me there. I am drowning in my sorrows.*

"Fine. What do you want?"

"You're a girl, aren't you?"

"Last time I checked... yeah. Is that your question? Because it sucks."

Grayson leans towards me, lowering his voice. "I want to surprise Sophie for her birthday, but I have no idea what to get her. I was wondering if you had any ideas."

Sophie practically worships the ground that he walks on. I'm sure she'd appreciate anything he got for her—a dozen roses, a fancy bracelet or anything that sparkles in the sunlight, preferably a golden amulet or something similar. It's not like Grayson can't afford it.

"Just buy her a bunch of flowers."

"That's so lame! I want to make the experience special for her."

"Flowers ***are*** special."

I've never received any in my lifetime, but it shows a great deal of thought and helps to communicate an emotion that would otherwise be left unsaid. I sometimes wonder if Sophie is with Grayson because she genuinely loves him or if she's more interested in the social status he provides.

"Maybe I'm asking the wrong person here," he mutters.

"Go and ask Shelly Matthews, then. I'm sure she'll be happy to help you out."

"I'll talk to her after lunch."

I glance around the cafeteria and spot her sitting at a table a few rows from ours.

"I've got a better idea. Why don't you go and talk to her right now? Save us both the trouble."

A frown touches his lips.

I've made it painfully apparent that I don't want him around, which I'm starting to feel slightly bad about.

"Fine. I won't waste any more of your time. You can be such a viper," he says, storming over to Shelley's table and returning to his side of the lunch hall where he belongs.

Part of me feels guilty for being such a grouch, but I don't have much time to think about it because Josie slides into the seat next to me. Her smiling face could be detected from a mile away. I didn't ask her to join me for lunch. She invited herself along, although I'm still struggling to understand why since I'm not the friendliest person in the world.

"Hey! How's it going with Grayson? Are you two finally getting along?" she asks, wiping her rose-coloured glasses with the end of her sleeve.

"Nope. We still hate each other. I'm supposed to meet up with him in the library later. How's it going with Eddie?"

"He's not *that* bad," Josie says, smiling and sipping her caramel latte.

*I know that look.*

*I'm not stupid.*

"Have you been sleeping with him?"

Josie starts choking on her latte. I'm tempted to pat her on the back, but that would only cause more of a scene.

"We have not—" She glances around the cafeteria fearfully and quickly adds, "We haven't slept together. That would be so unprofessional!"

"Sorry. It's none of my business anyway."

She sighs and looks down at the floor. "It's fine. Besides, I like someone else."

"You do?"

"Yeah, but he's got a girlfriend and barely even notices me."

I take a long, hard look at Josie. Maybe if she got rid

of the pigtails and weird clothes, more boys would notice her. She is a pretty girl, but Josie is young at heart. That's not a bad thing. I worry that she will get taken advantage of.

"Is this boy in our class?" I ask, taking a big bite from my ham and cheese sandwich.

"Yeah. I know he doesn't feel the same about me, but a girl can dream."

Now I'm wondering who her crush is. Not many boys are on our course, which narrows it down to only five possible suspects. I'm just glad she hasn't fallen for Eddie's charms. He's such a player.

"Have you ever had a boyfriend, Josie?"

"No. I know what you must be thinking. How can an eighteen-year-old still be a virgin, right?" She quickly looks away, cheeks turning pink.

I wasn't expecting her to say that out loud and in the worst place imaginable. The cafeteria is crowded with people eager to hear the latest gossip. Rumours spread like wildfire. For her own sake, I hope nobody overheard.

"I'm not embarrassed. I believe two people should be in love when they have sex. It's a big deal, especially to me, and I've never been asked out. I'm not pretty enough, I guess," she continues.

We live in a society where 'looks' don't always matter, but they do fifty percent of the time. As a female, I compare and contrast daily. There will always be someone prettier, more skilled and more talented than me, but I've realised I don't need to compete or prove anything to anyone because that's not a healthy way to live.

“Don't let anyone make you feel you're not pretty or good enough, Josie. It isn't true. I've slept around. It's not something I'm proud of, and I regret it, but if I could start over and wait, I would take it in a heartbeat. You’re being sensible,” I tell her.

She fixes me with a grateful smile. “Thanks for being so understanding, Skye.”

We return to eating our food, and my mind flashes back to all the times my mother's relationships crashed and burned. I know that she didn't love any of the men she dated. They were just decoys.

Now that I think about it, I have never actually witnessed a positive, healthy relationship. I have no idea what it feels like to be in love, and I already know that I'll never get to experience it because who could fall in love with a girl like me?

* * *

“Don't touch my radio.”

Grayson has been rude to me since I entered his expensive-looking Bugatti. He led me to his car when class ended and insisted we try something different for today's study session. I think he was looking for an excuse to avoid returning to the library, and I'm okay with that.

“Do you have an audio input?”

He keeps his eyes on the road ahead. “I have one, but I can't be bothered to link my phone to it.”

“Can I connect mine?”

He lets out a heavy sigh, clearly not thrilled with the

idea. "Fine, but don't go playing any girly music. It'll cramp my style."

"How do I connect my phone?"

"Just give it here."

"No way! I'm not going to let you drive and go on my phone. That's against the law."

He clutches the steering wheel and glances aggravatedly at me.

"Go to your settings and click on Bluetooth. Click on where it says Grayson's car, and it should connect straight away."

All the power is in my hands in seconds, and a *Feeder* song fills the car, instantly calming me. I hum along, pretending Grayson isn't there. That would make this experience far more enjoyable.

"You like Feeder?" Grayson's voice carries a hint of surprise as he angles his body slightly towards mine.

I stick my head out the window and land back in my seat when I can sense him watching me.

"Yup. Big fan over here."

"I listen to them all the time. I've got their music on Spotify." His enthusiasm shines through.

"Oh my gosh! We have something in common! Can you believe it?" I squeal, making him laugh.

"What's your favourite song of theirs?"

I stare out at the road unfolding ahead of us. "Probably *Just the way I'm feeling*. I can relate to that song so much. I could listen to it on repeat, and I'd never get bored."

His eyes widen. "No way! That's my favourite song, too."

"This is getting freaky now. By the way, I meant to ask, how long have you and Sophie been together?"

"We've been dating for two months now."

*Woah, I thought he was going to say that they were high school sweethearts. Two months isn't that long.*

"How did you meet?"

"At Lakeside College."

I wait for him to elaborate, but when he doesn't, I hold a hand over my heart and say, "Wow, that's the most romantic story I've ever heard, Swain. Someone hand me a tissue. I might cry."

Grayson rolls his eyes at my dramatic display. "We liked each other, so we got together. It's as simple as that."

"How lovely. Thanks for boring me to death with all the details."

He shoots me a questioning look. "Why are you suddenly so interested in my relationship anyway?"

I lower my eyes to my lap. "I'm not."

"Kind of seems like you are."

I throw my hands up in exasperation. "Well, sorry for attempting to start a conversation."

I deliver him the best glare I can muster, although it probably looks like I'm straining to use the toilet because he hasn't stopped laughing.

"You annoy me," I moan.

Grayson nods his head, smirking. "The feeling's mutual. Don't worry."

"I am so disappointed that you're my partner for the project."

"Right back at you, class viper."

"You–you just..." I search for the right word and end up repeating myself. "You annoy me."

"Yeah, you've already said that."

I slump down, pouting. "Whatever. It's the truth."

Tapping his finger against the steering wheel, he steals me another glance. "I believe you, but since you're keen to delve into my love life, let's focus on yours for a second. Are you dating anyone?"

"No."

"Has the class viper ever been in love?" he questions, teasing me further.

"No," I snap defensively.

Realisation dawns on his face. "Ah, I think I get it now. You got cheated on by your ex, didn't you? Is that why you're so cold to everyone? Because some guy came along and broke your heart?"

There is a line.

He just crossed it.

"I don't want to discuss this with you, alright? I'm done with the Q and A."

I must've fallen asleep along the way to Grayson's mystery location. My eyes pop open, and I wipe away a pool of saliva from the side of my mouth. I slept awkwardly because every muscle in my neck is aching.

Grayson pulls into a familiar lane, and my heart picks up speed. I look up at the large sign above the gate, trembling.

**TRINITY STABLES**

*He's brought me to work?*

Grayson stops the car, shuts off the engine and turns to face me.

"Oh, good, you're awake," he says, glancing over at me. "This is my dad's farm. I love coming here because it helps me to forget the business of life for a while. I bet you expected me to take you somewhere more flashy, right?"

I consider this, chewing the inside of my cheek anxiously. "No. I mean, yeah–" I trail off, unable to finish my sentence without stammering.

Grayson smiles, oblivious to my sudden burst of anxiety. "Come on. Let me give you the grand tour."

I have no choice but to unbuckle my seatbelt and follow him toward the warm glow of the stables. I could tell him the truth—that I work for his father. Maybe he'll understand.

"We recently hosted an event at the farm, and I took first place with my horse, Luna."

*I know. I was there. I saw the whole thing.*

"I don't come here as often as I used to, but I have so many good memories of this place. I thought it might help if we got a glimpse of each other's lives."

My thoughts swirl while I try to think of a way to bring up the work thing. This is pure torture. I'm struggling to find the right words and the best way to tell him.

"About that... there's something I need to—"

"We bought Luna from a farm just on the outskirts of Lakeside," Grayson continues, making it impossible to explain. "She was frail and timid initially, but she's become one of the strongest racehorses at Trinity."

"That's great, but—"

"All thanks to a bit of hard work and dedication," he finishes, cutting me off.

"Grayson, I need to tell you something."

We turn the corner, and neither of us notices Rory walking straight towards us down the path, pushing a large wheelbarrow in our direction. We make direct eye contact, and he propels forward, trying to swerve around us, but it's too late. Grayson's feet are swiped from beneath him, and he falls into the wheelbarrow head-first, legs dangling in the air. He looks like an injured seal, writhing in his filth.

Grayson sits up, recoils, and spits on the ground several times. It takes him another few minutes to fully regain his balance and jump to his feet. The look he aims at Rory is one of complete fury.

"Are you blind, stable boy? Look what you've done, you *idiot*! This is going to come out of your paycheck." He motions towards his clothes, covered in horse faeces and hay.

Rory steps forward, glaring at him. "Hey, *you* walked into me. I'm just trying to do my job."

Grayson spits on the ground again, grimacing. He spins to me when a chuckle rumbles at the back of my throat. I know I shouldn't laugh, but I can't help it. Tears are streaming down my face, and I don't feel bad. If the roles were reversed, he would be laughing at me.

"Do you think this is funny, Skye?"

"Uh... yeah. It's hilarious."

He holds a hand over his mouth. "I'm going to be

sick," he says, rushing off to the toilets and leaving a trail of curses behind him.

"What an airhead," Rory mumbles, lowering his gaze to mine. I pick up on his frustration now that we're alone. I get the strangest feeling that he's angry at me for some reason.

"What are you doing here with Grayson Swain?" he demands, confirming my theory.

"It's complicated."

"I thought you weren't a fan of the guy."

"I'm not."

"Have you told him that you work here? Does he know?"

I shake my head fiercely. "Not yet."

His eyes bore into mine. "One minute, you're telling me that you want to keep your job a secret from Grayson, and then the next, you're hanging out with him at the farm. It makes no sense."

"I understand that none of this adds up, but I'm only here with him because we have this college project to complete and—"

"I don't care if you're enemies or friends with benefits." His tone is cold and cutting. "It wouldn't surprise me if you were sleeping with him. You've had your fair share of one-night stands, right?"

His comment lands with a painful blow, striking deep within me. I feel a surge of vulnerability as if I've been cast aside on the school playground and rejected by a group of children, except this is far worse because Rory is using my past to hurt me, and it's working.

"Do whatever the hell you want. I'm just the stableboy, remember? Have fun playing pretend. It's what you're best at, after all," he continues.

He grabs the wheelbarrow and guides it back into the barn, the doors closing behind him with a resounding thud. Embarrassment and the hot sting of rejection slay me down.

Grayson and I are attempting to study in the field an hour later.

So far, it's not going well, but what's new?

My brain is too occupied and filled with thoughts of my last conversation with Rory. I can't seem to concentrate on much else. I keep reliving everything he said.

*I don't care if you're enemies or friends with benefits.*

*It wouldn't surprise me if you were sleeping with him. You've had your fair share of one-night stands, right?*

*Have fun playing pretend. It's what you're best at, after all.*

I'll never be able to escape my past. It'll always be there, ready to trip me up when I least expect it. I would be happy if I never had to speak to Rory again, but it's not that simple. Working together has its disadvantages.

"I've still got that horrible taste in my mouth! It won't go away!"

Ever since the wheelbarrow incident, Grayson has continued to make a long list of complaints. He also had to pop into his house to change into a new set of clothes, which cost us valuable time.

"Agh! You've got to be kidding me!" his voice cracks through the air again.

“Oh, what's wrong now? Have you broken a nail?” I snap, rolling my eyes.

“My phone battery is dead,” he says, throwing his phone onto the grass.

“Seriously? You're ridiculous.” I shake my head in disbelief.

“Well, considering I just got run over by a wheelbarrow, landed in manure and smell like a horse, I think my complaints are pretty well justified.”

“Yeah, but now you're just feeling sorry for yourself.”

He glares at me. “It's that bloody stableboy's fault. I bet he did this on purpose.”

“Why would he go out of his way to do that? He'd be putting his job on the line, not to mention he has no possible motive.”

“He humiliated me! That's motive enough.”

I reach for my notepad and lie in the grass, stretching my legs out in front of me.

*Rory Keaton is the last person I want to be talking about.*

“Moving on. I have a question for you.”

“Go ahead. Do your worst.”

“Why do you compete? You have all the money in the world. You aren't doing it for the extra cash. So, what's in it for you?”

He shrugs. “I love horses—always have. It also helps that I'm good with them, and they like me.”

*I have no idea why.*

*It's a mystery.*

“When did you start competing?”

Grayson picks at the grass, avoiding my gaze. “I

must've been about five or six. My dad used to compete, and he's won so many trophies and awards. I saw his achievements growing up and wanted to be just like him."

There's a pause as our eyes meet.

"That's nice."

"Yeah. He's great."

I want to mention that I think he's great, too, but I'm not even supposed to know his father. How will he react if he finds out that he has employed me?

"I want to introduce you to someone," Grayson says, jumping to his feet.

Extending a hand, he helps me off the grass, and I stare after him curiously.

"Where are we going?"

"You'll see."

He doesn't release my hand as we walk to the barn. The lights automatically switch on when we're inside, and I didn't realise how happy I'd be to see all my new friends again. Dante waves his head in our direction, eager to greet us. Albatross is busy eating out of his food container. Luna is trotting around, flaunting herself. Henry is lying down, enjoying his own company, and Dijon rolls back and forth across his straw bed, loving life.

I check the barn for any signs of Rory, but he's nowhere to be found.

*That's a relief.*

"This is my horse," Grayson proclaims, staring at Luna with nothing but love.

"She's beautiful," I tell him, feeling incredibly guilty

that this is not the first time I've been introduced to his horse.

Without a shadow of a doubt, Luna is one of the healthiest-looking horses at Trinity. She was born to race and will go on to do great things. Considering she's already won several races, she is proving to be the star of the show, but Dante still has what it takes.

"Yeah, she is something special, isn't she? I always ensure she's given nothing but the best care, don't I, girl?" he coos, earning a satisfied response from Luna.

"It's weird. Usually, Luna goes crazy when she meets someone for the first time. She hates Sophie."

Sophie is uptight and wouldn't dare mount a horse in case she messed up her hair. What Grayson doesn't know is that I've already met Luna. In the beginning, she wasn't keen on me either, but she must be getting used to seeing my face around the stables.

While I stand there and listen to Grayson talk about his experiences on the farm, I should be pleased that I'm gaining a lot of information for the project, but why do I feel like I've somehow cheated my way to the top?

# Chapter Fourteen

I'M BACK AT THE STABLES BEFORE I KNOW IT, AND I CAN HEAR Mr Frost shouting every word under the sun at Dante as he gallops across the field at a rather disappointing speed. His performance is all over the place. He's as fit as Luna, yet something is holding him back.

"I've had it with this horse!" Mr Frost declares, taking off his cap and throwing it to the ground in a temper tantrum.

I abandon Mr Frost and approach Dante. His head whips up to look at me instinctively, and I reach to pat him on the neck.

"I don't get it. You have all it takes to become a great competition horse, but you don't even try. Why is that?" I ask him softly.

Of course, he doesn't reply, but looking into the pupils of his tired eyes, I can't help but feel a little bit sorry for him. The poor guy is being ordered around constantly, and it must be physically and emotionally exhausting having to take orders from Mr Frost. Dante might not be exceeding his expectations, but there's got to be a reason for that.

"I don't blame you for being annoyed with that stubborn old fart, Mr Frost," I whisper, earning myself a deep-throated chuckle that doesn't belong to the horse.

My cheeks flame red when I turn around and find Mr Swain standing there, grinning.

"Uh, Mr Swain! I was just–"

"Stating an opinion?" he guesses.

"I'm so sorry. You weren't supposed to hear any of that."

He doesn't look angry with me for throwing shade at one of his most prominent investors. On the contrary, he seems rather amused by it.

"It's probably best Mr Frost never finds out that his horse isn't fond of him. I've picked up on their strained relationship myself. Your secret is safe with me," he says light-heartedly.

*That's good to know.*

Mr Swain scrutinises the horse, a flicker of intrigue dancing in his eyes. "We don't know much about Dante's background, but we know he was mistreated. The horse has been through a lot. I can imagine that he was quite a force to be reckoned with at one point."

I'm glad someone else has recognised Dante's potential.

"I think he could be Luna's equal if he gave himself a chance."

"Yes. Maybe. He seems to have taken a shine to you."

I never thought I'd form an emotional bond with a

horse. Part of me doesn't want to say goodbye to him when my time here is up.

"Have you ever thought about riding, Skye?" he asks, his unexpected question catching me off guard.

"Uh, not really."

"Training plays a huge part, but the way I see it, the relationship you have with the horse is far more important than earning yourself a trophy at the end of the day. From what I've gathered, you are a natural."

I blush bright red. "Oh, thanks, sir."

Mr Swain's phone rings, disrupting our conversation.

He glances at the screen, eyebrows drawing together.

"I'd better take this, but think about it," he says, walking further away.

I cast a glance around the yard.

Mr Frost has wandered off somewhere, and I don't particularly care where Rory is. I take a deep, rattly breath and gently ease myself onto Dante's saddle, following his movements so we're in sync.

Once I feel more confident, I urge him to go faster by squeezing his flanks with both heels to get him moving. The horse understands my language and naturally picks up the pace. My heart gives a little skip when Dante's galloping turns frantic, and I worry that I will fall again or suffer a severe injury this time. The doctor warned me not to mount a horse without supervision, but Mr Swain is nearby, so it's not like I'm entirely alone.

I hadn't thought about riding until Mr Swain mentioned it, but everything about this moment felt right. I have to keep telling myself not to get too comfortable, though.

This isn't permanent.

Nothing ever is.

* * *

I charge through the large wooden doors of the stables, the intoxicating smells of horse manure and hay hitting me straight in the face. It's not something you ever get used to, but as time passes, you begin to tolerate the smells since they're unavoidable.

I waste no time getting straight to work, ensuring the horses are well-fed before replacing any bedding and mucking out after them. Somewhere between tackling wheelbarrows and balancing buckets, I spot Rory leaning against the barn with the same girl I saw him with on my first day at Trinity.

She's wearing a cute pair of denim shorts with a low crop top. High-knee boots cover most of her legs, but there's still enough flesh for her outfit to be considered a bit revealing for a trip to the stables. She is pining after Rory like a lovesick puppy. Whether he's figured that out or not is undecided.

I watch them flirt while I continue working through my lunch hour. The girl whispers something into Rory's ear, and I roll my eyes at their overly affectionate display.

*They seriously need to get a room.*

Rory's gaze suddenly shoots up, and his eyes meet mine. His previously relaxed expression instantly sours. Whenever I'm around, I seem to bring out his serious side.

Heat floods my body, and I quickly avert my eyes.

Deciding to give them privacy, I jog back into the barn and walk towards Dante's stall.

"When I leave this place, I'm going to miss you the most," I say softly, a tinge of sadness in my voice.

My solitude is short-lived because Rory steps directly into my path and says, "Hey. Are we cool?"

I grit my teeth, determined to ignore him the best I can. Approaching the gate and swinging it open, I step into Dante's stall. Rory follows me, but there isn't enough room for both of us, so I'm forced to constantly sidestep and manoeuvre around him.

"I'm sorry if I upset you the other day. It wasn't intentional."

I finally turn to acknowledge him, emotion welling up at the back of my throat.

"What are you apologising for? Making me out to be a desperate, attention-seeking whore?"

Rory breaks eye contact, and I figure that he's either feeling guilty about what he accused me of, shocked that I'm choosing to confront him at work, or wants me to think all of the above so that I'll forget about it and move on.

*It is not going to happen.*

"I was out of order," he admits uncomfortably.

"You were a total jerk!"

He buries his face in his hands and glances at the ground. "Can you blame me for assuming the worst? Seeing you and Grayson together was a bit of a shock. You'd specifically told me you couldn't stand the guy. It made me feel like I was part of a secret. That's why I reacted the way I did."

*I'm not in a forgiving mood.*

"Has it ever occurred to you that maybe I've changed since high school? I might be damaged goods, but I no longer want to be branded as easy or desperate. You brought back all the painful memories of my past and threw them in my face, especially when you accused me of sleeping with the boss's son. That was a new low, even for you."

The sympathy reflected in Rory's eyes makes me feel vulnerable and transparent. I'm not trying to earn his sympathy, so the fact that he's showing me some is not doing him any favours.

"Anyway, I've got work to do. Let's keep this short and sweet, shall we?" I manage to say, abruptly storming away from him and blinking back fresh tears.

I get home late, in desperate need of a cold shower. I fully expect to find my mother sitting on the couch, reliving episodes of *Tipping Point*, but I'm met with stony silence, and it seems to follow me like a shadow.

My eyes fall upon a broken bottle, its fragments scattered across the carpet in the living room.

Fear washes over me.

"Mum!" I shout, my voice reverberating through the silence.

"Mum! Where are you?" I try again, louder this time.

She doesn't respond.

It's too quiet.

I sprint upstairs, my feet carrying me straight to her bedroom door, which hangs ajar. I push it open, and a chill surges through my body when I notice my mother lying on her bed, sobbing uncontrollably into her hands.

My entire world is crumbling.

Curling beside her on the bed, I listen to my mother break down repeatedly—the monster claiming its hold.

My mother sleeps soundly throughout the night, having cried herself out. I've made at least three cups of tea when morning comes around, and I fully immerse myself in deep cleaning the house. I scrub the windows, wash the dishes, vacuum the floors and take the bins out. Finally, when there's nothing left to do, I collapse onto the couch and rest my eyes.

It's scary how my mother seems fine one minute; the next, she drinks herself to death or cries for days on end. I'll never fully understand her, but I know what it's like to wear a mask and hide behind a smile because I always do it.

I remember that my mother was supposed to be at work this morning but is still in bed, recovering from last night's emotional escapade. I'd better ring them to explain. I call her work number, and on the third ring, a woman's voice echoes down the line.

"Hello, this is Keira from Wendy's Bakery. How can I help?"

"Hi, my name is Skye Clemons—Julia's daughter."

There's a short pause.

"Oh, hi," she finally says.

"Sorry to disturb you, but my mother isn't feeling very well today. She won't be coming into work."

"Um..." Keira hesitates. "Your mother doesn't work here anymore, Skye. She quit three months ago."

I clutch the phone tighter, tears pooling in my eyes.

"*What?* I don't understand."

"I'm sorry... I thought Julia would have told you."

I can't believe I didn't realise any of this sooner. It makes sense why she hasn't been able to pay the rent. She's been out of a job this whole time.

"Can I ask what happened? Why did she quit?"

"She wasn't showing up to work—it's like she lost her passion for baking. She used to be one of our best. I don't know what happened," Keira reveals.

*Me neither.*

By the evening, my mother looks miles better and even has a spring in her step. She's dressed, wearing a fresh face of makeup and looks ready to conquer the world, which I know isn't true. She's disguising her emotions once again. She's not getting better. She's self-destructing.

"Can I talk to you?"

She glances around nervously, avoiding eye contact. "Can it wait?"

It's painfully obvious she hasn't been going to work. I haven't seen my mother in her uniform for a long time. The truth hid under my nose, but I wasn't looking close enough to see it.

"You quit your job, didn't you?"

I don't care if she answers me or not. I only want her to acknowledge the truth.

"How—how do you know about that?"

"I rang the bakery, and they told me you quit months ago. Please stop pretending to be okay when we both know you're not."

My words linger for a while, creating an invisible curtain between us, and my mother lets out a shuddery breath, opening and closing her mouth like she doesn't know where to start. She's broken beyond repair. Bit by bit, piece by piece, my mother's life is falling apart, and mine is slowly beginning to catch up.

Where will we be five years from now?

What does the future look like for us?

At the moment, I can't see a future.

I look at her, searching for a glimpse of my mother, but the monster has taken over. I can't see past its walls.

"It's just a job. I can always get another one," she says dismissively.

"I thought you loved working at the bakery."

Another moment passes.

Her face shrivels up like she's about to cry.

"I did, but..." She trails off, burying her face in her hands. "Things change. I've changed. I wasn't enjoying it there anymore."

My mother's greatest passion is baking. She's always had a natural knack for it. Hearing her talk this way is worrying. The things that used to bring her the most joy no longer exist in her world.

"I'm really worried about you. Let's reach out for help," I suggest.

"I don't need help. I'm fine."

"Stop saying that you're fine! You're not fine!" I

shout, tears falling down my face. “I know you better than anyone. You’re depressed, you’ve been depressed for a long time now, but you don’t have to deal with this alone if you just—”

“Stop! Just stop! Don't tell me what I need, Skye. You have no idea!” she screams, and I don't know if she's shouting at me or the monster, but it's alarming.

“Tell me what's happening inside your head then, so I can *try* to understand. Just talk to me!”

Mum gives me a long look. There's so much emotion behind it. I already know that we're not going to get anywhere tonight. This conversation is going downhill fast.

“You're making it worse. You make everything so much worse!”

“*Please...*” My voice cracks, barely audible.

“I don’t want to be here anymore.”

“Okay, well, that’s fine. We’ll find another place to live. We don’t have to stay here.”

She sighs, clutching her head. “That’s not what I meant, Skye. I don’t want to be *here.* I’m not living. I’m just existing.”

I freeze for a second, the weight of her words slicing through me like an unshifting knife.

*She doesn’t want to be here.*

*She’s not living.*

*She’s existing.*

I’m not enough because she is telling me that she doesn’t want to be here... with me.

How on earth am I supposed to process that?

Without another word, my mother rushes out of the

house, slamming the front door behind her, and I'm left alone, drowning in a suffocating silence that lingers long after she's gone.

In my mother's defence, she has been seriously hurt and hasn't released this hurt in the best way. That feeling of adrenaline never lasts. It doesn't carry her into the next day or lift her burdens. Instead, it drags her down until she faces a million other issues she can't resolve.

I can't force my mother to go and get help, and I can't force the monster to go away, but am I just supposed to stand by and watch the depression destroy more parts of her, or do I try to take matters into my own hands?

I cling to my imagination because that has always been my primary source of comfort. It's easier to imagine that I'm someone else, not this troubled teenage girl who yearns for a normal life. For once, I wonder what it might be like to live in Grayson Swain's shoes, but then I tell myself off for wishing I had what he has because money, glitz, glamour and everything that comes with it is overrated.

*'You're making it worse. You make everything so much worse.'* My mother's words swim around in my head, and that familiar urge to do something reckless consumes my every thought.

I glance at my savings pot, which sits on the mantelpiece above the fireplace—tempting me. The money I've earned from working at Trinity is tucked away inside it, and I know I shouldn't risk spending anything, especially not when we're on a strict deadline to pay the rent back, but before I can stop myself, I'm already reaching in for two twenty-pound notes.

With the money safely in my hands, I rush upstairs and tear through my wardrobe, selecting one of my shortest dresses that leaves little to the imagination.

We can't run away from our past, but we can certainly run towards it, even if it's ultimately the wrong decision.

# Chapter Fifteen

I SOAK UP THE FAMILIAR ATMOSPHERE OF THE NIGHTCLUB.

Hot lights shine down from above, creating shapes and casting streaks of light across the dancing faces and bodies below. There is a stage for the DJ, and a few bar staff are walking around with trays of drinks, encouraging people to take shots with their friends.

The adrenaline hits me.

I have forgotten how much I craved it.

My heart is racing. The music is too loud.

Within these walls are no boundaries, no lingering projects, and no mother to fret over. Just for tonight, I can be whoever I want to be. I can be friends with my worst enemy.

Anything is possible.

I jump higher and higher into the air, feeling invincible, like I'm floating on a cloud. I never want to come down, but when something unfolds in the pit of my stomach and bile rises to the back of my throat, I push through the crowds and rush to the nearest toilets. I barricade myself inside the cramped cubicle, shutting the door behind me, my head hovering over the toilet seat. Waves of nausea surge through my body, forcing me to throw up not just once but three times.

"Are you done in there? My friend needs to use the toilet!" A voice shouts from behind the door.

With a resigned sigh, I gather my strength, flush the chain and swing the door open. Two girls stand there, and they giggle as I exit the cubicle.

"Ugh, it smells of vomit in here!" One of them remarks when they finally shut the door behind them.

"That doesn't surprise me. Did you see the state of the girl who just came out of here?"

"Hah! True. What was she even wearing?"

"She looked desperate if you ask me."

"Slut."

My stomach somersaults.

That word alone is enough to send me back to my high school years, and a flashback crosses my mind without warning.

*Being called a slut was not the nicest feeling in the world, but I would never let them see me cry.*

*I hid in the girl's bathroom and spent the remainder of the afternoon locked inside a toilet stall, so I didn't have to face further humiliation.*

*Everybody knew I slept with Jarrett Baker–one of the most popular boys at school. I thought I meant something to him, but he had clarified that I was just someone he could use for the night and throw away when it was all over. Today, he had distanced himself from me as if I didn't exist.*

*My body stiffened when I heard the bathroom door creak open and footsteps approaching fast.*

*"Can you believe it?"*

*I recognised that voice all too well—it belonged to Vicky Monroe.*

*Vicky was born on the more affluent side of Barnett and happened to hate my guts for reasons I still didn't understand. I had earned my fair share of enemies in high school, and she was undoubtedly one of them.*

*"Jarrett said that she was all over him. It's embarrassing."*

*My heart started thudding.*

*"She's so pathetic," another girl said with a snort.*

*I assumed it was Vicky's best friend, Ava. They were always hanging around each other, gossiping about everyone and everything.*

*"Why would Jarrett want to sleep with someone like her anyway? She's not even pretty and has slept with half the boys at school. Talk about desperate," Vicky said, her words piercing my heart.*

*"Skye Clemons is such an attention seeker. I don't feel sorry for her at all. She deserves what's coming to her," Ava added venomously.*

*"Have you got a lipstick I can borrow?"*

*"Sure."*

*"I think we should leave Skye a little message to let her know exactly what we think of her," Vicky added with a cruel laugh.*

*From within the stall, I listened helplessly to the sound of the lipstick squeaking against the mirror's surface. I waited until their voices faded into the distance, and then I emerged, my eyes heavy and brimming with tears. Catching sight of my reflection in the mirror, my expression froze, transfixed by the bold letters scrawled across the glass.*

***SKYE CLEMONS IS AN ATTENTION-SEEKING WHORE!***

*A tear ran down my face, and I quickly swiped it away.*

*I didn't know why I slept with Jarrett, knowing what kind of person he was—a player, a manipulator. I had heard many stories about him, yet I still allowed him to use me and treat me like utter garbage. He didn't care about me at all, especially considering he was the one who started the rumour. Even though the story was true, he didn't have to say anything. He could have kept the information to himself if he cared about me, but I had been wrong.*

*I wished things weren't so difficult at home, but my mother's health was deteriorating. She was hardly ever around, and my house always felt foreign and unsafe. I hated being in that house, especially when my mother brought home a different man nearly every night.*

*I constantly searched for distractions to avoid being anywhere near that house, and I wanted to forget my reality so severely that I didn't care if Jarrett or other boys used me.*

*The truth is, I was using them back.*

*I was familiar with people staring, judging and criticising. I experienced it daily, and I didn't exactly help myself by choosing to sleep around.*

*It was my fault, so I was getting what I deserved.*

. . .

The flashback is over, but it takes me a little while to realise I'm still in the nightclub bathroom. I glimpse at my former self in the mirror, and a tear rolls down my face.

*What are you doing here, Skye? Go home.*

If it were as simple as listening to my conscience for once, I would be on my way home right now, but I don't see any point. I don't want to go home because there's no home to return to.

"Do you have a mint?" I ask the girl standing next to me, my throat sore from all the vomiting and hours of crying.

The girl nods, handing me an entire packet of chewing gum. I tell her I only need one, but she insists I keep them anyway. I know my breath smells terrible from the vomit, but what is she trying to imply? Do I stink that much?

The girl dips her head and leaves before I can ask that question, and I understand why I might be considered a freak show right now. Mascara lines are trailing down my face. My pupils are dilated. I look manic—hideous.

I throw chewing gum into my mouth and thoroughly rinse my face before entering the madness again. I join the crowd of dancers, and tears blind me for a second, but nobody here cares. I'm falling deeper and deeper into a familiar kind of sadness where nothing seems to make much sense anymore. I should stop before this gets out of hand, but I can't. I'm getting caught up in the past, or it's catching up to me.

*It's time for another drink.*

I shuffle towards the bar and flag the barman down,

passing him a twenty-pound note over the sticky countertop.

"Vodka and coke, please!" I shout over the music, swaying from side to side.

"Don't you think you've had enough?"

I stare at the bartender, wide-eyed.

Those words didn't come out of his mouth. They came from the one person I wasn't expecting to see tonight.

Rory is dressed in his famous black attire, green eyes focused and sober. His entire presence is threatening to ruin my night. The bartender reaches for a glass, but Rory slams a hand down on the counter, startling him out of his task.

"Don't serve her anything," he warns.

*Now I'm annoyed.*

"What the hell do you think you're doing?" I snap, losing my patience with him.

Rory's head turns to me sharply. He's downright furious, but I can still see the concern in his eyes. I'm shocked to find it there. I didn't realise he cared. Maybe he's just embarrassed *for* me. That would make a lot more sense.

"I should be asking you the same question, Clemons."

I fix him with an incredulous look.

"Bloody hell, calm down. I'm having fun! Isn't this what kids our age are supposed to be doing?"

"What happened to that heartfelt speech you gave me the other day about reinventing yourself?" I glance away from him, my own words returning to haunt me.

"Come on. This is the last place you want to be."

I immediately feel awkward and foolish that his opinion of me is beginning to ring true, but if he knew my situation and saw what I have to deal with behind closed doors, he might understand that this is my only solution. I hate to think that his opinion of me was correct, but I wouldn't be surprised if he still believes I am the worst person on the planet who constantly makes bad choices.

"Here's an idea. How about you stay on your side of the dancefloor, and I'll stay on mine? Stop pretending for one second that you care about me because we both know you don't give a crap," I slur, stumbling slightly.

He neither confirms nor denies that theory.

"Let me take you home, at least. You can barely stand upright."

It's a pity I'm too drunk to think or speak rationally with him. We're not on the same wavelength.

"That's such an exaggeration!" I cry, even though he is right. My balance is wavering, but he will be very disappointed if he thinks I will walk out of here willingly. He'll have to drag me away by force if he wants that to happen.

Seeing an opportunity, I let the crowds swallow me up. Elsewhere, I notice Rory is busy searching for me amongst them, but I've become entangled between a mountain of bodies as I retreat to a quiet corner of the club and lose him for good.

Why did Rory Keaton have to ruin my night?

Doesn't he have anything better to do?

I'd assume it was fate if Rory weren't pure bad luck for me.

I'm only standing alone for five seconds before an attractive boy walks up to me. His body heat emanates a warmth I wouldn't mind getting to know better. It helps that I'm a bit wasted. I am much easier to get along with when I'm drunk. Sober Skye is not approachable.

I wait for him to start a conversation, but he moves in at lightning speed, lips crashing down on mine, hands everywhere. My back hits a brick wall, and I'm trapped under his body weight.

Another memory enters my mind.

*Jarrett had shared the nude pictures I sent him with the whole school.*

*"Slut!" Someone screamed into my ear as we passed each other in the busy corridor.*

*"Nice pictures, Skye. Fancy giving me a full preview sometime?" another boy asked, causing my heart to beat wildly in my ribcage.*

*I noticed Vicky Monroe and Ava standing against a row of lockers, their laughter penetrating my eardrums.*

*"Pathetic," I heard Vicky mutter under her breath.*

*Faces were suddenly blurring into one.*

*Everything felt like it was spinning.*

*I could hear people laughing and talking about me. Their voices followed me wherever I went. I couldn't escape it.*

*I spotted Jarrett Baker, and my anger stooped to a whole new level. He was leaning against a wall outside one of the classrooms, holding his phone and showing my photos to a group of boys. They were laughing hysterically and making inappropriate gestures.*

*I stormed towards them, hands shaking, heart beating frantically in my ears.*

*Jarrett glanced down at me with a smirk. "Oh, look who it is, guys. Skye Clemons is back for more. She can't get enough of me."*

*His friends broke into laughter, and my heart shattered.*

*"Take those photos down* ***now****," I demanded.*

*He tapped his chin like he was thinking it over. "Nah, I'm good."*

*"I'm not asking you again, Jarrett. Take them down or–"*

*He stepped towards me, and I ended up with my back against the wall. "What are you going to do about it? You're the one who sent me those photos. It's not my fault you're a dirty little slut," he countered, the harshness in his voice taking me aback.*

*I didn't have to send him those photos. I probably shouldn't have, but I did it anyway. I regretted my decision. I couldn't rewind the clock. Those photos had already been spread throughout the school, and I could do nothing about it.*

*"Fine. If you're not going to take the pictures down, I'll have to report you to the police," I warned, receiving a chorus of 'oohs' from the crowd of boys, but Jarrett's smile faded slightly as I shoved past him and weaved through the crowd of students huddled together in the hallway.*

*That day, I swore to myself and the universe that I would never catch feelings for someone again. I was tired of feeling used—more importantly, I was done with old habits.*

. . .

Tears pool in my eyes once the memory ends.

The harassment didn't stop there. Sure enough, the photos got taken down eventually, but the damage had already been done. I was slut-shamed throughout high school, constantly targeted by groups of boys and girls, often on social media. I stopped sleeping around after that and tried to be invisible, but people could be so cruel. They continued to mock and body shame me every chance they got. That's why I can't have history repeat itself. I won't be taken advantage of anymore.

*No way.*

I raise my hands defensively, pushing the boy on the dance floor away, but he closes in on me again, pinning me to the wall.

I shove him harder.

"Hey! Cut it out!"

*Why can't this guy take the hint?*

He reels back. "Come on. You can't wear a dress like that and not expect to get groped. You're asking for it."

I stare at him, dumbfounded. He doesn't even know me and assumes I will sleep with him. After years of trying to earn a better name, I'm still giving off that impression.

If you think about it tactically, this whole sleeping-around scenario resembles a chess game. The king needs to be conquered to win, and without his army of knights, bishops and queen, he doesn't have much protection and can't fend for himself. I had nobody to defend me when I was put into compromising positions. I felt hopeless – like the King at the end of a chess match. He either wins or loses. Either way, he's still pretty much alone when the game ends.

The boy is kissing my neck, sucking, tugging, his hands all over me, free to explore my body however he pleases. His touch isn't pleasurable. It's rough, void of emotion and dirty.

*I don't want to do this. Not here, not now, not ever.*

I burst free from his grasp, but I'm not quick enough to escape. He yanks on my hand, and I'm flung back into his chest.

"Woah, where do you think you're going, Skye? We're not done here."

My eyes widen. "How do you know my name?"

"Everybody knows who you are around here. Got a bit of a reputation, haven't you?"

My throat tightens, tears threatening to spill from my eyes.

*You should give him what he wants.*

*That's all you're suitable for.*

"Take your hands off her."

I'm instantly met with Rory's impenetrable gaze, shocked to find no emotion in his eyes. I want to tell him I can handle this without his help, but my brain cells are shutting down. My body is a million miles away. I'm tired, mentally and physically.

The boy releases his grip, but just barely. His hand stays rooted around my arm like he's continuing to stake his claim on me.

"And who are you supposed to be? Her boyfriend?" he taunts.

"It doesn't matter who I am. Just let her go," Rory snarls, clenching his fists.

"Why should I?" the boy jeers, a defiant smirk on his lips.

Rory doesn't provide him with an answer. In one swift motion, he raises his fist and punches the boy's face, but instead of cowering, the boy retaliates, landing a blow to Rory's jaw. Rory's eyes darken, and he delivers a punch, which sends the boy crashing to the floor.

He grabs my hand and leads us out of the club. The fresh air hits me immediately, and I don't know how I end up on the ground, but now that I'm down on my knees, I can't bring myself to stand. My legs aren't strong enough to carry me.

"How much have you had to drink, Clemons?" Rory mutters under his breath, throwing me over his shoulder like I weigh absolutely nothing.

I'm drifting.

*He smells good.*

I let sleep consume me.

# Chapter Sixteen

I WAKE UP AT PRECISELY TEN IN THE MORNING TO USE THE bathroom. My plans are put on hold when I push the covers back and notice plain black sheets caught like a vice between my fingertips.

*These aren't mine.*

I glance around, panicking when I don't recognise my surroundings. I'm in someone's bedroom. It's tiny and has black walls with barely any furniture. The last thing I remember was getting seriously drunk last night and kissing a boy, or I think he might have kissed me, and I didn't like it. I haven't got any recollection of what happened after that.

My head swerves to the other side of the bed.

Thankfully, it's empty.

*Phew.*

"Thank God," I mumble, falling flat against the pillows.

My phone is resting on the nightstand, and it's on charge. If this was a kidnapping, I very much doubt that someone would have gone through the trouble of trying to increase my battery life. I must be in safe hands.

I swing my legs over the bed and land on the floor gracefully, searching around for my quickest escape route. I hurriedly step towards the door, and my foot trips over something. I tumble to the ground, landing forcefully on the wooden floor.

"Ow!" I yell, just as I overhear a second voice cry, "Argh!"

I hold a hand over my mouth and slowly turn my head, glancing into the eyes of a somewhat dishevelled-looking Rory Keaton.

*What am I doing in his bedroom?*

"Why did you kick me?" he demands, glaring at me.

"I didn't kick you on purpose! I tripped over your unconscious body, which I wasn't expecting to find on the floor or anywhere near me!"

I hold my head, wincing at every little sound.

I've forgotten what it's like to be hungover.

"What am I even doing here?"

"You don't remember anything from last night?"

"Not really."

Rory brushes himself off and stands up, sticking out his hand. Reluctantly, I let him help me up from the floor and wait for an explanation.

"I brought you back to my place because I didn't know where you lived, and you were too drunk to explain. I slept on the floor, and you took the bed."

Images of last night startle me wide awake. I remember stupidly spending some of the rent money I'd been saving up, and nausea creeps its way up my throat.

*I'm such an idiot.*

*Why did I think that would be a good idea?*

I also remember Rory got into a fight and carried me here. That must've been a struggle. For such a small-built person, I am heavy.

"You got into a fight... because of me," I say, noticing a small bruise forming along his jaw.

I must be staring at it awhile because he says, "I've been in worse fights. That was nothing."

He's trying to reassure me that it's not as bad as it looks, but I wonder how many fights he's been in. I know he used to get into many brawls at school, and I just thought he was always asking for trouble back then. It seemed like he wanted to inflict pain on people for no reason.

I groan into my hands. "Ugh, my head is pounding."

"I'll go and get you some paracetamol." Rory moves to leave, throwing me a fleeting glance before closing the door behind him.

I sit on his bed for a few minutes and decide to look around while I can. He has one cabinet facing his bed, an Xbox and TV stand proudly on top of it, and an old, withered plant. It's been abandoned under Rory's supervision. The walls are bare, with no photos in sight, except for the picture settled on his windowsill.

I walk over to it and crouch down to take a closer look. The frame holds a photograph of a woman staring into the distance at something off-camera, a contagious smile brightening her face. She must be important if Rory's got a photo of her in his bedroom.

"What are you doing?" Rory's voice rings out, and my heart jumps.

*He's back.*

*I didn't even hear the door open.*

I scramble to my feet quickly and turn to face him. "Uh, I—I was just looking at that photograph on your windowsill," I say, gesturing towards it.

I notice his jaw clench, his eyes becoming distant.

*Awkward.*

My cheeks feel warm as I try to think of something to say. An apology would be a good start. I shouldn't be nosing through his things, but the words refuse to come.

Rory studies me for a long moment, turning back to stare at the photo, a wave of sadness crossing his face. He doesn't want to talk about this–about *her*. I have to respect that.

"I'm assuming you'll want to change out of those clothes before I take you home," he says flatly.

"Uh, yeah."

"My Nan said that you can borrow something of hers."

*His Nan?*

I'd rather risk walking around in my disaster dress than wear his grandmother's clothes. I don't fancy finding out what concoctions she's cooked up in her wardrobe. That is all.

"Ah, it's alright. I'd feel weird borrowing your nan's clothes. Nothing against your grandmother! I'm sure she's got excellent taste in fashion," I blurt out, pulling a face.

Rory's gaze doesn't lift. He studies me a little more

closely and then starts laughing. It's the first time I've heard him properly laugh in all the years I've known him.

"Yeah, I can see why that might be a bit odd, actually," he says, easing some of the tension that had been creeping into the room just a few seconds ago.

"You can borrow one of my T-shirts and a pair of tracksuit bottoms. Freshen up, take a shower and do whatever you need to do. Come downstairs when you're ready."

Being a guest at Rory's house has its perks and disadvantages, one being his grandmother's determination to feed me. I could hardly refuse when she handed me a bowl of porridge at the breakfast table, and she wouldn't let me leave until I ate something.

Her tight silver curls bounce with every exaggerated movement, and her eyes possess a captivating green shade similar to Rory's. She doesn't look old and certainly doesn't play the part. I bet she's one of those super cool grandmothers who live life to the full, partaking in skydives and riding on the back of speedy motorcycles.

I find it unusual that Rory doesn't live with his parents, but it's none of my business. His shirt and jogging bottoms are too big for me, but anything is better than that awful contraption I decided to wear last night. I want to burn it.

*What was I thinking?*

"I'm so sorry that I've barged in like this. I'll be out of your way in no time," I say, reminding myself that I'm in uncharted territory and must be on my best behaviour in front of Rory's grandmother.

"Don't be silly. A friend of Rory's is always welcome in my house."

*Friend? I wouldn't go that far.*

Socialising is not my forte. I'm not very good at it. I peer at Rory for assistance, immediately picking up on his cold and wary expression. He wants me out of here as soon as humanly possible. Anne extended the invitation without getting a thumbs-up from him first. I'm not even a guest. I'm an intruder.

I glance sorrowfully into my bowl of dried-up oats and spoon some more into my mouth.

"You're young. You deserve to enjoy yourself. Be careful, that's all. I'm happy that Rory doesn't drink anymore..." Anne's words trail off as if she's revealed something she shouldn't have.

Rory and Anne exchange a look that hints at a secret only they share. This huge elephant is in the room, and I'm the only person who knows nothing about it.

I wonder why Rory doesn't drink alcohol. In this day and age, it's rare to meet someone who doesn't. He must have his reasons.

"Are you in college at the moment, Skye?" Anne fires at me while I struggle to swallow another batch of dried-up porridge.

"Yeah. I'm hoping to go to university to study journalism next September."

"You want to be a writer?"

"That's the plan... if I don't get rejected by the universities I apply to first."

“Who could reject someone as lovely as you? I may have just met you, but I know a good person when I see one. Please go out and chase your dreams before they expire. If I could rewind the clock, I would've chased my own, but love and other things got in the way,” she says, looking at Rory, who is particularly quiet.

“You mean Grandpa Ernie got in the way?” Rory speaks up, confused.

“No. I met your grandpa a little later on in life. Before that, I had a fling with an aircraft pilot called Alberto. I was madly in love with him. I gave up everything for that man—my home, livelihood and career. It was all for nothing because he left me for a much younger woman,” she says with a sad smile.

*Ouch.*

Imagine loving someone that much, dropping everything to be with them, only to get cheated on. It's so sad that this is our kind of world. Anne is a real catch. She doesn't look a day over forty, has a beautiful personality and can make strangers feel at ease, myself being one of them. Why would anyone want to trade her for someone better when she is the complete package?

Alberto was an idiot. He didn't realise what he had.

I've decided that I like Anne. She seems like a no-nonsense woman, and I respect honest people. You always know where you stand with them. If they have a problem, they're not afraid to voice it.

“I'm sorry to hear that. I won’t let anyone stop me from following my dreams. From a very young age, I wanted to be a writer. I've learned that words are solid, unbreakable, emotional and beautiful–they can describe every season of life. There are no limits. We all start with a blank canvas, and just like an artist paints a picture, the writer tells the story," I tell her, reverting to picking at my oats again.

"Wow. You *are* a writer," Anne says, making me blush.

"Thank you. I've got a long way to go yet, though."

"But you know what you want. That's half of the battle. With that attitude, the world is yours for the taking."

I'm not used to this much flattery, but Anne is good at it. Rory is watching me with a hint of disbelief, and I want to demand his problem, but that would mean drawing Anne into the conversation, and I'm not sure I want her involved.

"So, Rory told me you work together at Trinity. How is that going? I'm dying to know the details," Anne moves on, staring at us with a suggestive glint in her eye.

*I'm worried about what that look might imply.*

I throw a glare in Rory's direction.

What else has he been feeding her about me?

"Um, well, Rory and I go way back. We've had our moments, but we've survived so far. He's good at his job, and it's safe to say that working with him has been a pleasant surprise overall."

He nods in agreement, a blush slowly flooding his cheeks with warmth.

"Do you have a boyfriend, Skye?" Anne asks me directly.

I let out a surprised laugh. "No. I don't—have a boyfriend, that is."

"You're a beautiful girl. I'm sure you've had plenty of interest."

This is the first time I've ever been called beautiful. It's a word that sounds so foreign to my ears. While I've never had a hard time receiving attention from the opposite sex, I've always had trouble maintaining it. I'm just another number to them. I'm not girlfriend material. Relationships are complicated, and I avoid them if I can.

"I'm a bit of a handful. No one has ever taken me seriously enough to pursue a relationship. I wouldn't even know how to be in one," I admit, lowering my eyes to the floor.

"Ah, you just haven't met the right person yet, but you will find him."

*What if I don't want to find him?*

*What if Anne is kidding herself?*

I don't believe in soulmates, 'the one,' or mushy crap. Romance novels and movies about a boy meeting a girl and falling in love at first sight are based on fiction. They're not real. Those stories have set the bar high for men and women across the globe, painting this idea that love is so glittery and fabulous and right around the corner, yet most people are still waiting for their charming prince to arrive. The harsh reality is he might never show up on his trusty noble steed.

I've decided not to rely on a man to make me happy. I'm not expecting someone to come along and sweep me off my feet. I won't let it add or subtract from my worth because my worth isn't based on what a boy thinks of me in the first place.

"Do you regret meeting Alberto?" I ask, worrying that

I might have overstepped the mark by asking that question. Being so outspoken is part of why I don't have friends. I hope I haven't offended Anne by bringing back any unresolved feelings.

"Yes and no. Yes, because I threw my ambitions away for a man who didn't love me and no, in the sense that it's made me who I am today. I learned a lot from that experience, and it prepared me for my next relationship. I don't regret it."

That is a mature answer.

Mistakes should not have the power to define us for the rest of our lives. We all have a chance to start again on a fresh, blank canvas.

I rarely click with someone immediately, but it's as if I've known Anne for a lifetime. We've talked each other's ears off, and I've gotten a bit carried away and have outstayed my welcome.

Anne pulls me into a heartfelt hug when we part ways at the doorway.

"Remember to visit again soon," she insists.

I feel a stab of guilt because I know I won't be returning.

"Thanks so much. It was lovely meeting you."

"Same goes, sweetie. You're welcome here anytime."

Stepping out onto the pavement, I freeze when I find Rory seated on his sleek motorbike, expecting me to join him on the back of it.

How many girls he has taken for a ride on this same machine?

*I won't be classed as another one of them.*

"I think I'll just walk home," I tell him, watching his eyes dart to mine, wide and alert.

He makes an impatient noise. "What's the point? I can drop you there. It's not a problem."

"I am perfectly capable of getting myself home," I say more determinedly.

"I don't doubt that for a second, but it'll be much easier if you just let me take you. What is the problem?"

"Look, I'm grateful for everything you've done for me within the last twenty-four hours, but I'll be fine now. There's a bus stop not too far from this area. I know it well."

Rory's face holds equal parts of frustration and surprise. I don't give him a chance to say anything else because I'm worried that if I stay here any longer, he'll convince me to change my mind.

Crossing the road, a speck of rain bounces off the tip of my nose, but I think nothing of it until another drop of rain taps against my forehead, followed by a chorus of raindrops. The bus shelter is five minutes away, and my shoes are already starting to rub against the heels of my feet, causing them to swell and blister in places.

The rain is getting heavier, and Rory's oversized T-shirt and jogging bottoms stick to every inch of me. In the distance, the faint hum of an engine catches my attention, propelling me forward. Thunder rumbles above, alerting everything in its path, and I keep wiping rain out of my eyes, even though it isn't helping.

I'm getting drenched.

"Skye!"

My body tenses.

Rory's motorbike skids to a stop by the edge of the pavement. Rainwater glistens on his skin as he holds out the spare helmet.

“Jump on,” he orders.

Stubbornly, I shake my head. “I'm not scared of a little bit of rain!”

On cue, the thunder roars once more, scaring the life out of me.

“Just get on the damn bike already!”

“No! I didn't ask you to come and save me from the storm!”

Rory jumps off his bike and charges toward me. His hand clamps onto my shoulder, and I’m lifted effortlessly from the ground. I kick and flail, desperate to break free, but his grip remains unyielding until he gently places me on his motorbike’s plush, black leather seat. With this hangover, it’s not worth fighting him anymore, so I reach for the spare helmet, clumsily securing it to my head, sulking.

Climbing on, Rory pulls back the throttle and the engine roars to life. He glances over his shoulder, chuckles at my grim expression and starts moving my wrists to his chest. Hesitating, I hold onto him as he speeds down the road. The breath catches in my throat, not just because of how cold the wind is, but because I’m incredibly aware of how close his body is to mine.

I shock myself by breathing in his scent. It reminds me of the farm, and not in a bad way—musky, earthy, masculine, with a minor aftertaste of cologne.

“Where do you live?” he asks from over his shoulder.

"My house is near the old industrial estate—the one by the abandoned car wash."

"I'm familiar with it," he says.

I lose sight of where we are and can only focus on the sound of my beating heart that is close to bursting out of my ribcage. I am tempted to rest my cheek against his back, but it wouldn't be appropriate, and he'd probably tell me to get off. My grip tightens around his waist as we round a sharp corner, and I slide towards the edge of the seat. It's good that we've got helmets on because I would hate for somebody to spot us together and get the wrong idea. We both have bad reputations, but mine has always been under more scrutiny.

Relaxing against him, I close my eyes and let the wind blow my hair into a frenzy. I can't believe I'm on the back of Rory Keaton's motorbike, but it's fair to say that this experience has taught me what real freedom tastes like.

When he stops outside my house ten minutes later and shuts off the engine, I'm disappointed that we've arrived at our destination so quickly. We step onto the pavement, and I remove my helmet, only to find Rory's gaze locked on mine. I stare back at him, a large knot forming in my throat.

"Well, thanks for the ride," I utter, walking towards my front door.

"Skye—" His voice forces me to stop where I am, and my body swivels back to face him.

"Yeah?"

"I've heard a lot of stories about you over the years. It

painted this idea of who you were but didn't necessarily make any of it true."

I glance down at the floor. "Okay... so what exactly are you trying to say?"

"I was wrong about you. I'm sorry for everything I said back at the farm. You were right. I was being a jerk. You didn't deserve that," Rory admits, leaving me momentarily stunned.

I will not be able to get those words out of my head. They'll be spinning on rotation for days.

"I don't understand. I thought you hated me."

"I've never hated you, Skye. Hate is a strong word. I didn't respect or like you very much at one point, but that was before I started spending time with you at work. My opinion is different now."

I never hated him, either. I just convinced myself that I did. Then again, I declared the whole world my enemy before they could get to know me. Keeping people at a distance has always been my safest option, but it has also felt like the loneliest.

I may have misjudged Rory the same way he has misjudged me. It's so quick and easy to assume that he's a troublemaker, no good, a womaniser, but there is a reason behind every action, and I'm beginning to wonder if Rory and I are not so different. I'm oddly touched that he took me under his wing last night. I'm not saying he was my knight in shining armour, but nobody has ever helped me like that.

Rory sucks in his cheeks, averting his gaze sharply.

"Right, that's all I wanted to say, so I'd better get going."

Taking a significant step back, I say, “Oh yeah, of course.”

Rory jumps back on his bike and adjusts his helmet. I watch as he revs the engine, my heart beating pretty loud in my ears.

“Hey, Rory!” I call out before he speeds away.

He looks into my eyes briefly.

“I'm sorry as well. You're not what I expected either.”

This moment has altered our relationship forever. Maybe, just *maybe*, we can draw a line under the bridge and start over. As the old saying goes, never say never.

Rory drives away, and just as the sound of the engine fades into the distance, the front door of my house bursts open.

“Where the heck have you been?” My mother demands, standing in the passageway, arms crossed.

I’m suddenly exhausted and have this strange urge to apologise, but I’m not even sure what for.

“I stayed over at a friend's house,” I explain, rubbing my eyes.

“You mean you stayed over at Rory Keaton's house? I saw him drop you off.”

*So she's been watching us from the window.*

“Rory isn't as bad as everyone thinks. He saw me at the club and felt sorry for me, so he let me crash at his place. It was a pretty decent thing for him to do.”

She blinks and takes a step back. “You hardly know the boy. Anything could have happened to you last night. Don't you realise that?”

I went to the nightclub because she made me feel like I made everything worse by simply existing. I expected her to react badly, but I've been in multiple vulnerable positions growing up. She doesn't even realise how many people have used me—how many boys took advantage of me without understanding my willingness to give my body away. Nobody is interested in digging deeper to see what's hidden behind the action someone makes. They look at a person's exterior and what they can see in front of them. What people saw back then was an easy target and someone they could sleep with—no strings attached. They failed to see a scared, lonely, naive teenage girl who wanted to belong somewhere. Anywhere.

"Where did *you* go last night?" I question, wanting some answers of my own.

"I met up with my friend. We went out for a drink."

"How can you afford to do that? Where are you getting the money from?" I question, confusion working through me.

"I've been selling some things on eBay," she responds convincingly enough, but her eyes avoid meeting mine.

"What kinds of things have you been selling?"

"Just some jewellery and a few bits and bobs—nothing important."

"I'm too tired for this conversation. I'm going to bed," I say, brushing past my mother and entering the house.

She whirls around and grabs my arm to stop me from going further.

"I'd like to think you would confide in me if you ever encountered a problem. I may not always be–" she pauses, eyes to the floor. "I know I haven't been the best role model, but I'm still your mother. The truth is, I don't want you to end up making the same mistakes that I did."

I had to grow up before I was ready to. I was responsible for preparing my lunch boxes at school because she was always too hungover. I had to buy a new school uniform while she was confined to her bed. I learnt how to cook food when I was eight because she was hardly ever around. Most nights, I had to stay up late to ensure she didn't choke on her vomit.

It's frustrating how I'm always there for her, no matter what, yet she's never there for me when I need her most. Maybe if things had been different back then, I would have told her what Jarrett Baker did to me, but I couldn't—not when she was barely holding herself together. Instead, I kept my head down and pretended everything was fine, except it wasn't, and now I'm paying the price for bottling up my emotions for so long.

"I'm old enough to make my own decisions, and have you ever stopped to think that maybe I'm nothing like you?" I snap, years of built-up frustration pouring out of me.

My breath catches when I see the hurt on my mother's face. Guilt consumes me straight away. There's a tugging in my chest as her eyes lower, and she lets go of my arm, retreating quietly into the house.

I officially feel like the worst person in the world.

# Chapter Seventeen

ENTERING THE LIBRARY, I NOTICE GRAYSON LEANING BACK IN HIS chair and using my seat as a footrest. I receive the most alarming looks from students sitting at computer desks because I look like a walking disaster who seriously needs to declutter her wardrobe twice.

Grayson laughs under his breath when he sees me.

"Bloody hell, did you bother to look in the mirror before you left the house this morning?"

I throw him a pinched smile. "Haha. Very funny."

"Thanks to the class viper, we've lost twenty minutes of study time."

"Wow. I didn't realise you were counting down the minutes until I arrived. How sad."

"Well, we are on a tight schedule, or did you forget?"

*That*, I can't disagree with. The deadline is approaching fast, and in a couple of weeks, we'll be standing in front of the class, presenting our work to them. Compared to everyone else, we're still miles behind.

"I have something for you," Grayson says, searching his bag and pulling out an old DVD.

***The Lord Of The Rings Trilogy.***

"Thanks for buying me this, but my birthday is still a few weeks away."

A snort escapes him. "I didn't buy these movies for you! Don't be absurd. I wouldn't go out of my way to get *you* anything."

"That's good to know because your money doesn't interest me."

His eyes narrow. "I just thought we could watch each other's favourite movies."

"There's no way I'm watching *Lord Of The Rings*. Isn't that on for like three hours?"

"Three hours and forty-eight minutes, to be exact."

*Oh, the horror.*

"If you want, you can waste three hours and forty-eight minutes of your life, but I won't be doing the same."

"Tough luck. If you want to get to know me and pass this project, you've got to watch it. You'll thank me once you realise how much of a masterpiece it is."

I let out an exasperated sigh. "Fine, but considering *Lord Of The Rings* is on for such a long time, it's only fair that I get to pick two movies to make up the difference."

Grayson curls in his bottom lip, and a smile overtakes his face.

"I'll agree to that, depending on what you decide."

"For the first movie, I'd like you to watch *Mean Girls*."

He physically shivers.

"That is every guy's worst nightmare," he moans.

"We'll be watching it from start to finish. No toilet breaks."

"And you must sit and watch *Lord Of The Rings* without falling asleep or daydreaming."

"I don't daydream."

He gives me a long, pointed look.

"Fine, I tend to daydream... on occasion. But that's beside the point."

"What's the other movie you had in mind then? I'm just dying to know," he says sarcastically.

"*Batman Returns.* Everything about it is just phenomenal. It's my favourite Batman film of all time."

He rolls his eyes. "You're so obsessed with Batman. I should have seen it coming."

"He's the best, that's why."

"I've never watched any of the Batman movies. I don't get the hype."

My mouth drops to the floor. "Are you being serious? Why haven't you watched them before?"

He shrugs. "I don't know. I guess they've just never interested me. I am a Batman virgin."

"Wow."

"I'm more of a Marvel fan, to be honest."

"Prepare to be amazed, my friend, because tonight you will lose your Batman virginity card."

Grayson grimaces. "You can come to my house after college today, and we can start watching the movies. I've got a cinema room."

*Oh no. No. No. No. Hell no.*

I am not going to Grayson's house when Mr Swain could be there. It's too risky.

"How about we watch the movies at my place instead? You'll see where I live—not that it's anything special."

He raises an eyebrow. "That could work."

"Great. I'll send you my address."

Disaster averted, or have I just created an even bigger disaster waiting to happen?

I get home and spend half an hour cleaning the house from top to bottom. I ensure no dirty dishes are piled up in the sink, every room smells fresh, and all the doors upstairs are tightly closed so Grayson can't snoop.

My mother left me a note saying she would be home late. We haven't spoken since our last conversation, and I know she's been avoiding me. Anyway, here we are – here I am, waiting for Grayson to arrive outside my house. I've lost my mind, but anything is better than wallowing in self-pity and troubling myself with thoughts of my mother and where she might be spending her time.

I answer the door in my black jeans and long blue shirt. Grayson is standing on the other side of the threshold, wearing a pair of smart trousers and a cashmere overcoat. He folds his arms neatly across his chest and dips his head.

"Aren't you going to invite me in? It's bloody freezing out here," he chatters.

"No, I might leave you there a bit longer just for my satisfaction."

I roll my eyes and open the door wide. He walks

through, hanging up his expensive-looking coat on one of our old pegs. It's not strong enough to carry all that cashmere, but it's not my problem.

"Would you like something to drink?" I ask him, desperate to leave the room while Grayson's in the middle of browsing. He's probably noticing every fault with the place already. I bet he feels relieved to be in such a wealthy position and doesn't have to live in such poor conditions.

"A cup of tea would be lovely, thanks," he says, checking out the fireplace, which hasn't worked in years.

*Splendid.*

I quietly slip into the kitchen, taking my time to prepare the tea as Grayson comes to terms with his new workspace in the other room. I can't hide here forever, so I grab the cups and march towards him. He spins around instinctively, and I offer him a cup. He rubs his ear, and I find myself tapping the rim of my cup, unable to keep still.

*What now?*

I wipe a lock of hair from my face and watch him take a large sip of his tea. I just remembered that our kettle has a habit of boiling the water at a million degrees, and it's always wise to let it cool down before attempting to drink anything. Grayson has already decided to swallow a mouthful, so it's too late to give him a heads-up. His cheeks turn a deep shade of red, and he spits the scalding tea all over me.

I let out a high-pitched shriek.

"My tongue! I've burnt my tongue!" he exclaims dramatically.

"You ruined my shirt!"

"Oops."

"You're not even sorry!"

"I didn't mean to do it!"

"Stay here. I'm going to change into a new top."

"Well, it's not like I have anywhere else to go. Can I have a glass of water? I wasn't lying when I said that I burnt my tongue. Show *some* compassion, at least," he mumbles, returning to his usual arrogant self.

I stop halfway up the stairs, expressing my annoyance with an eye roll. "There's a cup on the counter in the kitchen that you can use. Try to avoid running the tap for too long, though. We like to save our water supply for special guests."

Grayson mutters something undecipherable under his breath, his face nothing but a rigid scowl. I get to my room and remove the damp shirt, replacing it with a stripy jumper. I twirl my hair into a bun at the top of my head so it's out of my eyes and join Grayson in the living room again. He's setting his notes on the small coffee table and his *Lord Of The Rings* DVD collection.

I sit down, noticing his eyes travel over my jumper before returning to his notes on the table.

"This is what I've written down about you so far," he starts, clearing his throat loudly. "You don't like dogs, but you have a cat, Batman, who I still haven't met."

"You don't want to meet him," I'm quick to say.

"Why? Does he have a contagious disease or something?"

"No, but he's a bit of a misfit—doesn't like people. It'll be much safer to show you a photo of him instead."

I reach for my phone, flicking through a collection of photos until I find a decent one of Batman. The image is slightly blurred because he never tends to stay in one place for long, but it still captures his towering, shadowy presence and piercing green eyes in the darkness.

With anticipation, I scoot closer to Grayson, eager to show him the picture. He leans forward, his gaze fixated on the screen.

"Woah. He *is* a bit frightening, isn't he?"

"Still want to meet him face-to-face?"

Grayson shakes his head viciously. "No, thanks."

"I didn't think so."

He returns to his notes. "Anyway, as I was saying... I've also learned that you don't have any brothers or sisters and are most grateful for your mother."

I glance down at my lack of research.

"What I've learned about you is that you fear death, you're most grateful for the house you live in, you have a dog named Buckie, you enjoy horse riding, and your girlfriend's name is Sophie."

He blinks hard, and then his expression changes. It puts me on edge, and for a good reason, because what he says next makes me wish I had thought about what I would say before saying it.

"Hang on, how do you know I've got a dog? I've never mentioned Buckie, have I?"

"Uh, yeah, you have mentioned him! It was ages ago, though, so you've probably forgotten."

"My memory is amazing. I would remember telling you about Buckie."

Now, he looks suspicious.

I can imagine how the conversation would go if I could finally admit the truth, but I can't tell him yet. We need to stay focused on the project. We can't afford to fall out over this and waste more time arguing.

*Come on, brain. Think of something convincing. Think!*

"Uh, I overheard Sophie talking about Buckie in the cafeteria. She's very loud."

Grayson scratches his jaw, eyebrows drawn. "Hm."

"What?"

"It's just... Sophie hates Buckie."

"We're wasting valuable time here. Can we forget about this and get to work?"

"Sounds to me like you're trying to create a diversion."

"I'm not! I'm serious, Grayson. We need to focus."

"Fine. Ask me anything you want, and I'll answer it truthfully."

I rub my hands together like an evil mastermind. "If you could have anything in the world, what would it be?"

"If I could have anything, I would ask for a sibling. It's not the same when you're an only child. My parents would buy me whatever I wanted, which was great, but I remember feeling quite lonely. I may have had the best toys and clothes, but it was hard to distinguish who my real friends were. I wondered if people were using me for my money and status or if they genuinely liked me for me. I started believing that I was worthless without those things," he says, surprising me.

Grayson's eyes pull away from mine as I stare at him open-mouthed.

"You'd better start writing that down because I won't repeat myself."

"What you said about yourself is untrue. Just because you have money and status doesn't mean that those things have to define you. It's who you are as a person that counts," I comment once I've finished writing his confession on paper.

Grayson watches me closely, a warm smile emerging on his face.

"See, this is what I like about you, Skye. You're always so brutally honest with me."

*Eh...*

My guilty conscience returns and gives me a little wave, reminding me that I haven't been as honest as he thinks.

*I feel so bad.*

"Yeah, anyway, it's your turn to ask me a question," I say, glancing away from him.

"Do you have any regrets?"

There's no backing out of this one now. Honesty works both ways; I must be prepared to do the same if he's willing to open up to me.

"I regret some of my behaviour in high school. I used to sleep around a bit."

He inches forward. "Why did you do that?"

"I was acting out, I guess. I had a lot of stuff going on at home. Things only got worse after that."

"What do you mean? How did it get worse?"

"I slept with the wrong person, and he..."

I swallow the raw emotion, finding it hard to talk about this. No matter how long it's been, I will never fully recover from what Jarrett Baker did to me. I'll never get over the pure humiliation I felt when he shared those photos I sent him all over the internet. That's not something I can get over. I will have to live with it for the rest of my life.

"This boy shared some nude pictures of me online. That experience gave me a wake-up call, but the emotional scars haven't healed. I didn't have a single friend in high school. I was practically all alone for most of it. Everybody hated me, and to be honest, I hated myself," I explain, sighing heavily.

I remember Grayson is listening to me say all this, and my senses kick in.

"You must find me so repulsive."

His expression softens towards me, and it's not the kind of reaction I had expected to receive from him. "No. Far from it. I'm just sorry you had to experience that. It must've been awful."

My cheeks flame an even more obvious shade of red, and the urge to run away grows stronger by the second. I glance at the TV and pretend to act distracted. I'm not going to start crying in front of Grayson Swain. We've done enough talking for one night.

"Should we start this movie marathon so you can bugger off home?"

Grayson playfully wiggles his eyebrows at me. "You want to get rid of me that badly, huh? The audacity."

"We've outdone ourselves for the night. My brain hurts."

"My tongue hurts."

Our gazes meet, and we burst out laughing.

. . .

Watching *Mean Girls* for the hundredth time has made no difference to my personal life, but watching it with Grayson has made it feel like I'm experiencing the film for the first time. His reactions are priceless, especially during the scene where Cady attacks Regina George in the cafeteria, and they start acting like a pair of animals.

Grayson has continued voicing his opinions, which I've found both annoying and endearing all at the same time.

"Why doesn't anybody just stand up to her?"

"Ha! She hit him in the head with a boombox!"

"I can't believe Regina George got run over by a bus!"

At six-thirty, the end credits roll, and we sit in comfortable silence until Grayson fills it by saying, "Well, that wasn't as bad as I thought."

"It's a good movie if you look past the typical high school stereotypes. I knew you'd enjoy it because you are the male equivalent of Regina George."

He looks down at me, eyes dark and intense. "Well, if I'm Regina George, who does that make you? Cady Heron? I somehow doubt it. Aside from the hair colour, you pair have absolutely nothing in common. I think you're more of a Miss Norbury. Do you like to push people?"

A small chuckle rumbles from deep in my throat. "Somebody's been paying attention to the characters."

"I have a photographic memory, remember?"

Grayson reaches for the *Lord Of The Rings* disc and

pops it into the DVD player. I was hoping he would have forgotten all about it.

"If you need the toilet, I suggest going before the film starts. We're going to be here a while," he says, causing me to frown.

Maybe I'll become another *Lord of the Rings* fan club member.

Who knows?

* * *

I'm functioning on five hours of sleep.

I'm struggling to keep my eyes open because *Batman* and *Lord Of The Rings* were on all night, and after we watched the first movie, we had to watch the second, which escalated from there.

Grayson finally left at two o'clock in the morning, and we both suffered from major sleep deprivation. After giving him my number last night, I received a series of texts from him early this morning.

GRAYSON

Gah. Who said watching Lord Of The Rings was a good idea? Brain = fried 🧠 😩

SKYE

I feel your pain.

GRAYSON

I need some caffeine before I pass out from pure exhaustion.

SKYE

Same.

GRAYSON

The Hobbit is next. It's going to blow your mind.

SKYE

My mind is already blown.

GRAYSON

To be continued 😜

Exchanging texts with Grayson has never been a thing until now, and I don't mind it. Technically, we didn't study much, but I still learned more about him last night than all the other times combined. We managed to get along for once and didn't throw many insults at each other. It's a step in the right direction.

I pedal to work in a positive mood and take a shortcut to Lakeside. It's a lonelier route, but it'll be worth cutting some corners to get to Trinity on time. Turning onto a narrow stretch of road, I get the strangest feeling that someone is following me.

I glance over my shoulder and gasp when I see a black car moving slowly down the road. It's too far away to recognise who is behind the wheel, but this isn't the first time I've felt their presence.

Why are they driving so slowly? This is a forty-mile-per-hour road. There's no need to be moving like a snail.

*I should pick up the pace a bit.*

I can hear the car speed up from behind me, and

that's when I realise I am definitely being followed. Anxious knots start forming in my stomach. I'm getting so worked up that I'm not paying attention to the road ahead, but I somehow manage to stay on track. Noticing the Trinity sign, a massive sigh leaves my dry throat.

*I've made it.*

I sharply turn into the farm, my bike clattering against the metal railings as I abandon it in the car park. Seeking safety, I run into the barn and lean against the wall, trying to calm my racing heart.

I take Dante to the field for daily exercise and place my feet in his stirrup. He seems more animated today—eager to get moving. I push some loose curls away from my face, adjust my helmet, and hold Dante's reins tightly, gently rubbing his ears.

I encourage Dante to go faster, and he doesn't disappoint. Excited, I cling to him as he negotiates every turn, speeding around corners with such force my heart begins to leap into my throat. I'm half terrified and half thrilled. This will either end well, or I will end up on the ground again, injuring myself if I'm not careful.

We approach the picket fence at such a reckless speed I'm almost positive we're going to crash into it, but, recovering, Dante manages to swerve around any obstacles blocking his path, and we're back on track again.

I can tell he has raced a lot in his lifetime because he runs as if his entire existence depends on it—that he has no other choice. It saddens me to think that his previous owner placed too much pressure on him to succeed.

Could that explain why he struggles to compete?

Does it remind him of darker times?

Once we've finished our exercise for the day, I start walking Dante back to the stables. My face is numb and stretched from the wind, but I don't care if I look like a slob. I wouldn't be able to stop smiling if I tried.

Well, scratch that.

I may have spoken too soon because a familiar face puts the world on hold.

Standing outside Trinity Stables is our cranky landlord, Robert Knowles.

# Chapter Eighteen

SEEING THE LANDLORD AGAIN WAS ALWAYS INEVITABLE, BUT I never expected it to be so soon or that he would arrive at my workplace. Recognising him is like a punch to the gut, and I feel I'm about to walk straight into a trap. Any trace of a smile is completely wiped from my face. Fear overcomes me—paralysing my body from the top of my head to the tips of my toes.

He closes in on me, and I shuffle away.

"What are you doing here, Rob?"

"I came for my money," he declares.

"We've still got four weeks to pay you back."

I move closer to Dante, shielding myself from Rob's view. I look around the yard, hoping to see a familiar face, but I'm also afraid that someone will end up witnessing this exchange.

"I've changed my mind. I want the money now," he snarls, his tone growing more aggressive.

"Well, I don't have it."

He takes another step forward, stopping when he

finally seems to notice Dante beside me. His eyes travel from me and back to the horse again, a flash of excitement lighting up his face.

"That's a good-looking horse you've got there. I bet he's worth quite a bit. Could easily sell him for a good price."

Panic works its way to my chest.

His threats are too big to ignore. My professional relationship with Mr Swain could be jeopardised if he did something to harm Dante or the farm. That wouldn't just hurt me, but it would also harm a lot of other people. I can't drag anyone else into this mess. I'll do whatever it takes to make Rob disappear, even if that means agreeing to his terms.

I force myself to look at him, and with every ounce of strength I've got left, I manage to say, "I'll sort the money out. Just leave Dante and the farm out of this, okay?"

Rob smirks triumphantly, and I dart my eyes to the ground. "I want another two hundred by the end of next week—on top of what you already owe me. If you fail to meet the deadline, I'll pay you and your little friend a second visit."

I stand there, my head truly scrambled. I may as well accept that there is no possible solution to Rob's demanding requests other than to give him what he wants. The bad news is that I only have under a thousand pounds in my savings pot, which doesn't even come close to his request.

Now that he's added another two hundred to the original amount, we will struggle. I could ask Mr Swain for more hours, but that would mean sacrificing college life and all I've worked hard for these past few years. I would have to give up my dream, but I'm simply out of options.

A strangled cough comes from behind me.

Startled, I spin around, noticing Rory several feet away. Hot fury burns behind his eyes, nostrils flaring, his jaw tightly pulsing with anger.

"Who the hell do you think you are, blackmailing one of our staff members on private property? You have no right to be here," he confronts Rob.

Amusement dances in Rob's eyes. He's not the least bit threatened.

"Stay out of this. It's got nothing to do with you."

"Skye is part of the Trinity family. If she's in trouble, whatever bothers her becomes my problem."

Embarrassment floods my cheeks, and sharp tears sting my eyes. Emotion overrules me to the point where I feel completely exposed and naked. I never let people see this side of me. I keep the emotion bottled up until it eventually simmers, but I can't pretend to be okay when I'm carrying too much baggage.

"I'm sure the police would be interested to hear that you've been threatening and blackmailing a minor," Rory continues, more anger seeping into his voice.

I'm reminded of the few times I felt I was being followed to work. It makes me question if that was Rob all along.

"Don't forget to add stalking to the list. You've been following me around, haven't you?" I speak up, relieved to have found my voice again.

"You're not exactly difficult to find. Let this be a

warning. I'd better have my money back by next week. Otherwise, you can kiss that house goodbye," he roars, storming away.

I don't know whether to be relieved to know that my stalker wasn't looking to kidnap me or if I should feel seriously disturbed that my landlord was trying to make it seem like that was the case.

I'm sitting in the staff room, my mind half asleep. Rory has gone to get me some water, and I let myself cry some more. I would nap, but hitting the hay at work wouldn't be wise when my boss could surprise us all with an afternoon visit. Knowing him, that's precisely what he would do. Mr Swain is the most unpredictable human being on the planet.

"Here you go," Rory says, entering the staff room and passing me a bottle of water.

I open the lid and take a quick sip, satisfied I won't die from severe dehydration.

"Thank you."

"How are you feeling?" he asks, settling beside me on the recliner.

"Not great. I can't believe Rob showed up here."

"What's the deal with that guy anyway?"

Can I tell Rory the full story, or will he choose to share what I say to Mr Swain when my back is turned? I don't think he'd throw me under the bus. He did defend me against Rob and acted like an overprotective friend.

"Rob is my landlord. We are at risk of being evicted from our house. That's basically why I applied for the stablehand job. This was never going to be permanent. I just needed to earn enough cash to cover our backs."

"So, you were going to quit eventually? Is that what you're saying?" He sounds hurt by this, and I don't know why. Surely, he wouldn't miss seeing my sorry face around the stables. Weeks ago, he would have thrown a party in my absence.

"Yes," I admit.

"Are you still going to quit?"

I feel a new wave of tears, but I'm quick to blink them away this time. "No. Besides the fact that I enjoy it here, there's no way I can leave now. My mother has lost her job and hasn't been able to pay the rent, so I've got to find a way to support us both because she can't do that alone."

Rory looks at me for a while, with no judgement, no sympathy in his eyes, just complete understanding.

"So, what are we going to do about the Rob situation? He's not going to drop this."

I'm brought down to Earth again with one sharp jolt.

*Ah. Yes. Back to that.*

Rob will return next week, ready to cause more carnage and destruction.

"I honestly don't know," I say, feeling the weight of uncertainty pressing down on me.

"I think we should tell Mr Swain."

I shake my head roughly. "No way."

"Why don't you want him to know?"

"I just can't. Seriously."

Rory turns the ring around on his index finger, his lip caught between his teeth. "This isn't just about you anymore. Trinity is involved now, whether you like it or not. Let us help you. You don't have to deal with this on your own."

I know that Mr Swain will likely respond positively to my predicament because of the kind of person he is, but he's also Grayson's father, which complicates things.

"What if Grayson finds out?"

"You seem to care a great deal about what Grayson thinks." He's starting to sound a little jealous, but I know better. I must remind myself that Rory told me I wasn't his type a few weeks ago.

"This isn't just about Grayson anymore. This is about having to sacrifice my last shred of dignity."

"I don't know how I would react if I were in your shoes, but I would try to seek help, especially if I knew it was available. If you don't want to tell Mr Swain about this, that's up to you. I think you should hear what he says and then make up your mind. You'd be stupid not to."

Trinity is involved regardless of how I feel; I can do nothing to change that. Maybe it's time for me to accept defeat.

"Fine. Let's tell him today. Together."

Nerves eat me up all afternoon while I wait for Mr Swain to arrive at Trinity Farm. His blue suit makes him stand out against the stark contrast of Rory's dark tracksuit. One looks like they're about to jump into an important meeting, and the other looks like he's attending a funeral.

I stand tall, hold my head high, and brace myself for the most agonising conversation as we all sit in the staff room. I cross my legs, then uncross them, failing to get comfortable. Mr Swain leans forward, hands clasped together. The sun is reflecting off his Rolex watch, adding to its worth. His deep blue eyes are set on me, full of genuine concern. He isn't wearing his usual smile, which adds to my anxiety.

"Skye, I want you to know that whatever you tell me will never leave this room. This is a safe space, and you can trust me."

*Trust him?*

*That's a big ask.*

*I don't trust anyone.*

Swallowing my pride, I start somewhere at the beginning, leaving out any intricate details if I can. Mr Swain doesn't interrupt me once. He gives me all the time in the world to explain, and once it's over and I can finally breathe again, I wait for him to say something.

"Thanks for confiding in me. I will not allow that man to step foot on these grounds ever again or to come anywhere near you in the future. The police need to be informed, of course, and we have security cameras installed everywhere on the farm. We can use that footage as evidence," he says.

I take a long, shaky breath, relieved that he's taken this so well. My eyes flash to Rory's from across the room. Even he looks more relaxed now that this has all been aired.

"There's something else you should know. Rob seemed to take an interest in Dante. I don't know if he was trying to think of ways to threaten me, but he did mention that it would be unfortunate if anything bad happened to him," I say, palms sweating.

"Hm. I'll keep a close eye on that, don't worry."

My heart rate has slowed down considerably since this morning.

*Being honest has its perks.*

"I would like to help you out with the rent situation as well if you'll let me," Mr Swain says.

*I can't believe Rory told him about that.*

"Thanks, but I could never ask you to..."

"You don't have to ask. I'm offering," he interrupts.

Mr Swain might be persistent, but I'm as stubborn as a mule.

"I appreciate it. Honestly, I do. It just wouldn't feel right."

"Look, I'll make you a deal."

*Deals never end well.*

"How about I loan you the money, and then you can pay me back out of your monthly earnings? You'd need to keep some money aside to pay for the rent in future, but nothing will change. You'll still be working, earning and returning what you owe me in due course."

"But, I—I..."

"I won't watch one of my employees struggle like this. I'm willing to help if it means you are in a better place financially."

I close my eyes, pure relief filtering through me.

"This is crazy. Why would you do that for *me*? I mean, I'm nothing special. You could easily employ somebody else who doesn't have all my issues and is miles better at the job. I'm sure it would save you a lot of trouble."

Silence envelopes us like a cold hug.

"A couple of weeks ago, I asked you an important question. What makes you different from the last person I just interviewed? Do you remember that?"

He gives me a moment to gather my thoughts.

"Yeah. I remember."

"Well, I haven't forgotten your answer because it was the main reason I hired you. What I liked about your interview was that you didn't try to sell me something that wasn't real or suck up to me as so many others did. You were honest about your weaknesses, but at the same time, you were ready to tackle them if you happened to get the job."

He lets out a breath.

"I could hire somebody else at the click of a finger, but that person wouldn't be you. So, if you're expecting me to fire you or find a replacement, it won't happen. You're stuck with us, I'm afraid."

I've just realised the biggest difference between Grayson and his father. Mr Swain has never given me the impression that he loves money or that just because he's filthy rich and could buy my house and the entire neighbourhood combined, it doesn't mean he thinks he is automatically better than us. He's just a good guy who happens to be incredibly wealthy and is humble about it. There's not much I can fault him on.

I don't realise I'm crying until Mr Swain hands me a tissue. I dab the corners of my eyes with it repeatedly.

"I honestly don't know what to say, Mr Swain. Are you sure this is okay?"

"Of course. I will deal with Rob directly. You won't have to worry about him anymore."

"Okay. Well, thank you. Thank you so much."

The front door creaks open, and I step inside my house after a long day at work, collapsing onto our worn-out couch and kicking off my muddy trainers. Mr Swain's kindness has overwhelmed me, and despite being hesitant to accept his help at first, his generosity has just saved us from facing the threat of eviction.

I am forever indebted to him.

Leaping upstairs, I find my mother lying on her bed, engrossed in a movie. She notices me standing in the doorway and pauses the film.

"Hey. How was work today?" she asks, sounding more exhausted than I feel.

"Eventful. Robert Knowles showed up at the farm."

Surprise registers on her face, quickly transforming into a frown.

"What did he want?"

"He was asking for more money. My boss got involved and said he would help us with the rent!" I'm quick to explain.

Her puzzled expression deepens. "Why would he do that?"

"I have no idea, but it's one less thing to worry about, so I'm not complaining."

"Skye, we don't need charity from your boss."

"It's not charity. He genuinely wants to help us out. My boss is just a nice person. He cares about his employees and doesn't want them to suffer."

"I don't know. This sounds a bit suspicious to me."

I understand she has reservations, but Mr Swain has offered us a lifeline we can't refuse.

"I've been trying to save enough money to pay Rob back myself, but now that he's demanding more money, he's made that task impossible. This is the only way forward. Everything will be fine," I reassure her, hoping to put my mother's mind at ease.

She looks into my eyes, her worry evident. "I guess we don't have much of a choice."

There'll be some more challenges ahead, but at least Robert Knowles will no longer be one of them.

# Chapter Nineteen

SEVERAL TEXTS FROM GRAYSON FLASH ON MY SCREEN WHEN I wake up. I grab my phone, which slips out of my hands, landing on the floor with a thud. I groan and crawl out of bed to see how much damage has been done. I flip my phone over to find a few scratch marks on the screen, but nothing major.

I read Grayson's message, squinting at the screen.

GRAYSON

> Fancy coming over to my place? Since you've shown me your house, I think it's only fair to show you mine.

*Okay, now I'm awake.*

He's probably only suggesting we study at his place because he's had enough of seeing my old floral wallpapers, a cramped bathroom that you can barely fit one leg inside, and my bare feet parading around.

GRAYSON

Hello? It's eleven in the morning. Are you seriously still sleeping? That's so lazy.

*This guy can't even be civil for five seconds.*

I stretch out my arms and legs and bring up the keypad–not that he deserves a reply.

SKYE

For your information, I was sleeping. Thanks for waking me up! (INSERT ANGRY FACE HERE).

GRAYSON

So, you're a late bloomer? That's going in the project.

SKYE

And you're a jerk in all categories of life, but let's not go there.

GRAYSON

Are you coming over then?

I can't risk bumping into Mr Swain after he offered to help me with my landlord. If Grayson ever found out about that, he would think I was after his money all along.

SKYE

It depends. Are your parents going to be there?

GRAYSON

Nope. We'll have the house to ourselves.

SKYE

Fine. I'll come then. 😡😴😫😳

GRAYSON

Emoji overload. Will you be riding that disastrous bike of yours?

I jab my fingers against the keypad as I send him a reply.

SKYE

1. It's not disastrous.

2. Yes, I will be riding my bike.

GRAYSON

Splendid. 💩

* * *

**12 Crescent Road, Lakeside.**

*We meet again.*

There may still be time to turn around.

"Hey, Skye!" Grayson interrupts my plans to escape as he trots down the footpath, dressed to impress. His blond hair is styled into a perfect quiff, and a strong cologne wafts through the air, choking me to death. Meanwhile, I'm modelling a worn-out tracksuit that resembles sleepwear and a pair of scuffed white trainers that have long lost their shine.

Grayson's mouth curls up when he checks out my outfit.

"Why are you looking at me like that?" I demand, raising an eyebrow.

"Uh, no reason," he replies, trying to brush off his reaction.

"Come on. You've never been one to keep your opinions to yourself. Don't start now."

"It's just... where did you get that tracksuit from?"

"I got it from the charity shop."

"You wear other people's clothes?" he asks, his voice rising an octave.

"Yes, not everyone has enough money to buy things brand new, Grayson."

"But... don't you think it's weird, wearing somebody else's stuff? You don't know where it's been."

My heart pounds, irritation bubbling up within me.

*He's unbelievable.*

"Sorry, I didn't dress up specifically for the house tour. I didn't get the memo. I'll take my wardrobe with me. Bye."

I spin on my heel and start walking away, but Grayson runs after me and shouts, "Skye! Wait. I'm sorry. I didn't mean to sound patronising. The tracksuit is pretty cool. Not many people could pull it off, but you can."

Why do compliments always sound like insults whenever he opens his mouth?

I turn on a glare and twirl around to face him again.

"Is that supposed to make me feel better?"

"I'm sorry, okay? I wasn't thinking. I never think before I speak."

*I'm guilty of doing the same thing, so I can't complain.*

"Am I forgiven?" he asks, flashing his big, puppy dog eyes.

"If you promise never to make that face at me again, then yes, you're forgiven."

"Deal! So, what do you think of the place? It's impressive, right?" He glances back at his house and jumps about with excitement, reminding me of a newborn puppy—cute but annoying at the same time.

I cross my arms and scowl. "It's alright, I guess."

I'm being modest. The house is impressive. Grayson has probably heard this plenty of times, so he doesn't need to hear it from me. He's fishing for compliments.

"Leave your bike outside and take your shoes off when you get in," he instructs, walking back inside the house.

I stare after him, bewildered. "Seriously?"

"Yup. It's my mother's number one house rule! She's a neat freak. Also, the floor is porcelain, so we don't want to scratch the tiles!" he shouts over his shoulder.

I swallow down a bubble of laughter, follow him up the steps and walk into the mouth of his home. Grayson observes my reactions closely, and I'm making it evident that I love the place. That's until their dog Buckie leaps down the stairs and charges at me.

*Not again.*

I shriek and try to scramble away as Buckie continues to jump on me full throttle. He's a Labrador breed, so his paws almost reach my neck when he jumps.

"Buckie is harmless," Grayson declares, patting his head like he's proud of him for ambushing me.

"I don't care what he is! Just get him off me!"

Grayson grabs Buckie by the collar to lead him outside, and I catch a glimpse of the outdoor pool through the double glass doors.

*What **don't** these people have?*

It makes sense why the Lakeside students constantly complained so much when they first came to Barnett. They are living life to the extreme over here. They don't need to leave their houses because they have everything they could ever want on their doorstep.

Grayson was waiting for me to take my muddy trainers off, so I quickly placed them on the shoe rack and let him give me a tour of the house. He showed me the conservatory, games room, kitchen, lounge area and every other room in the building.

Opening the door to the study, he lets me take the first step inside. I gasp at the large balcony and window overlooking the freshly trimmed lawn. I press my head against the glass, taking in the countryside views.

*This is my dream writing spot.*

A large white desk occupies a spot near the window. An Apple Mac computer sits on top of it, a couple of books and carefully placed potted plants. Every piece of furniture in the room, from the walls to the carpet to the couch, is painted a fresh cream—immaculate and closely monitored. Making a mess is probably strictly forbidden in this house.

I walk across the room, drawn to the papers scattered on Grayson's desk. To my surprise, they are poems—something I never knew he wrote, but Grayson is swiftly stuffing them back into a drawer before I can get a better look.

"They're not finished yet," he says.

"You are such a perfectionist."

"What's wrong with being a perfectionist?"

"It must have benefits, but setting goals to an impossible standard will only bring disappointment if you don't get the results you were hoping for. Sometimes, being a perfectionist can be a curse and a blessing in disguise."

"I don't like to fail. My family has always put extra pressure on me regarding grades and stuff. If I came home with a C, it would be the end of the world," Grayson says while I turn to observe the abstract paintings on the wall.

"Seriously? I would be over the moon if I came home with a C. What's so bad about getting a C? It's still a pass."

"It might be a pass, but that doesn't make it acceptable, at least not to my parents. I've always had to strive for more."

His family sounds like they expect way too much from him. That must be challenging. I assumed that Grayson was living his best life and that his family supported whatever he chose to do, but I guess not.

"I'll never forget when I failed my first test at school. I'd never failed anything before, and at the time, I was getting bullied by this older kid. I had cried so much about it, and seeing a big F on my paper was the tipping point. I switched schools in the end, which made a difference, but I still felt like I was constantly striving for perfection and achievements. That might've been why nobody liked me because I only seemed to be looking out for myself. That wasn't what was going on. I just needed to prove that I could succeed and be somebody."

Mr Swain has already told me parts of Grayson's story, but to hear him speak about this from his perspective is proving to be quite powerful writing material. The fact that he's willing to share a bit of his past with me is incredibly humbling. This is all coming from the boy I had no intention of getting to know until I discovered that deep down, he's just like me—misunderstood.

Grayson sits on the desk chair, interlocking his fingers behind his head. "Believe it or not, I always stress out about essays and assignments, probably as much as you do," he confesses.

I would never have imagined Grayson stressing over academic work. He always seems to effortlessly complete assignments ahead of everyone else, leaving us to believe it's just a breeze for him.

"One thing Ricky always tells me is that I need to find my voice as a writer. I don't think I've found it yet," I admit.

"A great writer is willing to share personal experiences and tell a relatable story. Why do **you** write in the first place?"

I stare out the window, pondering the question. "I write because it gives me a purpose, and it helps me to release my emotions in a healthy, positive way."

"There you go! You've found your muse. Reflect on your life—be yourself. Stop overthinking it."

Grayson has turned my writing dilemma into something positive, and hearing a different perspective is refreshing.

"This is my favourite spot in the entire house," he says after a few silent seconds.

I understand why. This would be my favourite spot, too. I can imagine sitting at the desk and gaining inspiration from the surroundings alone. The sun is shining directly into the room, giving it a warm, gentle glow, and there is nothing but the countryside, green grass, rolling hills, and luscious mountains overlooking the houses below. I love everything about it.

"So, now that we've established you live in a mansion that looks like it's rolled straight out of a Beverly Hills movie and that I live in a building which is a dumping ground, I think we can both agree that our living situations are off the scale different."

Grayson leans back swiftly in his chair, which I could never do because I would probably end up high-fiving the floor.

"Oh yeah. I'm starting to understand why Ricky paired us together. I wasn't very nice to you at first, was I?"

"You were an absolute pig."

His mouth curls into an expectant smile. "I didn't see you trying to make amends, little-Miss-speak-your-mind."

Narrowing my gaze, I shoot back, "You acted like a spoiled little rich boy, that's why. Somebody had to put you in your place."

Grayson, raising his hands in mock surrender, concedes, "I'll admit I was a bit of a brat."

"Finally! We can agree on something."

• • •

"It's official. I am obsessed with Belgian chocolate."

I pick my way through a box of Belgian truffles, and Grayson laughs from across the kitchen island. Studying is fun when you have a huge mansion to keep you occupied and the best chocolates your taste buds will ever meet.

"I can't believe you've never tasted Belgian chocolate before," Grayson says, shaking his head in disbelief.

"Belgian chocolate is not cheap. Five pounds for a box of chocolates is way out of my budget," I say, grabbing another Belgian seashell and popping it into my mouth, chewing slowly to savour the taste.

"How do you take your tea?" Grayson asks, watching as I twirl around on the bar stool. He's probably worried I'll end up breaking the piece of furniture, no doubt.

"Somewhere in the middle," I explain, earning a quizzical look from Grayson.

"Huh?"

"I don't like it too milky or too strong. It's got to be just right. Otherwise, I won't drink it."

"You're weird," he says, shaking his head.

I watch him make the tea slowly, steadily, like he's got to be extra careful not to spill anything. This kitchen is larger than my house. It's spotless and any homeowner's dream. Yet, something about it unsettles me at the same time. It triggers questions about Grayson's upbringing, leaving me curious about the experiences he may have missed out on.

Was he ever allowed to get his clothes dirty, play freely in the park with other children, or experience the joy of carefree fun?

Has he ever climbed a tree in his lifetime?

I was an adventurous child, always willing to take risks and make a mess. Our childhoods were undoubtedly different, and it's fuelling my intrigue.

Grayson places my cup of tea on the countertop, his mischievous grin returning. "Is that good enough for you, class viper?"

Humouring him, I pretend to scrutinise the tea closely. "Hm. It could have been a bit stronger, but you did okay, I guess."

"You're acting like I haven't made a single cup of tea in my lifetime."

"You could've had *me* fooled."

"What's that supposed to mean?" he demands, the playfulness in his voice now replaced with a sudden defensiveness.

"Oh, come on, Grayson. You have a butler! How many teenage kids can say that? It's crazy!"

"Just because we have a butler doesn't mean he's treated like a slave or does *everything* for us. Fernando is part of the family. I may have an incredible house to live in, and yes, I have a butler, but sometimes this house can feel like the loneliest place in the world." His eyes pull away from mine, and he exhales.

A heavy silence descends upon us, threatening to turn awkward.

"Well, that's killed the mood," I'm quick to say.

"Yeah, it has, and unless you apologise, I don't think we can move on from this. I might have to deprive you of those Belgian chocolate seashells you've grown so attached to."

"No! Not the Belgium chocolates! I beg of you!" I exclaim dramatically, mimicking the voice of the gingerbread man from Shrek.

Grayson cracks a small smile, but he refuses to back down, and I feel bad that I judged him again. I need to stop doing that.

"I'm sorry."

He grins triumphantly. "You're forgiven, class viper."

I can't stop smiling as I drink my tea. "So... you're a secret poet, huh? What's up with that?"

Grayson glances down at the floor to hide the blush on his face. "It's nothing. I do it for fun."

"Will you let me read one of your poems?"

His jaw tightens, eyes widening in horror. "No! No way!"

"Why? I'm not going to make fun of you."

"It's too personal. I don't let anyone read my poems."

"That's too bad," I say, as the front door clicks shut and footsteps approach fast down the hallway.

*Oh crap. We have company.*

A woman with luscious brown hair appears in the kitchen archway, head darting to the person eating her prized truffles. I currently have one in my mouth, and it takes me a long time to swallow it because my throat has gone bone-achingly dry.

A man is standing next to the woman, juggling her shopping bags. It takes me a moment to realise it's Fernando, the butler. Even though I've finally learnt his name, I'd still rather call him Alfred. It suits him, so that's what he shall be called until further notice.

Alfred glances at me and does a double-take, recognising me from my interview with Mr Swain.

The woman is wearing an oversized fur coat and modelling trendy designer sunglasses. She's also rocking bright red lipstick, which makes her appear even more severe and tight-lipped. She glances me up and down, pulling a repulsed face at my choice of clothing. I regret not wearing a pair of smart trousers. I didn't know I had to dress up to be considered worthy as a guest.

"Mum... I wasn't expecting you back yet," Grayson says, looking slightly panicked.

Mrs Swain takes off her shades, exposing dark brown eyes underneath. They fix themselves on me, and I squirm. She's watching me like I need to be kept under close surveillance. It's a little uncomfortable.

"My afternoon meeting was cancelled. Who is this?" she demands, returning her attention to me.

I crawl into myself and don't utter a word.

Grayson glances at me.

"This is Skye. We're working on a college project together," he explains.

Mrs Swain shakes off her fur coat, revealing a bright green polo top underneath and a respectable long white skirt. I still can't believe that this is Grayson's mother. She looks way too young to be somebody's parent.

"Which side of town are you from, Skye?"

*The poor side.*

"I'm from Barnett."

I watch her expression turn sour, and it's the kind of reaction I expected from a Lakeside resident.

Mrs Swain turns to Grayson, casting him a disapproving look. "You should have told me that you were inviting Skye over. You know how I feel about strangers coming into our house."

*What did she think I was going to do, raid the place?*

*The fridge, maybe...*

Shame rushes to Grayson's cheeks. "Sorry. I forgot to mention anything. It was last minute."

"You'll have to get going soon, Skye. We're about to have dinner."

I wait for Grayson to say something, but when he keeps his eyes trained on the floor and chooses to stay out of it, I realise it's time for me to leave.

I hop off the stool and swing my bag over my shoulder.

"No worries. I was thinking of heading home now anyway. It's getting late."

"I can give you a lift," Grayson insists.

"It's okay. I can ride my bike."

Mrs Swain scoffs, rolling her eyes. "That explains who the dirty bicycle outside belongs to, then."

I grind my teeth together. "Yes. It's mine."

"Please let me take you home," Grayson says again, not taking no for an answer.

I should be thankful I don't have to pedal the forty-five-minute journey back to Barnett.

"I don't think your mother likes me," I say as we speed down the street in Grayson's fancy Bugatti.

He clutches onto the steering wheel, his knuckles turning white.

"She doesn't like many people, so don't take it personally. I was hoping to avoid the introductions altogether."

"Why? Are you embarrassed to be seen with me?"

Grayson sighs in exasperation. "No, Skye! Bloody hell."

"Well, did you see how she looked at me?"

"That is precisely why I didn't want you to meet her."

"I have never met anyone so stuck up and rude."

"Hey, that is my mother you're talking about."

Grayson's naturally defending his mother. I'm defending myself because nobody else will do that for me.

"Look, don't let her get to you, alright? She acts like that with everyone. Once you get to know her, she's not that bad."

"If I were rich, your mother's reaction would have been very different back there, and you know it."

"Yeah, you're probably right, but you're different from other girls I've brought home." He is saying all the wrong things. I'm different because I'm not as posh as Sophie or as privileged as Shelly blinking Matthews.

"Before I met you, I couldn't empathise with people or understand how hard life could be for them. It's made me realise how important it is not to judge someone so harshly at first glance. I know we didn't get on the best side of each other in the beginning, but despite our differences, I enjoy having you around. I always know where I stand with you."

Guilt eats me up, and my brain scrambles for something to say, but I have nothing.

*Come on, Skye. Just tell him the truth about working at the farm. Stop lying. It's time to come clean — confess everything.*

I'm not as straight-talking as he thinks. He doesn't know I haven't been honest with him, and it's only a matter of time before he finds out the truth.

"Grayson..."

"Yeah?"

The words get caught, and my web of lies refuses to reveal itself.

"Never mind," I utter weakly.

We stop at a red traffic light, and I notice Barnett Prison on the other side of the road, emerging from the fog. It's a sad-looking building. Extensive stone walls and barbed wires surround the area, reminding people that one wrong move could cost them the rest of their lives. It's where many kids from Barnett end up, caught in a cycle of crime and desperation.

My gaze flickers across the road, drawn to a boy walking out of the prison. His hands are shoved deep into the pockets of his hoodie, his head cast down. Each stride is fast-paced and determined.

The boy crosses the road, and I feel a pang of familiarity. At first, I thought my eyes were playing tricks on me, but it's him. The black clothing gives his identity away.

What the hell is Rory doing at Barnett prison?

# Chapter Twenty

It's easy to fall into my usual routine at work, but anxiety seems to follow me wherever I go. Letting my guard down means I won't be prepared for anything bad to happen, and lately, I've experienced too many unpleasant surprises.

Since I saw Rory leaving Barnett Prison, I've noticed that he's been acting strange. Whenever our paths cross, he tries to avoid me, and I don't understand his problem. I pass him on my way to the staff room, but he deliberately heads in an entirely different direction.

*Okay then... I guess I'll be spending my lunch hour alone.*

I'm still struggling to understand why he would be at Barnett Prison in the first place. I have no right to pry, but my curiosity is growing.

I eat my sandwiches and put my phone on charge. It's difficult not to think about Rory when nobody is around to distract me from my thoughts. Maybe he volunteers at the prison. Or perhaps he was visiting someone. A friend? Relative?

*Ugh. Not my problem. Stop obsessing over it.*

I throw the rest of my soggy sandwiches into the bin, and my phone lights up with a new message from Grayson.

GRAYSON

Fancy meeting tonight to work on the project + watch The Hobbit?

SKYE

Can't. I'm busy.

GRAYSON

Busy doing what?

SKYE

None of your blooming business, Swain. I do have a social life outside of college, FYI.

GRAYSON

Really? Does the class viper have friends to hang out with? 🐍

SKYE

Do you go out of your way to be highly annoying, or is that just something you were born to do?

GRAYSON

Ouch. Believe it or not, I am a very well-liked individual.

SKYE

Hah! And who told you that piece of information? Your Mother? Newsflash. She's obligated to like you, Swain.

GRAYSON

I'm surprised you have friends to hang out with if the conversations go a little like this one.

SKYE

Unlike other people, you tend to bring out the viper in me. I save my venomous words for you alone.

GRAYSON

Aw. That makes me special.

SKYE

Far from it.

GRAYSON

Is whatever you're busy with tonight more important than completing our project?

SKYE

I won't be home until half seven.

GRAYSON

Great. I'll see you then 😁

I've never hated the smiley face emoji more than I do at this moment.

"I heard Rory Keaton works here. Where can I find him?" A voice cuts through the silence, demanding attention.

Startled, I glance up and notice a boy standing there. He looks relatively familiar. It takes me a minute to realise he is the guy Rory was chasing down the corridor at college—the one that almost rugby-tackled me. You don't just chase people around for nothing. There's always a reason.

*What is he doing here?*

He's almost the same height as Rory, just a few inches shorter, and he's modelling a black jumper with matching tracksuit bottoms. He must be following the same trend that Rory is a fan of.

I stand up cautiously. "Uh, I'm not sure sorry. I haven't seen him."

"Fine. I'll find him myself," the boy says, leaving the room.

A few minutes pass, and I realise I can't just stand here and do nothing. If Rory gets into a fight at work, it'll jeopardise his future and potentially get him fired. I don't know why I'm so concerned, but maybe a tiny part of me has grown to like him just a smidge. I would hate to see him fall flat on his face over something that could have been avoided.

I leave the staff room.

Looking around, I pray for my heart to slow down. I'm nervous, mainly because that boy is here to cause trouble, and I allowed him to walk away. What if he's already found Rory, and they're having a throwdown? What if it's too late to step in now? Will I have to call security? Mr Swain?

I take hurried steps towards the barn, peep through the crack in the door, and notice Rory is carrying a fresh bucket of hay and leaning against Albatross's stall. Kyle is a few feet away from him and looks menacing.

I don't know whether I should get my phone out if this escalates and I need to call someone. I search through my pockets but can't find my phone anywhere. I must've left it in the staff room.

*So much for plan B.*

"I still don't get why you're here, Kyle," Rory says as I listen to their heated conversation.

"I'm here to finish what we started."

"There's nothing to finish. I'm pretty sure I kicked your ass the last time we ran into a problem, and I could easily do it all over again."

I'm annoyed he's choosing to rile Kyle up instead of trying to diffuse the situation. Does he want to get into a fight at work? That's precisely what's going to happen if he's not careful.

Kyle steps forward. "Well, you should put your money where your mouth is and give me a rematch right now."

Rory shakes his head and rakes a hand through his hair. "I'm a bit busy if you haven't already noticed. The fact that you've shown up here is an absolute joke."

"You might be able to put the past behind you, but I'll never forgive your father for what he did to my family! He deserves a life behind bars. He deserves to pay, and so do you. Sooner or later, everybody will see you for what you truly are–a danger to society, a lost cause, a waste of space, a ticking time bomb, just like your pathetic old man," Kyle spits, squaring up to him.

Rory moves fast. He drops the bucket of hay and pins Kyle up against the wall, breathing down his neck.

"You'd better shut your mouth!"

"Go on. Hit me. I *dare* you," Kyle challenges.

Rory raises his fist, and I expect him to throw a punch, but he surprises me by letting Kyle go.

"Go home, Kyle. I seriously don't have time for this—not today."

"You're such a coward."

"So, I'm a coward for wanting to do the right thing for once? When is this ever going to end for you? When one of us is dead?"

Words seem to fail Kyle. He turns to leave, but it's almost too good to be true because he quickly spins back around and says, "I'll be waiting by the train tracks from seven o'clock onwards. If you change your mind about the fight, meet me there."

Rory crosses his arms. "I won't change my mind."

"This is far from over yet. Deep down, you know I'm right."

I'm still staring through the gap in the door when Kyle barrels past and barges straight into me. He doesn't even apologise, but I'm not surprised since he didn't give me an apology the first time he almost ran me over. I can't expect one from him now.

Stumbling into the barn, I find Rory carrying on with his duties, acting as if nothing has happened, blissfully unaware that I've just witnessed his entire exchange with Kyle.

"Please don't tell me you're considering meeting Kyle later."

Rory stiffens, sending me a sidelong glance. "Eaves-dropping much?"

"I wasn't–" I scramble for an explanation, but I fall

short when I can't find one. “You're right. I was eavesdropping. I'm sorry.”

I watch Rory replace the old, soiled straw bedding and dump its contents into a wheelbarrow. He's fast on his feet, and I can't stop staring at his biceps as they work to lift and carry heavy piles of straw and manure from one side of the stall to the other.

“Do you need any help?” I offer, poking my head over the gate.

He wipes away some sweat building on his forehead and glances back at me, his eyes moving over my face slowly.

“Aren't you supposed to be on your lunch break?”

“Yeah, but I'm taking a break from my lunch break. I was looking for an excuse to leave my soggy sandwiches behind. This is my lucky day,” I joke, my laughter unreciprocated.

Whatever's on Rory's mind is creating a massive barrier between us, and I wish I had the confidence to ask him about it, but I don't want to push him further away. If life has taught me anything, it's that there is a time to speak and a time to stay silent.

“You still haven't answered my question, by the way,” I tell him, leaning on my tiptoes to view Albatross's new and improved sleep station.

“You wouldn't understand, Skye.”

“What's there to understand? Kyle wants a fight. You don't. Surely, you won’t give in to peer pressure and meet up with him later to prove a point. That would be stupid.”

He hangs his head. “It’s not that simple, okay? And I don't need to take advice from you.”

My stomach flips.

“What’s that supposed to mean?”

“It means whatever you want it to mean.”

“What is your problem? These last few days, you've barely even acknowledged me,” I say, swallowing back my emotions.

He looks past me for a minute, his eyes cold and hard.

“Maybe I don't fancy talking to you. Is that such a crime?”

“I thought we were friends.”

Rory swallows and folds his arms against his chest. “I don't have friends, Skye, and neither do you. There's a reason for that, remember?”

Rejection can feel as sharp as a bee sting, except it’s far worse than that—it’s more like multiple bee stings that have become infected and cause severe pain for days, but not even a single bee sting can justify the rejection people face daily. Words cannot be measured, and neither can the pain.

“We work together. We're coworkers—not friends,” Rory continues, his jaw tense and his stare ice-cold.

Tears burn my eyes, and his features harden severely. His words hurt more than I expected them to because despite us never putting a label on our friendship, I thought we were making some progress.

“I've got work to do, so if you don't mind closing the door on the way out, that would be grand,” he snarls.

Running out of the barn, I wipe my tear-stained cheeks with the backs of my knuckles.

*What a jerk.*

* * *

I've barely stepped into my house for five seconds before someone starts knocking frantically on the door. A stupid, tiny part of me hopes it's Rory coming to apologise, but Grayson barges in unannounced.

*I completely forgot that he was still coming here today.*

He hugs himself and shuffles around the living room.

"Bloody hell, it's like Antarctica in here. I can *see* my breath! How is that possible?" he moans, snuggling into his coat.

It's embarrassing that we can't afford to pay for our central heating, amongst other things, but we can't have the best of both worlds.

"Tea helps. Want some?" I ask casually.

"Is that a trick question?"

I step into the kitchen and boil the kettle. Grayson follows me in and leans against a counter, looking up at me with his cheeky grin.

"What does the class viper usually do after college? Are you living a secret life that nobody else knows about?"

Guilt wraps around my intestines and lingers there. It would be easy to tell him that I am technically living a secret life—working at *his* farm for *his* father, but how can I bring that up now? I've allowed this lie to multiply, and it feels like it's too late to come clean about it. We're just beginning to form a positive working relationship. The truth will most likely damage the progress we've already made. I will keep my mouth shut until the project ends, and then I'll tell him everything. Hopefully, he won't hate me.

“I live a perfectly normal life. Nothing secretive about it,” I tell him absentmindedly.

“Oh, well, that's boring.”

“What can I say? I'm the kind of girl that lays all of her cards on the table.”

*Most of the time.*

“Where's your mother? Is she at work?”

A sudden chill sweeps over me.

My expression tightens, and the air thickens between us. Just thinking about my mother brings uncomfortable pressure to my eyes. I don't know where she is or what she's doing. He doesn't need to know all the details, though. The less he knows, the better.

“She's gone out with a friend,” I say, a slight edge to my voice, turning my back to him to finish making the tea in silence.

Grayson is unusually quiet, and I'm grateful he isn't asking me a hundred questions.

“What is your family like?” I ask, handing him a mug of steaming hot tea and trying to remain calm. Internally, I feel like I'm about to enter hyperventilation mode.

He draws in a sharp breath and shrugs. “They're okay.”

“That's all you have to say about the people who raised you? Come on, Grayson, where is the story?”

His eyes roll heavenwards. “What else is there to say?”

“I don't know, but I’ll need a lot more than 'Oh,

they're okay' if I'm expected to write your story and get it right. It would help if you were a bit more specific."

Grayson takes a sip of his tea and sighs under his breath. "I have a big family, and they all have top-end jobs, so you can only imagine how busy life can get for them. Honestly, we don't communicate or spend much time together. Family reunions rarely happen. When they do, it's usually incredibly awkward and involves an argument. All my relatives ever talk about is work and business, which can get dull and dreary after a while. They're sort of like–"

"Self-righteous snobs?" I mutter, half-expecting Grayson to correct me, but instead, he nods as if that is the exact word he would use to describe them.

"I've always had the best of everything—shoes, clothes, toys. You name it... I had it. It never made me happy, especially when I wanted to find real friends who liked me for me instead of the money I had sitting in my bank account."

He looks away as if he's revealed too much. I should say something to reassure him that he hasn't, but this boy standing before me is not the same one who invaded my college class weeks ago. It's hard to compare the two now.

"Do you still feel lonely sometimes?" I ask.

"Yeah. I've had a lot of people lie to me over the years. As soon as someone gives me a reason not to trust them, then that's it. I haven't got time for secrets and lies. I'm done with all of the unnecessary drama it brings."

*He will hate me when he finds out I've lied to him.*

"Don't we all get lonely occasionally?" he adds as an afterthought.

"Uh, yeah. I guess we do."

I've experienced loneliness first-hand. From a young age, I remember feeling constantly left out. I was the girl who was never invited to birthday parties, sleepovers or school dances. Ultimately, my classmates' rejection of me became so real that I got used to being alone. That's probably why I struggle to make friends now because nobody has ever included me or stuck around long enough to get to know me.

Loneliness is like a never-ending train of pain. The hours tick by, and eventually, you forget what your voice sounds like because you have no one to talk to. I blink some unexpected tears away, hoping Grayson hasn't noticed. He's looking out the window when I glance at him, his attention elsewhere.

*Panic over.*

"What's your dad like?"

I wonder why I'm asking him this since I've already met Mr Swain and have made up my mind about him. I'm curious to know what he is like as a father.

"My dad isn't afraid to be human, unlike everybody else in my family who constantly tries to compete against each other to get ahead. I don't know where my dad gets his humbleness from because arrogance seems to run in the family, but he's a good guy. He even helped out one of his employees the other day—got them out of a financial crisis with their landlord."

*The guilt is back. Stronger than ever before.*

How can I admit to Grayson that I was the employee his father was talking about?

"What about *your* dad? What's he like?"

It didn't cross my mind that Grayson might ask me about my dad. I don't know which is worse, being questioned about my mother's whereabouts or having to discuss my non-existent father.

"He's not around. I've never met him," I say quickly, hoping to move past the topic.

Silence hangs between us, and Grayson's expression softens with empathy. "Skye, I'm so sorry. I wouldn't have asked if I'd known."

"It's fine. Please don't make a big deal out of it."

He runs a hand through his hair and blows out a sigh. "I don't know what to say."

"It doesn't bother me that much anymore. Honest."

That is partly true. However, it bothers me—way more than it should.

Grayson clears his throat. "So, you don't even know his name or what he looks like?"

"No."

"Wow. Like, seriously. *Wow*."

I suddenly don't want to talk about this anymore, especially not with Grayson. He can't relate to my situation because he's had his parents safely rooted at his side, and he wouldn't understand what it's like to come from a broken home. I don't know why I even revealed this intimate detail to him in the first place.

"Can we please talk about something else?" I request, averting his gaze.

"Yeah, of course. Let's get back to the project. There's something I'd like to ask you."

"Go for it."

"What's your dream?"

"I used to have big dreams, but once I grew up and saw the world for what it truly was, I realised life was far from easy and tended to throw curveballs into almost everything. I've always wanted to leave Barnett eventually."

"You don't like it here?" he guesses.

I shake my head gently. "No, it's not that. Opportunities are hard to come by, that's all. Pregnancy rates are high, poverty is rife in most areas, and the closest university is miles away. It's not like I'm spoilt for choice."

I'll have access to my father's money soon, but it's not like I'll use it. It would feel wrong somehow.

"There's a big world out there and so much to see. I don't want to limit myself by staying where I am, and I don't want to settle for less. Do you get what I'm saying?"

Grayson nods along, no trace of judgement on his face. If anything, he looks sad to hear about the harsh reality of my situation.

"Yeah. Sounds fair."

"We're lucky to have a college, but the sad thing is, most people give up on their studies as soon as they leave school. They decide to get a dead-end job because money is hard. That's just the way it's always been around here. What matters most is the heart of the community. We support each other. We're like one big family," I continue.

He smiles. “I have noticed that. You might lack opportunity, but it hasn't stopped you. It's what seems to drive you. That's inspiring, Skye.”

My heart warms. “Thanks.”

Is Barnett starting to rub some of its charms on the hard-to-please Grayson Swain?

I never thought I'd see the day.

I glance out of my kitchen window, watching a boisterous gang of youths pass by, their laughter and conversation filling the air. It must be nice to have friends like that—people to share life with. Making one friend is hard enough these days.

“Oh no. You’re daydreaming again. What’s on your mind?” Grayson's voice interrupts my thoughts, redirecting my attention.

I wave a dismissive hand in the air. “It’s nothing.”

“Sharing is caring.”

The more we dwell on loneliness, the more lonely I feel. I’d much rather do something fun and spontaneous. The night is still young, and I have all this energy to spare.

“Let’s climb a tree,” I declare, standing up confidently, resting my hands on my hips.

Grayson squints at me as if he’s struggling to determine whether I’m serious about the tree-climbing thing.

“You are the most random person I have ever met.”

“It’s not exactly rocket science, Swain. People climb trees all the time.”

“I’ve never climbed a tree,” he confesses.

I stare at his profile, a knowing look on my face. “It doesn’t take a genius to figure that out. Your clothes are always immaculate. I doubt you've ever intentionally gotten them dirty, have you?"

Grayson grimaces. "I could think of nothing worse."

"Have you got OCD?"

He lets out a surprised laugh. "No! I prefer to keep everything organised and clean. Nothing can be out of place. Order and structure matter to me."

"That sounds like OCD to me."

"I don't have OCD, okay? And there is nothing wrong with cleanliness."

"Nothing is wrong with it, but if you're scared of getting dirty, you have a serious problem."

"I am not scared," he retorts.

"Prove it then."

I move towards the front door and grab my coat.

"I'll be climbing a tree with or without you, Swain. So you can stay here alone or join me on the biggest climb of your life. What do you say?"

He looks at me, slightly amused. "You make it sound like we're about to climb Mount Everest."

"There's always next time," I remark, tapping my foot impatiently against the carpet. "Now, are you coming or not?"

He springs up from the couch, stretching his legs. "I'll come along because watching you climb a tree will be entertaining, but I won't be joining you."

*We'll see about that.*

"This is the one!"

I run over to the biggest tree in the park and glance at

the canopy of unscathed leaves. It's the perfect tree to climb because the branches look solid and smooth. If I jump, I should be able to reach the first branch and work my way up to the top.

Lost in my thoughts about the best approach to climb the tree, Grayson finally joins me, gasping for breath.

"This tree looks exactly like the last one we just saw. What's so different about it?" he grumbles.

"This one is way better. The bark is thicker. It'll be easier to climb."

"Do you climb trees for a living, like a real-life Spider-Man?"

"Something like that, but please don't tell anyone. My identity must be kept top secret," I say with a shrug.

Humour colours his face. "You're such a dork."

I drag my trainer against the tree trunk and give myself a little boost. I reach out for the first branch and pull upward, sitting on the bark comfortably. My eyes flash to where Grayson is still standing. He's rubbing his hands together, and he's blowing on them in an attempt to keep warm.

"Aren't you coming?" I call out to him.

He shakes his head. "No way. You'll see pigs fly before I attempt to climb a tree that high."

"I knew you would chicken out. That's a shame. You're not as brave as I thought," I taunt, watching his face screw up, his lips parting in protest.

"Pa-lease. I told you I'm not afraid."

"And I told you to prove it."

He stares at me silently for a long moment, contemplating his next move. Running a frustrated hand through his hair, he eventually breathes, "Fine. Do you want proof? I'll give you proof. I can climb that stupid tree with my eyes closed."

"Uh, I wouldn't recommend doing that. You might want to keep your eyes open."

Grayson rips off his coat like he's about to transform into Superman, and I howl with laughter. I laugh so much that I don't notice him leap to the first branch until it's too late. My eyes whip open in alarm as the branch starts to wobble, and I realise it's not strong enough to carry us both.

Grayson loses his balance, desperately grabbing the first thing he can reach, which happens to be my shoe. I let out a yelp when he topples backwards, dragging me down with him, and we tumble to the ground, landing in a mud puddle with a loud splat.

*Ow.*

*That's going to bruise tomorrow.*

I try untangling my leg, but it's trapped underneath Grayson's body weight, and his entire body has gone limp.

"That hurt," I moan, a little dizzy from the fall.

I glance down into the thick, treacherous mud surrounding us and do a double take once I notice Grayson's head is fully submerged.

I poke him, but there's no response.

"Oh my— Grayson, are you okay? Are you alive?"

He slowly lifts his head and emerges from the mud like a monster. I hold a hand over my mouth when a few giggles escape.

*What a sight.*

"Does it look like I'm okay?" he spits, wiping his eyes repeatedly.

*It's hard to take him seriously.*

"My mother is going to kill me if I walk through the house looking like this!" he cries, flicking clumps of mud out of his hair.

"Hey, calm down. It's just mud. It won't kill you."

"My clothes are ruined!" he exclaims, exasperated.

"You definitely have OCD, Swain."

"I do not!"

"What's the big deal, then? Did your parents forbid you from making a mess as a child or something?"

I see a flash of pain cross his eyes briefly. "Yeah, I guess you could say that. I had a strict upbringing. I wasn't allowed to make a mess."

A sad smile plays on my lips.

"Grayson, it's not normal for a child to be *that* paranoid about making a mess. Children jump rope, climb mountains, roll down hills, and dance in puddles. For someone so obsessed with staying clean, you choose to ride horses, which doesn't make much sense now that I think about it. How do you cope?"

He laughs momentarily.

"It's difficult, that's for sure. As a child, my mother wasn't happy when I told her I wanted to start accompanying my father to the stables. I tried to avoid getting dirty as much as possible, but I'd always come home covered in mud."

"So, that's where you get your OCD from—your mother. You said she was a neat freak."

"My father is pretty chilled, and my mother is the opposite, which might be why they work so well. I don't go to the farm much anymore."

"Why?"

"I'm tired of constantly living in my father's shadow. I want to make a name for myself—not live life through someone else's eyes, but I still want to please my parents," he admits.

"You'll be unhappy if you continue to live a life set on pleasing people. Half of the time, they never appreciate it anyway."

"It's not that simple," he says, his gaze shifting to the sky as he scratches the tip of his nose.

"Why can't it be? What are your goals? What do you want to do?" I ask, realising I haven't asked him about his dreams and goals for the future yet.

"I want to study literature. Maybe even write a book someday. I'm interested in learning about different cultures. I'd love to travel the world and meet lots of interesting people. I enjoy horse riding, but I don't think it's my destiny."

"I can't believe I'm about to say this, but I'm proud of you."

He looks at me in surprise. "For what?"

"Well, we've been sitting in this mud puddle for about ten minutes now, and you have finally stopped freaking out."

"Now you mention it, I want to get out of this mud as soon as possible. My skin is starting to itch. I hope I'm not allergic."

"Shut up, Swain." I playfully tap his shoulder, and he

laughs. "I still think you have OCD, though. You might want to consider talking to someone about it."

After spending the entire night studying with Grayson, I'm relieved when we finally go our separate ways because I am exhausted and reek of mud. I shower twice, head to my room and shut off the lights. My phone beeps, and I reach for it in the dark, noticing Grayson's name appear on the screen. Secretly, I'm excited to hear from him even though we only said goodbye a few hours ago.

It worries me a little.

GRAYSON

I've still got mud in my hair...

Suppressing my laughter, I cover my mouth with my hand as a picture from Grayson pops up on my WhatsApp. The image captures him pointing at his hair, which is thoroughly saturated with mud, and he's wearing an exaggerated pout that only adds to the comedic effect.

That's hilarious.

SKYE

Don't worry. You could always dye your hair brown to make it less noticeable.

GRAYSON

It's never going to happen. I'm pretty fond of my hair. It's part of the package deal. Girls love it.

SKYE

Wow. You are so full of yourself, aren't you?

GRAYSON

What can I say? I'm blessed to have this face and body. Have fun dreaming about me tonight.

SKYE

You'll be in my nightmares.

GRAYSON

Goodnight, Class Viper.

SKYE

Night, Swain.

I'm about to jump into bed when I hear loud footsteps on the stairs and muffled voices. I approach my bedroom door and open it slowly, noticing my mother stumbling up the stairs, and a man I've never seen before is glued to her side.

Their kisses are fast, sloppy, and desperate.

It triggers a bitter emotion inside me.

*So this is who she's been spending her time with lately.*

Mum breaks away for a second, and I hear her say, "We need to be more careful. Skye might hear us."

"Who's that again?"

"My daughter. Remember I told you about her at dinner?"

The mystery man nods absentmindedly but clearly

wasn't paying attention to anything my mother told him on their date.

"Don't worry about her. I'm sure she's out with her boyfriend," he says, making me dislike him even more.

"Skye doesn't have a boyfriend."

"That's what they all say."

My hatred towards this man has quadrupled within a matter of seconds. I watch them drunkenly stumble into her bedroom, eventually out of sight but not out of mind. My only source of company is Batman, who I'm caught in a staring contest with for a good five seconds before he also abandons me.

I can't stay here and listen to the high-pitched sounds from my mother's bedroom. I need an excuse to get out of the house. Even though I'm not his biggest fan, I can collect the stable keys from Rory and get out of here.

I don't even have to think about it.

My mind is already made up.

# Chapter Twenty-One

I STAND OUTSIDE RORY'S HOUSE, TAKE A DEEP BREATH AND knock on his door. I can hear babies crying in the distance, televisions blaring, and bustling traffic filling the street with life and noise.

After receiving no response, I knock again, this time with more force. Finally, the porch light flickers, and I hear the lock turning frantically. The door swings open wide, and Rory's grandmother appears, flinging her arms around me with so much force that I stumble backwards onto the road.

Anne draws away, hesitates and starts crying in the doorway. I've never been very good at comforting people. I never know what to do. Anne doesn't give me much time to think about it because she is suddenly leading me into her house, and before I know what's happening, we're sitting on her sofa, and she's bawling her eyes out in front of me.

I don't know whether I'm supposed to say something, so we sit there while she cries for ages.

*Rory, where the hell are you?*

*What have I just walked into?*

Anne blows her nose into a tissue and reaches for my hand. I don't know how she can act so comfortable around me when we hardly know each other.

“Have you spoken to Rory today?” she asks, dabbing her watery eyes.

“Yeah. We didn't speak much, though.”

“This time of the year is always so hard for him. He tends to go off the rails, and I'm worried he will do something stupid.”

It wouldn't surprise me if he did get into a fight with Kyle. They have unfinished business, but why can't they sort it out without using their fists?

“Why is this time of the year so difficult for him?” I have to ask, deeply confused by all of this. I figured that Rory's low mood was somehow linked to his recent visit to Barnett Prison. I mean, nobody ever goes to that place willingly. People tend to stay away if they can help it.

Anne takes a shuddery breath. “He hasn't told you?”

“Told me what?”

*We don't have heart-to-heart conversations, Anne.*

“It makes sense why he hasn't mentioned anything. Rory doesn't like to talk about it...” Anne covers her face, getting tearful all over again.

“It's okay. You don't have to explain,” I tell her softly.

“No, it's fine. It's not a coincidence that you've found yourself here tonight.” Anne hesitates and takes a deep breath. “Rory's father used to be a heavy drinker and–” she stops there, her voice catching in her throat.

I gently squeeze her hand, and she glances up at me gratefully.

"One day, Darren was driving home from the pub. He'd had a lot to drink and shouldn't have been driving. He fell asleep at the wheel and crashed into another car. The person inside it died on impact."

Her words hang in the air like a loose thread.

My throat goes painfully dry. "That's—that's awful."

"Rory visited his dad in prison a few days ago. It's the first time in years that he's been to see him. The conversation ended badly, and he's been upset about it ever since."

Pieces of the puzzle are slowly coming together—Rory's mood swings, frequent bust-ups, reluctance to drink, and his recent prison visit.

"He hasn't come home from work and isn't answering my calls. Maybe he'll talk to you," Anne says, startling me out of my thoughts.

"Wait. What? Why would he talk to me?"

"You're his friend, aren't you?"

*Not according to him.*

"I honestly don't think I'm the right person to–"

"I think he'll listen to you," she interrupts, tightening her grip on my hand.

Looking into Anne's red, puffy eyes, I realise she's relying on me because I'm the only person who can help her at this precise moment. I doubt I'll find Rory tonight or I'll be able to convince him that running away is not the answer, but he helped me when I was in trouble, and now it's my turn to do the same, even if I am rejected. At least, I tried.

An idea suddenly springs to mind.

"I think I might know where he is, but I need you to drive me there."

"Yes, of course. I'll go and get my car keys."

*Rory, please don't make me regret this.*

Anne steers the car to a halt near the train tracks, and together, we circle the area, our eyes scanning for any signs of commotion. The surroundings remain eerily calm. If there was a fight, we would surely know about it by now.

"Why did you think that he would be here?" Anne asks me once we're safely back in the car.

I buckle my seatbelt and explain what happened this morning, starting with Kyle's surprise appearance at the farm and how he wanted to meet Rory here to finish what they had started.

"Those two are going to end up killing each other one day," Anne says, breathing a shaky sigh.

"Why do they hate each other so much?"

"Do you know when I said the other driver didn't survive the crash?"

I nod along, suddenly realising where this is going.

"Well, that was Kyle's older brother. They've been at war for years over it, and Kyle can't move on. He blames Rory for what happened."

There's a small but weighty silence.

Kyle is hostile towards Rory and constantly wants to fight him because he's still grieving the loss of his brother, but he's taking it out on the wrong person.

"Is there anywhere else you think he might have gone?"

"There's only one more place I think we should try," I say.

It takes us half an hour to arrive at Trinity Farm, mainly because a flock of sheep decided to park themselves in the middle of the road, causing traffic to build up.

"You think that he could be here?" Anne asks as I scramble to get out of the car.

"I don't know, but it's worth a shot."

"Thank you, Skye. You're an angel."

I would not use that word to describe me because I'm about to break into Trinity Farm. It's not for the faint-hearted. Of course, it doesn't help that Mr Swain has taken this whole security measure to the extreme. If I even attempted to climb over the main gate, the alarm would go off in a heartbeat, and I'd probably be spending the night in a prison cell.

During my frequent visits to Trinity, I noticed a minor defect in its wall of defence. There's a slight gap in one of the hedges surrounding the area, and I'm small, so I may be able to crawl through it. I get onto my knees and peer into the small gap, earning my one-way ticket to freedom. Carefully, I slide through the opening and wiggle my way inside.

It's not pleasant.

Twigs and other sharp objects are digging into every inch of me, and I know I will come out of this experience with more cuts and bruises to my name. However, it's worth it because I manage to make it to the other side without attracting attention or setting off any alarms.

I walk around the yard for a while. A slight breeze whips against my hair, and I quickly force the loose strands into a high ponytail. I breathe in the cool air and glance around. From an outsider's perspective, nobody else is here, but this would be the perfect place to hide if you didn't want to be found.

I search the barn, inside storage cupboards and around the staff room. I even check inside the horse's stalls, but Rory isn't there. I search for his name on my contacts list, but then I realise I don't have his number. His mobile is printed on the sign-in sheet for emergencies, so I quickly rush to get it and punch his digits into my phone. The operator immediately answers and asks me to leave a message after the beep.

"Uh, hey. It's Skye. Where are you? Your nan is worried, and I think you should call her and let her know you're okay. Uh, please let us know you're safe and sound. Bye."

I pocket my phone and head out into the yard again. I wonder if it's time to accept defeat when I overhear a low whimpering sound from above, and I freeze on the spot, visibly shaken. After another few seconds, I hear it again —louder this time. The noise seems to be coming from the roof of the barn.

I glance up, but I can't see anything from down here. My only option is to climb the ladder to settle this once and for all. The other half of my conscience, the irrational side, argues that I'm imagining things and shouldn't start the climb in case a ravenous beast is waiting for me on the other side.

*The farm is very creepy at night.*

Slowly, I approach the ladder and bravely climb up. The higher I climb, the more I wish I'd worn a warmer jacket and a pair of gloves.

*If I die because of this, I will haunt you for the rest of your life, Rory Keaton.*

I step onto the roof, and my breath catches when I see it, or rather when I see him.

Rory is sitting there with his headphones on. He's sobbing into his hands. It's as if I've forgotten how to breathe—like I'm fully submerged underwater, drowning in his pain. I've never been very empathetic, but seeing Rory like this is tugging my heartstrings.

*My job here is done. I'll sneak away before he notices me, and Anne can take over. She'll know what to do.*

Something must grab Rory's attention because he looks up sharply, and time seems to slow as our eyes lock.

"What the hell are *you* doing here?" he demands, forcefully shoving his headphones and iPod into his backpack, his movements brimming with aggression.

"I came to the stables to look for you because your nan was worried that something might have happened. She's waiting in the car right now. You should probably go and see her—give her some peace of mind?"

Rory's eyes darken, and he reels back as if I've just slapped him. "Do you make a habit of sticking your nose in other people's business?"

"What? No, I... I wasn't expecting your nan to be so

upset when I got to your house. She told me about your father and the crash. I'm so sorry. I had no idea."

He laughs, but it doesn't create a nice sound. "Perfect! This keeps getting better and better. What else did you and my nan discuss while I wasn't around? Did she gush about what shampoo and conditioner I use as well, or am I way off base?"

"It wasn't like that. Emotions were high. I don't think she meant to tell me anything. It just happened."

"This has nothing to do with you, so why don't you just back off and leave me alone?" Rory is acting out of character, but that doesn't mean his words hurt any less.

"Please don't be like this."

"Like what?"

"Uh... well..."

"Come on. Spit it out. You've never been the silent type. You're not afraid of anything."

I narrow my eyes, anger simmering just below the surface. He's pushing my buttons, and he's always been good at it.

"I'm scared of everything, Rory. You're not the only one struggling with stuff, okay?"

"Okay. Let's talk about this *stuff* you keep referring to because I am dying to know what *stuff* Skye Clemons struggles with," he taunts, and a flush of embarrassment creeps up my cheeks.

He's undermining me.

"Stop it."

"Stop what?"

"You're being unfair."

"Why don't you leave then? I'm not asking you to stick around."

"You're angry and upset, and I get it," I say, trying to reason with him.

He raises a hand in the air, frustrated.

"No, you don't get it!" he cries, drawing a sharp breath. "You have no idea what it's like to have a dad who couldn't control himself around alcohol and ended up killing someone because he wasn't strong enough to resist a drink. He might've been imprisoned for what he did, but my family had to deal with the aftermath alone. The whole town turned against us. People I classed as my friends turned their back on me. We lost *everything*. So, please don't pretend to act like you understand my situation. You haven't got a bloody clue, Skye."

My whole body trembles with emotion. I've never heard him speak like this. It's as if he wants me to retaliate, which is not what he needs and not what he will get—at least not from me, anyway.

"Maybe I don't understand," I say, fresh tears falling down my face, "but I do know how it feels to be stuck in a difficult situation. From a young age, I watched my mother stumble through the door while she was drunk and trying not to choke on her vomit. I had no choice but to be an adult. You don't get to choose what happens to you in this life. Living in this world is a painful experience."

I'm about to tell him about my mother, and it's not because I have to. It's because I want to. For once, I want to rant and scream at whoever might be listening. In this case, it is Rory Keaton, who would not have been my first choice, but I'm willing to put myself out there if it means he will feel less alone.

“My mother has been ill for a long time now, and I am not comparing my situation to yours. They are two entirely different things, but for you to say I'm fearless—that’s not true. I worry about my mother because she is severely depressed, and I feel like I will lose her if she doesn't get the help she needs. I don't know where she will end up, and that thought alone terrifies me.”

I glance at Rory, but his eyes are elsewhere. Suppose we were stargazing, the lack of stars would be a total letdown tonight. There's still something quite magical about this moment, though. We're just two broken people, brought together by our brokenness.

“I may not have been through what you have been through. But I feel like I'm losing my mother every day. So don’t think for one second that I’m unfamiliar with pain or loss because I am—way more than you realise. I experience it daily. It never stops,” I continue, focusing on the sky above us so I don't have to look at him.

After an entire minute, Rory lifts his eyes to mine. I'm shocked to find so much emotion sparkling behind them. I hug my knees and glance down at the ground below us. I didn't realise how high up we were. It's turning my stomach to mush.

“I'm not very good at expressing myself,” Rory croaks after a long moment.

“Me neither,” I whisper back, unsure if he heard me, but it doesn't matter.

“Using my fists sometimes helps, but I'm trying not to cause any trouble for once.”

That faint scar above his left eyebrow looks like it was caused by a blunt object resulting from another brawl he found himself in over the years. The jagged edge of his nose stands proud but also paints an image of suffering. Deep frown lines tug at his forehead, and a sadness I'm all too familiar with seems to swim around in his green, glassy eyes. His knuckles are grazed and swollen, desperately needing medical attention.

"What happened to your hand? Did you get into a fight with Kyle?"

Rory bites his lower lip, then shakes his head furiously. "I was tempted to meet up with him. He kept messaging me—egging me on, but I chose not to go through with it. I did this to myself." He lifts his hands in front of him and clenches them together.

"What did you do?"

"I punched a brick wall."

He looks up, meeting my steady gaze. Something glints in them, making my heart beat violently in my chest.

"Aside from the wall-punching thing, you made the most sensible decision. Getting into fights doesn't solve the problem. It only creates a million other problems."

Rory nods, his eyes drifting shut. "It's hard to avoid a fight when it's all I've ever known. People expect me to lose control, and they don't even bat an eyelid when it happens because they're so used to it. I've been getting into fights for as long as I can remember. Like father, like son, right?"

The minute I steal a glance, his eyes meet mine instinctively, and my chest tightens. I swallow, trying to relieve the growing pressure that's building up in my throat. I was so quick to judge him for getting into fights, yet I was utterly blind to the fact that he wasn't looking to cause trouble—not intentionally. He was simply defending himself by fighting back, and I was too ignorant to notice or care at the time.

"I know this is not what you want to hear, and you've probably heard people say it a lot, but I am sorry, Rory."

"I'm sorry as well. I had no right to take my anger out on you when you've done nothing to earn it. I'm angry at Kyle, the world, and my father for leaving me behind. I'm even starting to wonder if Kyle was right. Maybe I am turning into my dad. Maybe I am following in his footsteps."

I shuffle closer to him. "Hey, I don't know your father personally, but I have come to know you, and you've got a good heart. What happened that day wasn't your fault. You were just a kid."

Tears pool in his eyes. "I've done some bad things, Skye — things I'm not proud of," he says, voice dangerously low.

"So have I. We all make mistakes. It's in our DNA."

Rory repeatedly wipes his eyes with the end of his sleeve, and then I do the most surprising thing and wrap my arms around him. He stiffens at my touch, and I immediately think it is the wrong move. I start backing away, but I'm pulled against his chest, and he's crying into my shoulder. He buries his head into my windswept hair, and I run my hands up and down his back, constantly telling him that it's okay—that *he will* be okay.

I don't know how long we stay like this, but at some point, Rory must realise that we're still holding each other, and he's quick to put a sea of distance between us.

"I visited my dad in prison. He kept apologising and told me I'd never left his mind. I sat there completely silent the entire time. It's like I lost the ability to speak. I could barely look him in the eye," he admits.

"I bet it wasn't easy seeing him again, but you did a brave thing. You should be proud of yourself."

Rory's gaze lingers on my face.

"Thank you," he finally whispers.

My throat constricts.

"What are you thanking me for?"

"You could've just left me here. You didn't have to stay. I was horrible to you earlier."

"It's okay. When we're going through a difficult time, we tend to push away the people who matter the most to us."

I watch his eyebrows rise, suggesting something I'd rather not know the answer to. I need to defend myself quickly before he starts getting the wrong idea.

"Not that I'm saying I matter to you or anything! I know that I don't. You care about your nan. She means a lot to you, so you're choosing to push her away because it's easier. Figuratively speaking, that's just what we do when we're upset."

Rory's hard lines fade away, and it's oddly rewarding.

"Thanks for the tip, Clemons, but just for the record... *you* matter," he says, nudging my shoulder playfully, and I'm relieved to see his old self return.

A hot flush creeps up my neck.

I'm thankful it's too dark outside to notice. He shouldn't have said that because my mind will now jump to various conclusions. My heart tends to do somersaults whenever Rory says something nice to me.

I wipe a fallen tear that catches me off guard.

"Ugh! Sorry! I don't know why *I'm* crying now. Please ignore me," I cry, wiping my eyes furiously.

"Skye, I was just sobbing while listening to *Angels* by Robbie Williams. I think if anyone should be embarrassed, it's me."

I cough out a laugh. "You listen to Robbie Williams?"

"Guilty is charged."

"Wow. Seriously?"

Rory leans in closer, eyes lighting up mischievously. "Hey, Robbie Williams is a living legend. Don't mock his musical abilities."

"I'm not a fan. Sue me!"

He chuckles.

"It's weird, isn't it?" I say, voicing my thoughts out loud.

"What's weird?"

"Well, who would have thought we'd be having this conversation? We couldn't stand to be around each other a couple of months ago."

"It is weird, but a good kind of weird."

Rory's eyes have captured mine, and the mood shifts. Slowly, he closes the distance between us, creating a clear path to my lips. I can't remember the last time I was *this* nervous around a boy. I'm worried that if he does kiss me, I'll be bad at it. It sounds pretty stupid since I've kissed many frogs in my lifetime, but those kisses meant nothing. It's different with Rory because we have so much history, and I've come to like him as a person.

It scares me to think that if he were to kiss me, it would change everything. I'm still determining if I want to explore the possibilities because once those boundaries are crossed, there is no going back, but before the tension between us can escalate further, Anne's voice slices through the air, breaking the spell.

“Skye! Where are you? It's been half an hour, and I haven't heard anything!”

Rory stands up immediately, reaches for my hand and helps me to my feet.

“Let’s go. We'd better tell her we're up here before she sends out a search party,” he urges.

“Yeah. Good idea.”

*Just let me catch my breath first.*

# Chapter Twenty-Two

MY BIRTHDAY IS IN THREE DAYS, AND MY ONE BIRTHDAY WISH IS to give Albatross a haircut. He's grazing further up the field, munching on grass and minding his business. My wish is never going to come true. Birthday or not, I don't think I'll get special dibs on that decision. Albatross might be destined to resemble a horse-like Bigfoot for the rest of his adult life.

*Poor guy.*

I'm hanging out by the pasture, watching Dante graze. He's showing off in front of the female mares, all watching him with growing curiosity. He's even attracted Luna's attention with all his hair flicking and trotting around.

*Dante is going to break a lot of hearts.*

At lunch, I skip into the staff room to take my afternoon break, but I don't expect to find Rory taking a nap on the recliner. He looks peaceful when he sleeps. I haven't seen him breathe yet. I step closer and lean over him. Sitting on my knees, I press my head against his chest, listening for signs of life.

His heart is beating frantically.

"Skye? What are you doing?"

My head whips up, and I notice Rory's wide green eyes are steadily fixed on me, his face a combination of shock and confusion. He's very much awake, and our faces are inches apart. My cheeks grow warm, and a rush of adrenaline shoots through my body. I hastily stand up to hop away from him, becoming increasingly flustered.

"Sorry, I didn't mean to wake you."

Rory sits up, stretching his arms above his head. "I wasn't sleeping. I was waiting for you."

"You were? Why?"

"I wanted to thank you again for last night. It meant a lot."

Yesterday's antics are still a bit of a blur. When Anne finally dropped me home, I couldn't stop smiling if I tried. I might've helped Rory in his hour of need, but he also helped me. I've never told anyone about my mother's depression before. It was nice to finally talk to someone about it when I have been battling to keep it a secret all my life. Sharing my burden has helped ease my conscience, and I feel much lighter.

I continue to stand there, even though my legs are starting to buckle. I have to keep shifting on my feet to relieve the growing pressure.

"Aren't you going to sit down?" Rory eventually asks, scrunching his eyebrows.

There is only one recliner, and he is sitting on it.

Considering my brain tends to get fuzzy whenever I'm too close to him, I wonder if we *should* sit together. Look what happened the other night. If Anne hadn't shown up when she did, we might have... well, I'm not entirely sure what might have happened, but I *felt* something in my gut—a spark, a connection. At one point, I had convinced myself that Rory might kiss me, but maybe I'd just imagined the whole thing. It was a vulnerable moment for both of us. It probably wouldn't have meant anything if we had kissed anyway, and I doubt he'd given it a second thought.

I need to forget about it since he's moved on. Besides, I can't assume for one second that he likes me as anything more than a friend because I couldn't bear to lose our newfound friendship over a mishap.

"What's the matter, Clemons? I don't bite," he says with a low chuckle.

Slowly, I scurry across the room and sit down next to him, scooting over to the furthest end of the recliner, which is the most uncomfortable part.

I unroll the foil around my egg sandwiches, knowing they don't smell the best.

*It's a bad day for egg breath.*

My phone vibrates on the table, catapulting me back to life, and I notice Rory's eyes linger on the lit-up screen before I can snatch it away.

The caller ID says **Grayson Swine**.

*I should change that at some point.*

I changed his last name to Swine ages ago because he was annoying me, and I was looking for an excuse to call him names.

"Are you going to answer that?" Rory asks, his forehead furrowed, lips drawn tight.

He's back to being serious all over again.

Grayson has that kind of effect on people.

"I'll call him back later," I say, switching my phone off.

Rory glances around, looking agitated, and I don't understand why. I fold my arms across my stomach, then unfold them. I can't stop fidgeting now that I've started. I don't know whether I'm supposed to say something or if he is, but he doesn't seem to be in the mood for any more chit-chat because he jumps to his feet and starts walking towards the door.

"I'll see you later," he mumbles, leaving me alone in the staff room.

Now, I need to survive another four hours of work without experiencing unnecessary drama.

Is that too much to ask?

Failing to mount Dante this afternoon, I head straight to the toilets to assess today's damage. My fingers are blistered from constantly dragging the wheelbarrow through the mud. I shake my hair out of my bobble and gasp. It looks like I've been electrocuted multiple times, and I smell so bad.

I glance back into the small, rounded mirror above the bathroom sink and apply lip balm to my chapped lips, wincing as my skin rejects the treatment it's receiving. I have a zit, and it's right in the centre of my cheek. Some giant spider bit me last night, or my body gave me a hormonal rain check while I slept. Regardless, the zit is enormous and has caused a red rash to spread to other areas of my face. I conceal it with foundation and use most of the bottle.

*Not a single beauty product can save me now.*

Outside, I see the big, red Bugatti parked near the farm entrance and realise it's too late to take a detour. I'm already dripping with sweat, and I can practically feel the thick layers of foundation peeling away from my skin.

Grayson appears from behind the car. Knowing him, he's busy observing the vehicle under closer inspection, checking that he hasn't scratched the paint.

*Typical Swain behaviour.*

I am surprised when the passenger door swings open, and Mr Swain's lookalike emerges. Sebastian Cole is glancing around, looking somewhat bored. The man is unbelievably intimidating, even from a distance.

*I wonder what he's doing here.*

An anxious knot forms in my stomach when they start heading this way.

My feet refuse to cooperate.

*If you don't leave now, you will face Grayson Swain's wrath, which won't be pretty.*

Mid panic, I feel a hand clamp down on my shoulder, and I'm forcefully turned around. Rory grabs my hand and tugs me towards the entrance of the barn. I struggle to keep up with him as he rounds the corner, opens a small storage cupboard, ushers me inside and locks the door behind us.

"That was such a close call. Do you think they saw us?" I ask, breathing heavily.

"I don't think so."

I sink to the floor. "Is this a good time to tell you you were right?"

Rory crouches next to me. "What are you talking about?"

"I'm such an idiot for thinking I could hide away forever. You told me that this would happen. I've dug myself a hole, and now I'm stuck. What am I supposed to do?"

"It's never too late to fix this, Skye. If it bothers you, maybe it's time to tell Grayson the truth."

"But... what if the truth is better left unsaid?"

"The truth is always worth voicing, even if it hurts at first, which it will."

That's the scary part—the truth will destroy my friendship with Grayson. If I don't tell him, the results will be equally soul-destroying because the lie will multiply.

*I have to tell him, but not like this.*

"Can I ask you a question?"

Rory glances at me, his shoulder brushing mine.

"Sure."

"If you were expecting a large sum of money, but that money was from a relative you'd never met, would you use it?"

"If the relative wanted me to have that money, I don't see why there'd be a reason not to accept it, but it depends on the context."

I'm tempted to tell him the full story about my father, but I can't.

*Not yet.*

"Let's say for argument's sake that the person receiving this money didn't know what to do with it because taking something from someone who never wanted to be in their life felt wrong. Would you still accept the money?"

Rory's stare deepens.

I've made it obvious that I'm talking about myself.

"I don't know what I'd do, but there's nothing wrong with spending money you are entitled to... even if that person wasn't around, they clearly wanted you to have it, otherwise they wouldn't have put it there."

*That's true.*

I'll be turning eighteen in a few days, and my father's money will be mine. I have never seen five digits to my name before. I have no idea how I'm supposed to deal with that sort of money, but I understand what it can do for people—it can transform lives.

Unspoken words hang between us, and I don't know what the hell is going on, but the fact that we're in a closed space is not helping the situation. We can barely move without bumping shoulders or butting heads. Our bodies will inevitably make direct contact at some point, no matter how much we try to avoid it.

There's a strange look on his face that steals my breath away. It's the same look he gave me when I thought he would kiss me on the roof of the barn. The space between us continues to shrink, the air charged with anticipation, but the moment is sabotaged when my phone starts ringing.

My anxiety skyrockets.

I take the phone out of my back pocket, and it slips out of my fingers, landing on the floor face-first.

"Crap!"

*It'll be a miracle if my phone isn't cracked after this.*

I flip the phone over and notice my mother is calling me. I reject the call just as the door handle starts turning, and I hear Grayson's voice.

"Somebody must be in here. I heard a phone ring."

"Don't worry. I locked the door. They won't be able to get in," Rory whispers to me comfortingly.

This fills me with relief for about precisely five seconds.

"No worries. I've got a master key right here," Grayson is saying.

My lies have come back to bite me, and I am not ready for Grayson to hear the truth yet. This would be the ultimate betrayal. I'd hate for him to find out this way. I close my eyes tightly, waiting for the door to open, inventing a list of apologies I'll inevitably forget when Grayson appears.

I sense Rory stand up, and my eyes flash open.

"What are you doing?" I ask him quietly.

"Just trust me," he says, opening the door.

Grayson and Sebastian are standing on the other side, looking mildly perplexed and suspicious. The door closes tightly behind Rory, and darkness surrounds me again.

"Hey, guys. How's it going?" I overhear Rory say, not a trace of nervousness in his voice.

"I don't know. Why don't you tell us how it's going?" Grayson fires back, sounding irritated.

"Everything's fine. No issues here."

"Well, what were you doing inside that storage cupboard? I heard you talking to someone."

"I was on the phone. I could hear a car pulling up, so I decided to continue the conversation somewhere private."

"Why was the door locked?" Grayson demands after a few seconds of silence.

"I didn't want anybody disturbing me. Sorry. I wasn't aware that either of you was coming here today."

"This is my dad's farm, so I think that gives me the right to show up whenever I want, with or without the stableboy's consent."

"I have a name," Rory says defensively.

Grayson snorts, and I'm seriously tempted to dive out of this cupboard and give him the jump scare of his life because he deserves it.

"I was showing Sebastian around. He will be responsible for the farm while my dad is on a business trip."

I'm disappointed that Sebastian will be taking charge of the farm. He seems like the kind of boss who would fire someone just because they failed to pick up his favourite coffee on their way to the office.

"Do you need my help with anything?" Rory is asking politely.

"We're fine," Sebastian's voice cuts through the air, charged and sour.

"Right. Well, I'll leave you to it then."

The voices eventually fade out, and I stand up to stretch my legs, bored out of my mind. There's not much to see in here except dust and dead flies.

What's the point of having a storage cupboard when it's not even being used to store anything?

I'm about to sit back down, but I notice a small box on top of one of the filing cabinets. I lean on my tiptoes to reach out for it, but, being the klutz that I am, I end up flinging myself against the cabinet with too much force, causing the box and all its contents to crash to the floor. I let out a startled gasp as another object tumbled onto me, its eerie, dark eyes piercing into the depths of my soul. For a moment, I'm paralysed with shock, but I'm quick to realise that it's only Dudley, the not-so-child-friendly mascot. I unintentionally dragged him out of his hiding place during my collision with the cabinet.

"Dudley, you freak me out," I mutter, flinging him back into the darkness.

I get onto my hands and knees and start putting the photos back into the box, but I find myself flicking through them, even though it feels like a total invasion of privacy. I reach for my phone and turn on the flashlight to view the photographs.

There are a lot of pictures of Grayson and Mr Swain from different horse racing events and shows. Grayson looks so young in most of them, and he's holding up all his trophies and medals with so much pride on his face. There are even a couple of pictures of him with Luna. It's lovely to see their relationship play out through the photos, and it looks as if Luna grew from a timid foal to a headstrong horse racing champion.

*She's a queen, and she knows it.*

I get to the last picture, and my eyes open wide. Sebastian and Mr Swain are both in this one, and a woman stands beside them. Her face is blurred from the angle of the photo, and she's wearing a Catwoman suit. It looks like they're at some fancy dress party.

*I wonder who she is.*

"The coast is clear."

Rory's voice startles me out of my daze. Light pours into the cupboard, and I react like a vampire exposed to the sunlight, quickly gathering the rest of the photos and putting them back inside the box. For some peculiar reason, I stuff the fancy dress photo inside my back pocket.

"Clemons, you've been caught snooping once again," Rory says, smirking.

"Well, what else was I supposed to do while you were gone? I've been stuck here for ages! I was bored."

"You've only been in the cupboard for twenty minutes. Don't you think you're being overdramatic?"

I gasp, which only makes him laugh.

"Twenty minutes is a long time to be stuck inside a confined space! Maybe you should try it out and see if the experience messes with your sugar intake!"

Rory's eyes twinkle with amusement. "I may or may not have something sugary up my sleeve. I think it might help."

"Gimme gimme!" I cry out, clawing at the air.

He throws me a packet of Haribos that he must've

bought from the staffroom vending machine. I rip the box open and stuff a couple of love hearts and gummy bears into my mouth, savouring the sugary taste.

A wry smile tugs at Rory's lips as he watches me stuff my face like a woman starved of oxygen.

"Feel better now?"

I chuck the last two gummy bears into my mouth and let out a satisfied moan.

"Yup. Massively. Thank you."

We step out of the storage cupboard, and I don't know why I'm still so jittery. Grayson and Sebastian have left the scene, yet what happened today is the perfect example of what could happen if I don't tell the truth anytime soon.

"I thought I heard Grayson say that Sebastian will take care of the farm for a while. Is that true?" I ask Rory while we return to work.

He nods, and the disappointment must be written all over my face because he quickly adds, "He won't be here long. Mr Swain's got another bumper race coming up next month. He wants to make sure that everything is running smoothly leading up to it. This place is going to get very busy."

"Mr Swain must trust Sebastian a lot."

"They've been good friends for years."

I smile at him weakly, immediately thinking back to that fancy dress photo. If I weren't aware they were friends, I would've assumed they were brothers. The resemblance is freaky.

"What do you think of Sebastian?" I find myself asking.

"I don't know him. He's a bit on the snobby side, but he seems alright, I guess."

There's something else.

Something I can't quite put my finger on.

I return to work, and I tell myself it's nothing. It becomes old news. By the end of the day, I forget all about it.

# Chapter Twenty-Three

SOME PEOPLE GET EXCITED ABOUT BIRTHDAYS, BUT NOT ME. I checked my account this morning, only to find that I am fifty thousand pounds richer, yet I feel indifferent.

Am I supposed to feel happy that I suddenly have a ridiculous amount of money? Is it weird that I don't care?

Paying Mr Swain back is my main priority, and once I've returned what I owe him, I feel like a weight has been lifted off my shoulders. I also agreed that we would go on a house hunt soon. If I use my father's money, I would rather put it towards a new home—something that will benefit us in the long term. I'll keep whatever funds I have left for uni, presuming I get 'in.'

Since applying to Sloanville University, I've eagerly checked my emails for that acceptance letter, but I haven't received any news yet.

My birthday mainly consists of my mother singing her version of 'Happy Birthday' to me at precisely ten in the morning, and then I head into college, acting casual. So far, nobody has detected that it's my birthday, and if I play my cards right, I should be able to keep this up for the rest of the day.

Unfortunately, Josie happens to be waiting for me when I get to class. She launches herself at me full throttle and starts choking me to death in the middle of the classroom. Her energy is contagious, and I don't know whether it should excite or worry me a little.

I blow some of her hair out of my eyes and pat her roughly on the back as she finally breaks away, allowing me to catch my breath.

"Why didn't you tell me it's your birthday?" she squeals, attracting my classmate's attention.

My stomach sinks to the floor.

"How do you know it's my birthday?" I hiss, annoyed that she had just announced it to the world.

*Now everybody knows.*

"It's on your Facebook page. I had a reminder pop up this morning."

I thought I had deleted Facebook ages ago.

I take my phone out of my bag, re-download the Facebook app and try logging in. I gawk at the number of notifications I've gotten over the years. I can't remember ever being this popular.

"Woah. You haven't used Facebook in a while, have you? No wonder you haven't been responding to any of my messages," Josie says, eyes fixed on the screen in amazement.

"I'm not keen on social media."

*Not after I was publicly humiliated on every social media site known to humanity.*

"You're the only person I know who doesn't use it."

"It's not for everyone. Besides, why do some people want to share every moment of their lives online? What is up with people taking pictures of their food and posting about it twenty-four-seven? Just eat already. Nobody cares what you had for breakfast, lunch or afternoon tea."

Josie goes a bit red, and I can tell by her reaction that she's one of *those* people. I've just described her and probably most of her friends and family.

"Look, can you please not mention that it's my birthday to anybody else? I don't want people knowing," I plead, lowering my voice to a whisper.

"My lips are sealed!" she sings, returning to her seat.

*I'm not convinced.*

Grayson arrives late to class, which is the most surprising part of my morning. I have to check him twice because he's wearing designer glasses. Glasses suit him, but Grayson could wear a paper bag to college and still look good. I guess that is the perk of resembling a Calvin Klein model.

"Hey, what did I miss?" he asks, sliding into his chair.

"Oh, Ricky was just giving us a pep talk, that's all."

"Nothing out of the ordinary then."

"I didn't know you wore glasses," I blurt out, unable to hide my curiosity.

"I couldn't find my contacts this morning," he grumbles.

"Is that why you're running so late to class?"

"No. I hit some traffic on the way over. This herd of sheep came out of nowhere and started crossing the road, but it was an entire family, and they brought all their friends."

Giggles escape my throat, drawing the attention of a few classmates who turn around to see what's so amusing.

It sounds like the sheep have left Lakeside, and now we have to deal with them. How unfortunate.

"It's not funny! I was stuck for almost an hour! They wouldn't leave, not even when the farmer arrived to take them home. I've never seen anything like it," Grayson exclaims, puffing out a sigh.

I can't help but smile.

"Well, it looks like we've got a sheep problem. Better call the sheriff."

"We've always had a sheep problem. They're going to take over the world someday. I'm telling you."

"Bit of a stretch."

"It could happen. You never know," he counters.

"Somehow, I seriously doubt it. Of course, we shouldn't underestimate the inner workings of a sheep's mind, but they're not evil. It's the human race we need to worry about. We are the ones that are destroying our planet, not sheep and their tendency to block roads just for the sake of it."

Grayson is watching me, his eyes large. I rambled, but I always make my opinions known when I'm passionate about something.

"Bloody hell, who knew that talking about sheep could be such a sensitive topic," he says with a grunt.

"Shut up, Swain," I mumble back, grinning.

• • •

I underestimated how much can change within a week.

Confidently approaching the lunch table, I spot a new face in our group, making me question reality for a second. Did I miss something, or is Shelley Matthews associating herself with the 'Barnett College wannabes' as she used to put it?

Josie's eyes light up when I reach the lunch table, and she says, “Yey! Skye is here.”

*At least someone is happy to see me.*

Why is Shelly invading our table?

I try to say all this to Josie without moving my lips, but she's completely oblivious. I flick some hair out of my eyes and sit down, watching all the girls interact like best friends. I don't get it. We didn’t like Shelly the last time I checked.

“What's up with Shelly?”

Josie looks at me blankly. “What do you mean?”

“Well, she never usually sits with us.”

I don't know how I feel about this new seating arrangement. I'm not happy about it at all.

“Oh yeah, well, we're friends now.”

“Since when?”

*More like, why?*

“I'm not sure. This project has brought everyone closer together. I knew it would work out in the end.”

*This project is messing with people's heads. That's what it's doing.*

Grayson casually slides into the seat beside me, prompting me to reluctantly shift over and make room for him at the table.

*First, Shelly, now Grayson. Who's next?*

"Talking about me again, are you Skye?" he teases, nudging my arm.

I roll my eyes, determined not to feed his ego.

"Don't flatter yourself, Swain."

"I know I'm good to look at, but I'm trying to eat here."

My gaze turns icy and he starts having a speedy conversation with Shelly from across the table. She fires me a sneaky glare while nobody else is looking.

*That girl is so fake.*

Grayson spins to me again, disrupting the growing tension.

"I'm throwing a private party at my dad's lake house on Saturday night. You should come," he says casually.

*I'm starting to think Mr Swain owns half of Lakeside.*

If I went to his party, it would be too easy to fall back into old patterns.

I'm faced with some pros and cons.

**PRO** - I get to experience a proper party that doesn't just involve a couple of cans of beer and music playing from somebody's iPhone in the background.

**CON** - Grayson is going to be there.

**PRO** - It's a chance to get out of the house.

**CON** - Grayson is going to be there.

**PRO** - Who knows what Grayson will get up to and what I'll later be able to document?

**CON** - Grayson is going to be there.

**PRO** - I might have some fun.

I've attended many parties, but none were good experiences. They all turned out to be complete disasters, and I don't want to relive my past or get wrapped up in it.

"Thanks for the invitation, but I'll pass," I tell him, deciding that the cons outweigh the pros.

"Oh, come on, live a little. Let your hair down, woman," he insists with a playful grin.

"My hair *is* down."

"You know what I mean."

Grayson glances over at Josie, and it's not a good time because she is aggressively stabbing her milk carton with a straw. She has that serial killer look in her eyes, and it's incredibly worrying. Even Grayson seems a little weirded out, but then I see a ghost of a smile appear on his face like she's amused him.

"Hey, Josie!"

Josie's head shoots up in a million different directions, and she almost knocks the carton off the table when she realises Grayson is trying to get her attention. She pushes her glasses up so they're not hanging off the bridge of her nose and stares back at him, her face turning a deep shade of red.

"Pass me your carton," Grayson says, sounding suspiciously friendly.

*What is he up to?*

Carefully, Josie does as he asks, and Grayson stabs the straw into the carton with one quick swipe. He hands it back to her, and I'm convinced she is slowly turning into a lobster.

"Thank you," she mutters nervously.

"No problem. Happy to help."

He flashes her his most charming smile and returns

to eating his pasta, utterly unaware that Josie is still staring after him, a look of longing in her eyes.

*Oh. I finally understand.*

Grayson is Josie's crush.

How come I never noticed before? How come I never even considered that Grayson might be the boy she was talking about?

It explains a lot, but at the same time, I don't get it. I'm not attracted to Grayson, so seeing him through Josie's eyes is hard. He is good-looking if she's into the whole prim and proper thing.

Poor Josie.

Grayson probably hasn't even noticed her, especially since he's dating that wench of a girl, Sophie. She would be better off looking elsewhere and forgetting about him if that is his type. If we're going to be friends, I'll have to help her forget about Grayson.

"Hey, do you fancy going to a party this weekend?" I ask her as everyone starts heading back to class.

Josie nods enthusiastically, unable to hide her excitement. She jumps around, and her pigtails fly everywhere.

"Yes! Yeah! I'd love to."

"Great. You can come to my house on Saturday, and we can get ready together."

There's no backing out of this now.

*What can go wrong?*

* * *

Everything is totally and utterly wrong.

Josie turned up at my house on Saturday and brought

a selection of dresses to try on, but they were the ugliest I've ever seen. She also got me a birthday gift, which was unexpected. She bought me a pair of golden hoop earrings that will go perfectly with the outfit I have planned for tonight.

I've straightened my hair for a change, and I'm wearing a bold red, knee-length dress. I'm not aiming to impress anyone at this party, but that still doesn't mean I don't want to make a lasting impression and look the best I can.

I've just started moving on to my makeup when Josie emerges from the bathroom in the ugliest dress yet. It's a washed-out colour, and giant teddy bears cover the bodice. It looks like it was either born and bred in the Victorian era or made for a young child to wear.

I pull a concerned face.

"Don't you have anything else?"

She lets out an exasperated sigh. "This is all I've got. Does it look that bad?"

*Does she want me to answer that?*

I walk over to her, her eyes growing wide and innocent.

"You're a beautiful girl, Josie, but these dresses don't do anything for you."

I do a quick wardrobe search and pick out a simple black dress. It still has the tag because I've been saving it for a special occasion, but Josie needs it more than I do.

"Try this on," I say, handing the dress over.

Josie stares down at it, sighs and then disappears into the bathroom for the fifth time tonight. While she's busy trying on the dress, I cake my face with foundation and suddenly realise what a bad idea that was. I've never been any good at doing my makeup, so I'm not sure I can salvage this monstrosity of an attempt.

*I don't want to look like an Oompa Loompa.*

I get a wet wipe and scrub my face just as Josie reappears and says,

"What do you think?"

I automatically spin around, and a gasp leaves my throat. It's incredible what the right dress can do for a person. It hugs her in all the right places and brings out the green in her eyes.

"Wow! You look beautiful."

She blushes. "Really? Are you sure it's okay?"

"Yes! It's more than okay. You look incredible!"

Josie turns to glance at herself in the mirror and does a little twirl.

"I don't look like myself, do I? What are people going to think?"

"They're going to be amazed."

"Maybe Grayson will finally notice me dressed like this." Her hands shoot up to her mouth, and she closes her eyes, squealing. "Crap! I didn't mean to say that out loud."

"Don't worry. I already know that Grayson is your crush."

"What? How? Is it that obvious?"

"Um, yeah. You constantly blush whenever he's around and stare at him a lot."

She buries her face in her hands. "Do you think that he's figured it out?"

I shake my head. "No, but Grayson is the kind of guy

who thinks every single girl on this planet fancies him, so you might not be completely off the hook."

Josie holds onto her stomach, and it's my turn to panic.

"Ugh! Hang on a second. I think I'm going to be sick!"

She rushes out of the room, and I brace myself for a theatrical evening.

The taxi drops us off at the party quite late, and we're left gawking at the modern-looking lake house towering above us. It has a perfect view of the lake below, and it's tucked away from all major roads—in the middle of nowhere.

There are many people here that I don't recognise. Some are gathered around a fire pit. Others hang out by the lake and sit near rocks by the water. I hear loud, rave music ripping through the air and feel anxious. I have to keep reminding myself that just because I'm at a party doesn't mean I will make the same mistakes I made when I was younger.

*This party is an opportunity to embrace the new me.*

We walk along the steep path, up a small hill and enter the lake house. It's crammed with people and smells of body spray and sweat combined. It's homier than I imagined, maintaining its modern theme, but it still feels like a timeless classic—a place you wouldn't find anywhere else.

I recognise some Lakeside students, and they glance at us with bemused looks as we walk through the main family room, and I feel my confidence fading. We dodge some party guests huddled in an alcove and stop at a refreshment table in the lounge area. Josie reaches for a plastic cup and fills it with some punch. I do the same to give off the impression that I'm busy doing something.

I knock back the last of my drink and almost choke on it when Grayson comes into focus. I watch multiple people shake his hand and crowd around him like he's some form of royalty. Sophie isn't anywhere close by. She's either not here yet or hasn't realised that her boyfriend has wandered off to do some exploring of his own.

"Oh look, it's Grayson!" Josie cries, staring dreamily at him from a distance.

Some of the crowd parts, and that's when he finally notices us, hiding in the corner. He smiles and waves but rubs his eyes as if he can't quite believe the girl standing next to me is Josie from class. She does look different, but different in a good way. I watch Josie's face fall as Sophie arrives at the scene, landing a sloppy kiss on Grayson's mouth. He's quick to pull away, and maybe I'm wrong, but he didn't seem to enjoy that kiss very much.

*I am going to have to play Matchmaker tonight.*

"Let's dance!" I scream, dragging Josie away from Grayson and straight towards the group of dancing bodies.

She shakes her head frantically, refusing to cooperate.

"I can't dance," she admits.

"Me neither. That's the fun of it. Just pretend nobody else is here."

Josie awkwardly flaps her arms like a penguin and

bumps into the other dancers. Time passes, and we both become less self-conscious and more confident. It's surprisingly fun. I'm far from a skilled dancer. I'm clumsily shuffling my feet out of sync with the beat, but everybody's enjoying themselves far too much to care about my lack of coordination.

A Becky Hill song blasts through the speakers, and we wave our arms in the air, the room erupting into a wild frenzy. I twirl around and notice a boy has joined Josie on the dance floor. The pair of them are holding hands and swaying to the music.

*My matchmaking plan is working.*

I'm dancing in my little bubble for a while—getting sucked into the music and the electric atmosphere, but it doesn't last long because I feel a frantic tap on my arm, and I realise Josie has stopped dancing. Something seems to have caught her eye.

It's Grayson.

He's effortlessly navigating through the crowd, heading straight towards us. The boy who had been dancing with Josie a few seconds ago has ventured off to dance with someone else, and now she is biting ferociously at her fingernails, freaking out.

"Crap! Grayson's coming over here. What should I say? I'm not prepared! I always say stupid things whenever I'm around him. I can't seem to string two sentences together."

"Be cool. You've got this," I reassure her.

Grayson joins us, and she loses her resolve completely.

"Hi, Grayson! Hi!" she yells, deafening me.

"Hey, Josie. Is that a new dress?" he asks, being overly friendly with her, as per usual.

"Skye was kind enough to let me borrow it."

"It looks good on you," he says with a wink.

Josie starts fanning her face, which is turning crimson from the compliment. Grayson takes a long swig of his beer, his eyes finally capturing mine. Nerves tickle my stomach as his gaze subtly moves up and down my body, confusing me. He lowers the tip of the bottle away from his mouth, and I'm relieved to see his wicked grin return before things get weird.

"Skye! It's nice to see you're mingling with the rest of civilisation."

"Yeah, well, I thought I'd see what all the fuss was about."

"What's your verdict so far?" he challenges, his eyes twinkling.

"I'm still deciding."

His grin widens, and he gazes into my eyes for another long second.

"I'm glad you came. Will you be sticking around?"

"We'll probably be going soo—"

"Yes! We'll be staying!" Josie interrupts.

Grayson is quickly whisked away to do the keg while a boisterous crowd of people chant and holler together in the middle of the room. He effortlessly drinks a yard of beer like it's the easiest thing in the world.

*Why does he have to be good at everything?*

"He's so cool, isn't he?" Josie whispers, primarily to herself.

The keg madness continues, and I let my gaze

wander around the room. My stomach flips when I recognise a familiar face in the crowd.

Vicky Monroe faces forward, and her mouth drops open the moment she notices me. We haven't seen each other since high school, so it's been a while, and she looks just as surprised to see me here as I am to see her. I watch her turn to whisper to her friend, and now they're both staring over and giggling.

The room suddenly feels so small.

I feel like I'm going to pass out.

"I need to get some fresh air," I tell Josie, desperate to leave.

"Okay. Do you want me to come with you?" she asks, eyes still glued to Grayson's impressive keg performance.

I can tell she wants to stay. It would be selfish of me to drag her away just because I've seen a flash from my past.

"Stay here. I won't be long."

I go outside, looking for a nice, quiet place to sit and think. I start walking down to the furthest end of the lake and keep walking until the lake house is out of sight. I crawl onto a large rock overlooking the lake and watch the water crash against the rocks so rapidly and aggressively it is quite evident that a storm is brewing.

I take a quick photo of the scenery around me and post it to Facebook with the caption; **Calm before the storm.** I might be a social media critic, but I can see why people might enjoy being on it. On the bright side, you can stay connected with people. However, there are few people I want to remain connected with these days.

My inbox is full of conversations that I never got

around to reading. A lot of them are from girls spamming me with hate mail. I bet some of them are from Vicky and her friends. I spend the next ten minutes deleting people from my friend list, which happens to be the majority.

The breeze picks up, blowing my hair into a frenzy. I tuck some of it behind my ears, but fighting against the wind is ultimately pointless. I can't fight a battle that I won't win. The lake sounds like it's breathing, and I've noticed that the wind has picked up dramatically since I arrived. Being out in the dark is also terrifying, especially since this area is lonely, and I seem to be the only person around.

I sit there a little longer until the temperature drops and realise I've been out here for nearly half an hour. The thought of re-joining the party and seeing Vicky again is nauseating, but I can't keep trying to run away from my past. Eventually, I'll have to face it. If I don't return to the party, I've played straight into her hands. I need to show her that I'm not afraid of her anymore.

I clutch onto myself, jump off the rock and land awkwardly on the grass, twisting my ankle. I begin to limp my way back towards the lake house and feel a speck of rain hit the bridge of my nose, bringing my worst fears to life.

I look up at the cloudy sky and scowl.

*Why am I always caught in a thunderstorm?*

I rush up some steps, expecting to hear people chattering away to each other and for the loud music to introduce itself again, but I'm met with silence.

*That's odd.*

The firepit has been abandoned, and the lake house is still—like nobody was ever there.

The music has stopped entirely.

There are no cars.

I'm the only person here, which is alarming.

*What the heck is going on?*

*Where is everybody?*

A lightning flash brightens the sky, and I jump as the heavens open. A chorus of rain belts down at me, and I rush towards the lake house for shelter, my ankle throbbing with every step.

The door is locked when I get there, and I yank on the handle repeatedly.

"Hello! Grayson! Is anybody in there?"

The door is bolted shut.

*Crap. What am I going to do?*

My phone buzzes in my bag, and I see I've had a new message from Josie. I'm surprised the signal on my phone is still above one bar. I try swiping the rain off my screen with my finger to see what the message says.

JOSIE

Are you home yet? X

I bring up the keypad and start typing a reply. My fingers keep hitting the wrong buttons. They're starting to shrivel up.

SKYE

I'm still at the lake house. Where did everyone go?

JOSIE

OMG. Are you still there? 😱 X

SKYE

Yeah. What's going on? What happened?

JOSIE

The police showed up and evacuated everybody from the lake house. They mentioned something about a storm.

I can't believe I missed all of that.

JOSIE

Sorry, Skye! I thought that you had left because this girl called Vicky told me that she saw you get into a taxi x

*Ugh. Vicky Monroe. What a cow.*

She's still causing trouble after all these years. Some people will never change.

JOSIE

How are you going to get home? x

That's a good question.

I have no idea.

SKYE

I'll find a way. Don't worry about it.

JOSIE

Let me know when you've made it back safely x

SKYE

I will. Thanks x

First, I need to get out of the rain before I catch my death. My dress is sticking to every inch of me, and I don't even want to know what my hair looks like.

I run under a large oak tree and crouch beneath it, hoping the leaves will protect me against the torrential downpour. I could try to get a taxi, but getting one at this time of the night will be challenging. I could ring Grayson, but I don't want him to know I'm stranded here.

There's only one other person I can think of.

I dial Rory's number and wait patiently for him to answer. Luckily, his voice is introduced after the first ring, and his tired voice echoes, "Hello?"

"Hey. It's Skye."

This seems to wake him up.

He clears his throat. "Skye... Is everything okay?"

"No. Not really," I tell him, shivering.

"What's wrong?"

"I went to this party, and everybody left. So, I'm stranded. Is there any chance you could come and get me?"

I hear a lot of shuffling in the background, and hope rises in my chest.

"Where are you?"

"I'm at Grayson's lake house in Lakeside."

The line goes dead, and I worry I've lost him momentarily.

"Are you still there?" I check, growing anxious.

“Yeah. Send me the address. I’ll be there as soon as possible,” he says in a gravelly voice.

“Thank you so much!”

I glance up at the sky.

*It doesn't look like it's going to stop raining anytime soon.*

I end the call, quickly send Rory the address and cuddle up against the tree, rubbing my arms to get the blood circulation flowing in them again.

Finally, my eyes drift shut.

*Let's hope I don't die of hypothermia in the meantime.*

# Chapter Twenty-Four

I'M FLOATING, OR MAYBE I'M FLYING.

My eyes pop open, and I realise that someone is carrying me. Rory holds me up against his chest as he strides towards his motorbike.

"Skye, can you stand up for me for a second?"

I nod, but I don't want to lose his warmth. My entire body is frozen. I can't feel my toes. Slowly, Rory lowers me to the floor, and I wobble unsteadily. His eyes trace the contours of my body, starting from the tips of my pointed shoes, lingering over every curve and crevice of my damp red dress that clings to every inch of me.

I feel my body burn.

He's dressed in dark jeans, a black t-shirt that shows off his broad shoulders and a leather biker jacket. His dark, wet hair tumbles over his forehead.

*He looks good in the rain.*

Without hesitation, Rory removes his jacket, enveloping me in its warmth. He carefully zips me up, ensuring I'm snugly tucked inside. Placing the helmet on my head, I straddle the seat of his motorbike, my arms encircling his torso as he revs the engine and speeds off.

The rain hammers down from above like its sole purpose is to torture us, and once we're back on the road, I clutch onto Rory's midriff, shivering uncontrollably, my stomach rumbling.

"Are you hungry?" he shouts, reading my mind.

"Y—yeah," I mumble, barely able to get my words out because my body is wracking with shivers.

"There's a McDonald's a couple of blocks away. Should we stop there and wait for the storm to die down?"

At this point, I'd be happy to stop anywhere for some food and shelter.

"Sounds like a good idea."

Rory parks in a large car park five minutes later and turns off the engine. We leave the comfort of his bike, and I look through one of the McDonald's windows, happy to see that the place is practically empty. The automatic doors open and we step inside the building. Warmth captures me in a tight hug, and gentle music plays over the speakers.

The girl serving behind the McDonald's counter looks terrified of me. I probably look like I've been dragged through a hedge backwards. After placing our orders, I trail behind Rory toward a secluded table at the back of the room. Sinking into the plush leather seat, I'm relieved to be able to rest my legs finally.

"Thanks so much for coming to get me. I'm sorry that I dragged you into this mess."

"Don't worry about it. You would've done the same for me."

"Yeah. I guess. Although I doubt I could've transported us back to Barnett on my bike. Might've been a bit of a struggle."

Rory chuckles and inches his body closer. The motion causes his leg to brush against mine from under the table. It's an accident, but nerves still flood my stomach anyway.

"How's your mother doing?" he asks casually.

It's a simple question, yet I'm struggling to answer it. He already knows more about my mother than anybody else, so it's not like it's a highly personal question. I have nothing to hide anymore.

"Sorry. I shouldn't have asked," he apologises when the silence stretches out.

"No, it's fine. I'm just not used to people asking me about her, that's all." I glance down at my trembling hands and clasp them at the table. "My mother's not doing any better. She hasn't had an episode in a while, but I have to be strong for her when it all goes wrong, and it *will* go wrong—it's just a matter of time."

"There's got to be a reason why your mother acts the way she does."

"I'm not sure what happened. I think my dad had a lot to do with it. He left the scene before I was born, but he must've done something to hurt my mother because she never talks about him."

"My dad isn't around either, so I get what you're saying. Unfortunately, I *do* know who he is. There are days I wish I didn't."

"Is there any part of you that misses him?"

Rory's eyes ignite with so much anger and hostility I worry I've crossed the line by asking him that question.

"Not really. He caused destruction wherever he went. It was my father's choice to drink and drive that night, yet I was the one who was made to suffer because of it. Kyle wanted to fight me every chance he got—not that I could blame him. I was treated like a criminal for something I didn't even do. So no, I don't miss him."

"I'm... I'm sorry. I didn't even know about your dad or the crash when we were still in high school. I think I lived in an alternate universe where the world only seemed to revolve around me. I failed to notice anything else," I say, shaking my head.

"It's not like we were super friendly with each other back then anyway, and you had your own stuff going on."

"True, but I still wish I'd been a bit nicer to you."

He's quick to dismiss my sympathy. "It works both ways. I wasn't very nice to you either. I treated you just as unfairly. I had a reputation for getting into fights. You had a reputation for sleeping around. We both had our coping mechanisms, I guess."

"That's the saddest part."

He hangs his head. "Maybe you should look at your situation from an entirely different perspective. Your father's absence might have saved you from facing further disappointment. You don't know what type of man he is. What if you've dodged a bullet?"

*Wow.*

This is the first time I've thought about it like that. A

fresh perspective is always so eye-opening. Everything happens for a bigger purpose, and for whatever reason, my dad wasn't meant to be in my life. He wasn't meant to see me grow up in the world. I've always loved the idea of him, but what if Rory is right? What if I have been saved somehow?

Rory heads to collect our food, and I retrieve my phone from my bag, glancing at the screen. There's a single message from Grayson, sent approximately twenty minutes ago.

GRAYSON

Hey. Just checking in. The police showed up out of nowhere and rushed everyone out of the lake house. I should have texted you sooner, but everything happened so fast. I made sure Josie got home safe.

I smile at that.

*At least he has a conscience.*

SKYE

I'm still alive.

His reply is almost instant.

GRAYSON

Good. Btw happy belated birthday! 🥳

SKYE

How did you know it was my birthday?

GRAYSON

Josie told me.

I knew I couldn't trust her not to say anything.

GRAYSON

Do you fancy meeting up to work on the project tomorrow? It'll be our last chance to meet before the presentations on Tuesday.

SKYE

Sure. I'm free tomorrow.

GRAYSON

Great. Wear something casual.

SKYE

I am the queen of casual 💅

GRAYSON

I've noticed. I'll pick you up at 6 pm sharp. Be ready.

I'm on the verge of sending him another sarcastic response when Rory returns. We start eating, occasionally pausing to engage in conversation. I tell him about the project, and he doesn't interrupt me once. Instead, he listens to me talk as if it's the most interesting thing in the world.

Our conversation flows effortlessly, and there aren't any awkward spaces. It's natural and easy. Yet, my heart always seems to skip a beat whenever he looks at me. I can see why a girl might fall for him. I can imagine that Rory has broken a few hearts in the past, and for all I know, he might already like someone else. That thought alone is like a bitter punch to the gut. I need to stop fantasising. I don't even understand these feelings that resurface whenever I'm around him. It's best if I ignore them.

The next question rests on the tip of my tongue, and when I can no longer keep it to myself, I blurt out, "Have you ever been in a relationship?"

Rory's love life has nothing to do with me, but I am too curious to hear about it.

"I've dated different girls, but it was never anything serious. What about you?"

"No. Never. When I used to sleep around, I sometimes wished the boy would change his mind—that he'd *see* me for a change. It sounds stupid, but I regret it so much. All of it. You have no idea."

I glance away from him, all the memories flooding back. The breath sweeps out of me when Rory leans forward to grab my hand. The action itself surprises us both.

"Hey, look at me."

I drag my eyes up.

His face is a combination of warmth and understanding. It makes me want to cry.

"That's not who you are anymore," he reminds me, "and it doesn't sound stupid, so don't even think like that."

I wipe away a few stray tears.

I thought I was beginning to move on from my past, but seeing Vicky again has brought back all those familiar thoughts and feelings, which led me to believe I was nothing but a lost cause, a complete waste of space—that I'm dirty and worthless.

Batting my eyelashes, I hope it will eliminate the tears, but the emotion is too raw.

"I saw Vicky Monroe at the party tonight. It was such a kick in the teeth. I swear, the way she looked at me... it was like I was back in high school."

"Who cares what Vicky thinks?"

I lower my eyes to the floor. "I do. It might seem like I can handle anything, but I'm quite sensitive."

Rory shakes his head violently. "I wish I'd known you back then. I wouldn't have let anyone mistreat you. I can't change the past, but I'm here for you now. I'm not going anywhere."

He means it, but I'm used to people leaving me. I can't cling to his promise because there's a strong chance he will disappoint me, just like all the others.

"Do you remember Jarrett Baker?"

"Who doesn't remember Jarrett Baker? He was on the football team, right?" Rory recalls.

My chest tightens. "Yeah, he was."

Mixed emotions rush through me as I remember myself falling for Jarrett's charms. In the beginning, he showered me with affection and made it seem like I was the only girl in the world. I thought he might've been different.

"I was sleeping around way before the whole Jarrett thing happened, but I did genuinely like him. When word got out that I slept with *him*, it tarnished my reputation in more ways than one. The whole school made me feel like I shouldn't exist. Vicky and her friends were horrible—they made high school hell. Jarrett didn't exactly help by posting the nude pictures I sent him online. I was lost. I'd never felt so alone," I say, sadness overwhelming me.

Rory stares at me sympathetically. "I was hardly ever at school, so I don't remember hearing all the details, but I remember some parts. I never saw the pictures, although that was all anybody ever talked about for a while. No girl deserves to be treated like that."

A tear rolls down my face, and I quickly swipe it away.

"You're right. They don't."

Silence envelops us, and Rory's unwavering gaze holds mine captive. The rest of the world has become a complete blur, and all I can focus on is the brown-haired boy sitting in front of me, staring at me like I might matter.

"For what it's worth, despite how Jarrett and those other boys treated you, I finally *see* you, Skye. Clearly."

My heart just exploded.

After an adventurous evening, Rory parks outside my house, and the engine cuts off. We step away from his motorbike, and I slowly step towards my front door, spinning toward him.

"Thanks again."

"We seem to be thanking each other a lot lately," he says, patting me on the head and ruffling up my hair.

"I know. What's up with that?"

I remember that I'm still wearing his leather jacket. I take it off and hold it out to him. Creating a diversion is easier because I need to give my heart time to calm itself down.

"You'd better take this back before I forget."

He waves me away. "It's fine. Keep it."

"Rory, I can't. This probably cost you a fortune. Real leather isn't cheap."

"Consider it a birthday gift."

I freeze.

"How did you know–"

"We're Facebook friends. It came up on my newsfeed while we were at McDonald's."

"Seriously?"

*I should have deactivated my Facebook account when I had the chance.*

"Why didn't you tell me it was your birthday?"

"Because my birthday was on Wednesday, and I'm not a fan of birthdays anyway. It's not important."

His brows rise in disbelief. "It's supposed to be *your* day, Skye. I think that makes it important."

"Birthday or not, I can't accept your gift. It's too much."

"You need that jacket more than I do."

It fits me nicely and could pass as a gender-neutral coat.

"Are you sure?"

"Yes! It's yours."

"Okay, well, thanks. That's sweet of you." Glancing at my house, a sense of loneliness creeps in, and I realise I don't want to be alone. "Do you want to come inside for a cup of tea and some birthday cake? We still have plenty to spare."

Rory hesitates while heat creeps onto my face.

"How can I say no to some birthday cake?" he finally replies with a grin.

We step inside the narrow passageway, and I'm sensitively aware that Rory is right behind me. I can feel his hot breath brushing against my neck as we head into the living room. I switch the light on and shriek when my mother appears out of the darkness, standing in her pyjamas and looking furious. My eyes immediately focus on an empty wine glass on the coffee table.

"What time do you call this?" she demands, arms crossed, her expression changing once she notices Rory. "What the hell is *he* doing here?"

"Rory gave me a lift home from the party."

"I've already told you I don't want you hanging out with this boy."

"Mum... seriously, what is the matter with you?" I cry, utterly mortified by her behaviour.

"I think I'd better go," Rory says quietly.

"That would probably be for the best," my mother fires back.

I grab hold of his arm and stare up at him. "Don't go. I want you to stay."

"This is my house. He's not staying, and that's final," Mum declares, cutting across me, her voice slurred.

I fold my arms across my chest.

"Fine. We'll both leave."

Rory places his hand on my shoulder. "I would never do anything to harm your daughter, Miss Clemons. I honestly don't want to cause any trouble here."

"Well, that's a first. I've heard a lot of stories about

you, Rory. Trouble seems to run in your family by the sounds of it, and quite frankly, you are not the kind of person I want my daughter to be associating herself with."

I can't believe what I'm hearing. She's throwing a load of judgement in his face and hasn't even given him a chance. He shouldn't have to redeem himself or prove anything to anyone.

"If you've heard what people have said about me, and you believe them, then I don't suspect that there is anything I can do to change your opinion of me, Miss Clemons. Sadly, the truth can be twisted these days." His eyes fill with disappointment once he turns to face me. "I'll see you at work, Skye."

"I'm so sorry," I whisper as he walks away.

I wait for the front door to close before I unleash my anger.

"What is your problem?" I scream, my heart thumping wildly in my chest.

"I don't want you bringing boys home with you, especially not boys with bad intentions."

I let out a horrified gasp. "Do you hear yourself? I don't think you have the right to tell me who I can bring home. How many men have drunkenly snuck into our house over the years? I think I've lost count."

"That's not fair, Skye."

"Oh, and it's fair that you get to pick and choose who I can hang out with? Please. Give me a break," I shake my head incredulously and stomp upstairs, but her voice forces me to stop halfway.

"Where do you think you're going? You still need to eat your birthday cake."

"My birthday was three days ago. I'm going to my room because I don't feel like celebrating anymore."

I run upstairs and slam my bedroom door behind me. Batman watches me from my nightstand and then leaves me to drown in my tears. I turn off the light and throw myself into bed. I should text Rory to apologise for my mother's behaviour. He might not see it until tomorrow morning, but it feels like the right thing to do.

SKYE

Hey. I'm so sorry about what just happened.

I wait and wait and wait for a reply. Finally, ten minutes later, I shoot up from bed when I receive a new message.

RORY

Hey. It's okay. Are you alright?

I'm relieved he's not mad, but I'm far from okay. I'm angry, frustrated, annoyed and confused. Mostly, I'm disappointed that the night had to end on such a sour note.

SKYE

I'll be fine. I can't believe she spoke to you like that.

His reply takes much longer this time. Again, it puts me on edge.

RORY

Don't worry about it. I'm only a phone call or text away if you need anything.

SKYE

Thanks.

I send Josie a message to let her know I'm safe and sound, and then I shut off my phone and attempt to get some sleep.

My mother's footsteps shuffle across the carpet as she enters my room. I have no idea what time it is, but I've been awake this entire time. Her voice calls out to me in the darkness, and my eyes promptly fly open when she lowers herself onto my bed and cuddles up beside me, but I keep my back turned so I don't have to face her.

"I'm sorry. I've drunk too much wine. I overreacted," she apologises, burying her head into my shoulder.

I press my head into the pillow, close to tears, unable to hide my frustration. "Rory isn't a bad guy. He doesn't have a hidden agenda."

"I just saw code red. Seeing you together again made me panic. I thought that there was something bigger going on. I mean, why else would you bring him home?"

"We're just friends!" I spit out, speaking the words under my breath.

"I didn't mean to scare him off."

"Luckily for me, Rory isn't the kind of guy who gets scared away very easily. He's made it clear that he's planning to stick around for a long time," I say to her.

"You think that you can trust him?"

"I don't trust anyone, but he isn't looking to screw me over. I am one hundred percent certain of that."

She lets out a shuddery sigh. "Well, I guess you know him better than I do, but I have every right to be a little cautious. That boy has been causing trouble around town for years."

"Everybody wants to be Rory's enemy because they hate his dad, but he doesn't deserve to be treated like a criminal for something he didn't even do."

My mother's head dips in remembrance.

"The crash was all over the news. The whole town mourned Josh's death because he was such a well-liked and popular boy."

"Did you know his family well?"

"Not personally, but I did go to the funeral to pay my respects. I remember seeing Josh's younger brother, Kyle, break his heart when they had to say their final goodbyes. They were extremely close. The biggest surprise was when Rory showed up at the funeral with his grandmother. That's when it all kicked off. Kyle was furious."

A twinge of sadness tugs at my heart once I'm reminded of the lingering grudge between Kyle and Rory. Their feud only seems to have gotten worse as the years have passed, and they say that time heals, but in some cases, it doesn't.

"Initially, I felt sympathy for Rory," my mother continues, "he was only twelve when his father was sent to prison, and that must have been incredibly difficult to process, but as time went on, I kept hearing stories about him—that he was involved in vandalism after vandalism and constant confrontations, and I couldn't help but wonder if he was veering down the same destructive path his father walked. That's why I was anxious when I first saw the two of you together. I was worried that he might be a bad influence on you."

"I understand your concern, Mum, but I have my own mind. Rory's done some things he's not proud of, yet he's owned up to them and wants to move on. Doesn't everyone deserve a second chance?"

"Yeah, I guess they do."

"At the end of the day, every story has two sides. Yes, Kyle lost his brother, and that loss is immeasurable, but don't forget that Rory has also suffered. His life was destroyed in a matter of seconds, all because of a stupid decision his father made, and he's been judged severely for it ever since. This must've impacted him in ways we will never fully understand."

A fragile understanding emerges between us, and we lay there in complete silence for a good minute or two, a thought suddenly crossing my mind. I've got to voice it before I chicken out altogether.

"I've been thinking a lot about my father lately. I want to know how you met."

It's as if I've just told her we're in a nuclear war, but we've avoided the subject long enough. I deserve to hear the truth. All my life, I've had questions about my dad. I will constantly be wondering about him, and it won't stop.

"It's a long story, Skye."

"I'm sure I can keep up."

I find myself leaning towards her, ready to hear her version of events for the first time.

"I met your dad when I was eighteen. I gate-crashed a Lakeside party with one of my friends and bumped into him at the bar."

I was not expecting her to say that.

She met him on Lakeside territory, which changes things because it could mean my father is from Lakeside.

Does he still live there now?

Or was he gate-crashing himself?

"He offered to buy me a drink. He was handsome and seemed well off. I had no idea why he was standing around talking to me. One thing led to another, and we ended up back at his place."

I hear her swallow, and it forces my anxiety to spike. I grab her hand and hold it tightly, preparing myself for what's coming.

"Then what happened?" I ask, trying to control my breathing.

"I found out that I was pregnant a couple of weeks later, so I went to tell him the news, and he turned me away–said some awful things—that he wanted nothing to do with me or the baby. He demanded a DNA test and eventually agreed to send money to support you, but that was all he was willing to offer."

My hatred for this man has grown. He didn't want to accept any responsibility for his actions.

"Did you ever see him again?"

"No. Never. He kept his distance, and I kept mine."

"But did he ever message you to ask how I was? Was there no contact at all?"

"Our connection was cut off immediately. He changed his number, and I was cast out. From then on, everything went downhill. Getting pregnant at eighteen was not part of the plan, but once people found out, I was judged severely for it."

I move closer, cradling my mother's hand in mine.

"When you were born, you gave me hope and a purpose, Skye. I was responsible for caring for you—this new creation, and for that first year, I gave you as much love as I possessed. Things were good. A friend who lived a few doors down was supporting me. She was very encouraging, especially after I lost my job at the restaurant."

*Bad luck seemed to be following her around.*

"When you were about two years old, my friend moved away, and I struggled to cope independently. I started bothering with the wrong crowd, turned to alcohol and dated some abusive people who made me believe I was getting what I deserved. The thoughts became unbearable," she says, causing a few tears to sting my eyes.

"It was like I had lost something, but I didn't know when or where I last had it. Soon, I started to realise that what I'd lost was myself. I didn't recognise that person anymore. It was a living hell. I couldn't see a way out."

My mother is a sobbing mess, and I let her head fall against my shoulder in defeat. She stays like that while I rub her back in slow, circular motions.

"I've made so many mistakes. I've let you down. I wasn't there. I put you in dangerous situations where you could have been seriously hurt. I'm so sorry for everything."

We're clinging to each other, eyes sore, faces moist from our weeping, and I realise that if I don't open up to her about my past now, I never will, but I'm also terrified that she'll be disappointed to hear the truth.

I can't hide the tremor in my voice as I begin to open up to her in ways I never have before. Reliving high school and re-telling the whole Jarrett Baker incident is so hard but freeing at the same time. The more I talk through what happened, the less and less it hurts.

"Are you disappointed in me?" I ask when I have nothing left to say.

My mother presses her forehead against mine, tears rolling down her face. "I could never be disappointed in you, Skye. I wish I could have been there for you. Why didn't you tell me sooner? I would have understood."

"I tried to... on numerous occasions, but it was never a good time. You were too drunk to take me seriously, or your attention was elsewhere. It felt wrong to tell you because you were having a mental breakdown. I didn't want to worsen things, so I stayed silent."

Her head bows. "I'm the true disappointment. You could never disappoint me if you tried."

I feel my features relax.

"I've been thinking a lot about what you said — about reaching out for help. I feel that maybe it might finally be time to do that."

I suck in a sharp breath. "Really? You're not just saying that because it's my birthday week, and you're trying to salvage it?"

"No. I mean it. I can't go on like this. It's not fair on either of us. I'm ready to take that next step. It's time to move forward."

This is the best birthday gift she could have ever given me, and even though I've gotten some closure tonight, there's still one gruelling thought lingering in the back of my mind.

If my father lives or used to live in Lakeside, he might be closer to home than I originally thought.

# Chapter Twenty-Five

"HAPPY BELATED BIRTHDAY!" GRAYSON SINGS, HANDING ME A small gift box when I open his car door and sit in the passenger's seat.

I had a wardrobe malfunction earlier on since I wasn't sure where Grayson was planning on taking me for our last study session. I assumed it was nowhere fancy, considering he ordered me to wear something casual. I'm wearing my slouchy mum jeans, a navy hoodie with Batman's face printed on the front, and my trusty old trainers.

*Casual to its highest standard.*

Grayson specifically told me to dress down for this little outing, so why is he wearing something opposite of casual? He's ready to go to the Oscars while I look like I'm about to run a marathon.

I stare down at his gift, scared to open it. "You didn't have to get me anything."

"It's not like I can't afford it."

This probably didn't cost him a penny. His bank

account is likely still intact, but I was raised to appreciate whatever I was given. It's incredibly thoughtful of him to buy me a birthday present. I don't take anything for granted.

Slowly, I unwrap the ribbon on the front, but whoever tied this must've intended to do it up as tightly as possible. Grayson is watching me struggle to open the box, and he's starting to get impatient.

"Come on, what's taking you so long? I can't start driving until you open the damn thing."

I set the box down on my lap and scowl. "Well, if you hadn't gone to the extreme of gift wrapping it, I probably would have opened the box by now. I mean, seriously, did you have to use *that* much ribbon?"

He snatches the box away and picks at the ribbon with his fingernails. He even tries biting it off with his teeth, but it's useless. The ribbon is safely secured around the edges and will not budge.

"You've made it worse now!" I yell.

"No, I haven't! I've loosened the ribbon!"

I didn't think it was possible to form knots out of knots, but he's pulled it off.

"Here's one for the project." I quickly clear my throat and put on a funny voice. "While Grayson Swain may excel at most things, he cannot wrap a present to save his bloody life."

"Oh, whatever, like you could have done a better job. We'll sort it out when we get to the pub."

He switches on the engine and pulls away from the kerb, tapping his fingers along the steering wheel. Meanwhile, I'm sitting there, wondering why he chose such a busy and chaotic location for our last study session. It's unexpected.

"We're going to a pub?"

Grayson keeps his eyes fixated on the road ahead. He looks pleased with himself for some reason.

"That's right."

"No offence, but you don't strike me as a local pub kind of guy."

"I'm full of surprises," he says with a wink.

A tangy smell of beer is in the air when we enter the pub, and it weirdly smells like home. Most of the tables are taken, but I spot one at the back of the room and quickly claim it before anyone else can. I remove Rory's leather jacket, which has officially become my new favourite piece of clothing, and then I scope the room for Grayson. It doesn't take me long to find him since he's the only person wearing a shirt and tie in this room, and he's waving his bank card around, trying to get the bar staff's attention.

The Angel is one of the oldest pubs in Barnett, and I've been coming here since I was old enough to walk. It's a coincidence that he brought me to my favourite bar because I'd never told him about this place. I wasn't sure he knew that it even existed.

It's a lovely, old-fashioned building and a hidden gem within the community. A small TV hangs over the mantelpiece, and a few men are crowded around it, deeply engrossed in a football match. I stare down at the coasters on the table and rub my sweaty palms together.

I can't relax, and I don't know why.

This is the last time I'll hang out with Grayson before we submit our presentations. I'm nervous because this might be my last chance to tell him the truth about my job at Trinity.

Ironically, *It's Now or Never* begins to play over the jukebox.

I jump when Grayson's face appears in front of mine.

"I can't get over the prices of these drinks! Didn't cost me a thing!" He places a pint of Coors on the table in front of me, and I sit up straight when he pulls out a chair and sits on it, taking a quick sip of his lemonade.

"Why did you bring me here?"

His eyes snap to mine, and he looks at me strangely as if he doesn't understand the question.

"I thought that it would be a nice gesture. I was tempted to take you to a fancy restaurant on my side of town, but I figured you'd appreciate something like this much more."

*Oh. Okay. That is quite thoughtful of him.*

I might look like a slob compared to Grayson, but I'd much rather enjoy being around like-minded people who don't care what I wear. The fact that he's thought about all this beforehand and has taken my feelings into account is very unlike him.

"Did I make the right decision?" he asks, awaiting my verdict.

I squeeze my eyes shut, struggling to hide my smile.

"Yes. You did."

Grayson fist pumps the air. "I knew it! I'm a genius."

"Don't let it get to your head, Swain."

"I've been meaning to ask. How's your presentation coming along?"

Truthfully, I've barely even started writing my presentation yet, and it's due on Tuesday. I have all these notes on Grayson, but I still need to work on putting them into long, meaningful sentences.

"Uh, it's getting there. What about you?"

He gives me a single nod, nothing short of confident. I wouldn't be surprised if he's already finished his presentation.

"It's going well," he says absentmindedly. "I sort of know what I want to say about you now."

My eyebrows rise. "You sort of know?"

"No need to worry. I've got this thing nailed."

"Same," I lie.

"Great," he says, grinning at me.

"Perfect."

"Fabulous."

"Splendid."

"Amazing."

I let out an exasperated laugh. "What are we doing?"

"I don't know! You started it! Do you come here often?"

"Now and again. You?"

He shakes his head roughly. "This is my first time."

"No way! I would never have guessed!" I lean forward and bat my eyelashes at him, blinking freakishly fast. "Has The Angel met your expectations, or are you still deciding?"

He casts a glance around the cosy pub and swallows. "Well, it's hard to answer you because a guy is sitting at the bar, and it looks like he wants to skin me alive. Do you see him?"

He briefly nods in the man's direction, and my eyes widen when I spot him. He is sitting on one of the bar stools, blatantly staring at us with a deep frown. Maybe that's just his face, but he doesn't have a nice one. If that's his daily expression, I feel sorry for whoever accidentally bumps into him on a bad day.

"Don't look at him!" Grayson hisses at me, fear in his eyes.

"You told me to look at him, you idiot!"

"I didn't tell you to have a staring contest with the guy. Are you trying to get us killed?" he wails, aggressively running his hand through his hair.

I've never seen him get this worked up before, but I would also be scared if I were him. That guy could crush Grayson into a grape if he wanted to. He's full of muscle, and tattoos cover his arms.

"Haven't you ever heard of a term called profiling? Just because some guy has a load of tattoos and looks like a professional wrestler doesn't necessarily mean he's out looking for a fight. I bet he's a big softie underneath."

"Well, I don't fancy finding out. The man is cleaning his teeth with a pocketknife right now."

My eyes wander back to the tattoo man.

Grayson is right. He is using his knife as a toothpick.

"I'm going to die!" Grayson cries, headbutting the table.

"You're not going to die!"

"This is how it usually happens in the movies. I've become a target. I'll never see the light of day again."

I groan into my hands. "This is real life, Grayson. Why do you always have to be so dramatic?"

"I'm not being dramatic! Sometimes, we have no choice but to stereotype people, Skye, because if we don't, we could risk some serious backlash, like, oh, I don't know, get ourselves killed, for example."

I flash him a grin. "You exaggerate, my friend."

His eyes narrow. "I'm a realist."

"So am I, but I don't judge people based on their appearance."

"You judged me the first time we met, didn't you? Isn't that the same thing?"

"Technically, yes, but I was going to give you the benefit of the doubt until you opened your mouth."

This conversation could be better. We're supposed to be bonding and learning about each other's lives. Instead, we're getting into a heated discussion over a man who has an alarming number of tattoos and uses a pocket knife to clean his teeth!

*I've got to steer us back on track.*

*We don't have much time left.*

"Let's remind ourselves what we're doing here for a second. The presentations are due in less than two days. We need to refocus," I tell him.

Grayson nods, breathing out heavily. "Fine."

I notice a dart board in the far corner of the room, and my eyes light up.

"I know just the thing that'll help us to unwind."

. . .

"Ugh! This is so annoying!" Grayson yells after his dart sails through the air and misses every number on the dartboard again.

I have concluded that he is a sore loser and sucks at playing darts.

*Turns out he isn't good at* ***everything*** *after all.*

"You're doing it wrong, that's why."

I grab his arm and reposition it at a slightly different angle to change the direction of his aim. Grayson looks down at me in confusion, and I suddenly realise that our bodies are only centimetres apart. He smells of expensive aftershave, and it's very enticing. I find myself breathing him and his scent, and then I jump away quickly, a little stunned to have had such an inappropriate thought cross my mind.

Grayson throws another dart, and it gets stuck in the wall.

"Crap!"

I burst out laughing.

"Don't worry. Nobody's going to handcuff you. If they do, they'll have to search for all the other people who missed the board before you."

"I'm out of practice," he says, turning red.

The game progresses, and Grayson hits higher numbers each time, beginning to get the hang of it, but it's still not enough. I claim my fourth win when my dart sails through the air and lands on a double twenty.

I jump around with excitement.

"I win again! Whoop, whoop, chicken soup!"

"Whatever, that was just pure luck."

I place my hands on my hips. "You are such a sore

loser! Why can't you accept that I am naturally gifted at darts?"

"What you just achieved had nothing to do with skill."

"It's called mojo. You either have it or you don't, darling," I say, flicking my hair to the side.

He glances away, smirking. "How about we make this a little more interesting, then?"

"I'm listening."

"How about whoever wins a round gets to ask a truth or dare question? We have to commit to the game whole-heartedly, though. No chickening out. A dare is a dare."

I salute him. "Got it."

Grayson miraculously claims his first win of the night a couple of shots later.

"Truth or dare," he fires at me.

"Truth."

"Have you ever lied to me?"

According to my brain, I've lied to him approximately fifty times since I've known him, but who's counting?

"Uh, I've changed my mind. I choose dare instead."

I don't even have to look at Grayson to know he's shaking his head at me.

"No swapping. Your fate has already been sealed. There's no turning back now."

I scramble for an answer but only think about his ugly, mustard-coloured shirt. "Okay... if you want me to be honest, then I will. I lied when I said that I liked the colour of your shirt earlier."

His smile vanishes as he glances down at his shirt and frowns. "What the hell is wrong with it?"

“Sorry, but I can't stand the colour. It's dull.”

“Blimey. I'm starting to wish I'd given you a dare question now. That was brutal.”

For the next hour, we fire truth-or-dare questions at each other. Grayson dares me to howl like a wolf for two minutes, which is the most embarrassing thing I've ever had to do. I dare him to keep two ice cubes in his mouth until they melt. He lasts ten seconds before spitting them out onto the carpet. Grayson dares me to start dancing on the table. I dare him to shout the first thing that pops into his head.

“Bumfluff!” he screeches at the top of his lungs, receiving a bunch of disapproving looks from people sitting near the bar.

It won’t be long before we’re thrown out of here, but I don’t care. I’m having the time of my life. I can't stop laughing. I might’ve peed myself a little.

“Oh my gosh. Stop. I can't cope. What does that even mean?”

He's holding onto his stomach, howling with laughter. “I have no idea.”

It's fair to say that we've just about outdone ourselves towards the end of the night, and the bar staff are fed up with us.

“Okay, I've got one last truth question for you,” I say with a slur.

Considering Grayson isn't drinking, he still has the time of his life.

He clasps his hands and rubs them together. “Go for it. I'm ready.”

“Do you love Sophie?”

"Uh..." He hesitates, and realisation settles in. "Love is a big word," he says with a shrug.

My mouth opens wide. "You can't even give me a straight answer, can you?"

"It's complicated, alright? I've only been dating Sophie for a couple of months. You can't fall in love with someone that fast."

"Love tends to work in mysterious ways. Sometimes, it can creep up on you when you least expect it."

"Well, hopefully, that won't happen to me anytime soon. I'd like to know when I'm in love, wouldn't you?"

I slowly lift my eyes to his. "Yeah. I would."

Grayson pulls up outside my house a couple of hours later, and I'm disappointed that the night is over. He's stone-cold sober, and I feel like I'm walking on stilts. Everything is either too loud, too quiet, too fast or too slow. There isn't an in-between.

"I had a lot of fun tonight, Skye," Grayson says softly.

"Yeah, me too."

"Oh! Your present. I almost forgot."

He passes the gift box to me, but the wrapping paper has been removed this time, and I gasp when I open the box and find a necklace shaped like a Belgian seashell inside. It's so beautiful. I have to stop myself from crying.

I hold the necklace close to my chest. "Grayson! What the heck?"

He refuses to look at me. "I could see how much you liked those Belgian chocolate seashells, and I thought it made sense to buy you a necklace in the shape of one...

even though it's not edible, and I'm pretty sure that if you tried to eat it, you would choke and probably die."

"That's good to know. I'm only eighteen. Believe it or not, I'd like to see my teenage years through until the end."

Grayson twitches his eyebrows. "Yeah... Well, you've gotten this far. It would be a shame if you flunked out on me now."

A warm feeling settles in the pit of my stomach.

I will always cherish this moment because we have come so far. I mean, look at us. We're not attacking each other. Grayson is still Grayson, just a slightly more like-able, improved version. After this experience, I hope we will continue to be friends.

We stay seated a few minutes more, and as I open the car door, Grayson's hand shoots out to stop me. It sits there on my arm, and we both stare at it. My breathing turns scattered — entirely out of rhythm with the erratic sounds of my heartbeat.

*What sort of mind trickery is this?*

*Since when has Grayson Swain made me nervous?*

The car feels very small and confined.

Grayson breaks eye contact, and my heart rate returns to its average speed.

"I'll see you on Tuesday," he says, more reserved and distant than ever.

I yank on the car door too aggressively and tumble onto the pavement, my head colliding with cold, hard gravel.

"Ahhhh!"

Grayson immediately exits the car, laughing as he crouches before me.

"I shouldn't be finding any of this funny, but you weren't exactly modest about the whole wheelbarrow incident, so it's about time I got my revenge."

"You're such a meanie!"

His eyes dance with amusement. "Meanie? Really?"

"It's the only comeback I could think of."

"The class viper has finally returned. I was beginning to miss her," he says, attempting to pick me up, but he loses balance, and we fall back to the ground in a heap. Grayson's leg lands on top of mine, crushing my ankle into the gravel.

"Ow!"

He scrambles away from me.

"It's not my fault you weigh a ton! For such a small person, you are much heavier than you look. What on earth do you eat?" he asks, hooking his arm around mine and pulling me up off the ground for a second time.

Safely on my feet, I cross my arms and glare at him. "You really shouldn't tell a girl that she weighs a ton. It's insulting."

"I didn't mean it negatively. You're, well..." He gives me a good look up and down, not being discreet about it either. "You've got a decent-sized body. You don't need to feel insecure about anything."

I let out a hearty laugh. "Have you been checking me out, Swain?"

His cheeks are flushed. "No. Of course not."

"Hm. Are you telling me porky pies?"

"No. You're overthinking it," he says, looking irritated.

I skip to my door and spin to face him. "Night, Swain."

"Night, class viper."

The car doors close with an expensive clunk, and I hear tires skidding as Grayson drives away.

# Chapter Twenty-Six

On Monday night, I'm sitting crossed-legged on the bed with my century-old laptop perched in front of me, ready to write a killer presentation.

I have stayed in my room since Grayson dropped me home because I have a mission to complete, and I am not leaving until it is finished. Reaching for my notes, I read over them while waiting for my laptop to install pointless updates.

- *Sophie is Grayson's girlfriend. She's a snotty cow.*

Let's leave that piece of information out.

- *Grayson wears a lot of aftershave, and I mean a LOT.*
- *He's most grateful for his money (shallow).*

I skip some pages.

*· Grayson does have a sensitive side.*

*· Got bullied at school.*

*· He cares deeply for his parents and looks up to his dad.*

*. He is protective of his mother.*

*· His house is ginormous - his favourite room is the study, where he writes his secret poems.*

I still don't know everything there is to know about Grayson, but I've got enough information to build a presentation around him.

I spend the next few hours typing, deleting, and correcting sentences, telling Grayson's story as if he were the one writing it.

I pick out the main points and expand on them.

Who is Grayson? What is his story?

My mobile vibrates on the bed, and Grayson's name flashes on the screen.

"Swain, I was just thinking about you," I say, answering the call and putting him on loudspeaker.

"That makes sense. I tend to cross people's minds quite often. I am too hard to resist, after all."

I roll my eyes and continue to type up my notes fiercely.

"Sorry to burst your bubble, but I am not part of your little fan club, okay? I don't obsess over you like so many other girls do."

"If it makes you sleep better at night, keep telling

yourself that. It won't be long before my charms rub off on you."

"Keep dreaming, Swain. You're delusional." I quickly glance at the time on my phone and yawn into the receiver. "Why are you calling me anyway? Don't you have anything better to do?"

"I just wanted to check in to make sure you hadn't vanished off the brink of the earth."

*He's so dramatic.*

"I'm working on the presentation as we speak," I say, glancing down at my messy notetaking. I can barely read my writing.

"Same! How are we planning to present this thing tomorrow? Who's going to speak first?"

"You can go first, Swiney."

"You did not just call me Swiney."

"I did, and it shall be your nickname from this moment onwards."

"No way!"

"Yes, way!" I snort and grip my phone harder. "Is that all you were ringing me for? I've got a presentation to write."

"Don't forget to bring your notes with you tomorrow, class viper!" he bellows, making me cover my ears.

"I don't need reminding!"

The line goes dead, and so does my motivation.

*I need a coffee break.*

I swing my legs over the side of the bed, but a light tap on the door prevents me from going any further. Someone is clearing their throat, and it doesn't sound like my mother's voice.

"Hey. It's Rory. Can I come in?"

*What the hell is he doing here?*

*I'm so not prepared for this!*

My hair is a mess. I've got hairy armpits, and my throat is as dry as the Sahara Desert. Besides all those alarming factors, I am on my period!

*This can't be happening.*

Why did my mother allow Rory to knock on my bedroom door without giving me a heads-up first?

I'm surprised she even invited him in.

"Hang on a sec!" I squeal, quickly changing into my tracksuit bottoms and a t-shirt that doesn't have food stains on it.

*I'm such a slob.*

I check myself in the mirror and hold a hand over my mouth.

*It looks like I haven't had a bath in years.*

"Are you okay?" Rory asks, sounding worried.

I scramble for a hairbrush and quickly try to make myself look as presentable as possible.

"Uh, yeah, fine! Just..."

I stub my big toe on the edge of my dressing table.

"Ow! Ow! Ow!"

"I'm coming in. You don't sound so good," he declares.

"No! Wait! Don't come in! I'm..." I search for an excuse. "I'm naked!"

"*What?*" His voice continues to rise.

"No, I mean... I'm not naked! I'm sick!" I yelp, clutching my toe and trying my best not to cry.

It's red and throbbing.

"Do you need me to get you anything?"

"Ice!" I cry out accidentally. "Uh, I mean no! No! I'm good!"

"Are you sure?"

"Yes!"

"Okay. I'll leave you to it," he says, his voice moving further away from the door.

I limp over to it and yank the door open. Rory is standing on the staircase, about to leave. He whips his head around to look at me, a worried expression masking his face.

"Oh wow. You *are* sick. You look as pale as a ghost."

That's just bloody marvellous. Someone you like tells you you look sick when you're as fit as a spring bean—such a confidence booster.

Rory casually strolls into my room and glances around. He's seeing my living headquarters for the first time, and I haven't cleaned it for days. I watch his eyes zoom in on an old pizza crust. It has been left on the floor for goodness knows how long. I should feel embarrassed, but I'm too exhausted to care. This presentation is starting to take its toll on my body.

"You shouldn't leave your front door unlocked, by the way," he says, his voice taking on a protective tone.

"My mother usually locks it. I guess she forgot."

"Speaking of your mother, where is she?"

"I'm not sure. She must've popped out, but if she does happen to return anytime soon, it might be wise to sneak you out of the window before she sees us alone in my room together—might give her the wrong idea, you know?"

"Makes sense."

Rory sits on the edge of the bed and looks down at my laptop. The unfinished document is still wide open.

"What have you been working on?"

"Oh, it's just my presentation. I've got to hand it in tomorrow, so I've been stressing out a bit."

"I have the perfect thing to help you de-stress." He reaches into the pocket of his hoodie and pulls out a big packet of Haribos.

My entire face lights up. "Oh my... You didn't!"

"I did."

Before I can think about what I'm doing, I throw my arms around him, and we spend a whole minute hugging each other. It isn't so bad, but it would help if I knew what Rory was thinking. Maybe he isn't fond of physical contact. Some people don't like you invading their personal space. I'm usually one of those people, but Rory makes me want to touch him constantly. I always have this strange urge to push his hair out of his eyes. It's confusing the hell out of me.

I lean back, giving us plenty of room to breathe. I really shouldn't have hugged him with armpit hair. I smell bad.

"What are you doing here?"

"I thought I'd stop by to see if you'd like to hang out, but I'm guessing it's not a good time."

"Yeah. If you haven't noticed, I'm a mess and need to finish this presentation by tonight. I can't go anywhere."

"That's okay. We can stay here, and I can help you."

"How exactly do you plan on doing that?"

Our gazes collide. “Well, you need a second opinion, right?”

“I guess.”

“Read what you've written, and I'll give you honest feedback.”

The idea of somebody else hearing my speech whilst it's still in the early draft stage is scary, but having a second opinion may help.

“Alright. I'll read it to you,” I tell him, returning my eyes to my laptop screen and delivering what I've got so far, which takes roughly three minutes at most. “It's still ongoing. I've got more work to do, but what do you think?”

“I thought it was amazing. You seriously have nothing to worry about.”

I confidently type up the rest of my notes with that newfound encouragement. I can't remember falling asleep, but I must've nodded off at some point because I’m no longer in the same position on the bed when my eyes open. My head is resting on Rory's lap, and his head is bowed down, eyes sealed shut. I must be moving too much because he extends his arms and groans, his eyes popping open.

“How long did we sleep for?” he asks, yawning.

I glance at my alarm clock and immediately shoot up from his lap.

“We've been sleeping for two hours!”

“You've still got plenty of time left. Don't panic.”

Rory almost falls off the bed when he notices a dark shadow flee across the room and fling itself out of the window, Batman style.

"Blimey, what the heck was that?" he yells, eyes almost popping out of his head.

"Batman."

His face scrunches up. "Batman?"

"Yeah, but this is the cat version. I had a crush on Michael Keaton when I was a teenager. Slightly obsessed." *Still a bit obsessed.* "Batman does his own thing mostly. I provide him with food and shelter."

Rory looks terrified of that freakish encounter. Batman doesn't usually make very good first impressions. He's not an average cat.

"Is Batman going to be okay? I mean, he did jump out of a window."

"Yeah, he'll be fine. He does it all the time. Nothing phases him. I think he's got unlimited lives." A smile breaks out on my face. "Hey, your last name is Keaton."

"Yeah, it is. Why?"

"I don't know many people with that last name... aside from Michael Keaton himself."

"Well, sorry to disappoint you, but I'm not Michael Keaton in disguise."

I place a hand over my heart and fake my disappointment. "You're not? I thought I could be talking to the main man for a moment. How sad."

"You're funny. I seriously think your cat needs a haircut. Nobody wants to see that thing prowling the streets in broad daylight," he mutters, half under his breath.

"Batman won't even allow me to stroke him, so he won't let me give him a makeover."

"I can help."

My brows rise. "Are you offering to groom my cat?"

"Yeah, why not?"

"Okay. You can face Batman's wrath if you dare."

"I'm up for the challenge. How hard can it be?"

We wait for Batman's return, which seems to last an eternity. I spot him creeping in through the window and dive off the bed to scoop him into my arms. His attack is sudden. He tries to kick and bite his way out of my grasp.

Rory quickly rises to his feet, slowly backing away from me.

"Woah, doesn't that hurt?"

I shake my tears away.

*It stings like hell.*

"If you'd like to take him off my hands, please feel free to do so."

Batman is getting more aggressive by the second.

"Uh, maybe you should just put him down," Rory suggests, visibly on edge.

"I thought you were going to give him a makeover."

"I've changed my mind. That cat is terrifying."

Batman clings to my arm, digging his claws into my skin. I have no choice but to set him free. We watch him jump back on the window ledge and fling himself into the depths below.

"Well, that's the most physical interaction I've had with him for months. I should count myself lucky."

Rory's head swings in my direction, his eyes full of disbelief. "Are you serious? I've never seen anything like that. The cat's got anger issues."

I rush over to the window and peer out. Batman has

ventured off into the shadows. I doubt I will see him again, but he will return. He always does.

"Why can't we be friends, Batman!" I cry out, shedding a pretend tear.

Rory moves towards me, gripping my arm gently. "Those cuts are pretty deep. They'll get infected if you don't treat them. Have you got any plasters?"

Now that he's mentioned the cuts on my arms, I suddenly recognise the pain. It's sharp. Every time I move my arm, it feels like Batman is still clinging to it.

"Yeah. I keep a first aid kit in my drawer over there."

Rory walks over to my dressing table and opens the first drawer he sees, which happens to be where I keep all my knickers.

*Kill me now.*

His face is red.

He quickly shuts the drawer.

"Sorry. That was um–"

"The plasters are in the second drawer," I tell him, preventing another mishap. We don't want that to happen. The knicker reveal was bad enough.

Rory guides me back to the bed and instructs me to sit down. Kneeling in front of me, I roll my eyes and wince as his fingers touch my sensitive skin.

"I'll try to be gentle," he assures me, leaning in closer so there is no space between us.

My chest tightens.

He has the most intense eyes I've ever seen on a guy —the living translation of Batman. I'm still talking about my cat, by the way. However, it's best not to tell Rory he looks like my cat. It might offend him.

"I think Batman might be secretly working for the mafia," he says, making me laugh.

"It wouldn't surprise me. I bet he's living a secret life that nobody knows about. For all we know, his mistress could be on the other side of town."

Rory's mouth curves into a smile. "It must be tough keeping a cat like that. Aren't you afraid of what he's going to do next?"

"Not really. Sure, he can be vicious, but we adopted him from the animal shelter years ago. I don't know what he went through before that, but he wouldn't let us hold or play with him like a normal cat. He's been through a lot. The least we can do is give him a home to return to, even if he doesn't like us very much and wants to claw our eyes out while we sleep."

"Fair play. You've got guts."

I stare at him, unable to tear my gaze away. "Can I ask you something?"

"Go ahead."

"That photo in your bedroom—the one on your windowsill..."

He nods, his jaw tensing. "What about it?"

"Who is the woman in the picture?"

Rory falls silent for a long moment, and I worry that I've overstepped the mark, but I'm relieved when he finally says, "My mother."

"Oh. Right."

"She passed away when I was ten. Cancer," he explains, letting out a breath. "I think that might be why my dad drank so much — he didn't cope very well after she died. That's the only photo I've got of her, and she also gave me this beaded bracelet. I take it everywhere with me," he shares, extending his wrist for me to see.

I have noticed the bracelet on his wrist before, but I never thought to question him about it. It's made of weathered leather, a testament to its history and significance. I can understand why it holds such sentimental value for him. If I were to lose my mother and this bracelet was the last gift she gave me, I wouldn't want to take it off either.

"Wow. That's beautiful."

Our conversation is rudely interrupted by Batman's dramatic entrance. He catapults himself into the room, covered in mud and tangled in brambles, holding a rodent triumphantly between his teeth.

It's the most frightening thing I've ever seen.

Hissing at us, he retreats to his favourite spot under my bed.

*Trust Batman to show up at the worst possible time.*

## Chapter Twenty-Seven

MY PALMS ARE SWEATING WHEN I MAKE IT TO CLASS ON Tuesday. I was up until the early hours of this morning preparing my speech. Luckily, I managed to finish it just in time, but I barely got any sleep.

Grayson pushes his chair closer to mine, snapping me out of my thoughts.

"Stop panicking, Skye, you're projecting your nerves onto me, and it's stressing me out."

"I can't help it! Go sit somewhere else if I'm bothering you that much."

"Why would I do that? You're my partner. We've got to stick together. Stop putting so much pressure on yourself. We're going to go up there and nail this."

"Little piece of advice to you all," Ricky says whilst he's in the middle of setting up the computer. "These presentations are only a brief overview of what you've learned. It doesn't have to be in-depth because it's impossible to learn everything about a person over the short time that we've had. The length of the presentation isn't as important as the quality. Just keep that in mind."

I reread my notes repeatedly until the presentations start. The whole class is silent as they listen and clap when required. I'm sitting there, dreading when we have to present our work to the class.

*What if I mess up?*

*What if I forget what to say?*

*What if my mind goes completely blank?*

Josie and Eddie meet at the front of the class and smile at each other. Grayson watches Josie in mild fascination as she talks at one hundred miles an hour, hands flailing, eyes never staying in one place. I zone out for most of Eddie's speech, but before I know it, Ricky calls us to the front of the class, and it's our turn.

*This is it.*

*Brain, don't fail me now.*

Grayson grabs my hand and leads me to the whiteboard, where all eyes are trained on us. I'm glad that one of us has it pulled together because I'm slowly starting to fall apart.

"My partner for this project is Skye Clemons, AKA the class viper," Grayson starts, and I brace myself for what's to come.

*I should cover my ears.*

"When I first met Skye, we didn't see eye to eye. I'm sure we hated each other, as you already know."

The room erupts with laughter.

"I used to think we couldn't possibly have anything in common because our lives were so different, but as it turns out, Skye has taught me a few things about myself."

*Have I?*

"We each have our own story to tell. Those stories will never be identical, and I've realised that Skye is a powerful, fiery, yet selfless person. She keeps up a barrier, but there's a reason for that."

He is saying all the right things.

It's making me emotional.

"She gives the impression that you don't want to mess with her. To the rest of the world, we might assume that Skye is capable of handling herself, which she is, but that doesn't mean she's completely immune to any negativity thrown her way or that she doesn't have feelings.

"Getting to know Skye initially was challenging. This was partly my fault. I could have made the experience easier for her. It took us a long time to finally open up to each other, so we ran slightly behind compared to everyone else. I didn't think we would ever get along at one point, but eventually, we found a way to work through our differences. The more I got to know Skye, the more she surprised me.

"My childhood consisted of being lavished with gifts and money. I never had to worry about my financial situation. Being born into a prosperous community only makes you blind to the fact that so many people struggle financially. This experience has made me realise who I am, and truthfully, I didn't like what I was becoming.

"You may have already noticed, but Skye rides her bike to college daily, even if it's belting down with rain.

She deserves a round of applause for that alone," Grayson adds, prompting the class to burst into applause, and I blush bright red.

"I can openly admit that when I first came to Barnett, I was quick to judge you all, which was wrong. But, after talking to Skye and spending so much time with her, I came to know what she was the most grateful for, and her words spoke to me. I realised that love could defeat what money can buy."

I remember that conversation.

I smile at the memory.

Hearing all this from somebody else's mouth and having people hear about my life is so weird.

"A supportive community surrounds Skye, and she has people that genuinely care about her. In some ways, she has what I lack.

"Skye recently told me how so many people give up on their dreams before they even have the chance to chase them. It hit home because, despite everything working against her, Skye's dream hasn't died... it's only been strengthened by her sheer determination and hunger to fight for what she wants—to reach for the stars and never give up. That takes guts... it is one of the qualities I've grown to love about her," Grayson proclaims, and I stand there, listening to his well-prepared speech, completely mesmerised.

"There are many layers to Skye Clemons. I still don't know everything about her, and she will always be the class viper, but she's become a good friend of mine."

My heart warms at his public declaration.

*Friend. He called me his friend.*

"I'm happy we got the chance to work together, and I'm looking forward to discovering more layers as our friendship develops."

The room explodes into loud cheers and claps, and my heart feels full.

"That was beautiful. Thank you," I whisper, my voice charged with inexplicable emotion.

I realise it's my turn to speak when the class returns to silence, and the nerves kick back into motion.

"Uh, okay, so... Grayson was my partner for the project," I stammer, trying to push down the nerves, but they keep springing back.

I stare back at my curious classmates, take a deep breath and start reading from my notes.

"Think of your favourite perfume."

I can tell by everybody's expression that I've confused them. Even Grayson is struggling to understand where I'm going with this.

"The packaging is almost as alluring as the product inside," I continue. "You are tempted to spend money to keep up with the latest fashion and beauty-inspired trend that is so pleasing to the world. You get home with the fragrance you bought and spray the first touch of magic to the nape of your neck, where it leaves its watery mark behind. The smell lifts itself high into the air, and for a split second, you are satisfied."

I glance at the sea of blank faces.

"You believe this little bottle can add to your worth and beauty, as it gives people something to talk about.

Hearing the compliment, 'You smell nice,' is a common feature that works until you later discover the perfume doesn't define who you are. Eventually, it'll wear off, and one day, it'll run out.

"Once you've sprayed the fragrance a couple of times, it dawns upon you how wasteful the purchase was, as it did not bring you lasting happiness; instead, it burnt a hole in your back pocket. As a result, the fragrance has lost its magic, and you wonder why you yearned for it so badly in the first place.

"The point I'm trying to make is that even though Grayson comes from a wealthy background and has all the money in the world, it doesn't mean he's living the perfect life or hasn't faced his battles. Money and possessions can't buy happiness. They bring temporary relief. Therefore, I have learned that you can never judge a person based on their appearance or where they come from because it might not reflect their true identity.

"Some people pretend to be someone they're not, and I used to think that Grayson was just another wanderer — trying to find his way but falling short every time because he was never fully satisfied with what he was given. We did not get along for the first couple of weeks, which continued until a certain point. Things changed when I got to see the real Grayson Swain."

I place my fidgety hands behind my back.

"He's a tease, acts like he knows it all and can be incredibly annoying, but I have also discovered that he has a sensitive side. He can be kind and helpful when he wants to be, and once you've earned Grayson's trust, he will remain a loyal friend for life."

*You haven't been loyal to him, though, have you?*

*You don't deserve his friendship.*

I clear my throat, wishing my thoughts away.

"Grayson might've grown up in Lakeside, and his world might be very different from mine, but the only thing separating us is that he's more advantaged and privileged to a certain extent.

"It was interesting to hear about Grayson's family life – particularly how his parents pressure him to succeed. He has to go above and beyond to get *the best* grades. Otherwise, it just isn't good enough. I used to think he was an overachiever who only thought of himself, but I was wrong.

"In conclusion, whether you've been raised in a poor or rich community is irrelevant because what matters most is a person's character. It was fun getting to know Grayson, and despite our ups and downs, we came out of this experience a lot stronger and even matured along the way.

"I finally understand why we were paired together. We were a good match because of our differences and similarities. In the end, Grayson became someone I *wanted* to spend time with. He might bring out the viper in me, but I wouldn't have it any other way."

Grayson meets my eye, smiling like he's immensely proud and honoured to be the subject of my speech.

"From Opposite Sides has taught me to listen more and not to judge a book by its cover. It's helped me to find my voice as a writer and not to be so afraid to use it."

I finish there and wait for a reaction.

Nobody moves or says anything at first, but

suddenly, the class starts cheering and whistling. Grayson's clap is the loudest, and I let out the breath I've been holding in.

"Skye! You did so well!" Josie exclaims as we step out of the classroom.

The presentation feels like a blur, and I'm amazed I managed to make it through without stumbling.

"Thanks. You did a great job too."

"I loved the introduction part about the perfume. That was so clever. Where did that even come from? I swear you're so talented!" Josie gushes with admiration.

Shelly Matthews appears in the corridor, cradling her Gucci bag. Her blond hair nearly whips my face as she flicks it over her shoulder.

"Yeah, well done, Skye. That was unexpected, but you are quite unpredictable, aren't you?"

*Was that meant to be a compliment? It sounded more like an insult rather than a pat on the back.*

Shelly struts down the corridor and out of my line of vision. A hand on my shoulder distracts me from my current stare down with the back of her head. Josie is rigid and starts making goldfish faces now that Grayson has joined us in the hallway.

He briefly turns to acknowledge her. "Hey, Josie. Great presentation."

Josie's cheeks are glowing. "T—thank you. You were... I mean, you did... I thought your presentation was brilliant."

I watch them trade friendly smiles before she leaves us alone in the corridor.

"Are you doing anything over the summer holidays?" Grayson asks me as we start walking down an empty staircase.

"Not really. What about you?"

"I'm going away for a few weeks. My dad needs an extra pair of hands on a business trip. I offered to help him, so I won't see you until I get back."

At least I won't have to worry about bumping into him at the next bumper race, but I will miss seeing him throughout the week. He's become part of my routine. Not having him around will be strange, but now that the presentations are over, I have got to come clean.

*No more lying.*

*No more hiding.*

"Grayson... there's something I need to tell you," I say.

He stops to look at me, and now we're standing in the middle of the stairwell, and I've got his full attention. I rest my hand on the railing to prevent myself from toppling over and take a deep breath.

"I..."

His phone rings, throwing a spanner in the works.

I'm so fed up with modern-day technology, drawing people away from the real world and causing unnecessary distractions.

Grayson glances down at his screen, and I decide to keep going. If I don't say this now, I never will.

"Look, I haven't been completely honest with you and–"

He holds his hand up, interrupting me. "Can we take a rain check? Sophie is ringing me, and we haven't been on good terms lately. I'd better answer this to see what she wants."

"But I..."

"I need to sort some stuff out, but I'll speak to you when I get back, alright?"

I shake my head and bite down on my lip in frustration.

"Grayson, listen to me for one second!" My voice echoes as it travels, startling him. "I've been working at your dad's farm, alright? I wanted to tell you sooner, but I wasn't sure how you'd take it. I can't lie to you anymore. It's wrong, and I'm sorry for keeping it a secret, but it's true. I was employed by your father weeks ago."

I stare at him, waiting for a reaction. His face shrivels, and I prepare myself for severe backlash, but when he starts laughing, it throws me completely off course.

*Wait.*

*What is going on?*

*Why is he finding this funny?*

"Good one! You could be a comedian."

I shake my head in exasperation.

*I should have known he wouldn't take me seriously.*

"I'm not joking around, Grayson."

"Yeah. Okay... I seriously need to go," he mumbles sarcastically.

"Wait!"

He's already started moonwalking away from me.

"Catch you after the holidays, class viper! Don't be a stranger!"

"Grayson!"

Of course, when I finally pluck up the courage to tell him the truth, he doesn't believe me.

# Chapter Twenty-Eight

I RIDE MY BIKE TO LAKESIDE.

Nothing can dull my sparkle—not today.

The reason I enjoy riding a bike so much isn't just because of the freedom it brings. It's because I get to see the universe on a larger scale. I can see life through a different lens. I can pretend I'm not Skye Clemons, the girl with baggage. Instead, I can pretend I'm just a girl riding a bike, searching for her next destination.

I arrive at the farm in record time and don't even bother chaining my bike to the rail. I leave it in the car park and sprint towards the barn, sliding to a halt when I bump straight into someone. I glance up, and my excitement dissipates once I realise I've walked straight into Sebastian Cole.

His eyes go wide for a fraction of a second, and he narrows them like I've ruined his entire day. I almost ran him over, but does he always have to wear that murderous stare?

"Sorry, Sebastian. I wasn't looking where I was going," I say, in one mad rush.

His gaze doesn't waver, and I wish it would because staring at Sebastian is painfully unpleasant—not physically, because the man is flawless. There's just something about him that puts me on edge. I can't explain what it is.

Sebastian glances me up and down, sending me a look of complete disapproval. What I'm wearing right now is nothing compared to those hideous overalls I tend to wear to work. He should be counting himself lucky that his eyes haven't been exposed to something far worse.

"You look familiar," he says after a lifetime of silence.

"We have met briefly before. I work here. My name is Skye."

He glances away from me, and I take a large breath before his eyes lock on mine again.

"I wasn't expecting you today. You're not on the rota."

*Ah. He's got the rota already memorised, then. He sure doesn't waste any time.*

"I know. I came here because I wanted to talk to Rory."

"Who?"

"Rory is the other stablehand," I say, a little annoyed he hasn't memorised our names yet when he's pretty capable of it.

"If you want to speak to him, you'd better make it quick. He's out on the field with Mr Frost. They're in the middle of a training session."

"Okay, great. Thanks."

"Oh, and Skye?"

I stop and turn to him. "Yeah?"

"Please don't come to the farm unannounced again. Mr Swain might quickly let things slide, but I won't stand for it while I am in charge. I'm not keen on surprises. Are we clear on that?"

I try not to flinch at his tone.

"Crystal," I say, marching away.

I find Rory exactly where Sebastian said he would be, but he doesn't notice me for a while. That's partly because he's trying to get Dante to respond to Mr Frost's gruelling instructions, which isn't going well.

Dante's rebelling is nothing short of a surprise. This is slowly becoming an increasingly charged atmosphere, and I've shown up at the worst time.

"Skye! I'm so glad you're here!" Rory jogs over to me, his frown suddenly becoming a colossal smile.

"You are?"

"Yeah! We need all the help we can get at this point."

He wants me to help with Dante. I am the horse's favourite, but you have to catch him on a good day. By the looks of it, this is not one of those days. He's lifting a hind leg off the ground, his ears are flattened, and he's baring his teeth, indicating he's not in the right frame of mind.

"I wasn't planning on sticking around. I just came to–" I stop there, noticing Mr Frost charging towards me with sheer determination.

*Oh no.*

"Finally! We have someone here who can speak the horse's language," he says.

"I don't speak horse, Mr Frost."

"No, but you certainly have a way with them. Dante listens to you."

"On occasion," I point out. There have been numerous times when he's ultimately rejected me by throwing me off the saddle, almost biting my arm off during feeding time and refusing to let me mount him.

"Work your magic! Do whatever you need to do to get Dante's attention," he says, letting go of my arm once we're only a short distance from the horse.

I sigh, observing Dante. He is acting more like a foe than a friend in this instance. I don't think my presence will make much of a difference today. He's getting agitated.

"It doesn't work like that, sir. Judging by how Dante is acting, we should give him space. He's not in the mood."

"Dante will be competing at the race whether he likes it or not, and we need to get plenty of practice beforehand to ensure that he's prepared and ready. Time is of the essence. We only have five weeks to get him nice and fit."

"I'm no expert, but the horse looks exhausted. He needs to rest."

"He doesn't have time to rest!"

"I think Skye is right, sir. We're not going to get anywhere today. Let's try again tomorrow," Rory speaks up.

Mr Frost throws a tantrum but quickly composes

himself before his behaviour can be deemed unprofessional.

"Fine, but I expect to see both of you here tomorrow—bright and early."

"I don't work on Wednesdays," I tell him.

"Well, starting from today, my dear, you do."

***

Going to work on a Wednesday morning feels strange, but at the same time, I'm happy to be doing something other than watching reruns of *Gossip Girl.*

Dante isn't performing to the best of his ability. He keeps running directly *away* from us and his rider. It's a challenge, but I signed myself up for it because I believe in Dante's capabilities. If we can turn those weaknesses into strengths, there will be no stopping him on that Bumper course, but he needs to let us into his world so we can be part of it.

Mr Frost takes an important phone call, and I sit on the grass with Rory, the two of us watching Dante run laps across the field. He looks like a wild horse on the loose. His actions are frantic, chaotic and downright reckless.

"I just don't understand. This is the second bad day he's had in a row. What are we going to do?" Rory asks, sounding frustrated.

I lower my head and pick at the grass.

"I have no idea, but we can't lose hope."

"Maybe we need to accept that Dante can't be taught.

He's set in his ways. There might not be anything we can do to change that."

"You sound like you've already given up on him."

"I haven't, but we've got to be honest with ourselves, Skye. Some horses aren't meant to race."

"Dante was designed to race," I argue. "That's why whenever someone tries to mount him, he gets half excited and half agitated because even though he might've been mistreated before, his body is still eager to move—it's still used to competing."

"I know, but when is enough, enough?"

After a very unsuccessful morning, we haven't made any progress whatsoever. I spend my lunch break alone in the staff room, searching for different online training techniques. Nothing we've tried has worked out so far. We need to look elsewhere for an answer.

Later in the week, I head into the library across town to conduct more research. I borrow a few books and read them excessively every night before bed. YouTube is also a massive help, and I find loads of videos online about desensitising, which talk me through a step-by-step process on how to introduce Dante to everything he might be afraid of so that he can overcome his fears and realise he doesn't have to be scared of them anymore.

Dante needs to be entirely retrained, which could take months to achieve. The race is in precisely four weeks, so the chances of us being one hundred percent ready for it are very unlikely. However, we can still accomplish a lot within that time frame.

When I'm not at the farm, I read about horses or watch movies about them for inspiration. I'm in the middle of watching *The Horse Whisperer* when my bedroom door knocks.

"Come in!"

Rory steps into my room. Bags are under his eyes. He hasn't been sleeping, not that I've had much luck. His hair hasn't been brushed, and light stubble is growing along his jaw.

"Hey. Is everything okay?" I ask him, pausing the movie to avoid missing anything important.

"I've lost my beaded bracelet. I haven't been able to find it for days. Maybe I left it here when I came to your place a few days ago," he says.

"I'll help you find it."

I'm so glad I had a sort-out since he was last here. My room is in much better condition now. You can move around without tripping over something and falling to your doom.

"Okay... so, I'll check the floor over here, and maybe you can look under my bed. It's surprising what tends to live under there," I say jokingly.

Rory's face instantly pales, his eyes widening with fear. "When you say things tend to live under your bed, are you referring to a certain Bat?"

"Huh?"

He's lost me now.

"Like, the cat version of Batman, for instance? Am I going to find him hiding under there?"

Big, uncontrollable giggles leave my throat, and it only seems to rub Rory up the wrong way.

"Are you scared of my cat, Rory?"

He shakes his head for a few seconds, puffing out his

chest to make it seem like he's not afraid of anything, but I've already discovered his weakness.

It's Batman.

"You're allowed to be afraid. Batman *can* be a bit intimidating," I reassure him, even though it sounds like I'm teasing him.

"I'm not afraid," he utters with a snort.

"Yes, you are. Just admit it."

Rory turns his head away and starts sulking to himself. I've pushed him too far. You know how males can get when you question their masculinity. They either try to prove the opposite is true or get highly offended. He takes a breath through his nostrils, flexes his muscles and lowers himself down to the floor so he's at eye level with what's currently lurking beneath my bed.

*I've got to hand it to him. He's a lot braver than I am.*

I hope I haven't got any dirty underwear under there. Batman likes to get his claws into them whenever he gets the chance, so it would be very unfortunate if he happened to be storing them away in his Batcave somewhere.

"Any luck?" I ask, keeping my eyes trained on the window in case Batman does decide to show his face at some point. It's always better to be on guard. You never know when he might make his next grand appearance.

"Nope," Rory mumbles, sounding deflated as he stands up.

"Hang on a sec. I need to pee. I'll be right back," I say, skipping towards my door, but Rory beats me to it. He's blocking the exit.

"I'm coming with you," he says, as if we always do this sort of thing.

"Since when have we become toilet buddies?"

"I'm not staying in this room alone, Clemons."

"Ahah!" I wave my finger in his face triumphantly. "So you *are* afraid of Batman. I knew it!"

He pushes me away, giving me complete access to the door. "I'm not afraid... just a little uneasy."

"I'm pretty sure both words mean the same thing."

He glances towards my window and shivers. "Do you always have to keep that window open?"

"Well, yeah. If Batman does return, at least he can get in and out of the house easily. He's free to come and go as he pleases."

"Can't he just use a cat flap like a normal cat?"

"I've already told you. He's not a normal cat, and we don't have a catflap anyway."

He scowls at me. "I'll stay to prove I'm not afraid of your little black cat."

"Correction. He's not little—a bit on the chubby side, and he's part bat, part cat. Aka, Batcat, so, who knows what he's truly capable of," I leave him with that and hurry into the bathroom, giggling.

I've never seen Rory scared of anything before. This is just too funny. I enjoy messing with him, even though I probably shouldn't. He's upset over his bracelet. The least I can do is show him some compassion.

While I'm washing my hands, out of the corner of my eye, I notice something glinting on the windowsill. I go over to inspect the object, heart in my throat.

It *is* Rory's bracelet.

He'll be so happy I've found it.

Carefully pocketing the bracelet, I hear the loudest blood-curdling scream that seems to last a while. I rush out of the bathroom and crash land in my room again, eyes widening when I realise what I've just walked into.

The window is closed.

*Why is the window closed?*

Rory has backed himself up against it, ducking as Batman repeatedly attempts to catapult himself at the glass. It dawns on me that he must've been here all along, and now he's angry because his one-way ticket to the outside world has officially been cut off.

Batman pounces again, and his claws get stuck in Rory's trouser leg. Rory yelps, trying to shake him off, but the cat isn't budging. He starts hissing and biting through flesh and fabric.

"Hold on!" I cry out, running downstairs to find a solution.

"Where the hell are you going?" Rory's strangled voice echoes throughout the house.

This might be a total waste of time since Batman may have already eaten, but I've got to do something before he tears Rory apart, and this is the only thing I can think of. I chuck some cat food into Batman's bowl and dive up the stairs two steps at a time.

Returning to my room, I push the bowl towards Batman to lure him away.

"Who wants some din dins? Looks yummy, right?" I say, lowering my voice to a whisper and slowly creeping towards him like a weirdo.

"What are you doing?" Rory demands, eyes watering while Batman clings onto his leg for dear life.

"Ssh. I'm trying to distract him."

Batman glances into the bowl of slime and turns his head away, repulsed. Regular cat food doesn't interest him anymore. He'd rather feast on birds and mice and human flesh.

"Can you hurry up, please? I don't think your plan is working, and I'm losing a bit of blood here," Rory grinds out impatiently.

I sneak up behind Batman and prepare myself for what is going to be one painful experience. I scoop the cat into my arms, which is excellent news for Rory, but now I'm on the receiving end of the attack. I feel the sharp sting of Batman's nails greeting my skin, so I unintentionally throw him straight into Rory's arms. He cries out in pain, tossing the cat back to me like we're playing a dangerous game of pass the parcel.

"Hey! I don't want him!" I shout, launching Batman in his direction again.

"Neither do I!" he yowls, flinging the cat into the air.

Batman lands on my bed, hissing at us aggressively, baring his blood-stained teeth. While he's more than a little occupied, I rush towards the window and fling it open. After giving us that horrifying human versus cat throwdown, he dives onto my windowsill and jumps out whilst Rory and I struggle to catch our breath and recover from our injuries.

"Did that just happen?" I voice, gasping for air.

Rory bends over, struggling to catch his breath. "Yup. It happened."

"Wow."

"That cat is a bloody nightmare, Skye."

"He is pretty funny if you think about it, but in all seriousness, are you okay?"

He faces me, arms folded across his chest. "No. Your villainous cat just bit and clawed me. He's unsafe to be around. Maybe you should consider giving him a new home that doesn't have people in it."

"You caught him at a bad time, that's all. Closing the window was such a bad move. No wonder the cat was ticked off. He couldn't leave. He's not a villain in this scenario. He's just a poor, innocent animal."

"I was only going to close the window for a second, and then he just appeared out of nowhere, ready to pick a fight. He knew what he was doing, okay? The cat isn't stupid," Rory argues.

I reach into my pocket, retrieving the bracelet. "Maybe this will cheer you up."

His eyes brighten, and I hand the bracelet back to him. "Where did you find it?"

"In the bathroom."

He twirls it around. "I must've taken it off to wash my hands or something. Thank you."

"No worries. Now we've just got to pray that Batman doesn't have rabies."

Terror takes over Rory's entire face as I brush past him.

"Huh? What did you say?"

"Nothing."

# Chapter Twenty-Nine

"YOU WANT US TO RETRAIN DANTE COMPLETELY? ARE YOU insane?" Mr Frost shouts impossibly loud after I've just finished explaining what I've learned over the last few days. He is not responding well to the news, and I expected nothing less.

The sun goes down slowly, painting the sky with beautiful golden streaks. We only have three hours before the day ends, and we'll have to call it a night. I have got to convince him somehow.

"You're a knowledgeable man, Mr Frost, so I trust your judgement, and I'm not questioning it. Surely, it can't hurt to try. We have nothing to lose. If it doesn't work, we'll switch back to the old way of doing things. What do you say?"

Mr Frost seems conflicted with himself. I can see he's thinking long and hard about it because he can't disagree with me, but he's a stubborn old man, and I'm worried he will not reconsider to spite me.

I catch movement in the corner of my eye and notice

Sebastian standing there, watching us all with suspicion. He's mostly looking at me as if I'm the one he needs to keep a closer eye on.

"I thought I told you not to come back here unannounced, Skye," he says.

"I asked her to help us with Dante's training, Mr Cole. She is good with the horse. It makes sense to have her around," Mr Frost responds.

*I'm shocked that he jumped to my defence, especially after I questioned his teaching methods.*

Sebastian crosses his arms tightly. "Please keep it down then. I'm in the middle of writing up some paperwork."

"Yes, sir," we all say together.

He looks at me for one long, lingering moment, turns and heads back towards the stables.

Mr Frost nudges me by the elbow. "If we're going to do this, I want you to be at the centre of it. The horse needs to respect its trainer, right?"

I nod impishly, not entirely understanding where he's going with this.

"It makes sense for you to take control and lead the sessions."

"But I'm not qualified or experienced enough. I wouldn't know what to do."

"You've been doing your research. You know enough, and you won't be alone. We will act as your guide. Considering Dante already likes you, that is one thing we can tick off the list."

I look to Rory for some guidance. He's nodding and holding his thumb up, giving me the green light. This could go one of two ways, but I'm willing to take that leap of faith. Dante is worth it.

"Okay. Let's do this."

During the holidays, I spend every single second of my time at the farm, helping to provide the right amount of training so Dante can thrive. It isn't easy, and there are times when we all feel like giving up. We stay on the ground most of the time, as it's easier to regain Dante's trust that way, and once he can see that he isn't punished, it'll improve our relationship.

I speak to the horse constantly, generally being nice to him, giving him treats, and ensuring he's touched in a way that makes him realise 'touching' doesn't equal pain. Mr Frost sticks to his word and gives me complete control, even though I can tell he's biting his tongue occasionally. He's stressing about the time frame, but it's better to take things slowly rather than rush and get it wrong.

We eliminate options one step at a time. For example, when Dante disobeys, we leave him alone in the field for a few minutes, removing ourselves from the equation. Several sessions like this improve Dante's mindset. He's beginning to understand that acting silly around us is not desirable, and it helps him focus on pleasing us rather than doing the opposite of what we say.

I eventually mount him comfortably during the sessions. I can hardly believe our progress within such a short time. It might not be enough to crown him the overall race winner, but it'll certainly make him a worthy contender.

We reach the end of our third week of training, and the setting sun casts a warm, golden glow over the barn. I finish securing the locks, ensuring everything is safe and sound for the night.

“Hey, great session today,” Rory says, joining me on the walk back to the car park.

I raise a weak smile. “It feels like we're finally making progress.”

“Definitely. Dante's getting stronger every single day, and it's all thanks to you.”

“Don't thank me. I haven't done anything.”

His stare is unflinching. “You've done more than you know.”

“I couldn't have achieved any of this without you, and Mr Frost has been a lot nicer lately, hasn't he?”

Rory nods, running a hand through his hair. “Yeah. I have noticed. He respects you for standing up to him. Not many people would have the guts to do that.”

I feel weirdly pleased to hear this information.

“I wish Mr Swain could be here to see everything we're doing.”

“Sebastian's probably keeping him in the loop.”

At the mention of Sebastian's name, I immediately tense up. We've hardly seen him around the farm because he keeps to himself mostly, but there have been times when we've had no choice but to cross paths with him. I'm sure he has been keeping close tabs on us all—making sure we're not doing anything we shouldn't be doing. I could sense him watching us during our training session this morning, and I had to act like he wasn't there so I could stay focused. So far, every encounter I've had with that man has been negative. I won't miss him when he's gone. That's for sure.

* * *

I'm late to training the following week, but it's mainly because my mother had her first appointment with the doctor and I needed to be there. The doctor was unusually quiet while my mother talked through her issues, emotions overruling her. I held onto her shaky hands throughout, ensuring she felt supported. Opening up to a stranger couldn't have been easy, but there might be a silver lining, which makes it all worth it.

She's been referred to the mental health team. They said it could take up to six months for her to be seen by a professional, which is ridiculous if you ask me, but I have to trust that she won't get bad again.

I arrive at the farm a little after twelve, huffing and puffing as I join Rory and Mr Frost out on the field. Dante's ears prick up, and he trots towards me excitedly. This fills me with pure delight.

"Hey, buddy," I say, watching him stretch his neck and nuzzle his head against my shoulder.

"Where have you been?" Mr Frost demands, skipping the pleasantries.

"Sorry, I'm late. Something came up. I'm here now."

We work until the late hours of the afternoon. Dante has some good and bad moments. His speed can still trip him up sometimes. Because he tends to race as his entire life depends on it, this can cloud his judgement.

"I believe in you," I tell him while we're alone in the stables together. I'm hosing him down because it's been a sweltering day, and he's been training for hours. His body needs time to cool off before we jump back into the exercises.

"Don't worry about coming first or getting into the top five. All that matters is that you give it your best shot, okay?"

He nods his head at me, almost like he understands.

"Who taught you how to ride horseback?" A voice emerges from behind me.

I spin around to face Sebastian.

This is the first time I've seen him without a suit, although he still looks like a multimillionaire. He's wearing a blue shirt and tie with smart black trousers tailored to perfection. I don't know why he wears clothes like this to the farm when they're destined to get dirty or muddy, but he seems to do little handy work, so he doesn't have to worry. Besides, I bet he's got plenty of replacements in his wardrobe if anything were to go wrong.

"Uh... I wasn't taught."

He stares at me, eyebrows drawn. "What do you mean?"

"I picked things up through first-hand experience on the farm and taught myself. Horse riding comes naturally to me. It's almost like I was born to do it."

His stare deepens, and I take a significant step back as he walks towards me, craning his neck to get a better look at Dante. I'm sure I see some recognition light up in Dante's eyes. He's still on guard, but I wonder if he knows Sebastian.

"I'm not sure if anybody has told you, but Dante used to be my horse," Sebastian says, clearing up the confusion.

My eyebrows automatically shoot up to my forehead. "No. Nobody mentioned that."

"I bought him from a knackers' yard years ago. For the first couple of months, I tried everything I could to help Dante, but in the end, he became too out of control, and when I eventually sold him to Mr Swain, I thought that maybe he could give him a better life—the kind of life that he deserved. I was surprised when I learned he would compete again. I didn't think it was possible to train a horse like that, but you are proving me wrong."

He suddenly looks uncomfortable, like maybe he shouldn't have shared that with me, but I'm glad he did because hearing about Dante's past is fascinating. The horse has endured so much and has become my world within the past few weeks. The more we can try to understand his past, the more we can help him to overcome it.

"Anyway, I'm telling you all this because I've known Dante for a long time, and I've never seen him warm to a person. You've formed a special bond with him, and I'm just a bit frazzled by it all. I'm also pleased you haven't given up on him as easily as I did."

So that's why he has been observing us so much during our training sessions. He's got a history with the horse. I can't believe Mr Swain never mentioned any of this sooner.

I produce a smile. "You saved him from years of mistreatment and violence, Sebast... I mean, Mr Cole. If you hadn't bought him when you did, he might still be at that knackers' yard."

His gaze lingers on me for a second. "Yes, well... that's one good thing to come out of it, I suppose."

The silence is welcomed, but Sebastian walks out of the barn before it can get awkward.

*Maybe the beast does have a heart, after all.*

Rory enters the barn a few seconds later, and his face speaks volumes.

*Something isn't right.*

"Oh no. What's wrong now?"

"Dante's rider has pulled out of the race," he reveals.

My mouth hangs open. "You've got to be kidding me."

"I wish I was."

"Why has he pulled out?"

"He's been offered to run a bigger race. He couldn't pass up on the opportunity."

I shake my head, disappointed that our rider has chosen to leave us with less than two weeks to find a replacement. That doesn't give us much time to find a new rider, and I doubt they would want to gamble on a horse they know nothing about.

"What are we going to do?" I ask, panicking.

"Mr Frost has been trying to ring people to see if he can find a replacement, but it's too short notice. Nobody will take over, especially with Dante's track record."

This is not good.

Dante will automatically be pulled out of the race if we can't find a rider. I try to think of an alternative solution, but nothing comes to mind.

"There's got to be a way around this, surely."

Rory nods, and a burst of hope builds in my chest. "There might be. I've been chatting to Mr Frost, and we both think you should be Dante's rider."

My face falls, nerves immediately kicking in, along with a strong surge of doubt and uncertainty.

"I—I can't. I mean, I'm not ready for that."

Rory steps towards me, his gaze steady and reassuring. "Skye, if we didn't think that you were ready, then we wouldn't have suggested it in the first place. Dante thinks the world of you. The bond you both share is incomparable. Nobody can replicate the connection you have. It makes sense for you to take the reins on this one."

I shake my head and move away from him.

"You need to find someone else. I'm not the right fit," I protest.

"I know you're nervous, Skye," he says, watching me, "and you have every reason to be, but Dante trusts you. You're the perfect candidate, if not the best."

I can't believe this is happening, but if I don't agree to be Dante's rider, he won't be able to compete. If I decide to do it, I'm setting myself up for failure before the race begins. Either way, the outcome could be better.

"You might not win, and you might stumble along the way, but you'll come out of the experience even stronger. Dante is already performing a lot better than before, so he will only keep improving from now on. This might not be his race, but what's to say the next one won't be?" Rory continues, his expression warm and encouraging.

I chew along my lip.

"I'm just scared that I'll mess up or something. What if I let Dante down?"

Rory walks closer to me, his eyes firmly set on mine. "You won't. You can do this."

"You think so?"

"I don't *think* I *know*."

# Chapter Thirty

THE THOUGHT OF BEING DANTE'S RIDER AT THE RACE IS worrying enough, but I have to perform in front of a large crowd of onlookers, which is even worse. I make silly mistakes that impact Dante's training for the rest of the week, forgetting to put my helmet on multiple times, and my posture is awful. As the day ends, I sit with Mr Frost and Rory in a rowdy pub, and we solemnly stare into the depths of our beer glasses.

"Well, aside from a couple of blunders here or there, I think we did alright today," Mr Frost speaks up, breaking the stretching silence.

"Yeah. It went well," Rory agrees, keeping the morale up.

"Didn't you guys see how many mistakes I made? Dante won't even make it to the starting line if we perform like that next Saturday." I chug down the rest of my drink, unable to match their positive thinking.

"Skye, you have to start believing in yourself. Once you do, you will have a very successful career ahead of you. Trust me, I've been in this business for a while, and you're a rare talent," Mr Frost says.

I've had yet to think that far ahead. This was never part of my plan. I've invested so much time into my college course, thinking it was the only path I wanted to take. I hadn't even considered how much I would come to love working at the farm.

Is it possible to do a bit of both?

I would struggle to choose between them now, but hopefully, it won't come down to that. Hopefully, I won't have to choose.

Mr Frost eventually goes home, and I sit at the table with Rory. A few musicians are in the middle of setting up on stage. There must be a band playing tonight, which is quite exciting. I am trying to remember the last time I listened to live music. It's been a while.

"Ugh, I'm freaking out already," I moan, my voice barely audible over the increasing noise filling the room.

"Don't be nervous." Rory's shoulder brushes against mine, and it's distracting.

"That's easy for you to say. You're not the one who has to perform in front of a large crowd!"

"I guess not, but all you've got to focus on is Dante. Forget everybody else. As long as you stick to the basics of our training, you'll be absolutely fine."

The band begins to play, damaging eardrums and interrupting conversations. They are good, but I've heard better. I especially like the guitar player. He's got a lot of skill, and he is super good-looking. No wonder the band has attracted a large crowd of squealing girls who are officially acting like a pack of hungry wolves. You put a group of decent-looking males together in a band, and girls will go crazy. Even if their music sucks, it becomes less about how they sound and more about how they look.

*Sad, but true.*

Gangs of girls are fighting their way to the front, hoping to catch the band members' attention, but they seem so lost in the music that it will be difficult for them to compete. I chuckle and glance at Rory, who is already looking at me, his green eyes burning into mine with so much intensity that it steals my breath away.

*That guitarist might be cute, but Rory is off-the-scale gorgeous.*

I smile and drink more Diet Coke to drown out my irrational thoughts.

"Do you want to dance?" Rory asks, making me choke on my drink.

Some shoots out of my nose as it goes down the wrong hole.

*How attractive.*

"*Dance?*" I repeat, trying to make a smooth recovery.

"Yeah. I can see you're itching to get up there."

"Me? Oh no. I'm more of an observer. I like to sit and watch from a distance."

*Unless I've had a few beers.*

I'm sober and of sound mind.

The chances of me getting up to dance are zero to none.

Rory reaches for my hand and tries to coax me from behind the table. "Come on. You can't not dance to this song. It's a classic."

The band is playing Mr Brightside by The Killers.

*I do like this one.*

We make our way to the front of the stage, the crowd automatically parting for us. There's little room to move around. Somebody is going to injure themselves on this dance floor. It's just a matter of time. Rory starts throwing himself about the place, and seeing him not give a care in the world is beginning to rub off on me. I move my feet slowly to the beat, and when it gets to the chorus, we both belt out, "Jealousy, turning saints into the sea!"

Everyone is singing along and joining in. It's intoxicatingly fun, but what's making the experience even better is that I get to share it with Rory—one of my new favourite people. I've been missing out on so much over the years. Friendship is a beautiful thing. I wouldn't have wanted to experience this moment with anyone else.

After the fourth song, we collapse into laughter, and that's when the main singer speaks into the microphone.

"We're big fans of *Picture This*, so we're going to cover one of their songs next. It's called *Addicted to You*, a love song that captures the early days of love–how two people are perfect for each other but are too afraid to admit their feelings in case the other person doesn't feel the same way."

There are a couple of hoots and cheers from the crowd.

*Why has there always got to be a freaking love song?*

I glance at Rory, sensing the awkwardness. He seems to be just as surprised by the sudden change in music.

The atmosphere has become far more serious, and neither of us is ready to explore it.

"We should sit this one out," I suggest.

Rory steps closer, his left hand resting on my lower back, drawing our bodies together. A gasp escapes my lips as we instinctively sway to the rhythm.

We're slow dancing.

*I've never slow danced before.*

To the outside world, we must look like a real-life couple. Nobody would suspect we were just friends, especially judging by how we stare into each other's eyes. His face is inches from mine, and I don't know whether it's the song itself or the smoky lights, but lines are getting blurred here. Everything about this moment is romantic, and the more we dance, the more I get caught up in the idea that maybe we could be something more.

"I am addicted to you, and only you, and I am surviving on you. Only you..." the vocalist sings, holding that last note for effect.

I suck in a shaky breath, and my lips part with anticipation, realising I *want* him to kiss me, but that's when I'm suddenly shoved backwards, and I wince as my back hits a wooden table, a sharp shooting pain travelling up my spine. Scanning my surroundings, I notice Rory frantically walking through the crowd, determined to reach me.

"Are you alright?" he demands once I'm safely in his arms again.

I can't think straight because too much is happening, and the music worsens the dull ache in the middle of my head.

"I—I think so."

We both turn to look at three bikers who are standing close by. One of them bumped into me, and that's how I got crushed against a table.

"Wait here," Rory says, storming up to them.

A fresh wave of panic settles inside my chest. These guys look dangerous, but Rory's making it clear he's not afraid of them.

Ignoring his order to stay put, I creep closer.

"I'd like you to apologise to my friend. She could have hurt herself when you fell into her just now."

One of the men turns to face us and scoffs. "I didn't even notice her."

"That's probably because she wasn't throwing herself at you, John," another guy says.

John's eyes travel down to my chest, and he laughs under his breath. "Nothing to see in that department anyway, so she wouldn't have caught my attention."

Rory's face is turning red with fury.

I reach for his hand and tug on it. "Come on, let's just go."

John grins triumphantly. "Yeah, lover boy... Why don't you listen to your girlfriend? Take her to the build-a-bear workshop across town. I'm sure you'll both fit in just fine there."

I tug harder on Rory's arm. He looks down at me, his breathing sharp and uncontrolled. I've got to get us out of here before he does something he'll regret.

I start successfully luring him away from the group of men until one of them says, "Hey, aren't you Marcus's son?"

Rory tenses up.

The colour drains from his face.

“Oh, I can see the resemblance now! Isn't he still in prison? Deserves it after what he did,” another man adds.

*This is such a sensitive topic.*

“Imagine having a father like that—what a joke. I guess the apple doesn't fall far from the tree,” John sneers.

Rory whirls around, his fist hurtling towards John's face, initiating a rapid succession of punches from all three men involved. The crowd stops dancing, the band fades out, and some people start filming the fight on their phones. The first drop of blood drips from Rory’s nose, and my stomach turns.

I have no choice but to stand here and let these men continuously throw him around like a human punchbag.

Miraculously, one of the bar staff somehow manages to cool things off, and the three men back away slowly, giving Rory some space, but he tries to swing at one of the men again. The barman swiftly restrains him, gripping his hands and keeping them behind his back.

“Calm down, kid. That's enough. Don't be stupid.”

Rory scrambles out of his grasp and grabs my hand, marching us out of there, but my feet keep tripping over each other. It’s hard to keep up. The fresh air greets us, and Rory releases my hand, frantically pacing back and forth in the street. He grabs an E-cigarette from his back pocket and inhales a large puff of smoke. It's dark outside, but not dark enough to disguise the blood that's dripping down the side of his face. I want to reach out to him, but at the same time, I'm annoyed that he got himself into another fight when it could have been avoided if he'd just listened to me.

"What the hell was that?" I demand.

Rory spins towards me, using the end of his sleeve to wipe away the trickling blood. "Somebody had to put those guys in their place, Skye."

"You could have walked away."

"I wasn't just going to stand by and let them slate me and my dad like that."

"What if the fight had gotten out of hand? You have no idea how scared I was!" I realise I'm shouting at him now, unable to disguise the worry in my voice. "I thought you were going to get beaten to a pulp and that I would have to be the one to deliver the news to your grandmother."

"I'm still in one piece, aren't I?"

"Just barely! You could have gotten seriously hurt back there, and it's like you don't even care! I don't think you realise how worried—" I'm interrupted when Rory's lips press against mine, shutting me up.

The kiss is quick and barely lasts a second, but it happened, and it has left me utterly speechless.

*He kissed me.*

Rory pulls back slightly and looks into my eyes, his gaze travelling to my lips again like he's hungry for more. I gasp when he traces my bottom lip with the tip of his thumb, and I lean into his touch, my heart pounding.

"Rory... what are you..."

"Just don't think about it. Please... I need a distraction," he says, searching for a sign that I want this as much as he does.

All it takes is a single nod before his lips crash down on mine again with a sense of urgency. Our tongues dance together as we melt into each other's embrace, lips moving in a comfortable rhythm, constantly testing and tasting. His hands move to the back of my neck, and he pulls me even closer so that the space between our bodies is officially non-existent.

I grip his shirt, deepening the kiss, and he groans against my mouth when I dig my fingertips into his shoulders. I've kissed a lot of boys, but never like this. This is different. This is unlike anything I've ever experienced. I can feel the electricity—sparks flying—raw passion burning between us until we're standing in a moment of suspended time where nothing else matters.

Finally, we break apart, our eyes opening to reveal a shared vulnerability. Now we have to face the consequences of our actions, and I can't tell if Rory enjoyed that kiss or if he's regretting it already, but there are so many things I want to ask him.

*What did it mean?*

*Does he have any feelings for me?*

*Or was I just a convenient distraction for him?*

It looks like Rory is about to say something, but my phone vibrates. I reach into my back pocket, desperately trying to silence the person trying to call me.

*Talk about bad timing.*

I decline Grayson's call, but Rory has already caught a glimpse of the screen, and his stare is suddenly ice-cold.

"I'll take you home," he says, his voice expressing resignation.

I thought he would have mentioned the kiss on the drive back to my place, but he doesn't speak about it, not even when I'm standing on my doorstep, and we're presented with the perfect opportunity. He says goodbye, and that's it. He's gone.

That kiss is becoming such a blur. I'm questioning whether or not it took place, but one thing I do know is that I won't be able to sleep tonight.

## Chapter Thirty-One

My alarm clock reverberates in my ears until I roll out of bed to make it stop. I didn't sleep a wink last night because I couldn't get that stupid kiss out of my mind. It kept replaying itself repeatedly, instilling me with false hope.

*What if Rory thought it was a mistake? Is that why he hasn't called or texted? What if things are awkward between us now?*

I don't have time for breakfast, but my mother has made me some pancakes when I walk into the kitchen, and it would be a shame if they went to waste.

"Morning," she greets me warmly.

"Hey," I reply, sitting at the kitchen table and devouring the pancakes, which taste like heaven.

"How's training going? I've barely seen you."

I instantly feel bad because I rush off to work as soon as I get up in the morning, and when I get home, I'm too tired to function.

"It's going well. The race is on Saturday."

"What time is it?"

"Two in the afternoon. Are you coming?"

She rubs her arms nervously, and I can instantly tell that there's something else on her mind. "I don't think I'll be able to. I phoned the bakery the other day and asked if they would give me another chance. They want me to start on Saturday, so I'll probably be working all weekend."

I leap out of my seat, engulfing her in an embrace. "Congratulations, Mum! I'm so happy for you."

"Thanks, honey. You've been working so hard, and it's inspired me to go and do the same."

Of course, it would've meant the world to me if she could've been there, but it doesn't matter. I know she'll be with me in spirit.

I make it to the stables precisely a quarter of an hour later, and I don't even notice when Mr Frost arrives, but I do notice that Rory isn't with him. Although, come to think of it, I haven't seen Rory since I got here.

Maybe he *is* avoiding me.

Mr Frost talks me through some of the rules and regulations, and once he's done explaining them, he says, "Remember, there are no hurdles in this race, aside from the hurdles that you create for yourself. It won't be Dante's first time on the track, but it will be yours. So, forget about all of the other riders. They will try to steer you off course in this game but don't listen to them. They all want to win just as much as we do, but winning is irrelevant because it's not as important as taking part."

"Thanks for the advice, Mr Frost."

"Yes, well, that's enough of the idle chit-chat. Come on. Let's get back to work."

The farm is the busiest it's ever been.

All the horses participating in the race are undergoing intensive training. Some are stronger than others. Henry, for example, is shying away from everything and everyone. Albatross chooses to observe rather than participate in any physical activity, and Luna is in top form as usual. She won't be competing on Saturday since Grayson isn't here to grace us with his presence. I'm sure she wouldn't have trouble finding a rider if Grayson allowed it to happen. Plenty of people are eyeing her up, but Luna's absence from the race has helped us because she is undoubtedly one of our biggest competitors.

Grayson has sent me multiple messages that I need to respond to. I'm tempted to send him a work selfie to prove I work here. I finally told him the truth, and all he did was laugh in my face and assume that I was joking. Then again, can I blame him? I'm supposed to be this super upfront person, yet all I have done is lie to him.

During lunch, I make myself at home in the staff room, expecting to bump into Rory on my way there, but he has officially gone AWOL. I bring his number up on my phone, wondering if I should check in on him, but he has *my* number. If he wanted to contact me, he would have by now. I wouldn't know what to say to him anyway.

I eat the rest of my sandwiches in peace, refusing to

text him and think any more about him for my sanity. Instead, I fully immerse myself into the digital world of horse racing for the next twenty minutes, looking up tips and tricks we can adapt to our training.

I can't pinpoint the exact moment Rory decides to show his face, but he can barely even look me in the eye when he does. He doesn't explain why he's late but says he had to take care of something—whatever that means. If he regrets our kiss badly, I'd rather him be honest.

We work until the last hour, and at the end of the day, I head into the barn to keep Dante company while he's eating his food.

I stare up at him expectantly.

“Why do things always have to be so complicated?”

Dante whinnies in sympathy, or maybe he's annoyed that I keep interrupting his dinnertime. I leave him in peace and decide to go for a little wander around the yard.

This is my favourite time of the day—when the sun has gone down, and the air is just right. It's not too hot or too cold. The temperature is cool enough to wear shorts and a tank top. It’s a shame I'm not wearing anything of the sort. My dungarees are the closest thing I've got to shorts these days.

My phone beeps with another message from Grayson.

I read it this time since he will not stop bugging me until I respond.

GRAYSON

Class viper, have you been kidnapped?

I roll my eyes just as another message pops onto the screen.

GRAYSON

I'm not used to all of this radio silence. Please respond within the next hour, or I will have to assume that you are in grave danger and need rescuing.

I've missed our banter. I can't deny that.

I bring up the keypad and start typing a reply.

SKYE

I am only in grave danger of being stalked by you all day. Don't you have anything better to do than text and ring me twenty-four-seven?

GRAYSON

Correction. I am not stalking you. I am simply checking up on a friend. And trust me, when your Dad has to attend a ton of business meetings, things tend to get extremely repetitive and boring after a while 😪

I can only imagine.

SKYE

Well, you've heard back from me. I'm safe and sound. Rest assured; you can get some sleep tonight, buddy 😴

I move towards the side entrance of the barn and rest my back against the wall, smiling as I receive another text from him.

GRAYSON

How are you anyway?

SKYE

Fine. Yourself?

GRAYSON

Eh. I'm not complaining. But I thought that maybe when I get back, we could

I don't finish reading that sentence because I immediately see two people emerging from around the corner. They seem close, unable to keep their hands off each other. I have to keep blinking rapidly, hoping I'm not seeing things, but Rory is with a girl—the same girl who tends to show up at the farm from time to time, always practically dressed in her underwear.

I'm at a safe enough distance, so neither of them has seen me yet. I'm too afraid to move because the girl is blatantly flirting with Rory right in front of me.

My fingers freeze on the keypad when she leans on her tiptoes and kisses him. My heart breaks into tiny pieces as I watch from the sidelines. I lose grip on my phone, which plunges to the ground with a loud crunch. This gets the pair of them to stop sucking face, but the last thing I wanted was to be caught in the middle of it.

Their heads turn in my direction, and Rory's eyes widen with alarm. I can't bear to look at him, so I divert my attention to my phone, quickly picking it up from the ground to check its functionality.

The screen is shattered, and so is my heart–just a little.

"Skye–" Rory starts, his voice trailing off.

His mouth is moving, but I can't hear any sound.

This is precisely why I didn't want to get too close to him because once you start developing feelings for someone, you're giving them the power to hurt you, and this hurts.

Bad.

I immediately cast my gaze downward, attempting to conceal my disappointment and shield myself from further pain.

I have to walk away.

There's nothing else to be said.

*I am such an idiot for thinking that Rory might like me.*

*How wrong was I?*

"Skye!" Rory's behind me, trying to match my pace, but I'm making it virtually impossible. I don't want to speak to him. I've seen enough with my eyes. I want to go home and feel sorry for myself whilst listening to breakup songs, even though this isn't a breakup—far from it.

Do I have the right to be angry?

Is my anger adequately justified?

I must care about him because I wouldn't get this riled up. But how can he kiss me and then kiss someone else just twenty-four hours later?

That's what stings the most.

Rory grabs my arm, forcefully pulling me around to face him. His face is flushed, and he wears a look of deep concern. It's a pity I don't care in the slightest.

"Skye, would you please stop running away from me? I'm trying to talk to you," he pleads.

I shake my arm free from his grasp and meet his gaze head-on, daring him to reason with me at a time like this. I am not ready to hear him out.

"Listen, I don't know what you think you just saw back there, but–"

"You were kissing that girl. Your tongue was practically shoved down her throat. There's no other possible explanation, Rory," I interject, unable to contain my frustration.

"There was no tongue involved. Chrissie is..."

"Chrissie! So, she has a name!" I let out a bitter laugh. "Why did you follow me? Shouldn't you be comforting your girlfriend? That's probably why she's always hanging around at the farm, so you can hook up and sneak around together. Is that what you've been doing this entire time?"

I'm jumping to conclusions now, but I can't help it. I've never felt this intense amount of jealousy before. I've never experienced jealousy until this exact moment.

*I hate it.*

"She's not my girlfriend," he says defensively. "We had a short fling for a while, but that's all it ever was, and that happened long before I–"

"Long *before* or *after* you decided to kiss me?" I interrupt, stunning him into silence.

He runs a hand through his hair. "I stopped seeing Chrissie weeks ago. She turned up at the farm today and caught me off guard when she kissed me. I wasn't expecting it."

"Well, considering you were so surprised, you didn't act like it," I shoot back.

"Nothing is going on between us, Skye. I can't stress that enough."

"Who are you referring to now? Me or Chrissie?"

"What?"

I've confused him.

Tears well up in my eyes, but I'm quick to blink them away. "Don't worry. I didn't feel anything when we kissed either. It was..."

*Please don't say it. Don't say it. Don't say it.*

"It was a mistake." I keep my stubborn face intact, ready to deliver the biggest lie I've ever told. "I like somebody else anyway."

Rory's gaze drops, his head bowing in defeat. "If that's how you feel, then consider our kiss forgotten about," he snarls, his face red with anger.

"Perfect! Glad we cleared that up."

Tension continues to rise between us, and I want to get out of here severely, but Chrissie's return has made my decision easier. She rushes to Rory's side and flashes me a triumphant grin as I leave them far behind.

*So, it's true.*

Feelings really can creep up on you unexpectedly. It's just a shame that they aren't always reciprocated.

# Chapter Thirty-Two

THE DAY OF THE RACE HAS ARRIVED, AND I HAVE NOT SPOKEN TO Rory since our last conversation. Despite the growing tension, we have put our differences aside during our training sessions with Dante. We act as if nothing has changed, except it has. I may have just lost a good friend, which sucks, but maybe it's for the best. I'm still mad at him for how he handled the situation with Chrissie. If he likes her, he should have just been honest about it before he decided to kiss me, sending me mixed signals.

I open the gate and step inside Dante's stall. He moves his head towards me instinctively and immediately trots over.

"Hey, you. We've come so far, haven't we, boy?" I whisper, drawing my face towards his, feeling choked up about the journey we've been on, and it's only the beginning, I hope.

"I'm so proud of you."

Dante makes a deep snorting sound. If he were human, I'd like to think he would be saying, 'I'm proud of you too,' but maybe he's just letting me know he's hungry. He does love his food.

We make our way onto the track, and I take note of my competition. There's no harm in having a little look around, only now that I have started, I'm instantly regretting it. The nerves have kicked back in, and I'm experiencing weird heart palpitations and nausea.

The other riders are way more experienced than me. Their posture is impeccable, and you can see how much practice, dedication and hard work has gone into their training. I must remind myself that I only started horse riding a few weeks ago. I'm technically a novice, but I can't compare myself to anybody else here. I'll be setting myself up for disappointment.

I remember what Mr Frost said to me a few days ago.

*There will be a lot of hurdles in this race, but those hurdles will only be the ones you create for yourself.*

"Good luck," a deep voice says from behind me, belonging to a boy straddling his horse, grinning at me. He looks about my age. His Jordie accent is thick and laced with sarcasm. His horse is wearing the latest and most expensive-looking tack and rugs I've ever seen. Considering how well-groomed he is, that horse must be treated like a king. Lucky thing.

"Thanks," I say, offering up a friendly smile.

"You're going to need it," he mumbles smugly.

"Excuse me?" I demand, jumping to Dante's defence.

The boy snorts, revealing his true colours.

"We have all witnessed Dante's frantic antics and lacklustre performances in the past. He is not a race-horse. The fact that they've paired him up with some random girl who doesn't seem to have the faintest idea — Well, it is quite frankly a joke."

Mr Frost said this would happen.

He said the other riders would try to put me off.

"Sorry, I didn't catch your name."

"It's Leonardo."

"Right. Well, Leonardo, you'll be eating your words once we beat you in the race today."

Leonardo throws his head back and laughs. "Ha! That's the funniest thing I've ever heard. I can't wait to see you fall flat on your face and for Dante's racing days to end. It's going to be quite something."

He beckons his horse to start moving and flashes me a triumphant smirk as he trots away.

I turn to Dante, nostrils flaring. "Okay. Time to re-evaluate. It's not about winning, but today's mission has taken a complete U-turn. We have to beat Leonardo. It's our duty. Do I get an amen?"

Dante neighs and I take it as confirmation.

A large crowd has gathered at the farm, including some reporters. I can sense people's eyes burning holes into the back of my head. They're probably wondering who I am since I have yet to make a name for myself in the horse-riding world. Nobody knows anything about me aside from that I'm Dante's new, mysterious rider.

There's more pressure for us to succeed than ever before because Dante might be cast out from future events if he doesn't run a good race today. We must do our absolute best because people expect to see him fail.

They're used to it, so we must show them he can be a champion and has what it takes.

“Stay calm at all times. If you get too nervous, it'll impact Dante's performance because he'll probably start to feel nervous too,” Mr Frost says, although I haven't been paying attention to anything he's been waffling about for the past five minutes.

“It’s kind of impossible not to feel nervous right now, Mr Frost,” I admit, watching him walk away.

“Hey! Good luck out there.”

I instantly recognise Rory's voice and glance down to look at him. He's wearing a smile, but it's not one I'm familiar with. This is the first time we've spoken since falling out. I wish things were different, but his decision to kiss me has ruined everything. Now, we can't be in each other's presence without it being awkward.

He only kissed me the other night because he needed to get out of his head, and I was the only person who could distract him at that particular moment. The problem is, I think letting him kiss me was the biggest mistake I could have made because it only solidified my feelings for him.

“Thanks,” I mumble back quietly.

He looks like he wants to say more, but I'm quick to stop it because I'm too afraid that he'll voice exactly what I've been thinking, and I'm not sure my heart can take it. It's one thing to witness the boy you like kissing someone else, but it's another to find out what he thinks about you, and at this point, I'm not sure what he wants or who he wants.

“I'd better get going,” I say, dismissing him.

He bows his head. “Sure.”

Each rider positions their horse at the start line, and we wait for the signal. I search for Leonardo and find him a couple of rows down. He catches my eye and flashes me a wolfish grin.

My blood boils over.

“Come on, boy. Let's show everyone what you're truly capable of,” I whisper into Dante's ear.

My stomach jumps into my throat as the whistle is blown, and we're off, except we didn't quite get the message. Dante takes a little while to get fired up, which costs us some time, but once we get going, he glides across the field much quicker, and we eventually catch up with everybody else.

Here I am–here we are, officially participating in a race with roughly three hundred people or more watching. It's surreal and terrifying at the same time. I try not to think about all those eyes on us because it's a scary thought. I imagine it's just Dante and me out here, practising what we've been taught.

Dante whizzes past a chestnut mare, and I realise we're going way too fast. The trick of the game is to go slow at first so we can keep all of our energy before the last lap. We've struggled to get the hang of this during our training sessions because Dante is so set on pushing himself to exhaustion. If I can reel him back, we can save some of that energy for later.

I pull tighter on Dante's reins to slow him down, but he's fighting against it.

“Come on, boy. You have to trust me.”

Dante's flying around corners at such a reckless

speed. I'm worried I will fall out of the saddle again or that he will injure himself. I ease him up a little on the next turn, and miraculously, he starts slowing down, still maintaining a fast enough speed to keep us on track.

I can see Leonardo up ahead.

He's currently in fourth place.

"Let's go for it," I say, encouraging Dante to break out into one final run while we're on the home stretch.

We won't win the race but can still beat Leonardo and steal his place. Dante seems intent on making this goal a reality because we're now neck and neck with Leonardo and his horse, the finish line only a few yards away. I register Leonardo's shocked expression as we move past him and claim fourth place. We sneak up behind a tall, black stallion when we enter the final turn. The rider glances anxiously over his shoulder, urging his horse to go faster.

The crowd is cheering.

Cameras are flashing.

The adrenaline is pumping in my ears.

Dante is in the zone.

I look at the spectators, and my breath catches when I spot Grayson and Mr Swain among them, watching the race with eager anticipation.

*What are they doing here?*

*They weren't supposed to return until next week.*

Grayson's eyes lock on mine, and dread consumes me, but I've got to focus on the race since it's my top priority. I'll worry about Grayson later.

We've overtaken the stallion and have made it into third place. Sailing over the finish line, there's a massive uproar in the crowd. My vision blurs over, and it's only when Mr Frost appears by my side that everything returns to its standard rate.

I hug Dante by the neck, and a few stray tears run down my face.

"Well done, boy. You did amazing out there."

Mr Frost couldn't be more excited, but I can't fully immerse myself in joining the celebrations because Grayson just saw me compete in a race I was never meant to run. He's bound to have a ton of questions.

*Please just let the ground swallow me up already.*

I dismount Dante, and Rory jogs over to take control of the horse while we're both cooling off. He catches my eye and smiles brightly, making me temporarily forget about Grayson.

"Congratulations. That was incredible, Skye."

"Third place isn't so bad for my first race, right?"

That disappointed feeling suddenly ignites in the centre of my chest, and I'm quick to digest this moment for what it truly is: awkward and charged with an inexplicable amount of emotion. Rory closes the distance between us, fidgeting nervously, shifting his weight from one foot to the other, but before he can say whatever's on his mind, a swarm of reporters descends upon us, bombarding me with questions and thrusting cameras in my face.

I don't understand why they're paying so much attention to me when we didn't even win the race, but it's good publicity for Dante and the farm.

"What's your story? How old are you? Where are you

from? We haven't seen you before," one of the reporters says in one breath.

"My name is Skye Clemons. I'm eighteen, and I'm from Barnett."

"We're all familiar with Dante's past performances. What did you do differently this time? What's your secret?" Another reporter asks eagerly.

Mr Frost handles the rest of the Q and A because I cannot do anything other than gawk and stare. It's starting to freak people out.

"It was a team effort," Mr Frost explains, "but I have never seen Dante bond with anyone as he has with Skye. She has helped us massively during our training. I'm very proud of the progress we have made. Dante's journey has only begun, and I'm sure you'll also see more of Skye in the future. She's a rising star."

The press goes wild and starts adding to their list of questions, but I decide to lead Dante back to the stables so he can get some well-deserved rest. I also need to take a break from the press because speaking to them is overwhelming, and I can't handle any more questions.

I don't expect anyone to be in the barn, but I wasn't the only person who decided to take a break from all the hustle and bustle currently going on outside.

Grayson is leaning against Dante's stall.

He glances up at me, and I can't figure out if he's angry, confused or a bit of both. All I know is that I'm about to find out.

My throat burns.

He stares at me with overwhelming accusations.

I open my mouth, but nothing comes out.

"Why didn't you tell me you've been having horse riding lessons at my dad's farm?" he demands, not sounding angry but pretty close.

I'm about to explain everything, but Mr Swain walks into the barn.

"Skye! There you are. Congratulations. I've never seen Dante race like that in all the years I've known him. Sebastian has been telling me all about your training sessions and how well they've been going, so I had to show my face. I couldn't miss it."

Heat spreads across my cheeks.

"Thanks, sir."

"Everybody's talking about how one of my employees rose to stardom. You are officially the shiny new toy."

"What the heck is going on? Why are you calling my dad, sir and... dad, why did you call Skye your employee? Am I missing something?" Grayson barks.

I can't hide the unshed tears that are building in my eyes.

*I am well and truly screwed.*

Mr Swain glances at me in bewilderment. "Oh. You still haven't told him, Skye?"

"Told me what?" Grayson repeats in frustration.

"I—I work here," I say quietly.

"*What?*"

"I've been working at Trinity for months, Grayson."

His mouth drops open, nothing but betrayal on his face. "I don't understand. How come I'm only hearing about this now?"

"I did try telling you at college, but you didn't believe me."

The air around us grows thick with emotion.

It's too much for me to handle.

"Wait... please don't tell me that you're the employee my father was talking about—the one he lent all that money to."

I nod my head slowly, sadness overwhelming me.

He laughs, but there is no trace of humour behind it.

"Are you kidding me right now?"

Mr Swain decides to remove himself from the situation, which sucks because I hoped he might've backed me up a little or tried to be the peacemaker. He doesn't want to be involved. This isn't any of his business anyway.

I move towards Grayson, desperate to explain.

"Grayson, it's not what it looks like. Your father only lent me that money because he knew I was in a difficult situation with my landlord. I didn't even want to borrow it, and I've paid him back every last penny."

"Don't try to make excuses for yourself. You could have told me about this ages ago but chose not to. You've been sneaking around for months, keeping this a secret. Am I just supposed to shrug it off and move on? Act like you haven't been lying to my face every time I've seen you?"

Another tear falls onto my cheek.

"I—I didn't know how to tell you."

"You didn't know how to tell me?" he repeats, his voice clipped, brimming with disappointment.

"Grayson, I was just–"

"You were just what? What's your excuse this time?"

"I was embarrassed, okay?"

Grayson's stern expression hasn't changed, but I have rendered him speechless. I can only try to explain my side of the story and hope that he understands I never set out to hurt him intentionally.

"I was in a financial crisis when I first accepted this job. I didn't expect to get it, and at that particular time, we didn't get along, so I had no reason to mention it. I didn't want you to know because I thought you would make fun of me. I convinced myself that I was doing the right thing by not telling you, and then it became this big, white lie I had no control over anymore. I kept it a secret, and I'm sorry."

I wonder if I might be getting through to him, but I notice his scowl deepen until too many lines cross his forehead.

"How many times have you rehearsed that speech?"

I take another deliberate step towards him.

"That wasn't rehearsed, Grayson."

"How do you expect me to believe anything you say now? I don't trust you."

"You *can* trust me."

"I told you about my past and how much I struggled to trust people, and you betrayed me way more than they did. You're not who I thought you were."

"Grayson, I—"

"Save your excuses for someone who gives a damn because I don't. Not anymore," he says, his words punching me straight in the gut.

I can see he is not prepared to forgive me, and there's

nothing else I can do.

*I'm going to lose him.*

My stomach tightens as he storms away, and I simultaneously tackle a million different emotions.

*Regret.*

*Anxiety.*

*Guilt.*

*The all-too-familiar ache of abandonment.*

Although I'm used to being abandoned, I never saw my dad leave. Seeing Grayson walk away from me is heartbreaking on so many different levels, but it's not like I don't deserve it.

"Skye, is everything okay?"

I'm shocked to find Sebastian standing behind me. He must've snuck into the barn when I wasn't looking. He is the last person I want to see right now, but the fact that he's asked me if I'm okay is unexpected and strangely appreciated.

"I argued with Grayson. I don't think he will ever speak to me again," I say, wiping my watery eyes.

"I doubt that's true."

More tears automatically start falling down my cheeks.

"I messed everything up."

I can tell Sebastian doesn't know how to deal with an emotional teenage girl, but he's showing no signs that he wants to get out of here unless he's that good of an actor.

"We all make mistakes. It's in our DNA."

My eyes dart up to his suspiciously.

*That's what I always say.*

"Grayson will come around, but you must give him

some time to cool off. Nothing is going to be resolved tonight."

I doubt Grayson will want to speak to me soon, but maybe Sebastian has a point. I need to give Grayson the time and space he requires.

"Come on. I'll take you home," he says.

I don't have the strength to decline.

The conversation could have been more present during the car ride home, but I don't think Sebastian knew what to say and vice versa. It wasn't awkward. I've been in worse situations.

We finally arrived at my house after I used up most of Sebastian's tissues and the remainder of his petrol. The journey was smooth enough, but I wouldn't be surprised if his car has paid the price.

Those potholes are a killer.

I feel bad, even though I shouldn't. It's not like I vandalised his car on purpose. My street, however, I can't vouch for. It tends to have a mind of its own.

We step out of the car, and he reaches for my folded-up bike in the boot, handing it to me with a slight smile. I say slight because Sebastian doesn't smile very often, so it's hard to tell if that's what's happening. I choose not to look into it in case I'm making a big deal out of nothing.

I fish around for my house keys, which are not in my handbag. I thoroughly search my pockets and let out a long sigh when I realise I don't have them on me.

"Great!"

"What's the matter?"

"I don't have my house keys."

"Oh. That's not good."

"My mother is at work. I'll see if I can get hold of her."

I bring her number up on my phone and dial it, but I'm immediately introduced to the dial tone. She must have her phone switched off.

"It's no biggie," I say, trying to sound optimistic. "I'll just pop down to the bakery where she works and get the keys off her there."

"Jump in the car. I will take you to her."

I wave at the air frantically. "It's alright. You've done enough for one night."

"It's getting late. I don't think a young girl like yourself should be walking the streets alone at this hour."

Five o'clock is not that late. Then again, nobody should underestimate the inner workings of Barnett's residents. The minority are usually up to no good.

## Chapter Thirty-Three

THE 'WENDY'S BAKERY' SIGN IS CROOKED, AND THE BLUE paint could use a fresh coat. Nevertheless, some locals are tucked away inside, drinking their cafe lattes, sipping hot chocolate and munching away on some of the most delicious cakes and cookies my eyes have ever seen.

My mouth is drooling at the thought of buying one, but I am here for one reason only, and I've noticed that Sebastian is beginning to get a bit restless. He's probably late for something and needs to be somewhere. He's too important to be waiting around and driving a helpless teenage girl from one place to the next.

I start walking towards the bakery and hear Sebastian's footsteps behind me.

Slowing down, I spin toward him. "You don't have to come in with me. I'll be quick."

He nods, relieved that he doesn't have to enter such a run-down building that could collapse at any moment. He doesn't want to leave his expensive-looking vehicle unsupervised, either. One should not leave a car like that in a place like this. The likelihood of it getting stolen is not even negotiable.

The bell chimes as I enter the bakery. It's ludicrously warm inside, and the room smells of coffee beans and freshly baked bread.

*Yum.*

One of the employees walks up to me and says, "Can I help you?"

"Hi. I need to speak to my mother, Julia Clemons."

"You must be Skye. I can tell that you're related to Julia. You could be sisters!"

"We get that a lot."

"She's in the kitchen."

"Great. Thanks."

There's a small crack in the kitchen doorway, so I quickly glimpse what's happening inside. I find my mother standing over one of the counters, deep in thought. Her apron is covered in flour and cake mix, bringing happy tears to my eyes. Knowing she's in a safe environment and doing something she adores brings me relief.

Mum's eyes light up at the sight of me, and she comes rushing over.

"Skye! What are you doing here?"

"I came to get the house keys."

"Oh. Right. Well, how was the race? Did you win?"

"We came in third place."

"Wow! That's brilliant! You should be so proud of yourself."

"Thanks. I wish you could have been there to see it."

"Me too, honey. It's just awkward with work at the moment. I'm trying to build bridges again and prove to people that I can be reliable," she says sadly.

"I know. I get it. Don't worry."

She grabs my hand and gives it a light squeeze. "Shouldn't you be out celebrating with your friends right now? Why so glum?"

I sigh, feeling close to tears again.

I had finally allowed myself to make some friends, only to lose them.

"My friends don't want anything to do with me," I admit solemnly.

"Why? What's happened?"

"I'll explain everything when you get home, okay?"

"Okay. Well, I won't be long. Maybe half an hour, tops. I'm so proud of you," she assures me, her eyes full of emotion.

A few minutes later, Sebastian is pulling up outside my house again. He kills the engine and follows me to the door. I fumble with the keys to unlock it, hear the familiar little click and gently push it open, switching on the light so we're not surrounded by darkness.

"Thanks for all your help," I say, entering the dimly lit porch.

"No problem. I will see you back at the farm. You did great today."

"Would you like to stay for a cup of tea?"

I've shocked the poor man to infinity and beyond. I'm

a little stunned that I extended the invitation myself. I mean, since when have I enjoyed hanging out with the guy?

"It's okay if you don't want to. I just thought I would ask because you've come all this way. It's the least I can do," I'm quick to add, taking some of the pressure off.

He lingers in silence for a brief moment, contemplating the idea, a blankness enveloping his features, devoid of emotion.

"Sure. Why not?"

I open the door wide for him to squeeze through and lead him into the living room, where the temperature drops. I rush towards one of the heaters and crank it up, noticing Sebastian visibly shiver. He hasn't taken his coat off, but maybe that's because he's not planning to stick around for long.

I don't blame him.

It's freezing.

"How do you take your tea? Any sugar?" I ask, making my way into the kitchen.

"No. Just milk, please," I hear him call out.

I pop my head around the doorway. "Strong or weak? Do you have a preference?"

He wrings his hands together, glancing at me from over his shoulder. "Somewhere in the middle."

I peer into the living room, eyes wide.

"What did you say?"

"Uh, I like it to be in the middle. An equal balance."

I blink rapidly at him and realise I've been staring at him too long. He probably thinks I'm acting weird.

"Sorry. I've just never heard anyone say that before. I

usually tell people that I like my tea to be in the middle. It's strange to hear it from somebody else's mouth."

Sebastian nods tightly, and while he attempts to creep closer to the heater, I get busy making the tea. I place the two cups on a tray and return to the living room, setting the tea on the coffee table. He thanks me quietly, and I settle into the armchair opposite, the silence returning. I'm worried it will last a while since I don't know what we could talk about, but thankfully, he has an idea.

"So, what happened with Grayson earlier? Why are you convinced he won't talk to you again?" he asks, making himself more comfortable.

I tell him everything—how and why I got the Trinity job and that I never told Grayson about it. Once I'm done explaining, even Sebastian looks exhausted after hearing all of the details.

"I can understand why Grayson is feeling upset. He might seem the confident type, but he struggles to trust people after the experiences he's had in the past. I'm sure he'll come around in the end, though. It would be a shame to throw your friendship away."

I doubt he will forgive me anytime soon if he's been hurt that much. Sometimes, it only takes a lie like this to destroy a friendship.

"We were getting along so well, and then I went and ruined it."

"I will talk to him for you if that helps, but I can't guarantee that he'll listen to anything I have to say. Give him a few days. He can't stay mad at you forever."

This is Grayson Swain we're talking about. He can hold a grudge for eternity. How much time should I give him anyway? How much space does one person need before I'm meant to chase them down and beg for forgiveness?

"Are you going to stay at Trinity for a while, or do you have any other plans or commitments for the future?" Sebastian asks me, moving the conversation along.

"My lifelong goal has been to become a journalist, to publish my work and share impactful stories with the world," I reply contemplatively, "but lately, I've developed an unexpected love for horses. It's a newfound passion that I don't want to let go of. Choosing which path to take is going to be difficult."

He nods, observing me, his stare deepening. "You're still young, Skye. You have plenty of time to decide what you want to do."

"But what if I make the wrong choice?"

"We can all make bad choices along the way, but they can still lead to beautiful destinations. Only you get to decide what you want to do. Nobody else can make that decision for you."

His words repeat in my mind.

*He gives good advice for such a cold and aloof person.*

"I must admit, seeing you out on the field earlier today... you showed a great deal of potential. You were up against some big names in the industry and handled the situation like a true professional. Whatever happens and whatever you decide to do, you've always got a future with horses."

Thoughts of Dante, Rory, and Mr Swain flood my mind, representing the three unique bonds I've formed. Trinity has become my home, where I finally feel a sense of belonging.

"Do you have any brothers or sisters, Skye?"

I return my attention to our conversation.

"No. It's just my mother and me."

A shadow briefly clouds Sebastian's face, vanishing before I can analyse its meaning.

"What about your dad? He's not around?"

My eyes burn as I try to explain. "My father is a bit of a mystery to me. I've never met him."

"That must be hard... not having your dad in your life."

"Yeah, but I try not to think about it. You can't miss something you never had," I mutter, feeling drained.

It's been a stressful couple of weeks. Sleep is finally catching up to me, and it feels like something heavy is sitting on my eyelids. Sebastian appears to notice and swiftly finishes his tea.

"Thank you for the tea. Well done again for coming in third place in the race. You deserve it after working so hard. I'm sure Dante will be exceeding our expectations soon enough," he says politely.

"I don't doubt him for a second. He's going to do great things."

Sebastian smiles. "Yes, he's fortunate to have you by his side."

I check my phone, and it's good I did because I've lost track of time. My mother will be due back any second now. I'm deciding whether to cook us my famous bean toasties when Sebastian's voice cuts through my thoughts.

"Who is that?" he asks, sounding a little strange.

He's completely transfixed on an old photograph hanging on the wall—a picture of me and my mother at a waterpark when I was only four. My mother's youthful appearance resembles mine, with her untamed and wild hair. She still looks the same now, practically my double.

"That's my mother," I reply casually.

Sebastian's head shakes frantically, and his eyes widen in disbelief.

"Oh, God."

On that strange note, I hear the front door opening and realise my mother is back. I can hear her shuffling about in the passageway, and Sebastian stands beside me, frozen. Initially, I don't pay much attention to his shift in behaviour, but as my mother enters the living room, her smile disintegrates into a million fragile pieces upon seeing him, and the atmosphere grows uncomfortably tense.

*Why is Sebastian staring at my mother as if they've already met before?*

"What the hell are *you* doing here, Sebastian?" my mother demands, not responding well to this little reunion because she's unable to look at the man without grimacing. I'm scared because I don't know what it means. I don't understand where the emotion comes from, and I'm unsure I want to.

*Who knew inviting someone in for tea could cause so much drama?*

Attempting to explain himself, Sebastian takes a

hesitant step forward. "I had no idea that you were Skye's mother. I swear if I'd known then–"

"What would you have done differently if you had known I was Skye's mother?"

"Well, for starters, I would have found some other way of bumping into you—not like this. I'm just as shocked as you are."

"How did–" she pauses, takes a deep breath, but doesn't finish that sentence. Instead, she glances at me, and it encourages Sebastian to do the same. A mutual look passes between them, one of pure recognition and awareness. Feeling overwhelmed, I step back and distance myself from the unfolding situation.

"How do you know this man, Skye?" Mum asks.

"He's just my boss's friend," I explain nervously.

"I can't believe you're here. After all these years."

"None of this was planned," Sebastian says urgently.

"Have you known who Skye was this entire time? Or have you only just found out? Tell me the truth."

His gaze lingers on me, but I can't return it. I have no idea what is happening, but my heart is sinking to the ground, making the ache ten times worse.

"I did think there was something about her that seemed familiar, but the idea of her being..." He stops like the word he's searching for is too difficult to say. "I wasn't expecting this at all."

"I don't think we have anything else to say to each other, Sebastian," my mother retorts, lowering her head.

Sebastian thrusts his hand in his hair, choosing his following words carefully. "Can't we just sit down for a minute and discuss this properly?"

"What's there to discuss? You didn't want to be a part of Skye's life. Those were your exact words."

"I did what I could to support you financially."

*Bluebell.*

*Sebastian is Bluebell.*

I'm not allowing this new information to sink in because I don't want it to be real. I'm just the bystander in this scenario, and this is not a conversation I was ever meant to hear or witness.

"It's not like we were in love. It was just a one-night stand, a mistake," he continues.

My heart crumbles to hear this.

*Mistake.*

*I was just a mistake—a result of a one-night stand.*

"We weren't committed to each other. I was young. I wasn't ready to bring a child into the world. I was still a child myself. I didn't know the first thing about being a parent," Sebastian adds.

Mum scoffs.

"And you thought that I did? I was *eighteen*, Sebastian. My whole life changed when I had Skye. I could have just abandoned her like you did. I could have neglected my responsibilities or refused to play the part, but instead, I chose to step up and become a mother because I knew that was the right thing to do."

I had just started to accept not knowing who my dad was, but then Sebastian Cole swoops in, and suddenly, he turns out to be the one person I have spent years despising.

I can't accept it.

I won't.

Refusing to let the truth sink in, I turn away and flee from the house. I have to escape because the truth is way too difficult to digest. I'll imagine that my dad's identity is still undiscovered or that he's halfway across the world. This is a much better explanation than having Sebastian Cole as my father.

# Chapter Thirty-Four

"HIT ME AGAIN, PLEASE, KEV!" I SHOUT AT THE BARTENDER, raising my empty beer glass and waving it. By now, I've become well acquainted with the bartender, Kevin David Butler, to be exact. In my slightly intoxicated state, I have proclaimed him my new best friend, although he doesn't seem to share my enthusiasm.

Kevin glances at me in annoyance, wiping over the bar. "Don't you think you've had enough for one night?"

I laugh at the wall.

*When on earth did that get there?*

"No! I am perfectly perfect! I am completely sober. Ask me how many beers I've had, Kev. Ask me! Go on!"

Kevin exhales, clearly not in the mood to be dealing with me. "How many beers have you had?"

I try to count on my fingers, but it's hard.

"Seven. I've had seven!"

"What about the one you've got in your hand right there?" Kevin queries, pointing at the glass I'm currently holding.

"Oh. Eight then. I've had eight beers."

"But you want me to pour you another one, which would make that nine?"

"Well done, Kev! You're a lot cleverer than you give yourself credit for."

*Is cleverer a word?*

*I don't think it is.*

Kevin shakes his head and attends to another customer further down the bar. I stare solemnly into my empty glass, eyes tired. I'm not drunk out of my mind yet, but it won't be long before standing on my own two feet will become an issue.

I wait for Kevin to come back and serve me, but he doesn't, so I glance around the lifeless pub to find only a few punters. Two older men are having a game of pool. Another man stares into his glass, looking just as miserable as I am. One guy is sitting on a chair closest to the toilets, mouth open, cap on his head. Everyone else might assume he's watching the TV, but he is sleeping, and I'm not far behind myself.

Taking out my phone, I absentmindedly scroll through my Facebook newsfeed and notice that I've been tagged in a post on Trinity's Facebook page. In the picture are Dante, Rory, Mr Frost, and me, all smiling brightly for the camera. Before everything went downhill, this was probably one of the best days of my life, and now it's officially the worst.

If only I could transport myself back to that moment. I would never have invited Sebastian to my house. Never in my wildest dreams did I imagine that someone like Sebastian Cole could be related to someone like me, but despite feeling angry and confused, shouldn't I feel a glimmer of relief now that I might finally know who my father is?

A message suddenly flashes on my screen.

It's from Rory.

RORY

Hey. Mr Swain told me about what happened with Grayson. Are you okay?

SKYE

Hey. I'm in a pub called The Cracker. I'm having a cracking time LOL!

Three little bubbles pop up on the screen.

He's typing.

RORY

Are you drunk?

SKYE

Nope. Why would you think such a thing?

RORY

Don't go anywhere. I'm coming to get you.

I twirl around on the bar stool and receive some odd looks.

SKYE

How heroic of you.

RORY

How much have you had to drink?

SKYE

Too much. I'm soberrrrrr, but I'm also a bit drunk. I need to burp.

I'm clicking send before I can think about what I'm saying.

RORY

I'm on my way now.

SKYE

Don't bother. I'm about to fall asleep.

My phone beeps again, but I quickly switch it off and lower my head onto the counter. My hair falls around me, and I take slow breaths, giggling. I must have lost consciousness at one point because it feels like time has passed when my eyes flutter open again.

"Skye, I think it's time for you to go home," Kevin says.

"Kev! I didn't think I'd ever see you again!" I cry, trying to wrap my arms around him and falling short when I grasp at thin air. "Where did you go?"

Kevin places both hands on the bar and leans forward. "I'm going to call for a taxi, alright? You have outdone yourself for the night."

I watch him move towards the phone.

"You're so good to me, Kevster! You're the bestest friend I never had!"

Kevin turns his back to me, talking to the person on the other end of the line. I let my head roll back, trying to gain more control over my tired limbs that don't want to cooperate. I pick up a placemat and flip it around, wondering how I will walk in a straight line after this. I don't think I'll be able to put one foot in front of the other or remove myself from this bar stool.

The pub doors burst open, and Rory charges through, scooping me into his arms.

"What am I going to do with you, Clemons?" he rasps.

I raise a hand to pat his cheek, running the other through his messy hair. It feels incredibly soft.

"You have such a pretty face," I tell him.

His eyebrows shoot up in surprise. "Okay... that's not really what any boy wants to hear, but I'll let that slide since you are completely off your face and don't know what you're talking about."

"If I could put your face in a frame, I would."

Rory laughs and says, "I'm truly honoured."

"You're welcome. You have perfect skin, and those lips aren't too shabby either."

"Alright, I think it's time we got you home," he mutters, guiding me towards the exit.

"I'm not going home. Please don't take me back there," I quickly protest, panic setting in.

Rory looks down at me, eyes filling with curiosity, and then Kevin quickly shouts, "The taxi won't be long! Do you want me to cancel?"

"A taxi sounds like a good idea. I don't think she's going to last much longer."

Rory was right about me not being able to last any longer. We piled into the taxi, and I fell asleep on his shoulder, cuddling into his woolly jumper, his strong arms holding me steady against him.

I jolt forward when the taxi pulls up on a curb, and the driver informs us that we've arrived at our destination. Rory comes to my side and helps me out, but I wobble as I place my foot on the ground, causing him to react quickly. He grips me by the waist and leads me into his house, assisting me in removing my shoes and coat. I try to plant a kiss on his lips to express my gratitude, but I end up kissing his chin or maybe his ear. My vision has become hazy.

"Come err. I want to kiss you," I moan, sounding like a needy child.

"No kissing tonight. You have no idea who I am right now."

"Yes, I do! You're Rory Keaton! And I like you. I like you very much!" I yell, reaching for the back of his head and attempting to pull it towards mine, but he's much stronger than me and barely budges.

"Come on, let's get you to bed."

I flutter my eyelashes at him.

"You can take me to bed any time, Rory."

He rests his forehead against mine, swallowing hard. "That's not helping."

"But it's the truth. You are one sexy human being—an absolute snack."

He breaks away, amused.

"Did you just call me a snack? What have you been drinking exactly?"

Rory lifts me, and I squeal in his arms. Bridal style, he carries me up the staircase to his bedroom, gently lowering me onto the mattress. I stretch my body across the sheets and encourage him to join me, but he quickly covers me with the blanket, keeping my arms under the covers in case I reach out for him again.

"Oh my gosh. Is she alright? How did she get into such a state?" I hear a small voice ask from the doorway.

It's Anne.

"Anne! Hello!"

Rory is saying something to his grandmother, but I can't hear him properly because it feels like he's a million miles away. Eventually, he leans over me to wipe away my tears, and I realise I've been crying.

"I was a mistake," I say, my eyes fighting to stay open.

His stare hardens.

"What? What are you talking about?"

"I was a mistake," I repeat quietly.

Before I lose all awareness, I'm sure I feel a pair of lips touch my forehead, and Rory's velvety voice says, "You are not a mistake, Skye Clemons. I'm lucky enough to know you."

I wake up, and I'm reminded of how clingy I was towards Rory last night. I'm forced to relive the entire ordeal.

*Did I kiss his ear?*

*I think I even attempted to get him into the bed with me.*

I quickly crawl under the covers, hoping to hide my less-than-presentable morning face from Rory when he enters the room. It can't be a pretty sight.

"Hey, sleepy head. How are you feeling?" he asks, sitting on the edge of the bed.

"Like a herd of elephants has trampled on me," I groan, wincing at the soreness that resonates through my body.

He winces in sympathy. "Ouch. That's got to hurt."

I touch a hand to my forehead and groan. "Oh, trust me, you have no idea."

"What the hell happened last night?"

My shoulders sag down as I process the question, and it feels like something heavy is sitting on my chest.

"It's complicated. I've got a lot going on."

"Do you want to talk about it?" he asks, tucking a loose curl behind my ear.

"Not really." I rise to my feet and begin searching the room for my shoes. Spotting them shoved underneath the bed, I quickly slip them on. "I've got to go. I'll see you later."

Rory moves to block the door, looking directly at me. I'm scared of what he's going to find.

"What's going on with you, Skye?"

I run a hand through my hair in frustration.

"Nothing!"

"I know you. Something is wrong."

"I don't need a counsellor."

He reels back. "I'm not saying you need one. I'm just letting you know that I'm here for you."

"Well, I don't need you to be!" I shout defensively.

"Are you still mad about that kiss I had with Chrissie?"

"No! You can kiss whoever you want. I don't care." The words spill out of me, but the weight of the moment hangs heavy in the air, only adding to my restlessness.

"Just get out of my way, Rory," I warn, gnawing viciously at my lip.

"Skye, whatever is going on, I know you're trying to run away from it, but you don't have to."

"Just leave me alone!" I screech, shoving past him and running out of the house.

I'm not paying attention to my surroundings or the people in them. I speed up, angrily pushing forward with all my strength.

I'm fed up with all the secrets.

I'm fed up with being kept in the dark.

Sebastian Cole is my father. He didn't want me then, and he doesn't want me now. He's disappointed that I'm his daughter.

*I was a mistake.*

The tears come, and I lose concentration. I cry into my hands, heavy sobs that leave me breathless and vulnerable.

*Why did this have to happen?*

*What am I going to do now?*

*Why did it have to be Sebastian, of all people?*

I let the rain wash my tears away, and the emotion is beginning to choke me from the inside out. My legs carry me through the park, and I spot a climbing frame with a small overhead cover. I run over, leaning against the frame, teeth chattering from the cold and inner turmoil.

A streak of lightning crosses the sky, and my stomach rumbles. Bile rises to the back of my throat, and I throw up. I continue to vomit until it hurts.

*Everything hurts so bad.*

It feels like barely ten minutes have passed when I

hear someone calling my name in the distance. I turn halfway and notice Rory scanning the park, searching for signs of life. As soon as he spots me, drenched in sweat and tears, he wastes no time and closes the distance between us.

My face scrunches up in pain, his arms wrapping around me. I cling to him, allowing him to hold me and support the broken pieces of me that have forgotten how to function.

"Hey. It's okay, Skye. It's okay."

He briefly pulls away, removing his jacket and draping it around my shoulders before drawing me back into his embrace.

"Ssh. I've got you. It's alright," he whispers into my ear.

"I'm sorry. I'm so sorry," I mumble between sobs, tears soaking into his shoulder.

He kisses the top of my head tenderly. "You don't need to apologise."

"I shouldn't have yelled at you. I just... I don't..." I can't even finish that sentence.

I shudder against him.

Everything is still so raw at the moment. I don't know how to explain, but I need to talk to someone. I feel like I'm slowly withering away — that I'm going insane.

"Sebastian Cole is my father," I finally confess, forcing the words out.

Rory gasps. "What? Why would you think that?"

"I found out yesterday. I invited him back to my house after the race, and it all kicked off when my mother came home. They have unfinished business."

Rory and I sit close together, our backs against the climbing frame wall. I wipe away fresh tears cascading down my face, and instinctively, my head leans into the warmth of his hand as he wraps an arm around me.

“I don't know how to deal with this, Rory. We can't return to normal because everything has changed. I honestly don't know where to go from here.”

“Did Sebastian explain himself? Did he tell you why he wasn’t present for all those years?”

“He just said he wasn’t ready to commit and that I was a mistake. I didn’t stick around to hear the rest.”

Rory shakes his head, fury burning behind his eyes.

“That’s what you kept saying to me, over and over last night before you passed out—that you were a mistake. I didn’t understand what you meant at the time, but now it makes sense.”

“What am I supposed to do?”

“Take each day at a time. That's all you can do.”

My mobile beeps.

I've had a Facebook request and a message from my mother.

MUM

Please come home. I’m worried. Let me know if you’re safe.

I open Messenger to accept the Facebook request.

To my surprise, it's from Eddie.

EDDIE

Hey, Skye. Have you heard from Grayson at all? His dad asked me to contact you. He's been AWOL since yesterday, and we're all a bit worried. He's not answering his phone, and nobody knows where he is. Let me know if he gets in touch.

I stare at the screen for a few seconds.

*Grayson is missing?*

"What's wrong?" Rory asks, looking concerned.

I tear my gaze away from the screen and take a deep breath. "It's Grayson. He's gone off the radar, and this boy from my class wanted to know if I've seen him or heard anything."

"Are you going to text him back?"

I shove the phone into my coat pocket and shake my head. "No. I'm the last person Grayson wants to see right now. I'm sure they'll find him eventually."

*Without my help.*

The rain has died down by the time I get to my house.

Sebastian's car is gone, and I'm relieved I don't have to see him. I open my front door and notice my mother sitting on the couch with the house phone pressed against her ear.

"I'm so worried about her. She hasn't called or texted. I don't know what to do."

I walk into the room, and her eyes meet mine. She jumps to her feet and shuffles over to me, quickly whispering into the phone, "She's back. Thanks for looking anyway. Bye."

*I'm curious about who is on the other end of that phone call.*

"Sebastian has been out looking for you all night and this morning. We were both worried."

*So, there's a 'we' now.*

"What did you expect? I couldn't stay here and listen to you two talk about your one-night stand and how much of a mistake I was."

"You were never a mistake, Skye. I understand that this has all come as a shock. I'm so sorry you had to find out the way that you did. It's the last thing I wanted."

I furiously wipe tears from my eyes.

"Sebastian has been living on the other side of town this whole time, and the fact that he has never even tried to reach out to me is the most heart-breaking thing of all. How am I supposed to see him as anything more than a villain in this scenario when that's all he's ever been?"

She stares at me, a terrifying amount of understanding crossing her face.

"Skye, nothing has to change if you don't want it to. You don't need to have a relationship with him. Judging by his reaction and our talk after you left, he might want to make up for lost time, but you have the final say in that decision. It's completely up to you."

A whirlwind of thoughts and emotions races through my mind as I contemplate the possibility of seeing Sebastian again. I owe him nothing, but perhaps, just perhaps, meeting him could offer the closure I've yearned for all these years.

# Chapter Thirty-Five

MY HEART CLENCHES IN MY CHEST AT THE THOUGHT OF SEEING Sebastian again, but if I don't hear him out, I'll always wonder what he has to say for himself. I try to steady my nerves, reminding myself I can walk away if things turn sour. I'm old enough to make my own choices. I'm the one with all the control.

As I make my way towards the park where we agreed to meet, the gravity of the situation finally hits me.

*I'm about to have my first conversation with my father.*

I spot someone sitting on one of the benches in the distance, and I approach the bench with caution, my knees wobbling with every step. Sebastian is slumped forward on the bench, head cast towards the gravel. He's fiddling with his hands, and I wonder if he's just as nervous as I am.

His head flips sharply, and once his eyes settle on me, they soften immediately, and I have to glance away.

"Thank you for meeting me," he says formally, a burning sensation welling up in the back of my throat.

I stand there, rooted in place, unable to move or speak. My body feels frozen, and I struggle to look directly at him because we must share some physical similarities.

"I... don't know where to begin, but I suppose I should apologise for... well, being absent for starters," he says when I fail to find my voice.

His apology should hold some meaning. I wait for the relief to arrive, but it never comes. A simple apology won't repair the damage already done. His absence hurt me and my mother, leaving her to shoulder all the responsibility of raising me alone. Perhaps her mental health wouldn't have suffered so much if he had taken some accountability for his actions.

"This is just too weird. Just the other day, you were Mr Swain's friend, and now you're so much more than that," I mutter quietly.

"It's strange for me too, but I'd like to get to know you better if you allow it," he says, making it sound as though we can pick up from where we left off, but it's far more complicated than that, and I need to make that clear to him.

"There are so many things that you've missed. So many birthdays, Christmas's, and school plays. I'm not sure we can have a relationship when you know nothing about me."

"I can't change the past, Skye. I know I wasn't there for you growing up, but I want to be there now."

"It's not that easy."

He sucks in a sharp breath. "How can I make it up to you? We could go on a trip somewhere, just the two of us? I could hire a yacht for the day. It'll be a great way of getting to know each other."

I breathe out an emotional sigh.

Once again, he's trying to buy my affection.

That's all he's ever done.

"I don't want your money," I snap.

He closes his eyes, then opens them painfully slowly, and I can see part of myself in his mannerisms—how he chews on his lower lip when he's anxious, how his smile curves at the edges, producing a barely-there smile. His eyes are just like mine–a startling blue. There is no denying this man is my father, but it will take a while to accept.

"Look... the truth is, when I met your mother, I was young and selfish. As I've matured, there have been times when I've regretted my decision not to be present in your life. I used to wonder whether it would be worth reaching out to you somehow, but at that point, I thought it might have been too late. I convinced myself that you would be better off without me," Sebastian confesses.

I allow his words to sink in.

"If you wanted to find me that badly, you could have. That's what I'm struggling to grasp."

He runs a hand over his jaw. "I honestly didn't know how to make things right. I hope that you will be able to forgive me someday. I would also love to have a relationship with you, but I understand if you don't want to have one with me. I've made my bed. Now, I've got to lie in it."

My thoughts all muddle together, bringing more chaos to the table.

I have two choices here.

I can give Sebastian a second chance or pretend that this conversation never happened.

It's a big decision to make.

The knots in my stomach are growing.

"Why are you so interested in playing my father now when you couldn't care less the day I was born? What has changed?"

"I've changed, but, more importantly, you are wonderful and deserve better. I know I was a little hard on you when we first met at the farm, but that's because you reminded me so much of myself, and it scared me. Even the way we ride horseback is similar—that's why I watched you so much during your training sessions with Dante. I guess I was... curious."

My thoughts scatter again.

"Did you truly not know who I was when you first met me?"

"No, but the more I saw of you, the more I became suspicious. I kept telling myself I was overthinking it."

Sebastian might have figured out the truth sooner if I had written my last name on the sign-in sheet, but I was always trying to remain unidentified.

Reaching into my back pocket, I take out the old photograph I stole from the storage cupboard a few weeks ago. It's a little crumpled up from being in my bag for so long, but I held onto it for a reason. I didn't know why I had taken it then, but now I understand.

The woman in this photo is my mother.

It must've been taken the night she met Sebastian–at the fancy dress party.

I hold the photo out and watch Sebastian's eyes slowly move over it like he's trying to process what he's seeing.

"Where on earth did you get this?" he asks.

"I found it in a storage cupboard at the farm."

"Michael must've kept it after all these years," he says, shaking his head. "When I first met your mother, we were both attending his house party, and there was a photographer who asked to take a group photo of us. That's probably why it got mixed up with Michael's things."

Tears stream down my face now, and Sebastian rises from the bench, enveloping me in a hug.

*It's like I've forgotten how to hug.*

I slowly let my head rest against his chest.

*So, this is what it feels like to be held by my father.*

Now that the truth is out there, I can finally move on, but do I want this man to be in my life? That's such a tricky question to answer.

"Was I a mistake? Do you regret having me?" I ask fearfully.

"No, of course not. I should've taken action sooner, but I'm not going to give up on you again, not now that I've found you."

Several moments pass before I finally say, "Let's see how things go. Baby steps."

"That's more than enough for me," he says, a glimmer of unshed tears dancing at the corners of his eyes, exposing the depth of his emotions.

It's a rare sight—seeing a proud man, full of pride,

reveal his vulnerable side. I know that life is too short to hold grudges. Poor Rory lost both of his parents in the blink of an eye. The fact that Sebastian is here and wants to have a relationship with me is a good start.

# Chapter Thirty-Six

The summer holidays are supposed to be a time to rest from the basic pleasures of being a college student. However, my holidays have been the busiest yet, and I have had no time to do anything besides going on a house hunt with my mother and arranging regular contact with Sebastian.

I still haven't called him 'Dad' yet, but I learn something new every time I see him. Secretly, I'm enjoying trying to figure him out because I know that part of him exists in me. That doesn't mean I'm making it easy for him. He does most of the talking, and I sit there absorbing the information, unable to get involved as much as I would like to. I'm holding myself back in case he decides he won't stick around.

I walk into the college classroom on Monday morning, and my eyes instantly search for Grayson.

His chair is empty.

*That's odd.*

I sent him numerous messages over the holidays, but he hasn't replied to a single one of them.

"Watch where you're going!" Someone cries into my left ear.

I glance up at Shelly Matthews, whose face is shrivelled up so tightly I wonder whether she's constipated.

"Sorry, Shelly, I didn't see you there," I say.

She scoffs. "Well, maybe you need to get your eyes fixed, Clemons."

"I've got perfect vision. You should be more aware of the people around you."

"Hey, girlies! What are we chatting about?" Josie says, joining the conversation. We've hung out once or twice during the holidays, and I've started to appreciate her friendship more. Aside from Rory, she's the only real friend I've got left, and I don't want to lose her either.

I'm relieved Josie is here because I can now retreat to my table in peace, but before I go, I'm quick to say, "We were just discussing Shelly's bowel movements. And don't worry, Shelly, I'm sure with the right treatment, that burning sensation will eventually die down."

Shelley's whole face drops, and I giggle as I sit at my table.

Throughout the lesson, I constantly check over my shoulder to see if Grayson has turned up. It's bugging me that he hasn't. Even at lunch, I can't stop thinking about him. Things might be different now, but they don't have to be.

"What's up with Grayson? It's not like him to miss a day of college, especially on the first day back."

At the mention of his name, I'm drawn into the girl's

conversation at the lunch table.

"Yeah... it is strange. Do you think he's alright?" Josie asks, sounding worried.

Shelly shrugs. "I had this weird message from Eddie during the holidays. Grayson went missing for a day or two, and nobody could find him."

My head sinks to the floor.

*I hope his disappearance didn't have anything to do with me.*

"I had the same message," Josie speaks up.

"Grayson is going through a bit of a hard time according to... inside sources," another Lakeside student comments.

*Inside sources? What is this? The Daily Mail?*

"Sophie said she thinks Grayson's parents are getting a divorce."

The girls exchange glances, and I tear a used napkin absentmindedly, catching Shelly's suspicious gaze. I shoot her an unappreciative look, which she only uses to her advantage.

"Maybe we should be asking Skye about this since she's been spending most of her time with Grayson lately."

"I wouldn't know. Why are you all so concerned about where Grayson is anyway? The guy has one day off, and you're acting like it's the end of the world. Calm down. He's probably just ill or something. You're making a big deal out of nothing."

I register their shocked faces and glance at the floor awkwardly.

Josie clutches onto my arm as I stand up. "Skye,

where are you going?"

"I've lost my appetite."

I take my tray and dump the contents into the closest bin before heading into the library to spend the rest of my lunch hour alone.

* * *

It has been an entire week without a trace of Grayson. He hasn't shown up for a single lesson, and a sinking feeling tells me he may not return to college.

During lunch, I scan the canteen for one person in particular and spot Sophie sitting near the front windows, surrounded by a large group of girls. Her smile fades once she realises I'm responsible for the disruption.

"What the hell do *you* want?" she snaps.

"Can we talk, please? It's urgent," I request, hoping she'll agree.

She laughs bitterly but doesn't say no as I lead us to a quieter part of the lunch hall.

"Have you seen Grayson recently?"

Sophie's eyes lift towards the ceiling like she's enjoying keeping me in suspense. "No. I haven't seen him since he decided to break up with me."

"What?"

"We're not together anymore," she states matter-of-factly.

I didn't see the relationship lasting very long, to begin with. Sophie was always very protective, and Grayson didn't seem to like that about her.

"I thought you would have been the first to hear

about it since you're close," Sophie comments.

"It was never like that between us, Sophie."

"You've had your sights set on Grayson the moment you were paired up for that stupid project."

*She's got this so wrong.*

"No, I haven't. We're just friends."

"How could you not like him? He's good-looking. Most girls want him. He's perfect."

Grayson is far from perfect. Sophie is only interested in his physical appearance. She hasn't gotten to know him as I have. She doesn't understand why he loves to write. She probably couldn't list all his fears, wants or needs because she bases her facts on what's in front of her.

"There is more to a person than their outer appearance, Sophie. Just know that your break up had nothing to do with me anyway."

"Get over yourself. I mean, why on earth would he choose to downgrade? That wouldn't make any sense."

I'll let that comment slide since she's clearly in the early break-up stages, and I'm in the firing line.

"Look, have you heard from him? Do you know if he's coming back to college?"

*Please be helpful for a change, Sophie.*

"We haven't talked since our argument. He said that he was leaving town for a while, though. He needs to sort through some stuff, whatever that means."

"Has he already left?"

Sophie rolls her eyes, clearly frustrated that I'm bombarding her with questions. "I don't know! I'm not a mind reader."

My feet are already moving towards the exit.

"Hey! Where are you going?" Sophie calls after me.

I don't bother replying. I am only set on getting Grayson to change his mind before he chooses to run away.

I just hope that I'm not too late.

I pedal the familiar road to Grayson's house. I place my bike against the wall and march up the steps, ringing the doorbell maniacally. Nobody answers, not even after the sixth ring fades away. I rise on my tip-toes amongst the shrubbery to peep inside the window. My fingers lose grip on the ledge, and I topple backwards into the flowerbed, landing on my elbow.

"Who's out here? I'll call the police!" A male voice demands as I struggle to free myself from the bushes, continuously falling back into them.

Footsteps draw closer, and Grayson stands over me, his eyes wide with surprise.

"Skye? What are you doing in my mother's flowerbed?"

I fling my arms in the air, exasperated.

"I got stuck. I was trying to look through the window but fell and ended up down here."

Grayson extends a hand to help me up, and once I'm back on solid ground, I brush off the dirt, thanking him quietly under my breath. He steps back as if being near me is painful for him.

*He doesn't want to be anywhere near me.*

Grayson starts heading back toward the house, and I stumble after him, my heart pounding.

"Is it true that you're going away for a few months?" I ask sharply, watching him tread up the steps.

He turns around, fixing me with a cold stare. "Who told you that?"

"It doesn't matter who told me. Are you really leaving?" I ask, desperate for answers.

"Yes."

My lips part in disbelief.

To say I'm disappointed is an understatement.

"Why?"

"I have nothing to stick around here for, and my mother needs me right now."

"Are your parents divorcing?"

"They're not getting a divorce. They are just taking a break," he clarifies.

"But what about college? You're just going to give up on your dream?"

"No. I'll finish studying abroad. We're going to stay with my aunt for a while."

"For how long?"

"I don't know, Skye! As long as it takes!" he cries, his voice raw with emotion.

I storm towards him.

*There is no way I'm letting him leave.*

"You are not going anywhere, Grayson Swain."

He laughs in my face, and fear ignites in my stomach at the thought of losing him for good.

"I think that's up to me to decide."

"Look, I'm sorry that I let you down. I should have

known better, especially after you opened up to me. You're right. I had plenty of chances to tell you the truth about Trinity. I didn't want to ruin our friendship because I care about you, Grayson. I'll miss you if you go."

He turns his head to the side. "My parents might be separating, Skye. You couldn't possibly understand what that's like since you're about to get your happy ever after story."

Sebastian must have told him the news, and I guess it's better this way. At least there are no more secrets between us anymore.

"Grayson... I'm not living happily ever after. Don't forget, I was born into a broken home. Just because I've found out who my father is doesn't mean things will be smooth sailing from here."

I take a deliberate step towards him, but what he says next sends my heart plummeting. "Is that all you came here to say? I need to continue packing. We leave tomorrow."

My mouth quivers, and a tear trails down my cheek. Grayson shows no remorse. His hands are in his pockets, and his hair blows in the wind. It's clear he's unprepared to forgive and forget. There's nothing else I can do.

This might be the last time I ever see Grayson Swain.

"Please don't go," I plead, my voice barely above a whisper.

I swear I see a flicker of pain in his eyes, but I could be mistaken.

"Have a nice life, Skye," he says, slamming the door in my face and, quite frankly, on my heart.

# Chapter Thirty-Seven

Sitting in the coffee shop with my dad and having a normal conversation about life is becoming second nature to me.

"It's just so sad that Grayson is choosing to go halfway across the country."

Sebastian hovers his hand over mine, and it's oddly reassuring. "It is a shame, but I'm sure his decision to leave has nothing to do with you. It can't be easy watching your parents fall out of love with each other."

I sip my caramel latte and glance out the window.

"I wish I could go back in time, you know? I would have told him the truth sooner; I could have been there for him. He doesn't like me very much at the moment."

"He'll come around."

I take a moment to gather my thoughts.

"I've still got some questions to ask you, by the way."

Sebastian straightens in his chair, removing his hand. "Feel free to ask me whatever you want."

"Do you have any other children or relatives?"

"I don't have any other children. My parents passed away a few years ago, but I have a niece. She is looking forward to meeting you. I won't introduce you to her until you're ready."

*Woah.*

It's exciting to discover that I have a cousin. I wonder what she's like. My mother was an only child, and her parents passed away when she was young, so it has always been the two of us. The idea of having extended family elsewhere is mind-boggling. I hope she likes me when I finally get the chance to meet her.

Sebastian drops me off at college, and I sneak into class to avoid drawing attention to myself.

"Sir, have you heard from Grayson yet? Is he coming back?" Shelly questions, making me roll my eyes as I sit by my desk.

*She is so obsessed with Grayson. It's unbelievable.*

"Unfortunately, Grayson will be continuing the course at a different college this term. I can't tell you why, as it's confidential. I'm afraid he will no longer be with us, but let's switch our focus back to the presentations for a second. I've got your results, so I'll start handing them out," he says.

Excited glances are traded around the room. If Grayson were here, we would both be eager to get our results back. We put so much work and effort into the project. It's not the same now that he's gone.

Ricky places my presentation results on my desk and winks at me.

"Congratulations, Skye. Exceptional work," he says.

Staring at the paper, I read over the feedback.

**<u>From Opposite Sides</u>**

**I was very impressed with your presentation, Skye. You have shown so much progress this year. I was waiting for this from you – an honest, in-depth piece of oral work. You delivered that. You are on your way to becoming a great writer. Keep being your authentic self.**

**Result: A**

It's a shame that the only person I'm excited to share this news with is no longer here.

Josie spins to me, a warm smile overtaking her entire face. "I got a B! What did you get?"

"I got an A," I mutter.

"Oh my gosh! Congratulations! Are you going to Jerry's house party on Saturday?"

"Who's Jerry?" I ask, puzzled.

"I have no idea," she laughs, "but he's throwing this fancy dress party at his place. It'll be the perfect opportunity to celebrate. We deserve it after working so hard!"

My mind flashes back to when I found that old photograph of my mother and Sebastian at a fancy dress party. I wonder if she still has that Catwoman outfit because I might need to borrow it.

* * *

Arriving home just in time for dinner, a smile lights up my face as I notice Tipping Point playing on the TV. The episode is already halfway through, so I settle down to watch the rest while scrolling through my phone.

I refresh my Facebook newsfeed and somehow find myself on Grayson's profile, feeling like an actual stalker. We never added each other on Facebook, so I can't see any of his posts or pictures, which is disappointing. My finger hovers over the 'add friend' button, but I hesitate, knowing he might remove me once he realises I've tried to add him.

My phone dings, indicating a new email notification. I open my inbox with little enthusiasm until my eyes catch the UCAS signature in the email's subject line, causing my chest to tighten.

*I'm about to find out if I got accepted to study journalism at Sloanville University.*

*Breathe, Skye. Breathe.*

This email holds the key to my future. Everything is riding on this acceptance letter. I'm scared to read it in case I've been rejected.

I click on the email and brace myself for the news.

Sloanville University

**Dear Skye,**

**Thank you for applying to Sloanville University. Congratulations! You have been admitted to study journalism in the new academic year.**

“Ahhhhh!” I scream, overwhelmed with joy and excitement.

I don't even need to finish reading the rest of the email. The word "congratulations" is all I care about.

My mother rushes into the room in a flood of panic.

“Skye, what’s wrong?” she asks.

“I got in! I’ll be studying at university next September! I can’t believe it!” I shout, jumping up from the sofa to do a happy dance.

My mother smiles, but it doesn’t quite reach her eyes, and my excitement dies right there.

Reality hits me like a punch in the face.

*Of course, I can't go.*

My reasons for staying in Barnett outweigh my reasons for leaving. My mother might be in a better place now, but that doesn't mean she's fully restored. She will need all the support she can get over the next few months, and if I'm not here, she could relapse.

"It's not like I'll be able to go anyway. I could never leave you," I say, lowering my head to the floor.

My mother steps closer, placing her hand on my arm, forcing me to look up at her. "Skye, I would never ask you to give up your dream for me. I'll struggle without you here, that's true, but I'll be fine."

"You need me, though," I say, choking on my emotions.

My mother's eyes fill up.

"You've got to go. Please do it for yourself, and do it for me. Don't let me hold you back. I won't let you."

My lower lip wobbles. "Mum, I..."

"You're going! End of story."

I walk into her open arms, and now we're both crying by the coffee table, knowing that soon we will be on very different paths, but our bond will remain unbreakable, no matter the distance.

# Chapter Thirty-Eight

JERRY'S PARTY IS IN FULL SWING, AND I FIND MYSELF FLITTING IN and out of social groups. The air inside the house is hot and sticky, throbbing with the pounding beats of rave music. People are dancing on tables, drinking, and engaging in passionate encounters in the dimly lit corners. I wouldn't be surprised if the police showed up soon because this party has already gotten out of hand. I'm expecting a noise complaint. It's bound to happen.

I navigate through the crowd, searching for Josie, but it doesn't take me long to find her because she's sitting on the sofa, casually snacking on a packet of Wotsits while dressed as a banana peel. Her outfit is one of the quirkiest of the night, but she wears it confidently. That's what I admire about Josie—her refusal to conform to being anyone other than herself.

Josie sees me and wobbles over, drawing giggles and attention from fellow party-goers.

"Skye! I'm so glad you made it!" she exclaims,

enveloping me in a tight banana hug. “Wow. You look great,” she compliments, eyeing me up and down.

My mother still had the Catwoman outfit. It was locked away in the attic somewhere, gathering dust. The cat ears are damaged, but the outfit is in perfect condition.

“Thanks, it was either Catwoman or Cousin It. I made the right choice in the end.”

We link arms and walk out onto the patio to get fresh air. The pool is fully occupied, and people dive into it, dragging their friends along. A flash of motion draws my attention away, and my jaw turns slack when I notice a tall, dark silhouette standing on the opposite side of the pool.

Batman is standing next to the buffet table.

I leave Josie near the pool while I approach him, pushing past half-naked bodies, Thing One and Thing Two and a guy dressed in a pinata jumpsuit. My eyes remain on Batman the entire time, and when I'm finally close enough to tap him on the shoulder, he twirls around and locks those dark, bat-like eyes on me.

My confidence crumbles, and so does my ability to speak normally.

“You... uh... hi.”

Batman's stare darkens until I can no longer make out his eyes. “Skye. I've been waiting for you,” he growls in his deep, Batman-esque voice.

It suddenly occurs to me how absurd this situation is.

For starters, how does he know my name?

Who the heck is hiding behind the mask?

“What's the matter? Cat got your tongue?” he asks,

firmly crossing his arms against his chiselled chest. I want to reach out and touch him to make sure he's real and not part of my imagination.

"Michael Keaton, is that you?" I accidentally blurt out.

This is so embarrassing. I'm living out one of my deepest, darkest fantasies and don't know what will come out of my mouth next.

*I hope nobody is watching.*

Batman burns out laughing, except it doesn't sound like his voice anymore.

"You're killing me! I can't keep this up any longer," he exclaims, laughing uncontrollably.

Batman's mask comes off, and Rory's face appears. Even though it was a long shot, I was expecting Michael Keaton to be under there. I'm slightly annoyed that Rory has revealed his identity in such a public place. The number one rule in any Batman movie is that Bruce Wayne's identity is always kept a secret. Hasn't he done his research? You can only dress up as Batman if you know the hard-core facts.

I turn on a pout and playfully slap him across the shoulder. "Talk about a sneak attack."

Rory chuckles. "I've never seen you so starstruck, Clemons. I might need to dress up as Batman more often."

My entire face burns.

"You must be frying in that costume. It's boiling."

Rory picks up a sausage roll and pops it into his mouth. Honestly, he looks even hotter than Michael

Keaton in that Batman suit. I'll never fully understand my levels of attraction for this boy.

His grin turns up a notch like he can read my mind. "Hm. It's time this bat went swimming with his favourite sidekick."

"What are you–"

Rory effortlessly lifts me off the ground, throwing me over his shoulder, and strides purposefully toward the pool.

Panic knots my stomach.

"No! No! Don't you even think about it! Put me down!"

*If only these cat claws were real.*

Rory executes a cannonball into the pool, forcing me to join him. The cold water crashes into me, engulfing my chest, and I swallow a mouthful of chlorine, emitting a high-pitched shriek. Gasping for air, I emerge from the water, my eyes stinging from the chlorine. Moments later, Rory's head surfaces, and I splash water in his direction, attempting to clear my eyes, but the burning sensation intensifies.

"You idiot! What did you do that for?"

"I thought you might've wanted a little cat bath since it's the hottest day of the year," he retorts, a mischievous twinkle in his eyes.

"That wasn't code for; Oh, let's throw Skye into the pool so she can cool off."

"Sorry. I couldn't help myself. You're just so cute when you're angry."

I blink slowly, my heart picking up speed as we trade glances. "Did you bring a date to the party then?"

The thought of Rory bringing Chrissie to the party gives me unnecessary anxiety. If he brought a date, I certainly don't want to know about it, so why did I ask that question?

My brain never ceases to amaze me.

"No," he says, raising an eyebrow. "Did you?"

I'm fighting a grin. "No."

"That's interesting."

"Why is that interesting?"

"Because..." His gaze drifts to my lips, and nervous anticipation flutters in my stomach. "I don't want to see you with other guys."

The blood instantly rises to my cheeks, and a bolt of surprise darts through me.

"I bet you say that to all the girls, Keaton."

I try to breeze past him, but he catches my arm, and his grip tightens as he pulls me closer, his warm breath tickling my ear.

"I don't, actually," he rasps.

My heart refuses to slow down.

His gaze burns into mine, and I glance into the water, cheeks flushed.

"What about Chrissie?"

He clenches his jaw. "What about her?"

"Well... you did share a kiss with the girl. It must have meant something, surely?"

"It didn't. I don't care about Chrissie."

"If that's true, why did you keep your distance after we kissed?"

Rory takes a slow, uneven breath. "Because I will never be able to compete with Grayson Swain."

Confusion grips me.

"What are you talking about? What does Grayson have to do with any of this?"

"He *always* seems to be there, Skye. He was even ringing you the night that we kissed. I saw his name flash up on your phone," he says, anger rolling off him in waves.

My mind takes me back to the aftermath of our kiss and how Rory's character seemed to change when Grayson contacted me. I remember he was trying to tell me something before that happened, but he never got around to it.

"Grayson is my friend... well, he was my friend before I ruined everything."

Without warning, Rory leans forward and cups my face, his touch sending a shiver down my spine.

"I can't get that kiss out of my mind, Clemons. You're all I've been able to think about these past couple of weeks. Please give me a straight answer. How do you feel about me?"

I stare at him, at a loss for words.

My fear of commitment, fuelled by my past experiences and the complexity of my mother's relationships, has always held me back from embracing a romantic connection. There is so much I want to say to Rory at this precise moment, but I know I can't fully commit myself to him. In a few months, I will be moving to Sloanville.

"I—I don't know," I lie, allowing my stubbornness to take root in my heart.

He makes a frustrated noise and shakes his head in disappointment, retreating from the pool. Leaving my stubbornness behind, I rush towards Rory and place my hand on his arm. He automatically spins around, eyes wide and questioning.

I'm struggling to express my feelings for him openly. I've always found it easier to express myself on paper. I'd have no trouble telling him how I felt if I could do it that way, but it is just too terrifying in real life.

"It doesn't matter how I feel because I got accepted to study at Sloanville University next September."

His smile drops to the ground, and he stares at me with a pained expression. "Sloanville... isn't that far away?"

"Yeah, so that's why there would be no point in starting something here when I'm going to be miles away."

"Can't you visit Barnett on weekends?"

"I plan to, but it will be difficult. I'll be moving to Sloanville for three years."

"Well, congratulations." He tucks some wild curls behind my ears, and I shiver. "What about the farm, though? What about..." he pauses as if he is about to say something he shouldn't. "What about Dante?"

I hadn't even thought of *everything* I would have to leave behind after moving to Sloanville. Everyone I care about is in Barnett.

"Just because I won't be working at Trinity anymore doesn't mean I can't visit."

"It won't be the same."

I try to swallow the emotion that is building in my throat, but it refuses to disappear. Before Rory came along, I was completely closed off. I had no friends or meaningful relationships, and then my life was suddenly bursting with colour. Without me even realising it, I was much happier sharing moments with someone else than ever at being alone.

That's why, after an eternity of standing there as Catwoman, I realise I've found my own Batman. What I'm feeling towards Rory is very real. He is the first boy I've ever felt this way about, and it scares me to death. I have strong feelings for him, but I know I can't act on them because there would be no point. I'm going away to study for three years. Anything can happen within that time frame, and I can't expect Rory to wait for me. Things could get ugly—messy.

“I care about you, Rory, but long-distance relationships never end well.”

He dips his head, blocking the sun shining into the pool. “Distance isn't going to change my feelings for you, Skye. No matter where you are, you'll always have a piece of my heart.”

*He is not making this easy for me.*

“You say that now, but you might feel differently in seven months when you're still here and I'm gone.”

“I won't. Life is all about taking risks, and I don't want to live with any more regrets. I'm yours if you want me.”

It feels like my heart is being squeezed repeatedly, and the realness of losing him almost knocks me off my feet. While I am studying in a foreign place, Rory will still work at the farm in Barnett. Our relationship will be put to the ultimate test. He could meet someone when I'm away. He could fall in love.

Silence hums between us, where words should be spoken. Neither of us says anything to fill the gap because Rory feels just as torn up as I am. The attraction is strong between us; that's undeniable. More importantly, we share a friendship that deserves to last. It's worth fighting for.

"I do... want you," I eventually manage to say, "but I'm terrified."

"It's not going to be easy, but this feels right, doesn't it?"

My mouth twitches, and a smile stretches across my face. "Yeah, it does."

Rory takes my hand and leads me out of the pool. We walk into the house, where the party is still lively. People turn to look at us, our dripping Batman-themed costumes attracting attention, but we don't even care.

Rory finds a cupboard under the stairs, and we pile inside, giggling as the door closes behind us.

His mischievous grin returns. "So... I've finally got you all to myself," he says, a wicked gleam in his eye.

"Hm. What are you going to do about it, Keaton?" I challenge him.

Rory intertwines his fingers with mine and backs me up against the wall, his eyes slowly drinking me in.

"Well, I think I'll start by doing this."

He softly places his lips to mine, and I lean into him, letting him take complete control. We cling to each other desperately, and he cups the back of my neck with one hand, hugging me to him with the other.

It's hot.

Fast.

Reluctantly, I pull away, both of us breathing hard. "So, what does this mean? Where do we go from here?"

"Well, since we like each other a lot, we should probably go on a couple of dates, and we'll figure out the rest when it happens. Let's leave the Batman-themed costumes at home next time, though."

I chuckle against his mouth. "Good idea."

"I'm going to miss you when you leave, Clemons. You have no idea," he utters, his words lingering in the air.

I playfully push his shoulder to lighten the mood, although I'm starting to feel a bit down in the dumps myself.

"Hey, why so glum? I'm not leaving yet. We still have plenty of time to spare. Let's not get all emotional at a party. We're supposed to be celebrating."

Rory's smile reassures me that we will be okay, but I don't even want to think about the endless possibilities–of what could happen during my stay at Sloanville. I'm terrified that my whole life is about to change–that the people I care about now might move on without me, and I'll be only a tiny fragment of their story.

All I know is that *my* story is still being written, and I am more than ready for the next chapter to begin.

# Epilogue

## SEVEN MONTHS LATER

A LOT CAN CHANGE IN SEVEN MONTHS.

I stand in front of the grand university building and prepare to embark on a new journey.

Sloanville University, with its brick and old stone structure, is situated amongst lush green grass, trees, and mountains, resembling a castle. Its remote location is the perfect place for studying because it's devoid of distractions.

*This will be my home for the next three years.*

I barely make it down the hallway when I hear a familiar voice boom from behind me, "Skye! Wait up!"

I turn to embrace Josie, relieved to see a familiar face. We had both been accepted into the same university, but encountering her on my first day was a surprise. She has become a true friend and the only person I stayed connected with from my previous college course.

"What uni hall are you in?" she asks eagerly, her excitement contagious.

I hold up the room assignment sheet.

"One hundred and two."

"Yey! We're on the same floor! This is going to be so exciting, Skye. We're going to have so much fun!"

Continuing down the corridor, I reach my room and open the door, revealing a cosy space furnished with a single bed, a desk, minimal lighting, and a centrally hung TV.

*It's perfect.*

I enter the room, dragging my suitcase across the wooden floor and placing it on the bed. Glancing at my phone, a message from Sebastian lights up the screen, instantly bringing a smile to my face.

SEBASTIAN

Good luck on your first day. Not that you'll need it. I'll see you soon x

My relationship with my father has improved, though I still can't address him as 'Dad,' but that might happen at some point. I haven't had the chance to meet his niece yet, but Sebastian speaks fondly of her, painting a picture of a lovely person. We're taking things slow for now, and I'm okay with that.

I shift my attention to a message from my mother.

MUM

I hope you have an excellent first day. I'm going to miss you so much. Love you x

We moved to a better neighbourhood, escaping the clutches of Robert Knowles. While my mother hasn't completely overcome her depression, she has found ways to manage her thoughts and regain control of her life. She sought help from the mental health team and regularly attends cognitive therapy sessions. She has also started attending church, which seems to be helping.

I am waiting to receive a text from Rory. I was hoping he would text me to see how I was settling in. We did say our goodbyes earlier in the week, which was incredibly difficult. The long-distance thing will be tricky for us both, and we'll hardly get to see each other, with Rory working at Trinity full-time and me being at university most days. Still, we've promised to find time for each other and fight to make our relationship work.

I sit on my bare mattress and start taking some clothes out of the suitcase, sorting them into different piles—socks, underwear, shoes, pyjamas, jeans/shirts and my best nightlife dresses, in case I'm tempted to see what these freshers' parties are all about.

Once I've sorted out my clothes, I pick up my small jewellery box and open it, drawn to the seashell necklace Grayson bought me for my eighteenth birthday. I haven't got rid of it. I think about him sometimes, mostly when I'm alone and have time to wonder.

*I hope that he's doing okay.*

* * *

My days at the university revolve around endless studying and attending classes that push my limits. Struggling to stay awake becomes a daily battle, and the constant strain of hunching over computer desks leaves my back aching—the homesickness intensifying with each passing day.

I am struggling to keep up with the rest of my classmates, and I knew from the beginning that this would be challenging, but I never expected it to be this exhausting.

After a stressful day of classes, I returned to my dormitory to find Josie comfortably seated on my bed.

*She spends more time in my room than I do.*

A smile lights up her face as I enter the room. "Hey! How was your day?" she asks cheerfully.

I collapse onto my bed and sigh heavily.

"Awful. I've got to complete another one-thousand-word essay by Monday, and I am so tired. Is this really what the next few years will be like for us?"

"Yup. We'd better get used to it."

There's a tap at the door.

We're not expecting any visitors unless Josie extended the invitation. I wish I could make friends as quickly as she does. She picks them up wherever she goes. Being a social butterfly, people *want* to be around you. I'm the opposite of positive, which means people tend to stay *away* from me.

There's another knock, followed by a male voice seeping up from behind the wooden door.

"I'm looking for Skye Clemons. Please tell me this is the right dorm room because I've been to at least four rooms and haven't had the warmest welcome."

Rushing to swing the door open, I find Rory on the other side and throw myself at him excitedly. Caught off guard, he stumbles backwards and hits the wall, our embrace visible to groups of onlookers in the busy corridor.

I take a moment to observe him. He looks even more handsome than I remember. His brown hair falls past his ears, and I long to run my fingers through it. He still carries a lot of that pain around with him—the kind of pain he conceals within himself, and often, I can see a hint of it in his eyes before it disappears as quickly as it arrived.

"What are you doing here?" I ask, butterflies fluttering in my stomach.

The giddy feeling never fades.

I'll never get tired of it.

"I thought I would visit you in person instead of calling. I wanted to see you," Rory replies, a smile playing on his lips.

"This is the best surprise ever!" I cry, flinging my arms around him.

I spend the rest of the day in my room with Rory, watching movies on Netflix and catching up on each other's lives.

Sitting in his arms, I fiddle with the string of his hoodie.

"I wish you could stay."

Rory pushes a stray curl away from my eyes, reminding me how much I've missed that simple gesture.

"Me too, but I want to hear what's been happening with you. Are you still excited to be living university life?"

I glance up at the ceiling and sigh. "Almost as excited

as I am to complete another three years' worth of studying. The partying isn't so bad, though. I never run out of things to do."

He looks at me worriedly, and I let my head fall against his chest. "Don't party too hard. You know what happens when you do... I'm forced to come and save you," he jokes, keeping his voice light.

"You'll have to continue saving me then. I don't mind."

"Might be a bit hard, considering I don't exactly live around the corner."

"I'm sure you'll find a way."

My heart flutters when he leans in, his minty breath fanning my face. I move to straddle his lap, and he plants a lingering kiss on my mouth. Electric bolts rush through me as his tongue explores mine, and I lose myself in the moment.

The door opens, and I jump away from Rory, accidentally kicking him in the groin.

He keels over. "Fudge!"

I try to rush to his aid, but he does not want to be comforted. Josie holds a hand to her mouth, throwing me a look of apology for potentially ruining the moment.

Time with Rory is limited, and we spend our final moments together exploring the campus. The stress and worries fade away in his presence, but the reality is that our lives are currently on entirely different paths. It wouldn't be fair for me to ask him to stay when he has numerous obligations awaiting him back home.

"How's your course going anyway? Have you made any friends?" he asks, swinging my hand against the wind.

"No. Aside from Josie, I don't hang out with anyone else. Making friends takes a lot of effort. I want to focus on getting through my first year."

"Those classmates of yours are missing out," he says.

"They probably think I'm a grumpy old... Well, I'm not the most approachable person, am I? Let's be realistic."

"It would be good for you to make friends. Don't be afraid to be yourself, Skye. The right people will love you for it."

"How's it going at the farm?"

I've competed in three bumper races with Dante within the last few months, and we've won two of them. Mr Frost is convinced we are ready for the next step—eventing, but now that I'm in Sloanville, I don't know if I can dedicate myself to training and studying.

"It's going great, but everybody's missing you," Rory says.

"I'm missing everybody, too."

We finally say goodbye, and I watch him speed away on his motorbike, my eyes watering.

*Pull yourself together, Clemons.*

*You can do this.*

*You'll see Rory again sooner than you probably think.*

Instead of returning to the dorm, I go to the library, scan my key card and enter a study area on the ground floor. Students around me are engrossed in their work, their attention fixed on computer screens.

I glance up at the elevated levels of the library and decide to head to the third floor. Navigating through the aisles, I am inadvertently drawn to the Religious Studies department. Shaking off the distraction, I prepare to move on when I glimpse someone familiar standing alone in one of the book aisles.

Surprised, I quicken my pace and head towards the aisle, but it's empty when I get there. Disappointed, I turn to leave, but I collide with another student, blocking my path. Prepared to give them a piece of my mind, I freeze as the boy turns around, his eyes locking with mine.

To my astonishment, Grayson Swain is standing there, dressed to perfection.

"You've got to be kidding me," he says, dropping the book in his hand.

THE END

# From Opposite Sides

1. From Opposite Sides - **Bryony Sier**
2. Addicted to you - **Picture this**
3. Just the way I'm feeling - Feeder
4. Danger! High voltage - **Electric six**
5. Mr Brightside - **The Killers**
6. Nothing else matters - **Metallica**
7. False Alarm - Becky Hill
8. Coastline - **Hollow Coves**
9. It's now or never - **Elvis Presley**
10. You can't always get what you want - **The Rolling Stones**
11. Angels - **Robbie Williams**

**Now Playing**

From Opposite Sides playlist

15:05 - 14:55

## Also by Bryony Sier

Coming soon...

The Sequel!

# The Opposite Effect - Sequel sample

"You've got to be kidding me," Grayson says, dropping the book in his hand, which leaves a startling echo behind as it falls to the library floor with a loud thud.

It has been such a long time since I've seen Grayson Swain in person, yet it feels as if it was only yesterday we were working on the *From Opposite Sides* project. I'm genuinely happy to see him because I never thought our paths would cross again, but he's not pleased to see me. After all, I single-handedly destroyed our friendship by breaking his trust.

Physically, Grayson's appearance hasn't changed. He's still got that luscious blond hair and those captivatingly deep blue eyes you can easily get lost in. I need to ask him what shampoo and conditioner he uses because he smells divine!

Coupled with his unfairly good looks, there is no noticeable physical defect on his face or body, and I've always been a bit envious of that.

*The boy has better skin than me!*

Grayson leaves me in the aisle alone, and I take a moment to consider my next course of action. Seeing him again has brought back some unresolved feelings and emotions. I may not be his favourite person, but that doesn't mean we can't rekindle our friendship and fix this.

Chasing after him, I find Grayson in the science fiction aisle, and his eyes flip to mine, a scowl taking over his entire face.

"What do you want, Skye?" he demands, making it painfully clear that he no longer has time for me.

Truthfully, I don't know what I want from him now. I'm annoyed that he avoided me for seven months, ignoring my numerous messages and calls. I'm also wondering what he's doing here when he should be on the other side of the world.

"Are you just going to act like we're total strangers?" I ask him, disbelief filtering into my voice.

"We *are* strangers," he snarls, casting me a disgusted look, his eyes returning to scan the shelves.

He's been through a lot this past year. His parents' relationship has been rocky, and despite my father's reluctance to share details, things aren't improving. The impact of their situation must be weighing heavily on Grayson's life.

"When are you going to be able to forgive me?"

"Skye, I'm busy, and I don't want to talk about this right now, so can you please just leave me alone?" he snaps, shouldering past me and charging towards the exit, the doors closing firmly behind him.

I lied for weeks about working at his father's farm. He

had no idea until he eventually found out at my first bumper race last year, and our friendship died instantaneously that day. Grayson disappeared for months, never returned to college after the summer holidays, and I didn't think I'd ever see him again, but fast forward seven months, and here we are—still stuck in the past.

* * *

"Grayson is just so infuriating! He hasn't changed at all," I dive head first onto my bed, shouting into my phone to express my anger.

Rory listens to me vent on the other end of the line.

I've not come up for air yet.

He's an excellent listener, which is why our long-distance relationship works. We ring each other daily unless other commitments hinder us. Late-night phone calls and weekend home visits are all we can manage these days. From seeing someone you practically spend every second of the day with to having no contact with them is strange. There's this constant ache in my chest whenever I think about him, and I don't know what it means exactly, but I'm not sure I like how it makes me feel.

"Okay... I'm done. Please say something," I finally say, releasing a sigh.

"Don't let Grayson Swain get to you. If he's not ready to hear you out, that's his problem. You've done all you can do."

This is why my boyfriend is so amazing.

He's always fair, and he lets me vent.

*That ache in my chest is gradually expanding.*

"Anyway, enough about Grayson. How have you been? How's the farm?"

"Fine. We have a lot of dressage events coming up."

That shouldn't worry me, but it does because we struggle to make time for each other now. If Rory works longer hours, communicating like this will be even harder, and we need to communicate. My university course is for three years, and I've always worried that we won't make it—that our long-distance relationship won't last.

"We've got a new stablehand. She's very experienced," he continues, causing a spike of jealousy to course through me.

*You can't be jealous just because a girl will be spending more time with Rory than you are.*

"Things aren't the same now that you're not around. I miss my co-worker," Rory admits, a smile tugging at my lips. I'm squealing inside, but I will not show him how excited I am to hear him say he misses me, too.

"Co-worker?" My voice rises a notch. "I thought you might miss your girlfriend, but oh well..."

"Hey, I miss all the privileges of being your boyfriend."

I sit up on the bed, grinning to myself. "Hm. What kind of privileges are we talking about?"

"Well, the fact that I can't kiss you is a big issue. I like kissing you."

I quickly scroll through my messages until I find his name in my contact list.

SKYE

A kiss from me to you, from across the pond 😘

I hear his phone pinging in the background, and after a few silent seconds, he sends me a message back.

RORY

😘🔥

We haven't said the 'L' word yet.

I'm not very good at expressing how I feel. Being vulnerable is not something I am comfortable with, but Rory is bringing out a different side of me I never knew existed—a caring, nurturing, softer side that isn't too overbearing.

I don't know if I love him yet, though.

*Is that strange?*

*I've never been in love, so how are you supposed to know when you are?*

Annoyingly, I'm waiting for something to go wrong because, so far, things have been too perfect. We haven't even had our first argument yet, and I'm not saying I want one, but it's healthy to argue. I'm self-sabotaging already, and I need to stop before I mess this up. I like Rory a lot, but it's almost like I'm not allowing myself to get too close to the flame in case I get burned.

"God, I'm tired," Rory says after we've been talking for nearly two hours. It feels like we've only been talking for five minutes, and I don't want this conversation to end yet, but it's late. I need to be up early for my classes tomorrow, and Rory's working an early shift at the stables.

"Should we speak again tomorrow at the same time?" I suggest, stifling a yawn.

"Uh, yeah. Tomorrow should be fine..." He hesitates as if he's just remembered something. "Oh, I can't talk tomorrow. I've got this thing."

"What thing?"

"Nothing important."

Nothing important is usually code for something you want to keep private. Maybe he doesn't want to talk to me because he's getting fed up with our conversations.

*What if he's bored? What if...*

"It's no big deal. I'll call you on Wednesday," he says, interrupting my intrusive thoughts before they can escalate.

*Stop overthinking this,* I remind myself.

"Uh, yeah, that's..." I cover my head with my hands. "Damn. Wednesday's not a good day for me. Josie has invited me to a quiz night on campus. I'm sorry. How about Thursday?"

"My grandmother wants to go out for a meal on Thursday. I can't bail on her now. She's looking forward to it. Friday?"

*Making plans is hard.*

"I've got an assignment to finish before next week. Friday will be my last day to properly work on it before coming home on Saturday. Otherwise, we could always see each other when I visit on the weekend."

We won't be able to talk again for the next few days,

but this is normal. Lots of couples don't talk or see each other often, and they're still going strong.

"Alright. Saturday it is. Let me know when you're almost home, and I'll meet you off the bus."

"I will."

"Sleep tight, Clemons."

We go our separate ways, and I turn off the light, repeatedly telling myself everything will be fine.

# Acknowledgments

I am completely and utterly overwhelmed to have published my first book at twenty-six! I started writing this story when I was twelve, so it's crazy that From Opposite Sides has finally been released into the universe!

This book has taken me so long to finish because I kept changing the plot every five minutes. It should have been released years ago when I first finished it, but I'm so glad I held off because it was not ready.

I REPEAT, IT WAS NOT READY.

After writing draft after draft and spending hours rewriting the story from start to finish during our first lockdown, I am happy to be able to share what I've been working on for twelve years.

I want to give a shoutout to a few people, but this first shoutout goes out to my mother for always believing in me. This book would not have been possible without you, mam. You have read every draft I've written, dating back to the first. All in all, that's a LOT of drafts!

Next time I'll have to let you read the finished version of my stories to save you all the trouble. I honestly can't thank you enough.

To my amazing friend Megan James — thanks for reading and editing one of my earlier drafts (before I decided to rewrite it again). The notes you gave me, and the feedback you provided were excellent, and I appreciated the time and effort you took to help me make the book flow better. By the way, I kept all of your suggestions and edits, which are still in the book now!

To my beautiful nan, Katrina Minney, who loves reading as much as I do. I remember you read an unfinished and very early draft of the book, and I will always be so grateful for your guidance and suggestions. I hope you enjoyed reading the finished story this time!

To my Auntie, Katrina Minney. Thank you for being one of my first beta readers. I was so excited when you rang me up and told me you couldn't stop laughing while reading about Skye's first experience on the farm. You have read many books, so I greatly respect your opinion. Your encouraging words filled me with hope and boosted my confidence. The fact that you told me you couldn't put it down was music to my ears!

To Eleanor and Claire Hope — you were kind enough to let me visit your farm, which inspired me to write this book. Thank you.

I also want to thank Writing Monteith, who was another one of my beta readers. You gave me fantastic advice and encouraging feedback.

Thanks to my amazing best friend and fellow author, Stephanie O'Neil, for encouraging me, helping with the publishing process and being one of my beta readers.

Thanks to Cheyenne Cooley for providing me with an in-depth proofread.

Thanks to Richie Evans for designing the font and cover background for the book cover!

To Jill Greenway, thank you for giving up your time reading my work and for the fantastic advice. I will never forget your kindness.

To my old English teacher, Mr Cope, thank you for bringing English lessons to life in high school. English never used to be a subject that interested me, but you were such a great teacher, and I started to enjoy the lessons when I moved into your class. You also helped me to catch up with everybody else since I was so far behind with my work. I don't know if you'll ever read this, but I just wanted to thank you for that.

To my beautiful family. You mean the absolute world to me. You inspire me every day. You're all so incredible, and I love you so much. Thanks for allowing me to chase my dreams.

Dear, YOU.

Thanks for reading my book. I hope you enjoyed it. I look forward to continuing this journey with you as I publish more of my work. This is just the beginning, and I can't wait to share what else I've been working on over the years. There is more to come.

There is a sequel on the horizon, as I don't think Skye's story is quite finished yet.

Lastly, I'd like to thank Jesus for giving me the strength to continue writing this story when so much was happening around me. I believe I was meant to rewrite this book because what took ten years to finish literally took me one year to complete once I had decided how it would end.

All Glory be to God.

# About the Author

Bryony Sier is an emerging author of young adult fiction. This is her first book. She is from a small town called Merthyr Tydfil in South Wales. She has been writing stories since a very young age.

After struggling so much in high school to fit in, she turned to songwriting and storytelling, which helped her escape the harsh reality.

Bryony would spend all her time writing stories and songs. When she's not writing books or reading, she is writing songs, playing the guitar and singing to crowds of people from all over the UK.

All images used within this book were designed in the Canva app.

facebook.com/BryonySierbooks

x.com/BryonySierMusic

instagram.com/Bryonysierbooks

tiktok.com/@Bryonysier

youtube.com/Bryonysier

Printed in Great Britain
by Amazon

39026270R00288